skywreck afternoons

Roger Coleman

Fomite
Burlington, VT

ISBN-13: 978-1-942515-76-0
Library of Congress Control Number: 2016961039

Fomite
58 Peru Street
Burlington, VT 05401
www.fomitepress.com

Cover art — Roger Coleman

the coffee meditations

You agreed with the buzz in your nervous system. If one thought was threatened all thoughts were threatened. What was the truth for? To fuck you over and how simple it was to be left in the dark? That it was easy to fall in love?

Relax the raven-haired woman said. It's just an old gunshot wound.

Yea you said there's no hurry to be normal anyway.

But you needed to check into the hospital again. Carrying two bullets inside you for forty-three years had a built in disadvantaged. Every year you got a scan and that scan decided whether or not they cut you open. The purpose for this invasion was to see if either bullet had moved and drifted closer to your spine — and to check if the dirty metal levels in the slugs weren't causing anything more than basic harm.

Blind Charlie set you up even before he was killed. He left you insurance. What did everybody else do when they were shot? They died. You owed Blind Charlie. Not for saving your life but for prolonging your life.

But was that a good thing? Was living longer worth the time that it took away from your day? You hated being shot. You hated seeing Blind Charlie shot. You hated seeing him dead on the sidewalk. You hated that — even more than seeing your own holes leaking blood onto 65th Avenue — you hated that moment — when you saw Blind Charlie die.

Where was Cripple? Where was Reds? Where was Rhino the Bob?

They weren't around that day when Blind Charlie was shot and killed. And they weren't around all the next day either.

*

You shared the windowless room with another man in a flimsy gown. He was reading a newspaper. He greeted you with a nod. With a slight acknowledgment he eyeballed you over a second time before flipping the newspaper in front of his face and disappearing from view.

You looked around for something to read — inspecting a pile of magazines on a small wooden end table. The choices seemed to be the usual suspects of crappy reading material left in waiting rooms.

Modern Maturity issues devoted to supplementing leisure time with cool gift ideas you can make for the grandkids. Or The Ten Things You Need To Know About Your Baby's Health — what's with that? There's not eleven or something more? Or an issue from a way outdated fishing hunting journal with the subscription label ripped off and with a fifty-foot grizzly bear on the cover attacking some guy armed with a pocketknife. After being chewed upon and clawed back and forth and then being rolled down a hillside and clawed some more the poor guy survives and walks five miles back to his truck but lost his keys in the fight. Or teen advice on acne from beautiful adolescents that don't have any face problems. Or celebrity escapades and all the sex that goes on while everyone's back was turned. Or why a famous person needs twenty cars to make his life right. Or The Male Diet And Why It's Going To Help or Toy Train Hobbies and Why They're Fun or you leaf through them all not paying attention as though you were back in high school passing time and waiting to walk out the door when the year was over.

You looked across the room at the man behind the newspaper. He drank something from a specialized hospital bottle with a prescription label — some concocted fluid that's probably necessary to what's wrong with him. Maybe it was cocktail hour for the doomed.

He noticed you watching him. Odd smiles were passed between us. Even if we meant to be sincere — so what? What we had between us was a delicate curiosity in a public setting that pitted privacy against an endless spinning inquisition. We made meaningless small talk but it went past our heads. It was too distracting to pantomime and listen to one another. He snapped his newspaper back to attention and sat behind it like a screen.

Yea — he said- life sucks.

Maybe as a state of mind — or even a verifiable place to find one self under — but what did that mean and what do you say to a stranger's voice from behind a newspaper?

Even if life did suck — it still was a temporary circumstance and much like sitting in a waiting room. Even when you die — that's still temporary. You can't go on dying forever.

And what did you know about it?

And what does he know about it?

If life were some believable process that birth stitches on your brain like a survival manual — kicking avoiding death and sifting all day long through a surplus of identities to worry about — you might even say yea why even breathe? Is that what he meant?

But what if life were like a blowjob where everyone agrees and it's like two spines sharing one person? What if under those circumstances the rituals were conducted with overt sympathy companionship and affection — wouldn't suck then be a good word to hang around? What answer did this guy want? And for all the diagnostic scans what were you prepared to give? But then it really wasn't a question...

Was it worse to lie? Should you feel worse for lying to the guy? You have a suspicion that the power of lying was wrong but that's what felt right. And why does it come down to this weird personal level? Maybe there was nothing to say and maybe he was just talking to the walls?

Make a note to the buzz: that whatever personal skills were needed to construct a dialogue with this fellow — you do not possesses them in enough variety at the moment. Given the luck of the draw and it being another Monday in the world it was just as easy to feel clueless and lonely.

Another note: as a human being you find this particular course of action unappealing — if not downright bogus and made you feel thin to the bones.

Make a note: as a personalized identity however — name history current address — sitting in a hospital room with no windows and the only thing you wanted was to leave — you found this conversational avoidance satisfactory and perhaps the quickest way out.

Dumb as it sounds — sitting in silence with the man behind the news-paper — did you say the wrong thing — were there wrong feelings — does this ever end — you decided to make an inventory as to what evidence you had to confirm or to deny what the guy behind the newspaper said: did life suck?

For starters who didn't embody suffering?

Would you ever believe you were bleeding internally unless it actually happened?

What did this guy think? Maybe he had some condition that threat-ened his life.

Maybe life was just arguing the facts? Nature turned you into a contrary being once you started walking. The ground did it. Those first few steps you took and you were just as treacherous as anyone else in the neighborhood.

Sky was breathless power.

But here you were in the suck of things possible and the guy behind the newspaper was so damn silent like he had blown a fuse or something and was setting off sparks inside his head and he couldn't bother with anything because he was reading the weather report or something.

You had this re-write for Star Trek. But Star Trek was way long ago syn-dicated so your idea was useless since nobody produced Star Trek anymore.

Maybe it was the serious crap that was nothing more than convictions of shit — in its own dark humored way. Sure there was evidence that we have hope or something. But evidence was muscle...

Captain Kirk and the Enterprise were sailing way beyond the neutral zone — warp speed after speed — beyond Klingon territory — boldly going where commercial television allowed us to have images implanted in those sub-level parts of the brain receptive to cool images — when the Enterprise picked up a message beaming faintly toward them.

On screen Kirk said leaning back in his chair — with that authoritarian voice — outwitting enemies and sleeping with alien women across the galaxies.

As an aside you put in space diseases you might catch or give. And wasn't balling the planet queen not only a violation of the prime directive — not to interfere — but also might leave the rest of the crew somewhat huffy about shore leave?

Faintly the message -gets decoded into Starfleet language — for the most part English since they all belonged to a federation of planets.

On screen were the words: What Me Worry. And a grinning Alfred E. Newman from Mad Magazine stared back at the crew.

Maybe worry was all what we were supposed to do.

The guy behind the newspaper was no help. Maybe you should dump it all back on him? That would be easy and sweet.

But then from nowhere — well you really saw it coming — and it was important to believe in spontaneous gestures — as much as you recognized it — a fret grabbing you by the ass — so it was a strange comfort — one you will never understand — but you believed in despite all the evidence that said watch out — and when a fall back moment hits and rippled across you — at the time it seemed like a cross section between the wilds of love-making and what radical paleontologists call the vanished body plan — when someone referred to as you — and you were stuck in a windowless room — when all of the you of you — and it does get stupid does it not to rely on identity — does not exist — never did — but you still wanted the sticks and stones of earth to play with — and a guy behind a newspaper you never met brought it up — yea life sucks — where were you?

*

Quite naturally when you think about blessings — the folly behind them when you count them — you and the raven-haired woman belonged together in time. Love and air and water and shelter and yes in arms and equations consumed what it was we knew and one night we were kids and walked away together and played the odds. We spent the night walking around place to place without a direction and hoping to find one.

All that aimlessness vanished near the old wooden causeway bridge. It was useless anymore — an ancestor in the shadow of the big new concrete span rushing traffic north.

Think about it she said. We've never driven over this bridge. And we never will.

Yea you said it rots in the bay. That's what it does. Some year it has an appointment with the water.

Water claims the world she said.

Sky claims water you said.

A slice claims sky she said.

And she had you — what sweet notions — let breakfast be like this — have us a pie when Da Vinci was closed. She had the key to the back door. What sweet notions to have and imagine: twirling that dough like a cousin: laying on great olive oil and a killer red sauce: hot pie. Too bad we couldn't fire up the big ovens. It was too early for them to get working Eden said. In the cooler we found nearly a dozens slices from last night. We reheated them in a microwave — made a pot of coffee — and had a feast. Maybe time dropped away from sight and we never saw the difference. Maybe we never cared if there was a difference. What mattered was the deepest possible silence we memorized together running our mouths through the dawn.

*

Not that you prayed but suddenly St. Jude was in the house. Haven't prayed for years.

But those times when you did pray you didn't find much beyond an obligation and the labor it required to become a supplicant.

But there was St. Jude — the patron of lost souls — strolling about and leaving footprints. Was there now a soul to think about — when did that arrive — plus the raven-haired woman whereabouts — and the guy behind the newspaper who mentioned he was tied into digestive knots?

Whoa. Hey Jude... take a sad song and all that...

And thinking about St. Jude that brought up St. Anthony — the patron of lost things.

Dear St. Anthony please come 'round — something's lost that can't be found.

Whoa. There were enough fairy tales kicking around in your head without the old school dementia popping up unannounced.

And how do you get these jobs being saints? Do you take night classes? Do you interview? You remember miracle works and grim martyrdom as like existing pre-conditions for someone getting named a saint least someone go out in a blaze of misunderstanding.

But hey you said — let's imagine for a moment you said to the guy behind the newspaper — that it's none too late for a second opinion.

He lowered the newspaper and said what are you talking about.

This was detachment by proxy you said.

What are you talking about?

Let's give up before we die.

I don't understand you he said and flipped behind the newspaper again.

Don't people ask you don't you feel this was unjustified you said?

The newspaper said of course this was unjustified. Who in the fucking world picks themselves out for a diagnosis? And you're telling me the answer was to give up.

Yes you said. Let it go.

What happens then he said. Assuming I let it all go... what happens — fuck man you don't know what happens — how would you — I don't think you'd know what a death star was from a fucking pink elephant — in the diagnosis of course. Okay he said. How do you give up? Explain that one to me.

Think about it like a grenade you said. You pull the pin out and then you relax.

You got a simple mind he said.

So what you said. What was *your* plan? Leave here and go beat somebody?

*

Well — suddenly you felt tired with two bullets inside you. All that why me crap got your head spinning in ends and karma and you lost it. You grabbed the metal colander and smashed it into your head. Salad greens shot out across the sink and stuck to the kitchen window. And the colander now had a dent in it from your skull — a fossil — a crater — a fingerprint from the space around your brain. You fell backwards — tripped over your feet — and the flat spot on the back of your head smacked into the floor. Impact with a colander and some inept shock wave that might embarrass the laws of physics took you by surprise and put down you on the floor where you sorry ass head hit the tile.

Stars flew around your eyes... late day October shadows cut you a profile across the floor... last night you watched The Untouchables and Elliot Ness was unable to answer the question what are you prepared to do because the old cop died and the scene faded away dramatically... the ceiling needed more joint compound... you needed to paint the walls before the cabinets went in... and before the cabinets went in you needed to run some wiring and paint the walls... you needed to buy the lights so you knew where to set the boxes before you did the wiring and you needed to paint the walls before the cabinets went in and your head knocked you silly against the tile and you stared at the ceiling and laughed and you couldn't remember what the paint color was... and you laughed and lay still and beneath a flicker of light coming from the window you closed your eyes...

*

But hey — the time you spent on the floor — that didn't seem so bad. You had gravity on your side. You were a body at rest.

When you finally came around you were flat on your back and holding a colander against you chest. Twilight reds and grays and the lost blue evening sky reflected in the kitchen window. Sanctuary — coming awake scared and hiding in a building — you manufactured your stars — one was deep natural breathing — another was cold vodka — another was the feathery sad time you took every day as every day tried to change your mind.

You sat up and tossed the colander into the sink. You owed the world several deep breaths at least. You poured cold vodka into a glass jar and measured it by the fist. Every day as every day it tried to change your mind.

The guy behind the newspaper — where did this guy come from — was he an accident? Was he waiting for you to happen? Was he a signifier? Or was he a liar?

Did life suck?

Did he plant that image in your head?

If you had the courage of your thoughts you'd ask him about it. But just like that he was gone. A nurse entered our windowless and silent man-cave — read his chart — and told him he was ready to go.

Wait a minute… you can't leave! Weren't we multitudes?

*

And it was like that once more — walking around the block for exercise. Cut back on your activities was the professional advice and let all the stitched together parts and pieces inside heal themselves again in good time. This was the fourth time the surgeons tried to get the bullets out. And it was the fourth time they failed without getting them out. The bullets kept working inward toward the spine like some osmosis.

In the evenings you stopped and watched kids play soccer in the park.

The match was knotted at zero. Team yellow had the ball…. team yellow lost the ball… then team blue had the ball… and then team blue lost the ball…. adults whooped and cheered … kids with undeveloped skills and sturdy legs… adults chanted names…kids ran forever chasing a ball across a field… adults admired themselves while they watched their children play… maybe they recalled a sweet night of fucking… the susceptible notes they had in mind…who they might be… maybe afraid who they weren't…

*

Simultaneous experience was not far-fetched.

Nor was it unreal to ride a bicycle through time on the boardwalk and ask in secret: what happened that night Blind Charlie died?

No more unreal than it was to sit on the back porch in a wooden chair — eating a long gingerbread cookie studded with dates and coated with a powdery sugar dusting. Than it was being a creature living the mythology of your own head and that kept reinventing you each time you thought about it — let's get out while we can — if you're not lost where were you etc.

The wooden chair was a deep purple wine color.

For recent days gold afternoons filled the sky.

9

Further on at dusk you were waked from the nod by a great noise above the neighborhood. Hundreds of crows in the pale evening sky yelling and screaming and disappearing west — and it was like they were flying into their own sound as they moved away and you lost them.

A bright half-moon climbed into the trees.

The materials of the day seduced you down to a question.

We could be heroes — right?

Or go R.I.P. and be missed.

*

Underneath the covers was a perfectly unclaimed place to wake slightly in the night and listen to the rain pound against the skylights. A perfectly nude body and a dreamy electrical ground slept beside you. The air felt the way the velvet seascape painting above the bed looked — lush soft and ritualistic — wide margins of happiness since we got it cheap.

We had all the details we needed. What to do with them — that was the question.

Revenge — if good was the standard perception — like love was the measureless tomorrow –qualities which take a long time to develop in somebody. Whatever will be will be was certainly something you could fuck with. Anybody's destiny was up for grabs.

But the nude body beside you underneath the covers quickly made you deeper than sex and excited mental states — the field around her gave off warmth and forgetting and a clock-less grace — relationship made volumes — and so it was easy to fall under the rain sounds and give up. What little resistance was left — the rain calling you back to sleep and curling around the dark spoon of her skin.

*

Lying naked and spooned out in bed — the vestige of unclaimed strangers — living the dream — a bed of thoughts — birds landed on the facades of flat tarred rooftops — thin weedy clouds blew past the window — the bus station loudspeakers and its busy chronic activity vibrated and rattled the old glass pane — unknown vanilla passengers left town — islanders in the great web of space came into town — we ate pancakes and drank coffee and looked over the matinee schedules on pillows — fucking the right reflections — ten thousand things made the world — each day started from scratch — pulled like a weed from an October garden — a marriage bed fifty thousand years old overlaid upon your torn bamboo sheets and some Jersey-land futon — felt great.

*

    pleasure drives consciousness
    it's like having a wish
    one gull one airplane the southwest rooftops
    shapes not names
    comic action figure partly
    gee whiz that's not going to invent the wheel
    the rain falls again
     beautiful and light

*

According to a television commercial — destiny will not find you.

Outside on the street you watched a personal family-owned vehicle the size of a tank squat in the road — standing off against a pickup truck whose wheels were like pushed to the curbs. Drive big. Drive delusional.

On the news you tried to size up what it meant when hundreds died in a single firefight in the latest Asian war?

Where do you put your money? On a smart bomb or a suicide bomber?

And would there ever be a car commercial telling the viewer hey no problem: be satisfied with who you were?

Once the little white pills kicked in... things were foolish and faraway and worth anything at all. Ghettos in Jakarta... speed bumps in Omaha... lonely damaged supermarket goods... real lottery numbers... more gas wells igniting in runaway Pennsylvania drilling... the homeland security chief and his dartboard… a grinning botox anchorman with hair more puzzling looking than there were reasons for his existence standing before a Mississippi flood… dance anthrax music from the club scene… by the time the M&M's came out you were reduced to some anonymous postal worker who after twenty-six years carrying a mail sack admitted to using steroids…

The raven-haired woman was doing a crossword puzzle and asked: what do you call a primitive people sitting in the dark eating dry spaghetti?

*

The evening turned rain gray and chilly along the St. Paul canal. What to do? You waited underneath a streetlight as the rain fell steady. Up boardwalk office workers hurried past tucked in long weathered coats and neat expensive shoes skipping around the puddles. You saw your own trader hurry past — head in his collar — a skeptic's bygone face that loved martinis — talking on a phantom line that did not exist. The market was closed. He needed more numbers. You called him over and asked what was up.

Rough day he said. But let me work it he said and I'll make it available in a day or so.

Nothing like cash you said.

Get out of the rain he said.

Thanks you said but no. You enjoyed standing in the rain.

Why he said?

That was a hard one to answer to answer. Do you believe in last minutes you said.

The empty lures- any reflective life — dazed beer hoodies that might rob you for a dime — Tibetan perfumes that slowed your breathing down where you saw endless memories like bright neon letters in shop windows — you had a sense of earthly feelings you said in raindrops as though this were as tender as it got — raindrops — what to do — what to find out — it's been years with no exception and kick-ass nuts to be alive and to be finally left standing in the rain below your own private streetlight — but something was wrong — something you couldn't name —

Closest I get to that would be a fool's errand he said and walked off saying he'd text you tomorrow with money.

You didn't know whether to say: no worries or plenty of worries. You weren't sure if it mattered.

Up on the boardwalk a dog took a crap and then trotted away happy and unleashed.

Teenage strays — all boozy earlobes and desperate cigarette smoke — rolled up to where you were standing. They wanted money or else they harmed you. Cool damp loops of foggy streetlight fell around them.

You gave them a few twenties and then pointed at some dumb kid's head and said get lost.

The homeless families were out walking their rounds — - begging in trash cans for their kids — maybe a cheap half eaten burger stuck to a wrapper with shabby ketchup — taking on thousands of year's worth of street water like body shots in a fight — maybe realizing that when the dead hit the ground they come from nowhere.

Money was god right? Money took us to the stars right? And money brought the stars back home right? We can't afford money but we keep doing it anyway. Money was rough dark and beautiful.

There was a food shack across Ocean Avenue — been working in Jersey-land for decades if not a dime — making the same food as ever — lasagna that never died in the pan and a green salad and garlic bread — wide meatloaf plates with mashed potatoes and gravy made that day with a side of peas carrots and sweet pearl onions — mac and cheese with sausage and peppers — lobster rolls on doughy white buns — and there was always a pot of chowder brewing on the stove like a taste from the pages of Moby Dick...

And weird as it was — technically you owned the place. However no one knew that.

You walked into the shack and slapped god down on the counter. See those people across the street you said to the cook: feed them.

We don't like the homeless around here the cook said.

You took more god out of your pocket and slammed more dollars on the counter. Feed them you said.

What's the use the cook said? They'll just come back. And besides he said: we don't want them in here.

There was a good thing about Friday that was always inside your bones. It was like you had a well-appointed dream to meet and the nerve to do so.

You took out more and more god and smashed the bills on the counter. Feed them you said. Make it take out you said. There's enough money here to overwhelm your conscience.

The cook shook his head no and told you to get the fuck out.

Why was there a problem you said? You're in the business feeding people. I'm in the business paying for the meal. So what's up?

The cook didn't budge.

Guess what you said.

You'll shoot me if I don't feed those people the cook said.

We'll never get it right you said. What about the garage in the back?

Nearly empty the cook said.

Fine you said. That'll be the dinning hall.

*

A green rainy mist curved off the slick tires from a delivery truck and sprayed you and the dog. Pigeon droppings washed away from the street and benches and car windshields. You recognized the spray paint tags on the delivery truck. Inky suited policemen approached and asked if the dog was legal. If not they said we run your mutt in.

The dog was legal you said.

Where's the collar then?

You showed the cops that you were wearing the collar. The dog went for a swim you said.

And so what the cop said?

The dog likes to skinny-dip you said.

Asshole the cop said.

Don't you worry friend you said to the dog. You have the moon in your eyes.

*

One lone blinking yellow traffic light in the rain — no secrets — no truths — one of these days you'll get it — you'll find a quiet in the world that was impossible to hold onto but it was worth the try to do so anyhow. Maybe optimism was just another poor excuse for lack of planning. The rain fell in ribbons through the streetlight's glow of the unknown. You put your ear set into the dog's pearl shaped earlobes because the dog liked to hear Pink Floyd while you walked together.

How simple would it be if you got away with it — like a tide rushing out and there was no fat chance or maybe that the tide wouldn't meet the sea and dissolve. If anything wasn't it time? Time to cut off that pound of flesh that Blind Charlie was owed?

You and the dog and Pink Floyd drifted around all night without any place to really go — like the way helium in a balloon got away from an inattentive hand. It was a tricky combination that you clung to stubbornly. Like that Japanese flower arrangement gig — the art of the imperfect — wasn't it the most natural thing on earth to want to hold onto time however it was arranged? But what if you died suddenly — what if those bullets closed in on your spine? What if you had no revenge? Was your life then make believe?

We bought beef jerky and canned spaghetti from a lazy convenience store at Ocean Avenue and Blaze Lane and we shared it together cold where the boardwalk ended north and where the Coast Guard security fences began — hanging out in the cramped neighborhoods of Jersey-land with the late hour bowling alleys to grab a beer and wear funny shoes and spring roll food carts with Asian boys trying to make a dime for the family in a bigot's world and third shift lamp factories making bright objects for the home and were made from poison elements that included chromium arsenic and lead and the compelling emptiness of sex workers being sold on the pavements.

What does an ordinary day look like anyway? Best wishes in the rain? Church bells that chimed late hours?

faster than gravity

We could have been anything — made anything- according to the luck of the draw.

How did you get to be?

You could have easily been a loon from a National Geographic special with its crazy haunting cry. Just as easily you could have been a grape vine whose fruit became destined for a wine cellar. Just as simple as an apple falling on somebody's sleeping head and suddenly an idea came into being.

Instead whatever you were in the first place — you became a child — and that was fine and all that — but where was it — where did you come from?

Working class origins. You and your mates were delivered into web-works of average households after another war and our job in the population boom was to replace the dead that were gone in battle.

What soldier fortunate enough to make it back to the home shores wouldn't want to fuck their memories off the ass and mate someone and settle down and have electric toasters and cocktails in the off-hours in the nest after that crude reception at Normandy?

Maybe you owed your existence to patriotic fucking?

Maybe life was feasible wonder bread at a cheap price to have and to have was God's shield for democracy?

You recalled things like they happened yesterday…. the gleams in Jersey-land eyes as the SAC bombers flew above the sky in formation against the godless threat from the drunken Russians… the smiling Kool Aid mandala on flavored sugar packets that when added to water turned into a vital fluid… hopeful images from commercials like the Oscar

Meyer Weiner-mobile maybe coming to your neighborhood and tossing out free dogs... Ed Sullivan's baggy morphine eyes... the encouraging blond hostess practicing television witchcraft craft pretending she used Kaiser aluminum foil... reality came enclosed in oval butch wax containers and Pep Boys automotive dogma and Mattel toy endorsement warfare and of course the lure behind Loretta Young's chiffon swirl.

Songs were being sung about just that: growing up abstracted and turned into file cabinet kids and then later turned into habitat vandals who never grew up. Ask too many questions and you were dosed with St. Joseph and his aspirin for children along with a cold caffeinated soda. Shit like that spread your smile pretty thin.

And you thought about nature? What was nature? Who was responsible? Was that another dead end you were brought to?

*

Your first encounter with a meditative state came one day in second grade during Miss Fraley's grammar class. All those verbs and tenses were made annoying — partly by her hair lip and powder brown Mickey mouse wig — and because they had to be perfected to use them. Miss Farley's grammar class took away time. She controlled all the action words — the funhouse mirrors of the body. What did she know about how past present or future behaved? She made you sigh — and need to find another place to sit — amidst the clocks and discipline — where not even the holy ghost flushed you out — and wish for crayon time to come up only a few hours away.

*

the coffee meditations

crows in the morning
last night's rain
toilet flushing

*

memory palace
episode town
collapsing roof

*

faster than gravity

Miss Farley was just another in a line who believed they had the authority over a heap of kids they were charged with. Every separate muscle twinge belonged to them and they enforced it. Freethinking among children was discouraged. Rather than amusement firsthand to get you settled on the road to life — we had to pass through the question of the ancients: why did god make us? How would we know the answer to that? Why were the kids continually picked on? Why was there an answer in Chapter One? An answer given and neatly wrapped for something we never did? Chapter One — the same book our grandparents used — while they were in school in the same building where you were in school to this day — always the same answer — like nobody who passed through the school halls had a fucking brain to deal with. What was it about god? What did god have to do with sentence structure?

*

On the way out and beside the classroom door was a poster-sized scene of the Adam and the Eve. They were all woeful looking and young and fig leafed covering up their junk and harassed by some pissed off Archangel waving a flaming sword over their sorry heads.

You didn't know how or when it figured out. There had to be sugar in this.

Miss Farley said there was a doorknob to hell. And we held it in out hands.

the coffee mediations

Evening again — time for chatting with Doctor Vodka.

a strange little boy's voice on the answering machine: I don't know what I'm doing so goodbye — what wrong number was that about.

Blue playground twilight in the window… clumsy histories at the time but they turned out unblinking in support for your attention and not all that stalled in your thinking so that little kid's voice on a wrong number from nowhere was like hearing a sound in a shadow — you saw the shadow and you trusted the sound — that's what stuck for a moment — this was ground hog day — a sad elegiac little kid's voice — played over on a machine.

Outside time…how many things do you figure were outside time — all ten thousand of them…?

reading Keats to the dog in a snowstorm
the text said we were already gone in this life
a lifelong habit stopping on a dime to catch fire

Two figures desiring the weather and carrying ice skates passed you on their way to the salt pound.

Unfavorable skies slapped the coast with unlucky tides — that was how the weather channel guy explained it across our phone channels. The dog was fascinated and crouched on the boardwalk and stared into the breakwater winds. Flood tides hit the boardwalk and the waves came up big and yowling and flew into the darkness and then crept down along the wind and froze onto an unplowed Beach Avenue.

Like those commercials for footpads in your shoes- the ones that made you feel like dancing — hooded diagrams for breath that were people with their heads down dodging car lights and wearing hero-like synthetic jackets walked ha-ha into the wind till the next subway stop.

Office windows up in the storm burned on like each window was afraid to turn off the lights.

How spiritual does the weather go?

Across the street the dog barked at a traffic sign that was digitally confused and kept blinking letters into the night of Jersey-land's biggest snowstorm since the heyday of the factory ages fifty years ago: WALK — DON'T WALK — WALK — DON'T WALK — WALK —

Today you saw immigrants on television — lonesome for bamboo forests — lonesome for the desert — lonesome for the songs of their homeland — they were being held like sheep in pens — waiting for a tattoo — a bar code officially shot onto their palms that once scanned at the state's borders would admit them entrance into Jersey-land.

Most likely you clear the stuff that bugs you — but then minutes later that stuff begins filling in your head again with all the stuff you don't want in your head again. We don't need more noise- just another mule to carry the load.

Somebody's grandmother pulled a little wheeled cart behind her filled with groceries bags and held onto with sad worn gloves and samsara horizons pushing the wind and snow at her back.

Soggy newsprint flipped against a construction site outhouse.

The dog listened to isn't it a pity.

Waves and waves ran ashore in repeating large numbers and pounded the shoreline. The whitecap spray spun across Beach Avenue and shook confused sparrows and their tragic feet clamped around phone lines. Don't sparrows have anywhere to go when things get shitty?

Each suggestion pulled you a little closer — to what you knew — the ridiculous empty beer can blown around in the snow — foolish adolescents all headphone smoothness laughed through the storm like it wasn't even there — trashcans blown around in the snow — two shadows under the boardwalk held on to each other as though they believed kissing lips were bridges over the cold and wind to the end of the world tonight — gray sidewalks piled into faded brick walls — standing there you were cold snow frosted — the dog had a companion — it was there for you to have — what you knew — but it was also easy to put off.

If you knew something then you faced the question whether or not you were going to do something about it?

Detective Shade once said don't you ever doubt the integrity of my lies.

You and the dog walked over to the park to get off the coastline wind and settled for a moment among the rows of planted Celtic oaks. Druid priests they were called. Pagan devils they were called. They were leafy shade in summer. They scratched against the clouds in winter. You gathered acorns when you were a kid. You imagined sky gave them to you like charms. You kept them in metal bucket you stole from Mr. Farley's hardware store — below a small bedside lamp where you slept in the attic.

What did you think? A lost television soul — because you had to think — you stared at a late night horror flick and rolled out pizza dough as a strategy? Magnifications of magnifications — what was that word the raven-haired woman used? Didn't it mean house lights?

Mostly likely you clear the thing and feel suspended. You handed the dog a slice. Everyone should have a slice. Maybe that was what you knew. Stop biting your teeth. Birds outside in the snowy trees slept like empty radios.

Namaste — that was it.

But there was something in the shadows and it was chasing after you.

Some ancestor — some fire dwelling creature — connected you backwards in time to horny ass cousins living in large muscular bodies and guided by small brains and who made monster sex in caves and gave off something like distant thoughts for future time to discover. How did that work? Forty thousand years old — afraid to be alive in the head — couldn't figure out why he was — and why do you know about it?

He twisted in the underbrush walking around the mountain. Oh no he was alone. Overhead long-feathered buzzards wheeled in the sky like angels. Rodents began stalking him. What he needed was a brainstorm and not just a spear to keep him alive

How does that work? What was it kept you walking through — or what keeps walking through you? Smooth as glass from sandlot memories of boy-time games to chain-smoking marijuana monkey shine time gaming the shit — smooth as glass from terminally unresolved lawn grass time to monster truck dervish credit card time with fucked up worries and a crowded modern silence that ponies up to a bank — smooth as glass and outrageous vanity and worthless market gadgets and the unsettled meditative tools we employ on the liquor glass margins to mark our idle naked time with and not to mention the theatrical mixed up skinny-dipping we equate with joy rides and story lines and love in the simple beauty of someone else's face turned back at you like a classic heaven that lost a found heart — smooth as glass — slippery fragile and connective — walking around and around a mountain — there was something in the shadows chasing after you like a movie scene much as you were chasing after it like you expected answers from the universe. Later on you sat on a cliff high above the trailhead and the parking lot below with its diminishing cars leaving for fantasies and tasty crab cakes and greasy baskets of fish and chips or shiny hamburgers with fries from the all purpose menu with those faint aromas of happiness if the kids won't stop crying as nighttime came upon and bulldozed the horizon into colors and then began placing stars one by one by the thousands to take up place in the backyards of the sky.

There was a murder of crows in the sky next evening.

*

A single beaten up and dented street lamp — with a shallow incandescent glow — hung on a splintered wooden pole by the grace of three rusted bolts. Dim ancient light shone down on the parking lot. Beach grass shifted in the mosquito free breeze. Short gnarly trees — shocked into odd growths after years out in the weather and the freaked out Atlantic storms — covered a footpath that twisted through the dunes and lead to the water.

It used to be the old fishing road. Horses and wagons hauled the catch of the day from the surf out to the docks to be sold.

Then it was paved for trucks and more lines in the water and the catch of the day got out to the docks quicker and bigger.

Then surf fishing as a living got replaced by boats the size of factories. Hooked drop lines stretched behind the boat's wake for half a mile and gilled anything in the way.

Soon after — the road was forgotten as a road. It shrank back down to footprints. And the dunes slowly crossed over — backwards and inward — dune upon dune — and filled in the road — and the broken asphalt debris like some absurd stand-in for glacial till — with ever- reverent sand and a moving wind and a primordial sense as to where the road belonged.

Maybe it was the off-season quiet that did it — salt air and molecules — even at a mythological best — you got it. You were never going to end up over the rainbow with a pot of gold. If anything you should go out and buy more foul weather gear.

*

Whatever it took — however myth-less we end up — there were slick dark seal hoods of identity to pass through and a universe of mirrors to crash — sans reservations naturally.

Swimming in the waves — rolling with the waves — floating on the waves and looking upward at the moon and stars — we had a temperament for living and a template for dying. Maybe the surprise was how love carried the years. How together we lived as a collective memory. Sure we had stars to get lost in and moonlight to guide us. Spellbound special effects — real as seawater on your teeth — what did we own after our karmic stumbles were used and put onto another rising generation? Did we actually get past the Nazi force fields and cracked atomic weapons and the real estate boom and disposable incomes?

*

How did we get here the raven-haired woman said riding a wave? What I mean is how do we get to this point?

We were restless you said and so they sent us over from central casting.

That doesn't provide much cover she said.

That's true you said. There are forces out there as we speak and they're prepared to do us harm.

Aren't we too old for all that she said?

Probably you said. There was only so much time to go around. Then we invent the rest.

We bobbed in the waves amidst so much flotsam and jetsam shit in the water that we might have been mistaken for leftovers from a shipwreck. Some dreams don't belong to us as individuals. They failed as property kept in a museum. They passed among us for safekeeping — malleable as lead — simple as a bar song that remained in your head for days. You hummed that tune — someone else picked it up and hummed that tune.

My hair is gray the raven-haired woman said spitting out the ocean after she'd gone under a wave.

Sure you said. But you still do the job.

We have more enemies than we eliminate she said.

You watched her across the moonlight ebb on the water — trying to avoid a short attention span — knowing how she was without her wearing a wet suit.

Let's emphasize the moment from central casting you said.

Sure she said going under a swell. What's the script?

You said that you were written in as a wounded soldier named Trevor. A darling sort of a character who smoked on the operating table and whose dance with battle experience had left him without an arm and now the camera replaced that experience with various angled head shots to imply not only loss but also the beginnings of hope and an unruly sense of rebellion that until his current misfortunes had gone on inside him for years both unheeded and unclaimed.

The raven-haired woman was a nurse named Gina. She too had lost something. And this loss — as she explained — she never had the words to explain — obliquely at first — then seductively throughout — using her descriptions of war and the injured in the early credit voiceover as the moral amplitude of the film — but then due to studio demands the camera loved her body more than she needed to explain what happened — her body as a well-rehearsed metaphor in cinema time — the nurse with the blouse.

And the first time Gina eyes met Trevor's eyes was at a harbor festival. It was a day belonging to a saint whose statue was roped to a buoy and decorated with garlands of flowers and bright cloth strips and written supplications on paper scraps all begging forgiveness and asking for a greater fishing season to come.

Was it supposed to sink — the saint I mean — the raven-haired woman asked?

Not really Trevor said. It's just supposed to float there and collect the facts.

*

… lone surfcaster at sunrise threw a line into the tide coming in … the curve of the earth stood beyond his cast … rosy red and gold at the horizon… closer to shoreline a smoky blue fog on the waves… we waved at him from a stone lined fire pit … coffee was brewing and technically our camp was illegal — but so was public nudity and having sex out in the open… hey yo pancakes in twenty minutes… were the surfers happy or did they just ride each day at dawn when conditions were right… and where does it come from… this happiness… how much money would you pay for it… and what makes you think that it was a deal… but where does it come from… it doesn't go anywhere… it's like having ideas about ideas and coming up with sleeping on the beach… the chase or the capture… concept or physical act or internal generated force… what we take for granted… do we cause it or does it cause us… the surfcaster threw another line… smooth and snap like… small exaggerations… simultaneous exclamations… does happiness radiate or do we swallow it like a pill in hopes …why was pain a bummer and happiness not… and why were those even considerations… or not even… or destination oriented even or a gut thing… a man walked along the water's edge and appeared determined not to have the waves touch his bare feet… when they come close he retreated backwards and nearly fell over… and that's how he walked down the beach…retreating backwards and nearly falling over … as though he were between the irrational and the enjoyable … another man and a young boy can't get a kite to fly and looked disappointed… they let it go and pitched rocks into the waves instead… was it to be aimless and meander… or to gather it up instead and hold onto it… what about god you once asked Miss Farley… looking into her face was like staring into castration… but what happened was we were all hit with obedience instead… you didn't understand it at the time but really… what was so terribly wrong… being young at the time suited you… like Superman's cape over Clark Kent's neurotic business suit … and what repeats… for sure there was going to be fooling around with this life… but what's on the leash… do we like happiness to be illusive so we need to look after it … the impossible dream… a lonesome walker with a tattoo on his spine that branched out to wings at his shoulder blades and down the backsides of his beefy arms… long tangled motorcycle hair caught in the breeze… what was comfort in thought… seaweed crashed about his ankles… what else worries the way we do… but where does the tide go that kid asked his parents… ooh this was such a good song Gina said and put the ear buds on the dog…

*

faster than gravity

There were invariables involved while growing up. There was always something new and unusual to look at in the gutter and this made walking to the store for bread and milk never the same sidewalk twice.

Did you ever see Miss Farley walking about?

What made it necessary for adults to figure they secured our feelings and measured every inch of our lives with yardsticks and pencil marks on kitchen walls?

One day we would meet the divine. That's how the old story squared things up.

Accordingly there was no problem with this line of thought.

But shit — it was difficult enough to try and believe if you had a soul or not — when a text was palmed off on you — and on page three you were shown here it was: your soul. On page three there it was: the picture of a milk bottle. So your soul was a milk bottle. White and clear meant full of grace. Dark spots or shadows meant sin. Did grace come in handy quarts or half gallons? And could you bless people with milk like it was holy water?

You remember saying to Herbie G. one time over a delicious slice — I hope there's pizza in heaven.

Herbie G. was a Jewish kid who lived in the neighborhood over on Colonial Street. He went to public school and his parents were divorced. Did Herbie have a milk bottle also? But what you were told was that unless Herbie G. was a true believer and unless he was folded into god's pocket in just that way — and not just a Jewish kid — or any other way like other public school kids — then Herbie G. was not getting into heaven.

What was this selective business — buzzing around out heads like flies eating on day old shit?

Didn't we all deserve great pizza and floating in atmospheres together and listening to music played by longhaired angel bands? How could Herbie G. get his act together in time and try and outdo his birth accident? How did that work if your parents weren't living together and he wasn't old enough to have a say so? Who the fuck was Herbie G. anyway and why did god even give a fucking care?

Every motive had a rule to guide it and a rule to destroy it. There was little room left to maneuver. Was it any wonder? How simple it was to dumb ourselves down.? You remember praying for Herbie G?. He moved away. You lost track for his whereabouts. The neighborhood was being destroyed anyway by the war between the others and the others so what did it matter — wondering about his descent into hell? But still — blessings and pressures come off the same stem.

Don't they?

*

the coffee meditations

We took a boat ride out to some islands. It was mostly as a tourist thing to do with our time but also we both felt a need to get off one land for another. It was an alchemy we were after. You looked over at the raven-haired woman and imagined how fortunate you were to be sitting opposite her on the tiny boat deck. Warm jelly daylight — that's how you remember the sky where it met the bay and seemed to fold back in on itself. It's silly like that — they were just reflections of light off water — but we always want something more and so why not have it? And it was like she wore nothing but sensual energy dots that outlined her body and a floppy hat that spilled her gray-dark hair onto her brown shoulders like Chinese water names for certain aquatic plants in old poetry.

We were dangerous she said over the choppy spray from the boat's motors.

Right you thought. A lodestar we followed that made each tomorrow not so obvious that it would return — guess the nervous addictions kept us alive.

Once on island there was a small general store at the harbor. The natives sat on the front porch — talking and smoking and drinking pots of coffee. That was how it was done you thought. The harbor parking lot was filled with work-beaten pickup trucks — many without license plates — this was an island — whose beds were cluttered with lawn mowing equipment and carpenter tools and lobster traps.

We walked along the one paved road like a couple of drunks who just cashed a two dollar lottery ticket.

Could we fit in here the raven-haired woman asked?

That depends. How far away do we need to get?

Oh I don't know she said. A place maybe to settle for a while — while things clear — a place oh I don't know where we didn't have to do anything special.

We'd be noticed here. Like a bad song on the radio gets noticed after it's been played awhile.

There was something curious in the air — like walking along and arriving someplace in the same motion without ever noticing a difference.

It's a smell the raven-haired woman said. Not a smell really but a scent. Odd isn't it?

It was. But then everything these days was odd. Maybe the years were starting to gain on us. All those years — the specialized employments — the lies — the graft of living where we made money while others had to die.

I know what it is she said.

What?

Lilacs and low tide she said.

And yea there it was. Bath-time fragrance and exposed mud flat — a cosmology of the nude and a mineral density baking in the sunlight — the perfect time of blooms and clam rot — and we as carriers of memory were woven into a fabric of springtime.

Ooh look at that one she said.

This was a given. The raven-haired woman pointed at a house and was now hypnotized by it. She was in love. With a house — with a sequence — what that house inspired. Multiple gables and intersecting rooflines and plain white clapboards with plain white trim with a veranda style porch that looked into the Atlantic beyond a small chain of other islands in the watery distance. It was all very karmic and extended. Towels on a clothesline lifted and fell in a sunny melancholy breeze. A technicolor riot of lupines and paper thin orange poppies lay on the sandy lawn in loose ends — some blooming — some gone by. Used tire containers filled with marigolds… green woods highlighted by dark spruce trees…. She stepped off the road and touched the house.

It's not trespassing she said.

No it isn't you said. And we've done much worse.

It's always the back door she said. That's the best.

*

faster than gravity

Red Dog and Cripple Beast left you off and told you to quit worrying.

They hopped off into the night like non-stop young boys breaking the corner at 21st Street. Reds D. lit up a cigarette like he was dying for it. Cripple B. flailed his arms above his head as he talked — explaining how the neighborhood was so fucking cutthroat cool.

You watched them fade around the corner at 21st Street — gone with the leaves blown across the streets by nickel-assed autumn winds. We were being swallowed by a menace that was as human as it was brutal. It was simple to see and hard to adjust. But we were out of time. Like game fucking over.

But thinking it over made you pause — pause to smile. But no one can see that. No one can see you smile. It's necessary both to smile and to keep that hidden.

And what to do at this hour but keep walking? Walk home — even though you knew in the deepest heart you carried — you knew you were not going home. Another night walking along the avenue like some refugee from a place where you weren't leaving. The more the cool air pushed against you the dumber you felt trying to squeeze the zipper on your jacket collar closed. Wasn't this the stuff we were supposed to grow into and become fucking legends about? Like in your own head — where all you did was to look over your shoulder.

But the wine… wine to a twelve year old made your legs rubber… wine to a twelve year old made you fashionable…wine made you scared someone else was going to bust in and crack your dream.

So you said hey to the others hanging out in the streets below the schoolyard. But you don't stop to talk. That usually doesn't happen at night. The language thing between others and others was a fear. So you just nod and try to be cool and flash hey we're all wasted and there's nothing to do here that means anything but to move through it without kicking up any more shit than necessary. And that works. Mostly. Even though there was a great undertow throwing us back into genetics and the other crap in the neighborhood that could ruin your life. Sad there were only words that kept us apart. Other kids versus other kids — but how do we make good unless everyone spoke freely? Things like this were handed down to us all from the elders. And in a sense all this shit we were given as truth turned out to be totally fucking wrongheaded. Why? For a simple reason — that it was not ours. We did not own it.

So you just said fuck it. And walked on by like a great soulful tune that played on the radio.

Down the avenue past the kiss and tell side streets where girls got pregnant and boys had a barking priest in their face swatting heads and wanting details. It was weird — but it was the same place where the junkies went to stab their arms and explode a moment's relief into their tired veins. A small corner of nowhere where the sidewalk heaved and burst where lonely sycamore roots pushed upward and tree branches reached into the pumpkin headed October sky and blocked the streetlight down below.

Stillness grabbed you — it always did — and that's what does it. We were always looking for greatness. Like that soulful tune on the radio there was this one house. It was like any other house among all the other row houses. A house to speak of because you lived and slept there and where hopefully all that happened outside never entered the door.

Other families lived inches away your room on either side of the walls. How did this happen? Why were you here? Who were these other people you lived with?

Somehow it seemed like a bribe.

But it was too early to go home. To actually go home and stay inside and say that was the story until tomorrow.

The clock in the real estate office said 12:49 glowing on a creepy pink face in the window. Who bought anything in this part of the world? How do you have a business like that?

But it was too early to go home. If you went home you'd meet your father. He'd be fresh off the K-bus like a zombie coming in the door off the dead shift from the factory. He'd asked questions that you avoided. Before you answered them his brain suddenly turned inside out and he'd be lost sitting and sitting and staring into the television and ignoring you. Why bother? When he drank he was ignorant and rude. When he didn't drink he was a simpleton churned away like butter.

So you waited and hung out on Opal Street.

Inside the rectory you thought the priests — huddled with sad memories — disturbed by nature — accomplished from sin — waited for time to pass like the rest of us. How was it like that?

Where the rectory lawn ended in thick hedges and a flat stonewall — there was a brown military colored mailbox- the storage kind where letter walkers tossed their bundles. How many hours? How long have you spent — sitting on a mailbox waiting for nothing to happen?

Just watching the street pull up on another funny street corner that only confused you — Opal Street and Avenue C — across from the house where you lived.

Where a house for sale nowhere was advertised in a phantom real estate office.

Where the church housed the poor box and the saintly purpose of relics. Where whatever said in the church was always told from yesterday — and fetishized a place that no longer existed.

Or assume that inside the mailbox was a letter addressed to you.

Across Avenue C was an empty storefront where Felix the barbershop used to be.

Where does it go? That soulful tune on the radio — walk on by — was that a place where you could live?

Down 20th Street a crowd gathered outside the Hell Belle Tavern. Everybody was grab ass talking to the moon and laughing with whoever listened. Everybody danced with transistors. Everybody was smoking dope. Everybody had a pint that got passed around.

Across 20th Street at Avenue S was Cheapy Kings used car lot. The worst cars in the world ended up for resale at Cheapy Kings. If the crowd at The Belle got too big then it spilled across the street to the car lot. The crowds then yelled at one another across 20th Street like a siren call in heat. The party might go on like that until dawn broke stupid in the east — or until the cops showed up on a house complaint and told the crowds to go home and sleep it off.

The number 6 trolley clanged over the familiar and irregular tracks on Ogontz Avenue. Ah — the number 6 trolley — like having a memory in the universe — the number 6 was the same trolley your grandfather used to drive. Would it be replaced? Would it go and be replaced by the now fashionable electric bus taking over routes in Jersey-land?

And that other young boy earlier tonight — where did he die — beaten curbside — DOA in time — and where does he end up — does he walk on by — kept in prayers and rap sheets and imagined in legend?

What did it matter how well you diagramed a sentence in school according to the rules of a grammar that no one really used in the world? What good was it that Thomas Jefferson treated his slaves well? How many times — how often — can a school year teach you battle plans against the physical universe — holy card obedience — and the history of empires — before we in the seats passed out from tales explained by well-intentioned but sedated idiots?

Rain began falling through the trees. Certain dreams do not belong to individuals.

*

the coffee meditations

The raven-haired woman stopped to pee- squatting in the morning heat behind a tall stand of sweet-smelling lilacs. You watched the road for potential embarrassing moments that might happen.

Someone told me life was a feeling she said.

Yea you said. You remembered Junior Clifton dunking a basketball on the neighborhood courts.

What was that like she asked?

The dunks were amazing.

No she said. You're talking about a kind of nothing. What makes you think you understand it one way or another?

Wasn't there always a taste of honey left behind in a sweetened cup? Don't we want the taste? Or was it up for grabs?

Up above — ospreys fished against a milky blue sky. Why do you care you asked?

It's not that she said taking a moment and looking about the road and the shallow fields of the island. But it does matter she said what we give up.

Yea you said — there was that lifetime thing you said.

But here's a funny thing you said: remember the holy trinity? We needed to memorize it but never understood it. So one day you had great news. You found the answer: how it was that the holy trinity existed.

And? — the raven-haired woman asked....

She hitched up her jeans after pissing and looked superb doing it.

Three-in-one oil you said. One oil and that was made from three different oils and together that made one oil from three and because that three made one and one made three and three was really one and one was really three.

You had this down. You owned it. Now you saw it. And if only others understood it like you did -three-in-one oil — that was the mystery of the trinity. You could buy it at Pep Boys for 89¢.

But no else saw it that way — especially in school.

Sister Crumble stared you down and asked: what did: what did you say?

The other day you were over on 20th Street and looked in to say hey to Mister Armstrong working in his garage. He was always doing handyman stuff around the neighborhood like fixing a door hinge or replacing a busted step. Anyway — there it was in his toolbox- with hammers and sad pliers and disorganized drill bits — a small tin of three-in-one oil.

It struck immediately you said. The holy trinity — three-in-one oil — they were made through the same process! And so wasn't revelation supposed to follow?

However- Sister Crumble did not see it that way.

She was so far up in your face that she did not look real — but was more like a rubbery Halloween mask — distorted and grotesque and looked funny. There was a mask yelling at you and damning you with breath that smelled like gunpowder. Her spittle flew across your nose. She screamed behind that mask that you blasphemed — and so in turn cracked you across the head from the right and then hit you back again from the left in case you missed something

But don't you care you said? The mystery was solved! Wasn't it great! That god had manifested in Mister Armstrong's toolbox? And was cheap to buy at Pep Boys!

*

faster than gravity

Thunder banged overhead — the park stopped and looked around.

A large cloud mass moved overhead — suddenly heavy rain drained a southwest sky.

Small lakes formed — storm drains backed up.

Spiky electric winds fractured the air.

Primitive atmospheres above the earth came apart and exploded on contact.

You just got a job as an odd job man for a hotel and lied about your age to get it.

Funny to think how lying was the absolute truth.

But to get the job you needed to be eighteen and you were not yet there.

Hallucinatory adolescence saved the day.

Not being truthful got you a place all your own to rent and money in your pocket.

One evening as a bus boy you lifted a MasterCard off a drunken table.

New radio — new bicycle — Chuck Taylor's — bought at the all-night store.

Impossible sunglasses — warm hoodie — gladiator sandals — you gave to Eden.

Shred the card — tossed what remained into the waves — like Blind Charlie would do.

Yea. This worked. This totally worked.

*

the coffee meditations

We were talking and walking along- happily lost together- passionate small talk to beat the day- disconnected far from the maddening schemes of the world — when suddenly some guy out walking his dog fell in beside us on the road. A beefy guy with short dark hair and beard and wearing jeans and boots in the early summer heat and it was odd the way he just appeared. One minute there's no one on the road but you and the raven-haired woman. And the next minute — there's this guy walking beside us and striking up a conversation like he'd been there all along since we got off the boat. How did we miss him? What did it mean? And did it mean we were now paranoid again and this guy was something that he wasn't?

He said he was born and raised out here. Eventually as he grew up he needed to move off island to look for work. Most people went through it he said. But after so many years living inland he got tired with it. Tired with chasing the money and getting none. He'd rather walk on the road with his dog and be poor etc.

It was a bit odd. Some stranger showed up and he immediately started telling us about his life. The repairs he needed to make each day...

We walked along and you heard the raven-haired woman thinking: whose life doesn't amount to a gesture?

He was married and then divorced and then as a consequence had huge bills to pay.

Maybe some trouble we thought. Maybe some violence took place.

Then he opened up. He shouted why... but it wasn't angry sounding or even a question... but was more like an ordinary voice — a voice you might have anyway... And that made us more suspicious.

He told us there was a bar stool and lots of cheap beer. There were faces all around him. And those faces asked what was the better option? They had eyes on the clock. But there was nothing to schedule. Tobacco smoke hung around their heads like a fog that wouldn't lift. Egg stained mouths he said before breakfast was even served — much like the bank loans they were outstanding on their lives.

You need to tighten your mind he went on and threw a ball for the dog across a meadow of wildflowers. The dog took off and chased it — like chasing a ball and bringing it back was the very idea of having been given an idea to do something with the idea in the first place.

Was this like a fall from grace the raven-haired woman asked?

People get hard he said. Sometimes they don't forgive themselves: for what they done you know? Sometimes he said people stray. They try and try again but it's no use. They can't. For what they try and do. They can't get back on the fold.

And then what the raven-haired woman asked?

Then the guy said what happens was: is that sermons come true. We're damned if we don't work. Or what happens when that work paid you less than for what you know how to do. That was the problem with sermons. They don't add up. But they keep the telling up and going until your head pops.

Do you think this guy's made us the raven-haired woman thought? Do you think he knows who we are?

Didn't know what to say. It was always the raven-haired woman's job to be paranoid.

How could this guy know us? We needed to be cautious. That's the first thing you learn. The second thing you learn was to forget spontaneity and always plan. And the third thing you learn was that if you forgot the first two then you were dead.

The raven-haired woman thought I'm going to ask this guy if his head popped.

No not really he laughed. But he said you had to wonder. You had to wonder how this life was exactly made... and then when it's made that way... what do you get for the effort?

But where did that leave the faithful he said? The trembling faithful

— those holy souls from every town and city — the holy souls who loved by fear alone and whose fear grew night and day — where did they end up?

Looked at another way — weren't they just a stand in for the guilty? Just what did we do? Why do we accept punishment?

This guy had something. It was easy to see. But not so much that it was simple enough to trust. Because you can't trust anyone that you believe was real.

Must be nice though to live out here the raven-haired woman asked.

Yea he said it is. What you end up doing was what you know. That's why I'm back out here. But what you know was all fucked up anyway… so in the end… it don't matter what you know. Because you always end up back where you started.

We stopped walking. The raven-haired woman grabbed the guy by the shoulders and stared into his eyes. We stood beside a meadow with wild-flowers and songbirds going nuts in springtime. So this cruel myth being alive — with nothing to show for it — made a mockery of us?

The guy didn't know what to say. He probably wasn't used to being grabbed by a woman.

No he said.

There was a gentle look that went forward through his eyes and played out innocently across his expression. But it also might be the same look Anthony Perkins had in Psycho when Janet Leigh pulled up on that rainy night.

Look he said. You get turned around.

Do you remember Tang the raven-haired woman asked? The astro-nauts breakfast drink?

Yea he laughed I do. Shit tasted terrible but we drank it.

Well that's what heaven tastes like the raven-haired woman said. Some old jar that was a substitute for the real thing and when you think about it- does that make you feel scared?

Then we weren't alone on the road anymore. A number of people came walking by either way. Summer people you'd guess judging by their clothes and their smiles. In groups they surrounded the guy. How was the winter out here? How'd that ear infection go? See you at the community hall later? ... Could you put on a roof on the cottage? There's a drainage problem if you might have a look at that? And a thousand other requests that mobbed the guy for household repair answers and counsel about what to do with seagulls shitting all the time on the back deck as if his life were stretched all the way back from infinity and the dead to just some guy trying to slow down the minute hands on a clock.

And you know- the raven-haired woman thought- this all was too demanding and way too sudden. I don't like this she thought.

Don't think about it you said. We need to walk away from this.

No she thought. There was something following us. There was a man here who does not belong- a man who does not keep to himself what he thinks despite what he says afterwards. And what's up with the PhD Thoreau bullshit?

Maybe you thought- as he implied- we're all employed by the same spearhead. We're tolerated and disciplined and trained to work like dogs and then left to see plainly for it. Where's that age that we all want? Where we enter the future for a fucking better world- where freedom and influence turn into something like mechanics and we're then heart-felt in the world?

Yea she thought. There was something glorious here. But it's just a paycheck. He knows who we are.

What if he doesn't? What if you're wrong?

Mistakes get made she thought. But this was not a mistake.

And so you looked.

Even if our place were already there — waiting there for us with all the anxiety Gary Cooper faced in High Noon — the one experiment with life rising above subjugation- the horizon stretching out like cracks in an old face- a life well lived- the long string of pearl mornings- it still ended up as a kind of electricity of being that nobody in their right minds would pay you a dime for. You felt sorry for the guy. He returned to his island a changed man. The trees still bloomed shade against the heat. Maybe he took in the occasional proverb.

But the raven-haired woman was a tough one to argue with. She shot him. Only once was what it took because she was a pro. If there were something personal she would have added a flourish.

It wasn't so difficult to imagine — as it was such a pain to have him on our hands.

We dragged the body across the road and tossed him behind a farm stand that still had plastic mulch tarps over the beds. The rest of the day we spent buoyant because what else was there to do?

We got back on the boat to the mainland pronto before anything negative blew up in our face.

Because we were terrified — because we did not care after the fact nor did we even care because of the fact — we were terrified by the explosive power of wonder and how that kept whipping and whipping our attention like a weather flag on the boat — because we were terrified — because we were able to walk away.

*

the coffee meditations

A clear balloon with a tiny heart message inside rolled and bounced across the sand with a long string attached.

It hung in the wind for a strange second and hovered across our camp — a strange second where it didn't move — hung there in the wind like a thought bubble. And because it was clear you looked right through it.

Then it rolled on with the breeze- tumbling along down the beach.

The balloon rolled along. Then it hung in the air again — glossy curious musical and nude. And it remained that way — brief as an elegy — turning on some invisible axis without moving.

You watched it through some binoculars that you stole from a dead man you met a few days before. Then it moved off — and whirled through crowds and splashy beach umbrellas like flowers planted in the sand- and passed over large expressionistic towels where delighted partisans — disconnected from the world — lay flat out on holiday spinal columns and asleep on vacation- while their jobs back home were being sold out to the hordes of youngsters who promised they worked for less.

Perhaps you should cue the love interest and wake the raven-haired woman and try and explain the balloon to her? She was sleeping like a jasmine stick that went out and all that was left was a little smoke before a window.

Did breath or kindness matter? We were being hunted. Maybe it was time to unbutton a deal that was owed us. We've kept running for years. The dog was listening to: wish you were here. And those years never end — they kept on — appearing in renditions — well elucidated and late in time. How to explain this balloon?

Gray blue clouds in scores like addictions were further out to sea and tangled on the horizon line. Looking at them you thought: god speed.

With the raven-haired woman napping- and you not wanting to disturb genesis- especially against the tides- the beautiful Atlantic- the first address — ridiculous airplane advertisements flew overhead for cancer products and casinos- you bent down close to her ear and whispered — doesn't someone need to wake up before it's too late?

*

Down the beach a man and a woman were tossing a baby up into the air. Everyone squealed as though delight were a built in reaction to the suicide is painless music from MASH. They fly their child. Up in the air and down. Flying as much as they wanted like blessed ignorance or maneuvers in cosmology.

*

We can't have profiles weighted around our hands.
We can't have curly-lipped prosecutors.
We can't have the cheap pine that creaks in coffins.

*

The last blue light we had fell off the evening and vanished into the horizon.
The best part of life was life's limitations.
Where was it said that we couldn't outdo them?

*

Three fishermen passed at the surf's edge — thirty feet or so from our camp outside the scratch lands and the oil workers' tents. Who were these people? Why did they talk so loud — about where to fish? What was incomplete here?

You looked at them and decided — they looked like they knew nothing — and right there- that was the problem.

Besides — they had a dog for a slave — and that fucking killed you.

Some drooling Siberian in a harness sweating its nuts off — pulling a fat wheeled cart — large boom box aboard playing cowboy music — beverage coolers stacked on the cart like adult Legos. And it's not the dog so much or the cowboy music or even men acting like crows — men do that — they act like crows — but what it really came down to was practically nothing at all that caught you on eye level- and that was what bothered you.

Actually you liked cowboy music.

But when you saw men acting like crows — first thought was best thought — and that thought was to watch your back before somebody behind your back cashed you in.

*

One day you thought — but that was another day — it was not today. Today we were true to another day because we needed to get some rest. The three fishermen didn't help. It was fine to be paranoid. But to be paranoid and active was something else. And that didn't help.

Gulls and terns glided over tides made from green white waves.

Little sandpipers ran nervously around an ocean foam bubbling into the sand — stop and go — advance and retreat — and picking at insects in the seaweed lines.

If we never came back — if we left today- if we lost our dreams — if we went unanswered — if we lived on that boulevard lined with houses with dual identities like downhearted and pleasurable and leafy shade trees in mind that robbed the heat from the sun and made the asphalt feel better — if you weren't scared — if you sat on a beach and there were three fisherman you did not trust — if everybody was within eyeball distance and not a lucky shot — if the raven-haired woman needed more sleep — if you were someone who needed both the money and the girl in the end — if you believed running in circles was fine as long as we got away with it — if we didn't kill anybody else — if there weren't three fucking bimbos dressed as fishermen — if only they didn't look insane and fake as lost souls about where to fish — when you looked up and down and sideways and said good — no one else was around — just you and cowboy music — if Mars was rising — if Mars floated in the sky a billion years ago and moved steadily over cold lengths of time to reach us today — if you understood any of this — if you understood the waves — if those questions robbed us — if indeed it was too late to be fixated — sans mammal — sans identification purpose — sans smart aleck — if evening accumulated in the sky and glorified our skins — if you had to pay a strange witness to three guys who could not bait a hook-if you had a walk away card no matter how it ended...

*

Why she asked?

Because it seemed like a genuine thing to do at the time you said.

We drove off underneath the stars and didn't look back at the outgoing tide. Nothing to lose there — but the question was — was there anything to gain?

Driving and heading further into the night — being in love and listening to the radio — sharing a pie — heading further into the night — looking for a hole in the wall of ten thousand things where we knew Jersey-land sheltered us — middle aged outlaws with a job to do — there was the joke -and the time we had left to do it there was the joke.

*

What we didn't understand was there was a hurricane rushing up the coast and tearing up everything in its way. Or as the radio said: damn the summer went fast! The forecast called for waiting in fear until the powerful storm arrived. But we needed taffy and tee shirts...

The raven-haired woman said I don't like the winds.

Are you scared?

Yes she said. But uncertainty means so much. It's like we're dreaming in public — even if it was by accident... but I still get afraid. Can we hurry? Before nature does us in and the last thing we know in this life was a weather forecast?

What if this was the time to leave and not come back you asked?

I don't know if that's possible she said.

There's a hurricane you said. Even if it's a bad cover maybe we count on getting washed away in a storm.

No she said. Don't count on that. We don't get missed.

*

We grabbed a motel room while everyone else ran for the hills.

No promises the woman behind the desk said. You can't flush the toilet — you're out of here.

*

a number of murders calm down tricking yourself of all things
sunshineflowers beach towels gratitudelittle shells
flotsam boat gearworthless punctured rubberized
everything dies everything comes back
love changes everythingthere's a point accept nothing less
you ask remember that?
 sand castles beach changelings butt naked sunburn
she asks again are you hungry?
the trouble signs she said
 the bad coffee we bought at the store
 the uncooked fish in the restaurant
 some motel dad next door whose entire child care vocabulary seemed
to consist of
 yelling NO in capital letters to three infants stupefied by genetics
everything waited on the storm
 around town people laughed and bought water and matches
the weather channel was everywhere
we buy water and matches also
one woman said she was so afraid for the trees

strange luminescent mist moving in across town like a ghost
one minute humid with a heavy hand the next cold and a dull pearly white
destruction was key but what destroys a storm? town folk optimism?
 she doesn't like it it's going to happen at night
 would it be more than scary not to see it in the darkness?
definitely night she said
have a good hurricane the waitress said after breakfast
worries about floods houses sliding off dunes boats getting crushed
will the windows in the room last?were the tress aware?
 in the clouds zephyrs gone bad
 walked out a road that said dead end we're day trippers spiritsso fuck it
 we emptied onto a small water land tall grasses stiff wind definitely
a place
 wading birds worked up celluloid moment soundtrackriders on the
storm
 heavy Darth Vader clouds
 surf heaving and heaving sky above like the crazed Atlantic below
 back at the room grilled cheese canned soup waiting till death do us part
 she doesn't sleep possessed by wind banshee outside she said
 pounding ocean rain
 shaken walls shaken doors like a nightmare wanted into your sleep
 water and matches heart to heart strike the unknown
 next day trees left standing blown apart at the leaves
 let's step outside party balloons twisted around torn zinnias liquid
sunlight
 shiny muscle tension walking beside someone else's life
 ten thousand simple acts it was clear it was impossible
 sunflowers and tomatoes uprooted and dumped in the street
 the skin was a mystery so were the wind chimes the warm morning
shadows

*

faster than gravity

The rain hung above the evening as the police hauled the kid away. Whether he would be dead later on was strictly- at this point in his ass kicked life- an academic matter.

Cripple said nothing staring from behind the hedge. On the avenue the trolley had long ago passed the sad bystander who questioned if he weren't better off dead than how he was alive. A small bustle of people appeared and helped him to his feet- pressing handkerchiefs to his banged up face and offered comforting words like any of it mattered.

It was definitely time to leave. But Cripple said we couldn't afford to be seen. So we sat in the rain and waited.

When the police finally cleared out- and the floodlights from Mulligan's were turned on- and the general dismay below us turned into another Friday night — we snuck away.

It was quickest to get through the alley on the backside of Colonial Street — before the dads got home and started getting drunk for the weekend and where fucked up dogs in shit-fouled yards snarled against their chains.

*

Cripple wanted to head over to Da Vinci's for a pie. And much that like immediate thought — a hot slice — what Cripple said lifted your spirits. The rain let up and was as much a drizzle as it was a mockery from above. A cool October wind picked whatever leaves that weren't rain soaked and scattered them in whirls across Mulligan's parking lot.

We ran through the alley — rushing toward a pie — Friday night happiness — escaping a crime scene — with an awkward ease known to young boys not knowing the difference.

*

Da Vinci's red neon light was on. The word pizza glowed brightly against the plate glass facade of the shop. Inside the shop — inside everyone's heads — rich tomato sauce and spices cooked on big iron stoves from a thousand year old recipe and killed the air.

A young couple entered and ordered a pie and two beers. Her eyes were as brown and as supple as the leather aviator's gloves were made from. His boots — half-eaten by cement — kicked a lunch pail underneath the table as he crossed his legs and took a tall pull from his beer. Maybe they couldn't afford twilight on the six other nights of the week — but not Friday night. Friday night rocked. They were out together and together they weighed less than a bird.

Row house life and its inhabitants were taking a breath and enjoying a break from the anxious and addictive forty hours that from one week to the next led to paycheck grandeur. Now it was Friday evening. The job was somewhere else. Two days forward it turned back into another lonely idea waiting at a bus stop.

You and Cripple looked out from the back room and saw Reds walk in. You knew this by heart.

Reds found a table inside the steady hum of the shop. He wished he were old enough to drink openly. He often wished for a great many things. But then he told himself he really didn't believe all this business about wishing. He stared out the window at a streetlight on Wyncote Avenue. The stiff brightness from the industrial lamp overhead the avenue made Reds want a cigarette. But Blind Charlie would throw him out if he lit one up.

He doodled a while to pass the time with a geometry problem on a paper napkin. He noticed the contended atmosphere and thought this was so fucking confused. He soaked in hot pizza slices held aloft by hungry neighbors- even as he cared little for any neighbors because he said neighbors were fools.

Elsewhere a medium looking man in a checkered sport coat went to town on a saucy meatball sandwich. Somebody else bit too ambitiously into a homemade Italian pepper and let go with a sizzling wow.

Teenage girls in bunches began to file in.

This pricked up Red's attention like a newly rolled reefer. Despite an annoyance he felt around girls — all the chatty talk about guitar players and acne — made him realize how much he need to blame someone else when he was uncomfortable. Reds stared at the young girls and their butts until his head wandered off like a loose screw. His thirteen-year old experience was limited. His closet moment with sex had come one evening in the big weedy overgrown space behind Da Vinci's that everybody called the Lots.

Abbey Saul liked Reds. But she was not having anything to do with his hands fumbling inside her bra. For Abbey love was all radio lyrics and a secret you might tell a friend one day over your first cigarette.

For Reds love was- well- unfound- like stealing the nudie magazines an uncle left around the house — and then sitting down somewhere private and grabbing yourself until the big thing happened.

A large woman with hefty bones walked up to the counter and announced like a church organ that she'd have a cheese steak- plenty fried onions to go- and make that in a hurry.

Reds turned his attention to a girl dropping quarters into the jukebox. His eyes locked on the fantasy world beyond her clothes. He knew what world was there. He'd seen the nudie pages. He thought he might talk to her — one day he might bump into her at school.

It was dark outside and Reds felt needy. Walking his sandwich to the table- the hoagie oil spilling off and swamping the plate- the lettuce shredded like the money- double spicy meats and two cheeses — a wave of tomatoes resting on an ocean of onions — Reds sat down supremely. He took bites with deliberate careful mouthfuls. He was famished. He wished he were eating with the girl putting quarters into the jukebox.

She ignored Reds and she went back to the table and joined her friends.

But that girl kept giving Reds eyeball problems.

Lonely and incomplete — a bell with no clapper- a cigarette without a match- he questioned when to leave and walk through the door. But he wanted something. And he thought: the idea about wanting something was so good to have. There was nothing better he thought than wanting something. But sensations were common — just fucked up reactions to experience- ghost-like things in his head. Reds went out for the night... however that night ended... his pockets were either full from stealing or he got caught.

You had to be all impulse and balls and that was the fucking plan. Without that- what did you have?

And that girl — the way she opened a pack of chewing gum — tore it open and then pulled one out from the pack and held it there — like she'd seen this before on television and were now imitating it — that did it for him — yeah that did it for him — and then Reds looked up and was thinking about that girl when -

Ace MacDonald's car showed up n the window.

Reds finished eating and then it was on to business. He left Da Vinci's feeling sad though. And he knew why. He passed by that girl's reflection. He looked out at the car and knew he had to pony up. But damn it all — he felt himself pass through her reflection on the way out the door... her reflection he thought... that was a start... that was sweetness even as Reds suffered... a girl's reflection superimposed upon a red neon sign that glowed and said pizza in the window.

*

Why Cripple had this thing he had for sitting behind the hedges and watching the fights went beyond you. Why it was you were there went beyond you. Fat and manicured and bunched close in like a partition — the hedgerow went half a block up Ogontz Avenue between Colonial Street and Avenue S. Between the hedges and the bad looking stucco wall of Mulligan's Funeral Parlor there was kind of a crawl space on the lawn- which sloped away and was retained by a high stonewall set in cement rising above the sidewalk. Barricaded by the lawn's angle and the tangled hedge growth- we were able to look out onto Ogontz Avenue and not be noticed from below. It was like the one-way mirror that stores were installing to help prevent shoplifting.

We watched this other man as he waited for a trolley. He strolled back and forth on a little island in the flow of the avenue. Every so often to increase the boredom from his waiting he swung the rusty chain guardrail — shaken by thousands before him as they once waited like him for the number six trolley to finally show up. The man's guardrail wobbled sadly-like an old cane dropped by someone who's suddenly had a heart attack.

The 6-trolley going north the other way rattled and clanked past-oblong as a bullet- connected overhead by a long metal antenna to electrical wires and the city's juice. You looked to see if you recognized the ghost of your grandfather in the driver's seat. A bell clanged heading for the next stop at 65th Street.

Across Ogontz Avenue there was an orphanage. It was a gloomy place with a deep porch all around with no chairs and gray stone turrets and buttressed cornerstones on rooflines that headed in all four directions. And those stained glass windows underneath the porch roof — did they ever admit light? Why does anyone put windows in the shadows?

Earlier in the century a wealthy guy donated the place. He wanted to give homeless kids a chance. A chance — didn't that sound like a good thing — a chance to have a meal and a bed before indifference caught them and wiped them out.

Maybe some were adopted and filled a need in limbo — for a couple with bacon and egg problems but who wanted a family.

Maybe they stayed lost — stigmatized — born from dead parents and left behind — until the legal age rang their bell.

When that happened — that scary thing called the legal age — if no one claimed them on the outside — then they were throw-a-way kids without financial support — let loose with ten bucks a handshake and a pair of shoes. Then either criminal dreams or the army had dibs on them — kids born from dead parents and left behind.

You didn't know anything like personal about the kids inside. You didn't know much about legal age that didn't frighten you.

Some afternoons on the walk back from Eden's house you'd stop and hang on the iron fence around the grounds and watch the orphan kids play football. A large green lawn incorporated trees for boundaries and goals. What was crazy was it didn't seem to matter how they played.

Didn't matter if you were tall or old or fast or slow. Looked like anybody who wanted to play was in. Little kids ran without purpose like distance was unconnected. Guys tough enough to be on a regular team ran the show — but it looked like no one care that much. Did they even keep score? It looked like they ran and ran and enjoyed running.

The man on the cement island swung on the chain. His feet scraped the ground with the tips of his shoes. His head drooped inside the collar of his imitation London Fog trench coat. He looked over his shoulder. Three busy streets met head on and ran through each other — a hyper-lunatic geometry that squeezed humanity and knocked pedestrians into the air — screaming car horns — broken windshields -

So much drove you nuts.

A cab box on a telephone pole nearby rang- and rang — it always rang — and would keep ringing because there was never anyone around to answer it.

The locked up blue metal newsstand — where you used to sell the evening paper after school — was long abandoned.

Across the street was the ruin from a gas station fire. Why not knock it down? What kept it standing? The building smoked in your head in time — because that night we lost Mr. Thant and his younger cousin Bobcat when the gas station exploded.

You figured the comic book man waiting for the trolley lived in some misty evening row house that he wished he were home for. A sad haired bumbler without a hat in the drizzle — swung on a rusty chain in his cheap threads — and who was perched in a no man's land getting toward four o' clock — when soon enough a gang from the funeral parlor side of Ogontz Avenue — and another gang from below the orphanage — were set to crash and fight whatever nameless other got in the way.

For sure — you felt sorry.

*

Eden sat next to you in class that year. She wore glasses but that didn't bother you.

Behind those lenses was what you knew. She had a soft pink face like an advertisement for a skin moisturizer. Clean dark hair curved to her shoulders and closed in toward her jaw line in a flip of sorts. You thought Eden was beautiful. Of course we've know each other forever- since like first grade. Eden was a girl you felt easy being around. It was like Eden was always there. You always hung around Eden or you always thought about Eden. Looking back upon it- you might say it was a sincere attraction- one that held onto your brain for the effort- and fluttered your heart without the usual girl embarrassments that you had.

Why she asked? Why do you think I'm beautiful? Why can't I be something else?

You hadn't really thought about it. You just felt you knew about it in a certain way. Like there was no answer to it that you knew. Answers were pressurized anyway. School church neighborhood — those were answers. Aptitude exams. The cocksure reign of god. Old boys on street corners were answers that carved things up righteously. No flaws. There wasn't any sense in that.

Sure your attraction to Eden was strange. But so what?

You told her you were hypnotized by the things she did. Like the way she listened to music.

And so that's beauty she asked?

You get excited about things. And you liked to watch how she got excited about things.

It's probably physical she said. What if I dyed my hair blond? What if there was a difference? What if I broke my nose? Or lost an ear or something like that?

You wouldn't look good as a blond you said — despite the commercials about having only one life to live. But no doubt- you said- you have a damn good face. It's a terrific face. It's a face like you feel when you're having a good slice of pizza. You don't need much else.

Pizza she said?

A slice of pie from heaven you said.

Besides that — Eden had a personality that was also informed by the movies. On Sunday afternoons we'd walk the thirteen blocks up Ogontz Avenue to the Renel Theater for the double feature matinee. Both our parents gave us money to spend. If this was life then we were all for it.

You remember her mechanically happy steps cutting lines back and forth across the pavement like a dance routine. We saw a rainbow together once in the dusty gnawed up sky between storms. Vincent Price — all laughter and violence and addiction eyes — had just brought down the House of Usher. Were all attractions meant to be that strange? If so then what were our bodies telegraphing?

We sat side by each in the shadowy space of movie house life without even holding hands. There were dark curiosities for sure.

But how do you explain to a girl? Everything that attraction was for you...

Being around Eden made your stomach hollow. Was that a good thing or was Eden something confusing about to happen? Was there a difference? Depending on who you talked to- going to a movie with a girl either changed your life and ruined it or else you got lucky.

You remember how she cleaned her glasses. Holding them up to the light with strong bony fingers and inspecting them as though juggling opinions. You remember those hazelnut eyes and how her thoughts reached toward your own. Eden was beautiful. If only you knew the reason why. But it didn't matter. And it wasn't enough to masturbate and then pretend you were bashful and intelligent about the whole thing. And it certainly was not acceptable to plan on anything beyond your next meal or the next allowance you got and used the money to either go the movies with Eden or by comic books with.

Sometimes you bought comic books for Eden. But this was eighth grade we were talking about. Things were changing. High school was on the horizon. What happened when suddenly you don't have at your exchange all that was familiar? Even the oddities we took for granted — walking along the boardwalk and kicking trash at gulls — the kiss good-night that began miles from her parent's house — and lasted from the deserted beach to the old King's highway where she lived — would now be changed into something heavy by us getting older from what we knew.

If the Russians allies dropped the bomb then we had a plan no questions asked.

We forget everything else and meet up at the Lots behind Da Vinci's Pizza and make a run for it. There would be no bomb shelters for us. No getting caught in the crossfire. No living in the tragedy. No parishioners saying their prayers and cursing the unthinkable in the frightened candle-light down in the church basement while assholes above went nuclear.

We were headed west like a slogan to some unimaginable place like Montana — which the geography books described as big sky country. We liked the sound of that. If we had to pledge allegiance to a new and desecrated world then it might as well be in big sky country- a place where if there were a lot of stuff falling down around you- then at least you'd see it happening.

Often in class- when Sister Crumble wasn't looking- Eden looked at you and crossed her eyes. You pleaded with her through furtive eye con-tacts — just give you the answer. Give you the answer to a question on page seven — or some old math question — or some old fucking history test. It all stared back at you from the page and performed a sort of pint-sized lobotomy on your behalf- blanking you out and seizing you with a dullness that would not allow your brain to work. You were not good with tests. There didn't seem a reason to be good with tests.

Eden shook her head and indicated the material was multiple choices. Just pick one her thoughts said. Even if it was wrong- just pick one or the other. And then she'd turn back to her paper and wouldn't say any-thing more until after class.

*

the coffee meditations

We watched the sun go down and downed Tupperware containers filled with vodka.

How did we ever get Tupperware.... did we buy the damn things or did we steal them... there was another filled with shrimp and cocktail sauce... and another filled with tomato avocado and celery... crusty bread from some guy we met in a parking lot... not a bad preview... kick on into the golden years... cruise unknown... we snapped up some digital memories... later on what we were at the time can be stored forever inside anyone's hard drive... it takes us outside the norm she said... you didn't see it that way and probably never will... photographs turned out to be nagging illustrations... one reason why you were afraid in the first place... and evidence you asked... it won't matter she said... the heat of the day faded into the bay water along with the sunlight... the sand began cooling to the touch... like running your fingers through silk... something bright appeared in the sky... a planet maybe... a glass delicate name...

Maybe it was our last night in town she said. Let's grab a sit down meal.

That was fine — but you knew otherwise — you knew there would be another night in town ...

Afterward we sat outside the crowded restaurant on a bench and dug our toes into the sand. Overhead the stars were visible by thousands or millions or whatever. It was just sight wasn't it? And looking up it struck you as odd that you belonged to a galaxy.

Looking out into the Milky Way felt like trespassing across some else's map. Here we were — among the user-friendly makeup of genetics — messed up by chance and left there beside one another — nothing but the slimmest parcel of time between us — holding us — the whole thing with entropy undressing — red shifting neighborhoods of stars — what to do but hold on — but you felt upside down staring into the night sky.

And somewhere out there — in dark space- across vast theaters of light — two other people sat on a bench on a world far away and listed to the radio girlie moons of their own star system. And staring outward into the twisted night — they looked back toward who would be us sitting on this bench as we looked back toward them.

And it was hard to determine- when there was a point- where nostalgia replaced comfort. You looked at the rows of potted geraniums placed around the benches and took comfort in that. But if you looked too hard then there was trouble. Nostalgia was like having a primitive amen said on your behalf. Like sitting inside your own ghost with a weakly formed smile and feeling unavoidably small with no redeemable coupons to speak of in the game of life. The raven-haired woman sat beside you- rubbing shoulders against you- reaching out and drawing down a collection of thoughts from the starry night sky. As though a love supreme were at that moment first written and put to music and language became weightless… no peculiar yesterday just a plate of oysters … replace all the blind holes with diamonds as we held hands… her shoulders pressed against yours… where was the reasonable end of things and where do we say goodbye… the brightness from the stars settled like a blanket… can't help staring… can't help how the raven-haired woman's heartbeat sampled your own…

We connect our bodies. We just rent the flaws.

*

faster than gravity

Old world sycamore trees lined the orphanage ground. They gave the place a deep and established presence- watchdogs with tall open branches- when contrasted against the pink flamingo crab grass lawns and carbon monoxide daises that tried to grow elsewhere on Ogontz Avenue. The cab phone was ringing again- louder and as always unanswered.

Where were all the cabs?

The man on the cement island checked his watch- looked Northward but saw no trolley- only the tracks set archaically in the cobble stone of another age. He paced like he wished he had a newspaper to hide behind. He looked like he waited underneath some meaty responsibility — a Protestant Gerber's face on his head.

*

the coffee meditations

You remember Michael Remey standing at the spaceship in the movie The Day The Earth Stood Still. He and the big robot were about to fly home. Before he leaves though he gives the earthlings a message from beyond the stars. If you people don't stop destroying and exploiting one another- then he and the big robot would come back one day and with no questions asked — they would go medieval and kick some serious ass.

*

faster than gravity

Cinder dust swirled across the empty parking lot of Mulligan's Funeral Parlor. Cripple looked like he was trying to raise a question from the dead. His wiry eyebrows turned like worms behind his glasses.

It's a show he said.

But don't you feel strange you said. Watching like this?

Fuck no he said. You got the war on TV news and everybody watches that with supper.

Friday night fights: everybody's father watches that.

Combat on Tuesday night and The Gallant Men on Saturday night after the Lawrence Welk disco.

But that shit's made up you said. They got stunt men on TV.

Cripple B. stared back at you- glasses thick as stones. So you watch all that pretend shit he said but you don't have the heart for what's real? Folks don't take the Clang serious.

Rain began falling again like the erratic dribbling from a man urinating that doesn't actually have to. Cripple crawled behind the hedge up to the far end of Mulligans — where the hedge ended near a porch with some chintzy metal railings- all fake curly things and some cheap factory design that looked a whisper might bend it over. You'd think a place with as much turnover as Mulligans could invest in more structural banisters. What's it say about the house of the dead when its appearance looked like cheap shit?

Hunched over like a rodent in a test maze- Cripple's nappy head stuck above porch level for a better look. He yanked himself down immediately and motioned for you to hurry up.

That poor motherfucker down there he said better hope his trolley comes in soon.

You heard shouting and trashcans knocked over — car brakes screeching — like an alarm clock violently come to life while you're sleeping. It was a sound that made you think. It reminded you that thunderstorms were pulled from the ground and then blew up in the sky.

Cripple watched like some hound from the future taking notes.

*

the coffee meditations

You remembered that sound — as though it were pulled from no-where and suddenly there it was before you in a puff — it was a subway sound vented through metal grates over openings in the sidewalks — a rumbling stink rising over caged holes in the earth — a low roar from below the street that met the air above with diesel fumes and wasted time and a fascination as it faded from your shoe top senses and rode down the line as you stared after it.

*

faster than gravity

Cripple said my god they're thick!

The Clang and Somerville ran at each other across Ogontz Avenue.

Arrows shot into the air behind castle walls... cannon volleys boomed across lowland troops... sword wielding emperors cut off peasant heads... machine gun mobsters wiped out the competition... homeland fascists kicked babies into the street... a dead man's wallet was stolen... dead women were raped... crosses burned on continental lawns... my god Cripple said they're thick!

The Clang ran Across Avenue S.

Somerville ran across Avenue C.

Was there anything left but dreams meeting senseless ambitions?

The war usually took place here.

Then there was the man on his cement island. You think why bother with a guy like that? Where was that fucking trolley of his life when he needed it?

One young boy had a sawed off baseball bat and spiked into the top were several loops of chains purely medieval looking and made for punishment...

Three Clang had a Somerville surrounded and methodically went about punching his lights out...

Bottles rained back and forth and car antennas whipped across bodies only deepened the sad world...

When it finally ended — and it really wasn't an end — to think it about as an end — well that was just a way to look at it — the war didn't end — the war got picked up later on like a half finished cigarette in an ashtray — the husky young boy with the bat chain was passed out in the street and crushed like a squirrel run over by a newspaper truck. The corners of the young boy's mouth were split apart and a bloody unconscious grin lulled over his mug. The young boy had been curbed. His jaw was destroyed. Teeth lay in the gutter. Ever seen someone curbed? What happened was you basically knock someone out in a fight and then you drag him over to where the sidewalk meets the street in a right angle of concrete and asphalt and sadness and filth. Then you open the jaw and position its flaps so it's like biting the curb. Next you take a few steps back. Then you run and take a few steps up and stomp down on the back of the guy's head. The guy's jaw explodes. Then you let out a war hoop in celebration and run away refreshed I guess by dedications to the ages... not so much dead but left near dead... tomorrow was always another day...

Cripple's face went white. His high clammy forehead sweated and highlighted the ugly red marks from his early acne.

*

the coffee meditations

You see what needs seen.
I think. Therefore I exaggerate.
Breathe freely. But so what do you do.
Get the fuck out.
Didn't make sense.
I want. Saying I want.
Tell something.
Tell something sundown.
Not fair.
I worry which was your worry.
Maybe this was crazy.
Why care you look at yourself.
You continue the fog of yourself.
Try and think clearly.
What did you do silly?.
Everybody get a bloody nose fable.

You and the dog stopped and watched a writer tagging a strange brick wall two floors high — but there was with no building attached to it — it was like the rib cage were taken from a body — just a brick wall and everything else around it was removed.

The air still had a summery ken on the days.

You asked the writer yo how does it end.

Don't know yet he said. Come back later.

Okay you said. But once upon a time you told the writer you had paint can dreams of your own so to speak. Picture window nudes that went pornographic on storefronts — and you had this idea for a glossy cartwheeling freak that spun along Ocean Avenue with the same grin until it splattered uptown into a paintball like an evolutionary dead end. You had to tell something. Like you were scared. If it was beautiful or if it was fucked up it didn't matter. Because it was locked down in the middle of thinking... and that was like stars with tiny pin pointy locations that kept moving the more things dropped...or running wild over a plate of spaghetti because you were hungry and lonely for a place to be quiet — beautiful and fucked up — but dogs barked in the evening and babies cried in the arms of strangers that one day turn into their parents and every lawn mower on the street fired up obsessively to cut the grass before nightfall after yesterdays' rain. So often you go blank because there are just too many feelings to have before you get tangled up in the shrieks of your brain and the zen-like distortions soft and material of your mind even if that act was dependent and worked against your better judgment what you wanted was to pull at memory and suddenly let it go.

Cool the writer said. Come back later.

*

Yesterday the raven-haired woman sent a text that said stay cool they won't find us.

For decades she's been saying that. They won't find us. But following so many years you worried. You needed to wonder instead.

Maybe it was not easy to stay cool.

Maybe it was great to stay cool.

Goldfinches flew off the fence the way tungsten went shinning in the night.

*

There was an evening where there was a brilliant blue sky.

Suddenly a wind picked up. The temperature dropped. One month was gone and the next month was visible. Up in the sky three turkey buzzards soared overhead. They circled directly above you. You recognized them — same buzzards from a month ago. You were certain they followed you home. They were simple narcissistic facts. Maybe you had debts to pay. Maybe it was fun to be an animal — split among qualities like anxieties and bargains and the raw biting tooth — but who knows?

*

You sat against a small dune — you and the raven-haired woman — enjoying a humid afternoon on a late summer beach. Waxed paper covered the sky — flimsy thin gray clouds hid the sun but not the sunlight.

What if there's no wake up call after surgery you asked? How long had those bullets been in your head as well as stuck inside your body? How long was it before these people stopped looking for us? What if the kitchen renovations never got finished?

She punched you in the arm. It was surprising how much heft she had to that southpaw.

What you said? What if after surgery you wake up and you're not the same? What if after surgery the whole thing abducts you like aliens were sitting in a parallel room and waited to abduct you? What if after the incision — and after they open you up — they find somebody else hiding inside you? What if your bones get stupid? What if things got creepy and they had to nuke you? So you asked her- would you still love somebody who glowed in the dark?

Let's have sandwiches she said.

Let's get distracted you said. Let's go down and flop in the waves — like Burt Lancaster and Deborah Kerr did.

Let's have sandwiches she said.

Then...seemingly... from nowhere...came the buzzards... We watched them silently move up the beach toward us... speechless in flight as we stared at them... without flapping gliding without noise... dispatched... sonic whisper... then circling overhead like buzzards do looking for remains...

Same buzzards. Same trio of ghostly dark birds who cursed the word survivor were looking down upon you with satellite vision. Same crimson heads looking for something dead.

Not yet. Not yet you said.

*

Before rolling it up and going to sleep- you wondered- how should you behave? Like the Paul Newman character in Hombre? As he's being shot up he yelled to the nasty bad character played with such glory by Richard Boone — ah hell we're all gonna die — it's just a matter of when.

*

In the dream you're carrying a boat on your shoulder down to the harbor. As you near the harbor shore the boat slipped from your grasp and went head first into the icy water. You tried and reached after it. But a giant cargo tanker passed and blocked you. You looked for a harbormaster to ask permission to go after the boat. First though you had to make breakfast for everybody else and rearrange the room because more guests were coming for the weekend. And all the while this went on you received pictures from the boat drifting away. Somebody said don't worry. You can always buy another. Yea. But that was the best boat.

*

loose change

Still as the tension left behind the echo from a kiss — one evening you lost some time.

Suddenly looking about- you had no idea where that time went. No idea to tell what was up or what was down.

Satellites high above the earth fed pictures through the television like cardiovascular currents in a muscle system. Partially naked bodies in swimsuit money sold alcohol and thinness and universal elation and the message was just get lost in these watery shores and have the first noble truth of suffering and desire turn out to be plain old ineptitude.

A student took a class hostage with enough ammo to fill a movie set.

Somebody backed a car over a sunbather's head and swore in tears it was nobody's fault.

The same government official wanted to explode an atmospheric test bomb again.

Maybe throughout the universe we've become a planet whose prime directive was its major quarrels and rhetoric poverty and lost chances...

So you went to the sink and ran some water. A cloudy nebula swirled in the glass like weak sour milk. It didn't even look like water. Didn't even look like polluted water. How many years had you been drinking this stuff? No wonder there were more taverns than churches in Jersey-land. Or maybe the water quality division from public works had given up and was now serving the enraged benzene itself and not an ancient fluid that life depended upon.

And holding this glass of tap water up to the kitchen window light to inspect — car horns on hot evening winds drifted in from the street

— you had this funny laugh. Why have a self? Mid-twenties — other male identity — according to the legal cards — part environment part pharmaceutical wonderment– one year this way — one year that way — it didn't matter so much until those years were you and began valuing counting devices — and at some point — despite attention and images wired to the gills like love — why bother?

Things rolled along. Little differentials. Efforts…Whereabouts…

One evening you lost some time. Watching television…

Back when we were kids Eden hid out and pretended she lived in the cemetery at Bay and Packer. She thought this was a highly inventive way to be — to play a part from somebody else's life that's already been played out before. One day she was performing one headstone and being family there- and then on another day it would be on to the next headstone and so on throughout the graveyard. Fictional psychosis she qualified later was a better alternative to have…

Like the moon landing- a cartoon Cinderella — Eden Jones dropped into worlds — and then — once there — found it hard to stay around for long.

Clouds molted through the window… a late light in a late blue sky burned way out in the sun- like some cosmic postal service delivering a concussion into your head…

Out the window across Third Street pigeons flocks rose from the sidewalks like paper trash in the wind and landed on the roof of the 20th Century Club. You never set out to be disillusioned… never meant for happiness and sadness to be painted on opposites sides of the same coin. Sure there were the ageless condom jokes and sure there were the old perfect voids… sure we were left scrambling and holding onto very little once born — but where was it — where did the high spaces of the heart put together a shelter for you?

*

Too much the dog thought.

Purple clouds reached the windowsill until you lost them. From your bed looking up they fell off into the strange distance over Jersey-land.

Purple clouds fell into the distance over Jersey-land. Synchronized each time you stared out the window clouds fell into purple Jersey-land. Slow balls not worth hitting… corneas hung on distant windowsills and Jersey-land cracked in the glass… good curve ball… falling in love was like tossing eggs out the window and hoping nothing broke… falling in love was like holding a lottery ticket but you missed the drawing… falling in love said empty space — empty space — empty space… long ball hit the right field pole and went foul…

Too much the dog thought.

*

Memories were unreliable the television special said.
The small of her back made for a perfect nesting place while you read.
Let's not repeat what we've already done she said.

*

When you first saw her after like a year not seeing her — you were sitting in a booth at the 20th Century Club and hearing last call from Fast Eddie.

She walked quietly into the club — but she walked right into you like a knife and cut you in half. She wore baggy jeans that gripped her hips like sailor's pants and an open throated sleeveless blouse and that killed you in white cotton. Did Eden Jones just walk into the room? Was that even a question?

Suddenly it was too early for last call. Maybe it was the sudden emptiness and quiet. Maybe the beer finally ran out. Maybe rock and roll eternity lived up to its name.

Maybe this was an illusion due to a paradox frame of reference where you believed what you saw or maybe this resulted because tonight life was a misadventure in the illegal substance trade but you were sure that if you blinked then she would be gone so guess what — no maybe's — you did not blink. And she did not move.

Her long dark hair was cut short from its forest creature length — a long sweeping bang crossed her forehead that she constantly brushed aside as she talked — and it was dreamy looking in a way — the way a shipwreck went under the waves and then rose from a storm with nothing but ghosts on board.

How about hot dogs at Fabians you said?

She thought about hot dogs.

Strange concoctions after midnight — since birth it seemed — forgotten animal parts — entrails glued together in pink industry casings — they turned on thin metal spears and cooked for hours past their prime time underneath a scorched and foul radiant light — unless they exploded inside a greasy window box on the boardwalk. Sad brown chili sauce and Jersey-land onions and that ugly yellow mustard you said.

Hot dogs were fine she said.

*

Between bites there was clumsiness hand to hand ...relearned material... the wondrous function of confusion...she leaned toward you... pulsing... catching your view... like a blue star... she wanted to go walking... wanted to see the titled trees and the wasted roadside exits of home... wanted to see if she was still infected from the days when she was born here.

*

Two days later Eden Jones got in her small brown car with all the dents and headed west- driving off into the sunset. She left you at the corner of Third and Mulberry with your breath turned over inside. She left a cell phone number. But really what good was that? Time kept disappearing just like that.

One day you woke up just like that wrapped and twisted in the sheets and she was there in bed sleeping beside you.

You landed somewhere from the sky.

*

Sister Crumble had her lumpy backside toward us and was writing instructions on the blackboard in blood. Supposedly we were taking a test but that hardly mattered. Your attention wandered. Eden was busy writing answers or something. Curious things happened. You kept at it. Despite the outside interference from Sister Crumble — you felt what you never known before.

*

You watched her breathing…curving up and away beneath the sheets… like a pitch no one got hold of…

Hummingbirds entered your thinking. Weren't they the only bird capable of flying in reverse?

And you saw orange day lilies in a glass jar. They bloomed for a day and then dropped. No matter. The roadsides were filled with large overgrown clumps of them multiplying each summer as though frightened or desperate- wildflowers you picked for nothing and then brought home.

Below the shabby apartment window a gross heat rose upwards from the sidewalk below and hit back with another amplified day off the charts — a sunny nuclear asphalt and touchy bus fumes that stank the air with cheap grade diesel and the daily chemical explosions from the scratch lands and the failed economics nobody tried to solve.

You smelled the ocean- resting your head on her back — and doing nothing to change or release the situation. An oscillating fan spun back and forth — its rusted grill raising the air above our heads with each turn.

You smelled the ocean — rolling on Jersey-land shores — rolling for centuries on waves that made us who we were- from horror creatures leaving the brine for ties to the sand

Maybe time was nothing — nothing more than a clothes optional day.

You tried as usual to convince her. She smiled as usual but said she couldn't stay in Jersey-land. Not enough firewalls — not enough protection since most of her family was shot and dead. Like wise she was in the neighborhood for a job and then needed to leave in a hurry.

At Frank's Playland By The Sea we hooked up with Mantis and Mister Jimmy and Pun Chow Elliot Chung and other assorted lovelies from the tribe and got stoned and were thrust loose into the shadows — hanging out beneath the pier while tourists walked crazy above.

Later we sat on a curb at Decatur Street. The curb ended where the sand began where the boardwalk ended and the long commercial hustle from the bar traffic stopped.

From drugs to people to cars to a fake new identity- if you roamed around where the curb ended on Decatur Street you were able to buy anything the heart desired. And because it was empty and fucked up we also found peace of mind there.

The remains from an old warehouse building stood nearby. One night it died almost cabalistic in a fire. The cause as ever in Jersey-land was un-determined. Wall partitions and burnt stair outlines were scratched onto one standing brick wall — as though scars were signatures — neurologi-cal reflections — accumulated nerve-ending desires. Yellow plastic signs were stuck to the wall. To date the notices –WARNING NO TRESS-PASSING — were unreadable- beneath the colorful waves of sprawling graffiti and dense pornographic images of whatever sex imaginable — dire and sweet anarchist's slogans like: DESTROY AND RISE — what-ever message intent was there in the first place didn't amount to boo.

We liked it here. It was wondrous and a confusing place.

Lightening rippled behind the dirty night clouds –blue cobalt streaks behind the chromium and cadmium plumes and the hot ash fallout that sizzled like a dragon's hiss when the shit hit the bay water.

Horseshoe crabs flipped over by the tide waited on their backs and couldn't move — waiting to bake in the morning sun and dehydrate — waiting for when the teenagers came and shot at them before class.

Late that night we went swimming... boulevards of hips wading in the surf... mission impossible eyes...the hoarse romanticism from a voice that's taken too much whiskey... a curve of the body like a ques-tion mark... love was never enough... never enough to hold the time...

Eden lay on her stomach — watching large container ships leave the bay channel for deep open waters. The air smelled like animal skin and weed killer and phosphorous. Her narrow chin rested inside a bowl she made from her cupped tattooed palms.

It doesn't show much respect she said.

For what you asked?

For whatever reasons they made it she said. And then they sank it.

Half sank you said.

All right half sank she said. A half sunk concrete boat. Explain that part again.

It was supposed to carry supplies to Europe during the war you said. But it never made it. So they hauled it back and half-sunk it here. It looks stupid but the fish liked it. And people come and put money in the telescope and look at it.

That was so messed up she said.

It was obsolete before it had a chance to do anything you said. How many class trips did we have out here? To learn our war lessons. It was like we had to have these weird memories given to us.

We never got the questions we wanted she said.

It was a combination of things really. We got half-truths covering a half-sunk boat.

We never got what we wanted you said.

Her dark night hair fell across her face in that bang that was driving you wild.

These bangs drive me crazy she said.

Eden stared at the Atlantic and low tide sloshing its ambient-like waves against the pebbly shore of Jersey Land. There was always a sweet volume to her voice- melodic and inviting- the way someone might sound behind a receptionist's desk whose normal day-to-day activities include greetings and being friendly to strangers. And it's not like we were just absent-minded sponges she said.

The more you rolled with it — you said- the more being in the dark seemed okay.

Maybe she said. But I can't stay here.

What's wrong with giving up and staying here you said?

You give up the dead she said. And then you see how that makes you feel. No she said this was a perpetual state — and we can't leave it behind. This was not bingo she said. No she said this was vengeance.

Take me with you then you said.

That's not going to work either she said. What are you doing?

Giving you the eye.

What eye she asked?

The detective story eye you said. Where the female character walks into some incredibly down on its luck office with few prospects and looks around and then offers obscure clues and tantalizing propositions about some missing identity that needs to be found. The detective looks you over in that tight black dress and heels and says- well then- tell me your troubles. It's the eye laid on an empty street corner beneath a dull and misty streetlight- watching the curtained upstairs windows of an apartment across the street- all the while knowing that behind his back certain cards are being played out to no good. It's the same eye behind a car wheel driving slowly across those rainy streets with low music in the background- knowing he's got to turn that missing identity to earn his pay- and all the while out of the corner of that eye he needs to be vigilant- keeping a make on the whereabouts of the clandestine femme fatale. It's a sex eye. An eye that wants to know better against what he sees. But against all judgments he gets involved too deep and his imme-diate world spins out of control. Yet he likes this feeling. It's a sensation he can't account for. A high if you will. Something that's brought him to heights he only wished he might remember had he actually done some-thing in the past. And so in the past he sought to kill those very heights he wanted by drinking heavily and not sleeping.

Sex eye she asked?

*

By then night reached around and pulled its hindquarters back from the outer limits of the horizon. The peep show of the stars — marking the history of eternity- closed down again for another day. How odd it always seemed to look at the stars as just tiny impractical flares?

Fishing boats pulled out to sea under a shapeless blue — generations of family business aboard getting busy with nets and the ghosts that circled the boats in the wind — followed by the almighty noise and shit of the gulls — and the rising power of the sky.

Falling in love was like living on the moon.

*

Over eggs over easy and a coffee pot and home fried potatoes and bacon that was too crisp and rye toast with butter and grape jelly at the 8th Street Diner around the block from the Vernon Street Apothecary where you cashed in your scrips — scenes like this happened regularly — one full earthly rotation around the sun you said — two people eat breakfast together and move on in case mistakes were about to happen.

What would you like me to do she asked?

This was the part where the female character re-entered you said. She causes sudden innuendo and unexplained disturbances. She hits the male character over the head with a hammer- and then dissolves behind sunglasses off screen as the credits roll.

And the male character goes dead from the hammer blow?

Actually let's make that a shot to the heart.

Actually she said let's make it this way: this was the part where the female character asks: aren't we perfect the way we are?

And having said that- she retraced her thoughts behind a sip of coffee. She will after all change her mind — like most people. And using the toast to sop up the remaining eggs on her plate- as a metaphor for hunger — close up head shot as she places her fingers in her mouth both suggestively and with an admiration for their own achievements — she intones with deliberate emphasis on the exhale — you deliver the goods the best way you can.

And the male character said: what if you can't help being easily influenced? What if despite all the drawn out personality glitches — the drowsiness and inactivity and the bafflement and suspicion through which he colored the world — what if- for the sake of giving him something to grasp after — after all what if his aim in life was to have an aimless aim so to speak — what if he saw he suddenly made it into the future. And what if this realization sets off inside him a fuse that burned with a heart popping velocity and he then reads the fine print — and what's really got a hold on him was this: this wasn't made from things he already knew.

So what is it Eden said?

It's like that geography film we saw back in eighth grade. Entire generations of ancient Chinese families worked on the same jade figure until it was done. Collective strength made beauty. And it lasted.

Those people were peasants employed by emperors who had big guys with swords and they dictated who did what or else they lost their heads she said.

Falling in love was like holding hands with the dead.

I guess there were stranger things she said.

The female character she said orders more coffee. She appeared indifferent to how late it was. Her eyes widen and sparkle like a knife blade opened in sunlight. Even before she made a move and went anywhere — she felt vulnerable. She might be tired from repeatedly explaining it- but she still believed there was something left worth accepting.

She tells the male character- she's leaving tomorrow. As in she's always leaving tomorrow. In fact she said — tomorrow might be her favorite word.

Before the male character can reply she beats him to the punch. She looked into his complicated and tired eyes and said — I know you want something.

The female character paused — and finished her coffee. Not everything she does had bearing on him.

This was the part where the male character senses how it was that things crowd in.

She senses material powers she has yet to enjoy.

Falling in love was like having an original thought. And having an original thought meant your entire neuro-disk had to misfire.

*

The problem was this — living the dream was a problem.

Falling in love was like being a portrait in a rear view mirror.

You reached out and held up a hand and penciled your name on the air.

Meaningless characterizations — instant money — party-hat sex — nervous energy — a butterfly landing on a flower — agile mobile ventricle — it's the affair with the world — the need to go home — a syndicated attraction between us and the sky and let's throw it across the universe like inventing the wheel each time — completeness fades — narcotic neutrality — going about like a human Switzerland — the problem happens and revisits the outposts inside your head — Hey Jude — don't let me down — if you want something — you never wake up and try to plumb it —

*

the coffee meditations

Hardly a wind moved the rainbow whirligigs — hanging on a thin wire stretched tree to tree across the yard. For kicks you plugged in a string of lights on the rose bushes. For kicks you fell in step with the sunflowers again. Dragonflies chasing each other sideways in the morning pulled up suddenly — hovered in the tiny space around them — and put together stillness and wings and dazzle.

You wanted more coffee but were too planted in a chair to fetch some. You needed socks because your feet were cold but you didn't bother. You needed to make a list but you said forget it because you might do that later on. It was like the air had slipped from one stage to the next and hadn't bothered to inform you. Flowers with tired and beautiful late summer colors... empty lawn chairs still held what were last night's party people.... leafy shade trees rode waves in the nearby sky... falling in love was like needing a fix... a cat hurried between shadows... a background like the solitary crow docked on a branch...you were old — an ageless fool who was willing to die — but was not ready to die yet — imperfect frightening and good to the end of the bone.

*

loose change

Falling in love was like having a strain of cancer waiting to attach itself to your body.

Pretty blonds walked along the boardwalk wearing the last seasonal cool white lines.

Funny teenagers in pith helmets passed among the video parlors at Frank's Playland by the Sea — talking at one another with high-octane voices and hormones in swing and the vacation freedom near the surf.

Jersey-land guys lay in the cool shadows of shade trees in a nearby park. They drank beer and smoked joints- indulging a pleasant lethargy after a double-header softball game.

Some strange dwarf orange flower bloomed in the broken wooden containers near the trashcans. Gulls fought and picked over the crumbs from a takeout meal left near an empty bench. A pale evening settled over the sea. Nothing was better than to be out and walking around. That's the mystery you said. Walking around together like it should be you said. Sharing a carton of noodles... Even if the noodles were laced with aped ginger paste and chromium shrimp...this was what we have you said.

The unreal weekend she said.

High white clouds across the dirty sky looked the way a farmer's blade turned the earth and heaped low matter into furrows. Irritants from the scratch lands morphed into fascinating colors.

Sandpipers retreated along the water's edge. Maybe the waves were too hot this evening....

Falling in love was like being a dog tied to a parking meter...

Let's just walk Eden Jones said.

Falling in love was like having a cameo appearance in a disaster movie.

What were you thinking she asked?

The hasty motions that went along with stifling a hunger pulled you back. You looked at the fake apple pie in its weak tin plate and questioned — do you want to eat this? But then- those factory phobias over mass produced foods were normally quelled by your appetite- and so you bit into it- and there it was again- a generic radiance- at peace with the world for the moment- all the while looking for the apples but finding instead a jelly-like strata — apple flavored but with extra lumps built into it.

Nothing has changed Eden Jones said.

Scented hypnotic winds blew in off the Atlantic. Grease packings hung in the air from all the diesel equipment that was forever rebuilding exit 47. Rusty machinery in weedy lots leaked plastic fluids onto the torn up ground.

Used forlorn factories with sad low fences spilling into bootless roadways and convoluted barrels of wasted metal organized by chaos settled into ditches and fire hazard buildings played dice with the gods and forget it and polluted raspberry bushes grew from the smashed windshields of long forgotten cars and the brilliant red sun went down among fragments and a jagged landscape that suffered from an industrial hangover.

Falling in love was like having a small copper wire exposed from your skull during a thunderstorm...

You doughhead she said.

*

We climbed to the top of the bunkers and watched the sunlight rise on another day.

Erosion cracks climbed through broken gun turrets. Fat reinforced concrete walls built to withstand a direct shelling from two wars ago buckled in places and shoved rusty steel bars out into the weather like veins on a corpse. The bunkers were now fortresses for spray paint writers and improve-towns for the homeless... garden settings for weed and strange bent trees... dank interiors and giant metal doors collapsed on old hinges and would never open nor close again... where dirty-haired oil workers dabbled on their day off... what once were shore batteries lined with troops and arcades of weapons defending the eastern seaboard now were home to nudie book heaps and the splintered roasted gulls and used alcohol containers thrown nightly by frenzied teenagers hopped on the latest psychotropic motor drugs all taking at once and scratching themselves and setting fires...

We looked out over the ocean and tried to remember — that color red — shinning over the horizon and onto the water — did it have a crayon box name? We tried to remember but came up empty and left it at that. What a red to have though.

Falling in love was like the twinkle — twinkle star rhymes.

Falling in love was like the red neon vacancy sign hanging in a Rt. 9 motel window.

Like reading a paperback book the next day riding the subways back and forth alone.

*

the coffee meditations

The car horn atmospherics — the impatience at being held up — crawling along red light to red light in a great traffic jam — we had business in Delaware City — what more evidence was there? None of us were getting anywhere on time.

A heavy twisted rain flew around the entrance to the tunnels. Nothing moved — even as the red lights changed — nothing moved.

Radio host ran theirs mouth across the dial and basically had the same message: you motherfuckers are stuck!

Car overlaps car ergo car fights car ergo cars fight cars — therefore drivers in cars have the fuck you not fuck me but fuck you — a well directed point of view was needed to be the car an inch ahead.

*

Taxis lost in the economy and doubled parked government vans that paid no attention and bus accidents leaking oil at the curb like dinosaur blood and nervous breakdown minivan dads and abundant payday rent-a-smiles and the industrial security breakdowns where formal names spun into census figures and what to believe when you had this reptile suspicion where you might not get enough from what was there...

*

I have to pee she said. It's cold today. Can I have some coffee?
Sure you said. We have plenty.

I don't like this anymore than you do she said.

If we go back we'll just have to get another car you said.

This won't be the end she said. But it will help. Then we get you to the hospital.

She wore a baseball cap with the words: OUT FOR TROUT — stitched across the front. She looked ahead and sighed — curling her mouth inward and biting her lip — the rainy cool weather that hounded the car — traffic lights never happened for her — the marginal enthusiasms from the disenfranchised motorists with cigarettes hung from their lips and phones tucked awkwardly on shoulders — stared back vacantly at her.

We shoot one of his cousins she said. Then we go to the hospital — leave the car in the parking lot — and check you in. Tonight — we catch the last ferry over the bay.

Why not kill Bobby Alfredo?

Oh I will she said. Bobby Alfredo has lived long enough to be an old man.

You looked at her — bunched in a five dollar over coat and a floppy afghan hat — and you knew she was right. That it was great to suffer — but it was also a pain in the ass.

*

… you explained it was the transistor sized memories kept you going. Real time had become a fuzzy state of mind. It was somewhat affectionless. Like you're walking down the boardwalk you said and you find a sandwich left behind on a bench — and you think should I eat this? Soon enough you're engaged in a tug of war between yes and no. It's just a sandwich but the potential decisions regarding it seemed endless.

She laughed and said maybe it's just a free lunch. Anyway she said — what happens when memory cheats?

We inched the car through the tunnel once we got into a single lane. Go ahead you said — give me a memory.

*

I remember one night being lost she said. I was driving all over the place and looking for 44th Road. I found 44th Street and 44th Lane and 44th Avenue. They all looked the same — dark streets with empty warehouse buildings — and no signs of music — or any dancing in the windows. I looked at the map some one drew for me but it didn't make any sense. Anyway I was about to give up and drive away when I looked up — and there it was — 44th Road — and there I was looking at a map.

So anyway — I went upstairs and had a drink. It was chatty and fashionable- which I liked- but I was looking out a window at the skyline. I had this thought- and it was some kind of thought but I didn't know what about. There was a bridge and that was all lit up. And there was a train going underneath the bridge and that was all lit up. People were dancing. People were excited and talking about themselves. Soon I was dancing and the music was loud and everyone was getting drunk and I forgot what it was I thought looking out that window.

I don't know what it was she said. But I remember having that thought- and how it felt- even if I can't remember what it was about.

It's about the end of the world you said. What happens when it doesn't last? Don't you worry about having — unconnected breaths?

You're not going to die today she thought. It's an old bullet wound. You'll get over it just fine.

And yea you thought — there were things to give up at the end of the line — cocktail hours and a love for the stars — the howling moon — everlasting sky where we had to get back. Why was that necessary? Why give up the delicate tents of air where we lived inside? Why give up bicycles or rhythm machines playing songs from open windows on an afternoon when the stock exchange meant nothing?

See she thought.

It's still all situations and no plot you thought.

Maybe you were dead she thought. Anyway- can we get some food? I need to eat.

Maybe you were dead? What did that mean? You didn't want to feel dead. But what would that feel like anyway? What reference do you use? Was it a simple matter where all you did was judge distance?

See she thought.

Right you thought. But don't you think about meat-faced politicians stealing your social security check? What about icebergs melting in Antarctica — do you still imagine hey it's a radiant future? What if we're living in one of those parallel string theory dimensions? The ones you thought that lived right next door while we're living in the world here? And so what if you're living next door and not living here and you've already had surgery and don't even know about it? Maybe you're in the hospital already and don't know it? Attached to litanies and mechanical extensions- hooked into various ports stuck into your body- oxygen forced up your nose and IV needles dripping sugars and anti-bacterial junk and shooting dope into your veins and some bright green snake-like catheter rising off the strange impressions from a urine bag and winding its way up your penis and disappearing inside a cavity behind a stapled up incision.

I'm cold she thought. I'm hungry.

But where's the world next door to the world next door you thought? What if next door there's another strange component? And what if in that world next door there's a chemical in the air? What if that chemical prevents you from healing? And what if while you're healing you're standing in line at a grocery store and someone gets mad at you and punched you in the stomach? What if you sneeze and blow yourself over and land on your back — arms and legs askew — and can't right yourself like somebody's pet turtle?

Good thing she thought that you're not worked up about this.

What if you thought this turned into a creepy horror show and the incision started to grow and takes a mind all its own? And then you turned into this Frankenstein guy with scars all over your body and a big old blockhead bolted together that cries out at night for angels to come and lift off your head and take it into the clouds? What if you're cleaning the house and the vacuum twisted around you like a boa and what if cleaning the house and the boa constrictor was really an infectious monster that starts eating through your rib cage with no other force guiding it but its own survival because in the world next door this actually was an organic condition? And so good thing now — because should you drop over from severe abdominal trauma — and because you've cleaned the house — the EMTs responding won't think my god this place is a mess!

You need to stop and think she thought.

Was it better if you didn't?

Okay she thought try something else

But what if there wasn't something else you thought. What if one day when you're living next door and things weren't around anymore? What if there were no more wind chimes or downtown noodle meals? And what if there were no more cold beer and sundown queries and the eternally soft fun playing with somebody else's ass? What if the surgeon works for some shady government agency? What if he packs the wound with explosives and sets you on your way with what you take to be a nefarious yet encouraging smile? And now what — you're walking around with a bomb inside and waiting to detonate?

Well she thought there are cousins everywhere. But it's too late to freak.

If that's the safe thing to do you thought — then what's dangerous?

Look she said- putting her arms around you- even sadness doesn't compensate for the loss you feel being alive.

You stared off into traffic and felt... a trace... overworked neurons failing again to get it done... thousands of years going about... a tomorrow to fill among the broken lawn chairs of Jersey-Land... her arms folded around your shoulders like candles in the dark... her eyes like warm pie... You muttered... don't puke in the wastebaskets...

What did you say she thought?

I was thinking I was a maid once at the Trade Winds motel you thought. There were maniacs everywhere. Droll-faced fighters with faces like grenades and kids who wore body bags as fashion statements. And there was this cat I remember — howling away each night like something worn out... and there I was changing sheets and vacuuming carpets and securing little paper strips across toilet mouths and leaving notes on the dressers that said if you drink too much please don't puke in the wastebaskets...

Maybe she thought these affairs represent movements. Something you don't even know about. Spirited creatures sent by the sky for your comfort.

But what if in the world next door this was all you had you thought?

*

faster than gravity

Da Vinci's Pizza made a fortune on Friday nights. What you wanted was a hot greasy pie and that was so simple it practically made you almost stupid with beauty.

Inside Da Vinci's Pizza you listened to all the jokes and beer laughter from a people who didn't take sin as a concept much to heart.

And as a matter of respect we went behind the counter to see how Blind Charlie was doing.

We opened the dusty door that was built into some cheap little wall to keep the noisy restaurant away from Blind Charlie as he got older. A little bell knocked and sounded atop the jam. Cripple limped in first. His genetic stomp- as he dragged a bad leg afterwards- was as recognizable as if we had first said our names out loud before we walked in.

Blind Charlie sat in an oily over-stuffed chair the color of perpetual newsprint with knitted covers on the arm rests that looked like spider webs. As we waited he looked up from reading delicately with his fingers. They whispered over pages in a book shot full of holes. Holy articles and religious paraphernalia decorated the walls and table. Blind Charlie watched us across the skinny carpet with something deeper than ordinary eyesight... that's the way it seemed...the way his eyes scooped presence and made images beyond those Ray Charles' shades... feeling air for disturbance... cool and scary...strange radar like some kind of spirit muscle...

I heard sirens earlier he said.

A young boy from the Ville got his head crushed Cripple said.

Blind Charlie spent most of his time now indoors- waiting for heaven to ring and make that personal call and drain what little color he had left in his face. In the interim — before death took him off to that sacred back room in the sky — he read and prayed and cooked pizza sauce and made sure at least once a day he gave Satan and his crew the finger.

Let's think for a moment he said.

Cripple shrugged his shoulders and said what? What you do was stay out of the way. You don't get hit.

Blind Charlie nodded. He rubbed a weathered finger over a small plastic stature of St. Francis on the table. Then it's another sad day on earth laying odds against the flaws in god's handiwork he said.

Sure Cripple said. But where do you go? Where you moving to?

Life's the kicker boys Blind Charlie said. That's where to put your money. Even if we trash everything twice over to find it...

Yea Cripple added shit fails each week just when you look at it... can't really say why can you ...

There was almost a lament to Cripple's voice- like he hadn't thought this out- and was now wondering about it out loud to see if it was true.

And Blind Charlie- smothered in his all day thoughts- tucked away inside his tweed gray reading jacket- a guy in the neighborhood since time began- a long family tree spread across bus routes and trolley divides- admitted yes we all needed a running start.

Oh yea Cripple said like Newark and shit.

No Blind Charlie said not that Newark — but a Newark inside our heads.

Aw man Cripple said how you gonna act with that...I got no place in my head for no place like Newark...

Blind Charlie said well it's tears from the sidelines anyways — and suggested we drop our worries lest they do us in. And let's have a drink he said.

Cripple worried about the food. But he always worried about the food. You might think Cripple never ate before in his life before he had his next meal. But what did he know? We were sitting in the back room at Da Vinci's — talking with the king of the sauce — and out front pies were made and sold and eaten and made and sold and eaten and so — it's like what — there's no food? It was fucked up to think that way.

And Blind Charlie had this thing with prophecy. Like he worked out some agreement with the future. Like when he told Ace MacDonald not to chase after his granddaughters or else he'd be shot in the back. Like how he threaded through a room without bumping a chair or stepping on the faithful dog passed out and breathing slowly on the floor like a weary rug and returned back to his chair with a bottle of wine and three short glasses. He poured us all a glass without missing a drop. We lifted our glasses around the campfire of neighborhoods burning down.

Blind Charlie toasted us. He toasted Cain and his smackdown on Able. He toasted the latest Asian war and Lenny the old head who wasn't around due to his walking into a minefield at the wrong time in history and came home to his mom wrapped in a handkerchief. Blind Charlie kept on toasting and the bottle got lighter — toasting everybody because we all end the same way he said.

And since an empty glass was better than a full one it became a simple matter to follow whatever reason was put forth — make that two empty glasses — let's toast the bloodstream — your body felt like the sky the more you drank.

But who was scoring Blind Charlie?

What was up with his odd hopes?

That one-day every robbery stopped and you rode the trolley in peace? A place where proverbial dreams fell upon you and was someplace where you screwed around until you got the fucking thing right?

Cripple suddenly slapped you across the back of the head. It was a move designed to wise you up and pull you back from the drift of your thoughts before you set up shop and stared the night away at like the hidden sky patterns in wallpaper.

But what was up with that?

We need to get Charlie some fish Cripple said.

What kind?

Flounder would be fine boys Blind Charlie said. And some coleslaw — and make sure they put in some rolls this time... last week he said there were no rolls... he tipped his shades up to his forehead and stared at us through the queer white burns that were his eyes — what's coleslaw he said without rolls... and he smiled... nobody in the neighborhood disappointed Blind Charlie when he smiled and asked for a favor.

So out we went. Another Friday night errand into Avenue C — to bring back fried fish in a little paper bucket for our patron saint and the guy in charge. Otherwise why go through all this business about souls?

Flounder was the other key Jersey-land Friday night meal to have. What made eating crucial to sidestepping sin? Why was fried fish better to eat than fried hamburger was to avoid? If you looked at a fish and if you looked at a cow would either seem less intelligent? So we're related somehow to cows but somehow not related to fish? So we're related to creatures that shit all day long and rarely move- but we're not related to creatures that work together in groups and navigate the globe underwater?

But it was Friday night on Avenue C. Nappy music funked the street corner at 21st Street riding and bouncing off streetlights. People filled the sidewalks like the whole purpose in being alive were to be out on the sidewalks in the night- clusters in time while you secretly feared getting lost in time so you motored around on time with a drunken head that you stole from god.

*

We headed down 21st Street past the Tropicana Lounge. The bar's neon palm tree sign and its gaudy colors vibrated and flashed against the night. How old were those colorful tubes? How many days does it take burning off an intoxicating message through gravity before someone else picks up on the other end? Chemical pinks and bright slimy greens and bloodshot electric reds all surrounded by a light blue that burned annoyingly around the edges gave off this weird halo around the bliss-faced and shifty men pitching sad faced pennies against a brick wall like a requiem for a rut.

Next door to the Tropicana was the Laundromat. It didn't have a name or any signifier. It was just Laundromat in fucked up letters above a big glass window.

Naturally the window was cracked — had been for years — no surprise there — nobody thought to fix the window- all that happened was the crack was taped together — had been for years — and the tape on the crack peeled off and blew in the wind and so more tape was applied over the tape that was peeling off and meanwhile the crack was still there only hidden away like someone insane took up handiwork and kept taping the damn thing.

Inside several women chain-smoked and played cards and drank quick snorts from a brown bag. The clothes dryers tumbled and sputtered round and round on their repetitive nickel-a –turn cycle.

Occasionally you hung out in the Laundromat. It wasn't like it was great or anything. But it was a place. You learned how hands were dealt. You helped the newspaper rats store bundles of dailies they stole in the morning and then sold back cheap in the evening.

You ran errands across the neighborhood when a card player asked you to go and fetch a message — like sex or bus tokens — or some other crap — too many details wrecked adults — and what you got from it was spare change and an idea — never be an adult. When they had complaints — and the card players always complained — you listened to them flap air and give meaning to the pursuit of happiness.

Outside the used furniture store the rain stopped. It was a chilly autumn night. Music blasted from Cadillac stereos parked at the curb and from big radios on the sidewalk propped on milk crates like natural beliefs.

But was the sky clear? It was impossible to tell — the permanent overcast — if it was prophecy or not …who had the answer when it came to those skyward questions? But still… fuck it… you could live it.

Stars were those faraway places like dreams. But you knew stars weren't candles god placed in the window to light up the emptiness. And stars were more than textbook reassurance that shit was definitely exploding.

Stars meant you were vulnerable and not yet put together properly. That's why stars meant tomorrow. We don't like the idea being shut inside. We need what happened out in the open…if there's elbowroom we take it… and whoever's next-door — well too bad for them if they haven't taken it first…

And looking around- what? Where was the room? Cars were packed on both sides of the street and traffic passed on both sides of the street as though the air had a thought and that thought was a tin lining. The K-bus groaned by. It barely squeezed through traffic and the double-parked motherfuckers along its endless circuit picking up and disgorging passengers like some monotonous appetite never quelled. The cardboard advertising on its sides were nearly wiped clean of meaning and painted over by graffiti artists seeking fame for the name. What was it we were supposed to buy underneath all that lettering? Maybe that's why we laugh… everything piled on top of everything else… cars on top of streets and people on top of cars having a party and the noises rises and the people rise to be heard above the noise and some utterly beat Coronet in the double parked purgatory of cars slowly rolled down a window and a shady guy in the passenger seat asked who wants reefer…

Nothing moved. That is nothing moved beyond a pace designed to keep up with going nowhere. Even when things happened- in that cancelling out sense where a step ahead meant a step back- you don't help — you ask a question — where does it go?

Just made the same loop day after day like the K-bus and you watching it pass day after day? You stared into the graffiti highlighted windows and wondered: was your father seated in the rear of the bus? Vaguely doing a crossword puzzle on the way to work? It would be time for the graveyard shift commute to begin. And he was always on time- a catatonic icon if there ever was one- misplaced in this life because he could be- arteries hardening and as poorly attended as an early Sunday mass. Maybe that's why there were troubles to begin with. They help us stay isolated while we ride the bus. Troubles gave your life a sense of accumulation. You gather woes around like old friends but nobody else cared. They were yours alone to deal with and yours alone to put to rest. Whose idea was that?

To get people to fork over time out of life — that would be money — you work difficult all week and then when Sunday came your payment was in kind and you got some fake absolution for having a lousy week. And then you had to do it again the next Sunday or else the shit hit the fan.

Whose idea was this? Did you really believe there was anything wrong way back when and there's been like this bounty to pay accounts in perpetuity? You could not wrap your head around this original thing. That business about being born with a curse… so now you had to pay to be alive like some fucking shakedown? Just because you were born and were now breathing so that means there was something wrong with us all to begin with?

Pay to be alive? Who's idea was that?

Original sin was some cruel joke palmed off on us from behind the dark curtains of sanctuary so we can ride the K-bus with troubles and think about it and feel bad till we reached our stop.

Maybe being born did require some duty but don't get your troubles handed down.

*

Who really cared about millennial old grievances between heaven and hell? You didn't start it and you weren't going to finish it. Nobody pats you on the back for dealing with it either. Mostly it exists — in the name of life — like how you pick up the shit you've knocked over and then once again trying to pay attention.

It seemed inevitable that's all. That some day you head for the hills and get out of Dodge like the panicky townsfolk do in a western before the shooting starts and hoping not to get blasted in the crossfire while running for cover. High Noon you'll never be. And you never shoot Liberty Valence either. That rough guiding spirit was missing and nobody else's rifle had your back. Besides those brave loner types had affinities in the script that weren't necessarily destructive but wind up gun-fisted in the end anyway. But maybe who knows? Didn't they always get the girl and the keys to the future? Maybe you just haven't seen enough movies yet…

*

So in the meanwhile there was… flounder to get for Blind Charlie… Friday night walking down Avenue C… don't walk around like a peacock… don't stumble around like an orphan either…find a cavity where you got noticed and in the same instant got forgotten… remember the brave loner… work both sides of the coin… you guess it was like the new math we were supposedly learning in school… where different sets meet and overlap… what was a set anyway… brain twisting inductions you were just going to memorize and then forget…when you finally got around to learning the material school passed you through and that was that... it was all a show... can't be tough can't be soft... you guessed it was like being confused about sex for the first time... but you can't walk around telling the truth... that would be taking it too far... it might leave an impression that you were willing to piss somebody off and then do something about it... you don't fuck with a young boy who comes up and says check your heart... you don't fuck with raggedy eyed wrecks drinking Thunderbird on the corner... and you never fuck with somebody spray painting a wall... you don't want any of that... but you can't walk around sorry headed either like a silly cracker who doesn't have shit together... you stay just behind the play... in touch with the higher powers like indifference denial and sabotage... we passed just atop the surface and not any deeper... floating along terminally cool and faking it... that's advantage... what we hear around us we become... we're shadows.... why bother and make things further than what they seem... because the neighborhood reflected the big world ... because everybody's father rode the K-bus and had their money taken by churches for endowments and by governments for wars... maybe in the end you find yourself caring... caring about something you never thought you could... but damned if you knew what ... what you imagine was there was a place... you're walking toward it... some place ... where invisible did not matter... invisible as a little kid who stuttered... a brief shining place...and laughing your ass off if you got there...

*

Links Fish House was the bottom floor of a wedge shaped building that jutted onto Avenue C from a dark corner off Woodstock Street. Underneath a streetlight that barely functioned- a dim sparking energy that was more like an excuse for electricity than actual light- paint flakes scattered in the wind. Delicious smells drifted outward — seafood from yesterday's haul prepared in a batter of downstream beer and backyard eggs and kitchen dust and Chinese flour — cheap thin potatoes — all golden fried in deep hot oil until it was common fare and debilitating to resist. What greeted you outside Link's dirty windows — what pulled you — was a scent vain and tasty.

Maybe that's where… stay in the neighborhood forever… marry Eden… start a window repair business… deliver hot pizza and golden fish…

Cripple slapped you across the back of the head again. Stop thinking he said.

*

So we crossed back Avenue C and stood looking at the upstairs apartment above Links.

We crowded around with the men and stared upward as though expecting the marvelous to greet our eyes. What we got for our trouble was seeing Wauneta in her underwear again- a rear view with her standing in the window backwards to the street.

She was down to big sad panties and was toying offhandedly with the three fishhooks that held her bra. She seemed to be watching something in the room. But that's how she does it. With her ass to the street and lit from inside Wauneta never showed any face. Swaying in the window like she might be humming to herself or swaying in the window like she might be clamped down or swaying in the window like she might be giving us some heartbreak we wanted and that she alone had leverage over.

Cripple said damn he had an ache. Enough to drive me crazy he said.

Maybe that was the problem… imagining an idea… what held you immobile…

Damned if I wouldn't want a twirl a man said.

Somebody had to testify. But what filled a poor sucker's eyes more — which twirl in the chain was a bargain — going upstairs and having Wauneta in the room or standing on a curb and having Wauneta fill your head?

Meanwhile a block over at 21th Street — the Ville gathered in small bunches in the shadows. They were not a happy bunch- not after what happened this afternoon- not after their young boy died. The pain from the dead had barely lost its beauty and now in the swing back the Ville were drinking and suffering whiskey in the alley next door to the consignment store. And were getting mean for their troubles…sometime later tonight they'd cross Ogontz Avenue and go pound on the Clang.

That's how it goes… a feud had needs… lonesome sweetness and vortex-like vengeance... crazy and kinetic... throw trashcans on the Avenue and beat on cars held up at streetlights... break some teeth... it's like we all tried to scare to death the thing that killed us... like we were given bodies and were then driven to frenzy ... what the hell you might as well stand up in a void and scream hooray for nobody...

That's some wound up shit Cripple said.

Can we go now you asked?

Everything's got reason Cripple said.

What was it that kept us from vanishing? Maybe what we were was just some business thought up by other people when they saw you... if the Ville had a stick then the Clang picked up another stick... stuff like that... like what if Wauneta ever looked back what would that mean...

*

the coffee meditations

...Just an old bullet wound she said...

Spectral-like figure — tired and weak — walking the hospital halls in a flimsy fucked up gown with your ass hanging out- pushing the ubiquitous IV station along — moving slowly and afraid to bust the stiches — moving slowly to be moving at all — underneath the fluorescent glare overhead and the strange antiseptic air crowded around — there was a window at the end of the hall and that's where you were barely moving — happiness seemed to be there — all the staff looked at you and smiled like they've been trained to — and it felt odd to feel friendly in return when tethered to a bloody urine bag — but was important was to keep walking — to get to that window — food service carts and medical carts and janitorial carts sped past on the highway of the ICU — patients with drained faces- some dying in adjacent rooms- some that looked like death with applesauce on their chins — stared out from their beds — television noise surrounded the door frames like mad auras — finally the window — the view was all worldly green and slowly turning autumn colors and a town activity below that from six floors above looked so grand — if only you could be there standing out in the open air you'd sell what was left of your soul — but no — no you said that was impossible — so you said let's take another lap and do that again —

*

...The sounds... lying awake deep into the night... all those carts passing and the wheels that needed lubrication and the trays flopping about ... the orderly who kept apologizing each time he crashed into the door... syringes filled with morphine demons who wouldn't let you think or breathe... they sat on your chest and howled...the high pitched screech and whine from the IV machine when the fluid in the bag ran out... the vulture calls from incessant beeping alarms... the huge room-mate wider than the gurney that wheeled him in post-surgery but was like compressed into a ridiculous short body like his skin wasn't enough to contain him and was stuffed to bursting with old pillows and a bean bag chair... and who snored so loudly the curtains separating the bed spaces shook with each exhale...and had seizures to boot in his nightmares and swung wildly at whoever approached so the docs had him sedated and strapped down... snored so loudly your own brain went concussive... there was a clock on the opposite wall... the second hand went round its errands with a silence that seemed mocking you... I can move but you can't it said... one minute round the face and then another it said be-cause you're locked down in bed with the machines and can't get away... who could forget the urinal flushing and the latex gloves snapped off someone's fingers as your bloody waste was poured into the toilet and disappeared via the science of indoor plumbing to get the shit out of the room and drooped six floors and was rushed through sewer pipes to the water treatment facility and finally melded out into the holding pomd where a month from now you'd be drinking the same holding pond water from the tap in the kitchen... and snored so loudly it was like having your head stuck inside an explosion that detonated at regular intervals... and who knew professional wrestling was on television all night long.... maybe the morphine make you paranoid and you heard things that you weren't hearing at all... maybe the roommate wasn't snoring... maybe he was like a powerful meditator or something and what you heard was like his essence counting his breath... and snored so loudly it was like trying to close your eyes against a motor's backfire ... wait did the new shift nurse just introduce himself as Larry... what if you need something and can't remember his name... what if he's psycho-nurse and doubles up the morphine and you can't call for help because your lungs collapsed like plastic bags because you been given an overdose by a sadistic nurse impersonator who's all smiles and said hi call me Harry... the strange fluted sleeves around your legs that acted like bellows... every thirty seconds they inflate and pressure your calves and then let go and wheeze... and starts again... all night long... the squeeze and the wheeze... rhythmically pacifying to a bizarre degree and totally fucked up to lie there and listen but hey it was more interesting than professional wrestling was to kill the moment... the morphine demons sat on your chest and howled.... it was all Harry's fault because legitimately things were confused and getting fucked up because Larry couldn't get his name right... and snored so loudly.... squeeze and wheeze like fairy tale arms grabbing your legs from underneath the bed... beeping alarms latex snaps squeaking wheels the toilet gurgling with an evil laugh that wanted more blood... maybe it was just lifestyle withdrawal and that was it... where's the pizza where's the video store where's the domestic embrace... oh-oh why were the walls crowding in... why was the room shrinking... why did the roommate the snoring creation get the window bed... how much would it take to bride nurse Barry to switch bed spaces... why were you stuck... stuck with oxygen tubes up your nose and needles in your veins and electrodes glued on your chest... stuck in a shrinking room with the snoring roommate sedated and restrained and going nowhere but more snoring and was driving Dante's subway straight through hell... it should be simple right... help me help me... like the David Hedison character in The Fly... that's what he said... right at the end... after David Hedison's head was grafted onto the body of a fly in a matter transporter accident... and the fly head on David Hedison's body crushed itself with some large industrial press... to spare the love interest the horror for sure ... anyway the David Hedison head on the fly body was trapped in a spider web in a garden and the spider slowly made its way toward him... and in the limited special effects the day offered what you got was this grainy weird shot of a tiny David Hedison head badly superimposed on a fly body and as the spider drew ever closer you heard this teeny little voice crying help me help me... would it be a bad thing to gag a snoring person.... he wouldn't know... he was knocked out anyway... how come Harry was a nurse... that sounded like a good question... first there were white pills in a small paper cup with a ginger ale chaser... they were like relaxants or some shit... to help take your head out of the game they said... what game... Larry you asked I had lot of nurses in my time and truly what you do... but wait... what you wanted was sincere...it was totally easy to be unexplained and that was cool and have universes switched on you through the pinhole of an IV port.... but morphine was like having cocktails with the gods only to understand the god's don't care... you tried to remember lullabies but didn't know any so it became twinkle twinkle little star crap but you didn't have the window bed to look out from and make associates... fucking snored so loudly... why didn't Barry take your money... you remember David Hedison was in love... and so you decide you'll be in love... that will help... love will carry the day... or night... whatever's left of it... you will lie flat and be stuck and be in love... remember adolescent pornographic daydreams and try and construct living scenarios from them... giving was better than receiving so you made a list and decided when the gods get out of your face you will do something... but given a hazy moment where you thought humanity's best you forgot what it was you were going to do but decide it was all right anyway because it's the thought that counts... you think this love business was pretty good... you want to remember so much but really all you wanted was sleep... you imagine rest was love and love was rest... and the silence and the air pulled from Harry's face when you pressed the red call button and Larry rushed into the room and you had to tell him you were serribly torry but you had just shit the bed...

*

Stoned musical winds blew through the bright gold and deep red leaves holding to the trees.

October evening hit you in the head- stepping around the block with the raven-haired woman on your arm- feeble pathological steps- looking for the future the way an old man might walk- or looking for a memory like a toddler first discovered the beauty from upright motion. Geese in the hundreds rushed away overhead and carved a wake in the rich blue sky. Little kids ran around the soccer field chasing after a rolling ball they never seemed to catch. Over-zealous dogs tore up the street behind us without leashes or handlers and marking the obvious that it was good to be alive.

There's a reason the raven-haired woman said reading your thoughts.

But it always seemed stupid you thought.

Seeing equals what she thought? A cliché? A faith in how serious your life's been?

It's intense you said. You never bargained for it in the first place.

Hey she said this is not a reality show.

No not that you said. It's the way the air won't let go.

Yea she said it's a ginger soup apple pie day.

Best corn bread in the Milky Way you added.

Ball game later tonight she said.

The air won't let go. Radiating sunlight overlapped the neighborhood. It was better this way. Even if it had to end it was better this way. Orange twilight clouds behind the spinning blades of the wind machine at the electric department dropped into a fetish-like sky at the bottom of Locust Street. It was crazy to think those blades were not connected to anything — like a grid — to power — but were only there for show and for making a good ocular accent in case anyone asked. The air simply won't let go. It held us both like a condition dependent upon the grace of others to continue. We held on and went walking and said we could get used to this. It was warm. Night was coming — an empty space never empties — the dark streets of stars were lined up in flickers to tramp upon — a fearful cousin planet where maybe rice and beans were also staples rose in the hemisphere — the fucked up force of gravity pulling us down since time and its carnival-bending light fell upon the asphalt songs of teenage skateboarders carving turns down the hill — the air won't let you go — won't let us go — mists of electricity rose up block after block and reflected from house windows — trash blew across the streets — a tiny red sunlight wobbled last in the sky — no wonder — we love sad songs.

*

Standing beside worn out marigolds and Chinese paper lanterns dense enough with the season and ready to explode- you felt a sudden ache- like being lost- as though memory dropped you off and then faded away. It all looked familiar but something was missing. How do you square something missing?

Was there a moment when you actually saw the leaves change color?

All that gold along the backyard trees brushing against the sky seduced you with movement and wanted surrender.

First though you waited for the little white pills to relax your limbs and change your head with a deep inner air. Have a little wine also and say fuck off to the new sobriety.

You imagine it might be spirited to call someone and explain the golden leaves. Something like longing appeared driving those explanations in the strangest way- like being propelled outward into the world and desires and away from the security of home and the leave-me-alone voices that rise when things go bad.

Besides what could happen? It can't be that dangerous to go for a walk by yourself? Just a short trip when no one's looking…

After a day at the job paying the bills for someone else further up the food chain- the soccer dads were out and heading home to microwave leftovers- driving massive vehicles over speed bumps- tank-like cars filling up with tired grass-stained teammates and older sisters with IPod soundtracks and heavy expedition packs from school.

Security moms were out and running the streets like honeybees in a swarm- running in hive-mind groups and wearing the latest in stretchy butt gear- running it seemed where they talked as much as they ran and worked over everything in mimeo while losing breath and keeping pace.

What did it mean to be back at the ranch and have a general handle on things?

Harley guys were still out in the sweet evening and dressed against the sky in dark leathers rumbling on Pine Street and roaring to the wind like geese in formation with that unmistakable sound that a television show called American Thunder.

Day care kids outlined the dropped apples from ornamental trees with bright pastel chalks on the sidewalk- making sunbursts and wavy hypnotic impressions and day-glow halos around scores of small rotten fruits and the reddish brown smears made from footprints stepping on them.

*

And does a bird stand on a wire? Does it squat on a wire? Perch on a wire?

There was a bird in a dream you had. Like a compact hawk with steel talons and sharp eyes it looked around at the ground and the air and then looked at you from the edge of a tree limb. The bird began talking. Whatever it said you couldn't understand. Probably because you were too far away or maybe the bird didn't want to speak loud but you needed to understand if this was a conversation. You had to be up in the tree. So you started to climb and get out of bed and that woke the raven-haired woman like a metal filing pulled by a magnet. She looked at the clock and groaned softly.

No worries you said. There was plenty space left in the big overnight urine bag with shopping handles and extra capacity. No reason to change over to the handy day-tripper bag that strapped to your leg. No worries at all you said. She flopped back under the sheets for some extra rest and some time breathing alone. Looking at her made you feel funny. In a good way no doubt because love was long and beautiful and uncomfortable and just might be equal to what you've spent together. Like how you remembered her sleeping in a dumb hospital chair while you fidgeted in post-surgical hell — and sleeping in a twist like a shoelace knotted the wrong way — and thinking what you really wanted to do was to get the fuck out and go for a walk and make footsteps with her atop the ocean of the present.

It was a bird you said. And it was talking. Maybe if you went outside you'd hear it again. That might work — to get outside and find the dream — get a different station here on earth.

Make coffee. Make toast. Ask the stars what you felt on a clear early morning?

Hell must be a place without bread you thought. A place where nobody brings you bread. A place with a literal state of mind you thought. Picture the demons as carbohydrate starved loners. Picture nobody around to have their backs. They must know that. Dreary and remote set off to brood in shitless cycles. All that eternal gyration with destiny and they can't find anyone around with enough fascination to lend them a bulky roll to make a sandwich.

Make toast and kill it twice with honey and butter. Brew coffee until the smell intoxicated the house and sang like those old percolating commercials from Maxwell House that played retro on cable.

What did the bird say? Bring back what from yesterday?

Did you ever imagine that you'd marry an assassin? And one day take a bullet for her?

Fall in love because it was her neurons that kept you together?

Once you shared a room with a demon. It was a rental house on Fillmore Street while the family was between housing digs. You had a makeshift room on the third floor in the attic and there was a small window with a view that looked to a bridge over the river. And that was okay. It was removed enough to get away from the difficult routines that belonged to any family. You had a place to escape from the feudal arguments over what Walter Cronkite said happened in the world that day and the jaded viewpoints from the latest Surgeon General's reports on a canned food diet.

Often in that room you felt something as you went to sleep. During the night you'd wake up and look at the window. A shape floated there against the bridge lights in the distance. At first you asked are you a fucking burglar or what? As the nights went on and you couldn't sleep you'd watch the shape and ask it questions. But it never answered. The shape floated in the room and gave off a silence that got inside your head. Mostly it gave off eerie vibes like it wanted something but found itself unable to deliver. What was so necessary? You slept in that room for three months. And each night you had conversations with a shape that would not answer. At first you were scared. But maybe it was hungry and lost and wanted to live inside you. Maybe it recognized you.

And you remembered Sister Crumble one morning in eight grade yelling at the class like a bellows — demons came in spades she said — the worst was sure to come she said — because we were young — darkness held a velvet tongue — and you pictured them attacking in formation — demons flying up from the skies of hell — fanged teeth snapping

109

like flesh eaters — red eyed nasty and screaming — much like Sister Crumble herself. Consumed as she was by doing god's work — handing out corporal punishment and taking the almighty's name — swatting kids in the head — juvenile things like talking out of place or not knowing an answer when you were confused doomed you. There was always something that pissed Sister Crumble off — and summoned the demons that brought the house down each day. Maybe she had a bad reputation. But who knew about those trusted with power — especially the bloody satisfaction that went with holy power?

But the last thing you wanted was the demons. Why have demons when you could make toast instead? Besides it was the demons' job to make things as ugly as possible. All death seemed ultimate anyway so why take the bullshit and be pulled around and fooled?

The glow from the toaster- an electric ochre on the putty colored cave of the kitchen walls- shone against the early morning shadows as light from daybreak gathered outside the windows. The alchemy — a piece of leftover bread — how yeast flour salt and heat combined and burned a little in the air — to release the stored energy in stale bread and make it crisp — was like catching a source and the affect afterwards was not only toast without interference but also a first thought best thought mystery you could not answer.

And so you made toast and coffee for the raven-haired woman and thought why not bring her breakfast in bed? Perhaps this simple act — liminal and synthetic — and the gratitude having an old bullet wound fixed — who wanted to die from the past and all that — might illuminate what nature had to offer — to get through a day without failure and leave things behind — without a trouble that wrote down your name.

But the question was could you walk back upstairs carrying a tray without losing your balance? What if you fell backwards down the stairs and spilled the coffee and ruined the toast? How do actions go — from love to calamity in an instant? How do you get stuck in the kitchen!

But what happened if you ate all the toast?

Was sleep better than toast? Where was that equation? The one that said first thought best thought?

The raven-haired was played out — from looking after your concerns — and ignoring her own. She wasn't used to playing Florence Nightingale. Who did play that role in the movies? That had to be a movie right? Otherwise what was history for if you couldn't make a movie out of it?

The old movie — the nurse's anxiety was a big chance and was reflected in selfless immediate acts- like how to save a man — where doubt was not an option and the sky was not moved by worldly failures. She affected other people — to the point where recovery gave definition to life.

In the up to date version — Florence Nightingale would star a stainless body actress as the fashionably smocked nurse savior — loosely buttoned and bending over embarrassed patients- chaste in motion — weepy designer eyes smoked and horny. In some other place and in some other time — that's where her mind was set best — wanting to be Somebody other than who she was.

But she continued tired-lipped and filled with a sad intellect. She laughed about everything — laughing at nothing at all — roamed the halls — cared for patients — the lonely hours — hospital time — almost right — talking with the mop squad who polished the floors.

And as she stared at their functional existentially useless jobs — looking out the window at another night short on mythology — she injected herself with a bag of heroin and fell back onto a convenient chair — shaking her long dark hair from a sad and youthful face and deciding silently that there was a tomorrow but what the fuck did it matter except for the dream of a lifetime?

*

Aside from the hopeful routines taken on to square things — the pain demons made your head a wrecking bar — your blood felt like boiled dishwater — you were able to keep time about you. Even if that time was walking on weak knees and stopping arms akimbo to catch a breath. Outside by your lonesome — removed from a team of specialists cutting you open and digging inside your body — the streets buzzed and twilight on the sleepy brown grass moved too fast.

Why change it?

Why thin out your fears unless you measure them?

Short winged geese flew overhead — limping in formations — toward the fouled marshes and the dirty oiled scratch lands. The sky washed down through inky blue colors on the atrium of evening. Unleashed mutts browsed in the weeds. Three small kids all rode on one bicycle. Peppy infidels with razor slick haircuts parked in wet dream cars and talked exhausted money codes into headsets. Opposing baseball caps jawboned at the bus stop like geographies in a civil war. Stupid lawns sign wanted your vote and your confidence. A bird on a wire was uncertain.

When you looked around — the things you saw — the warm emptiness — they pulled back at your gaze and grinned you a lesser hallelujah to walk on by. Bizzaro divine peels of information unwound around your head — electric tomatoes — holographic teenage eyes — tall asters bloomed and leaned over from the weight of cranberry petals and bright yellow stars in the centers of the flowers. Bees attacked the asters — gathering what was left because that's what bees do — they make other foods from the mess of a garden. The mad Syrian on Pier 19 was selling his apple pies in flimsy tins and his ground local fish and seaweed pate shaped into a brick and then dipped in blue wax melted down from plastic Slinky's and lobster floats. You needed it all. You bought an apple pie. You bought brick pate. You cut asters with Blind Charlie's knife and stole tomatoes from a yard across 2nd Avenue. You told the dog this will make us a fine meal.

When you got home — take your time the sky said — take another pill you said and bleach out — you settled in beside the raven-haired woman and watched a ball game in the pennant race.

*

faster than gravity

Links Fish House was a madhouse on a Friday night- packed to near standing room only- with long benches along the walls holding the weary butts of parishioners sitting and waiting for takeout orders to be filled. We ordered Blind Charlie his flounder and coleslaw and told the guy behind the counter we wanted fresh rolls also. He nodded like it all meant nothing. Whatever rolls were there- those were the rolls we were going to get.

While we waited — hungry fish law devotees ahead of us like hordes for the lord — the frying machines filled the air with the smell of heaven in a basket — deep fried and crunchy like what you might expect heaven to taste like. Cripple read the seafood chart on the wall from the Eastern seaboard- talking out loud- talking to no one and talking about shit he knew nothing about- like the pros and the cons of haddock and cod and mackerel.

An elderly woman sat on the benches. She told you about her son in law who was serving in the army and fighting in them strange awful wars.

You agreed it was bad.

She showed you her filling and told you about the dentist.

You agreed that dental hygiene was definitely important in life.

She told you she liked the Cleveland Browns over the Packers on Sunday.

You asked her if she'd give you the Packers and a field goal for two bucks.

Her eyes lit up and said you got it.

We agreed to meet next Friday evening to settle our debts.

Did you care about the Packers? No really. It was just something to say.

Did you care about the old lady? Not really. It was just something to do while waiting for a fish order. She peeked inside her shopping bag to see if the contents were still there and hadn't either vanished or been stolen. She closed the bag and straightened the handles getting it just so the way she wanted. Likewise when she creased the sides so they won't rip and started talking to you again.

Maybe the problem was you don't care. Or what you let pass for a truth… Maybe you should stay in the neighborhood forever and try and find some dignity and learn how to care…

By the time you looked up the sentient old lady and her fish eating soul grabbed her greasy paper bag and was headed out the door along Avenue C.

Was there a condition for happiness? What would hold up and withstand tonight's meal? Would the son-in-law make it home alive? You should have asked for at least a touchdown on Sunday's game. For all you knew- god was a Cleveland Browns fan.

Hey lady — what's that you got? Fish?

Reds held the door for the old lady and laughed as she walked away carrying her bags. He took a last drag from a cigarette and then flipped it off into the night. A crumpled gray sweatshirt hung on him like a sack filled with packing material. Reds wasn't exactly fat as he was adolescent and pudgy and contrary to fact thought himself muscular and defiant. The way he walked across the room and how he slowed his steps enough to be noticed was a check me out moment for everyone to see — but it was also painful to watch a fake symmetry in action that had no point.

You weren't in school today.

Thank you for the obvious he snapped back.

Sister Crumble said -

See my face Reds interrupted? Does this face look like it give two shits about what she said?

No you said it doesn't.

And it wasn't long in coming — tormented by kids stronger than he was — kids swung at Reds because he was there to be swung at — like for years Reds had his shoes pilfered right off his feet and placed on the trolley tracks to be run over and cut in half — while Reds watched —

fuck growing up and wasting time — then he had to walk home bare foot demonic and sad — that soon enough Reds fashioned the world into categories. Think about it — what creature enjoyed being prey? First there were those who did you wrong and they needed to be fucked over in some way revenge-wise. Second were those who had something worth stealing. And third were the assholes to ignore because they took up too much space. But he was your friend. Even if his worldview was a windy delusion that blew through his head — it was a kind of genius scam to be admired. Somehow Reds was convinced he already bypassed the pretensions — that he was a young boy — he was already a star strutting about the neighborhood. Swinging that right arm in the air like it was cool and untouchable and throwing a dip down with his left shoulder like he owned the whole Monopoly board of life. If he was a physically clumsy mess — then Reds had a mouth that ran smart against the odds. And if you bark sharp enough and long enough soon enough your shoes stay on your feet…Ah yea the worst was yet to happen…

Not true he said. I ran a favor today for Cousin Jimmy.

And that proves what?

Money proves what? Money proves what is what. Reds looked at you and said ah man don't go asshole on me. This is how it works. Some night you need a slice. I know you and with you it's like anything to get that slice … that would be you am I right? But on that night you got no money — and are we clear here what I'm saying? Oh Reds man can you do me up a slice? I hear this shit in my sleep. Because it's my money… that's how it works… Cripple's scheming — you're thinking — but hey it's me that's buying. So don't talk to me about school…

You guess he had a point. What if all your life somebody else bought your pizza?

Would that mean you never grew up? That you'd become defenseless and lost in time?

But that was like a situation that required no explanation. We had a single purpose and that was to get Blind Charlie his fish. It was neat and economic — we were the messengers — we brought back the material. No ideas no emotions no attachments. The

money thing was already taken care of. And that was the best part running errands for Blind Charlie. You went to places and didn't need money. Blind Charlie had tabs and marks all over the neighborhood. You walked into a place for Blind Charlie and you walked out with the goods.

But where did that leave you?

Sure it looked easy enough. Getting fish for an old man. Or running for cigars and newspapers. But it was the bundle hidden inside along with the fried fish coleslaw and rolls that was worrisome. The package you never looked at and never talked about. That package was Blind Charlie's business. And Blind Charlie could be as frightening a dude as he was a kind old man.

It might be simply intellectual — for some people anyway — because there was always something wrong– like getting killed — walking on the wrong side of the avenue — but truth was maybe someday you end up shot in half like a boy caught and already forgotten in some crossfire bullshit.

You began to see life in the eighth grade as a messed up go round that weighed a hand down upon your shoulder. Doing shit that brought you down — that was it — but also if you looked closely it was a shit that just might turn out to hand you over a soul. Maybe you should stay in the neighborhood forever — be a secret agent — a double agent — until the angles sang like money in the highest choirs...

Cripple motioned Reds over to the Seafood chart and said something in his ear. They were a loop — it was easy to watch them — in orbit — who was going to last — bring something — who had balls and verve — and what you heard Reds say in reply was no way that's too fucked up. Young boys were a sight to behold. They can't see the future. And as long as they stayed an arm's length from harm they believed in what they did and stayed true down to the bone.

Cripple said we cut it some.

Reds said bad move.

Cripple said who's not wise?

Reds said the package was stamped. And was sealed with signs in red wax like fucked up shapes you never seen before. Cripple he said no — bad plan.

Goddam Cripple said we need ours!

Yea Reds said someday. We get ours. How far ahead you think you get if you messed with Friday night and the fish. Check your fucking head…

It was easy to have obedience… a dog can be taught obedience…to have no look other than to avoid a smack in the face… but thieving was a business… when you get caught that was certain … and the streets were filled with people trying to bring home a little something extra…

Cripple said he had a feeling that's all. Tired he said with all this sincerity. We need to put up some truth. What? You want forgotten? Not me.

Cripple might be insane with big ideas. He might not get past his own little pocket change of circumstance. But who know that but him?

Bad plan Reds said again and grabbed Cripple in a headlock. Cripple's glasses went flying and crashed to the floor. Now he was practically blind — squinting through a scissor work of ceiling lights. His eyes moved back and forth inside his boney head like two bulbs loose in their sockets. But he was a funny kid. And he especially liked television wrestling gestures — like the kind with the fake forearm slam across an opponents head — like how he did to Reds and then flexed his arms and beat his chest like some wahoo working the crowd.

All right Cripple said. Maybe you slick and maybe you bad. Maybe you got nothing but the dumb ass way you walk. But you are dead-looking ugly. And the possibilities for your ugliness were plain endless. How you get up in the morning without breaking mirrors? And I know your mom was a religious person because each time she looked at you she said — oh my god.

Reds meanwhile had Cripple's thick glasses hanging on his nose. He paced around Links to counter-attack Cripple. Maybe an elbow chop to the skull…or if Reds got in close he'd put the sleeper hold on Cripple… then game over…

And one by one the Links Fish House costumers stood in line for their fish and fries — watching the commotion in the ring — and you knew for sure what they wanted — and that was only to go home and put the week behind. For sure they knew Cripple and Reds. They saw the act each week. Nobody wins. It just happens each week. But who was paying attention? It was — after all — Autumn on earth — where the dead who didn't make it and lived in purgatory as fake souls were trapped in no-man's land — an homely moment indexed between bliss and torment — and walked the ground once a year — scanned through the human ghosts of bodies they came across — starred them down -and eventually hoped to find their own lost residence and settle their own stupid eternal death and finally be done with it and nest in the hometown soil where they were born.

But what did you know?

Cripple slid up to an old woman sitting on the benches. And she looked old enough to maybe be the last living refugee set free by the emancipation proclamation. Cripple asked hey mamma what say you let me borrow your glasses? Can't see worth a damn here he said!

The ancient woman looked straight at Cripple — she looked sideways over at Reds — he's right she said to Reds — you ugly. And what's worse she said was you two clowning your damn lives away! She looked back at Reds. Give that boy back his glasses and put a cap on this nonsense!

Her words brushed past — the fried fish smell climbed over the counter top — hitting the ceiling fan- filled the atmosphere with good sensible food — a Friday night bag that kept the family in tune eating together and watching television. You had to wonder — what did a sad mysterious soul have to do — just what did put a cap on this nonsense?

Suddenly Mister Link banged the small bell beside the register that said our order was ready. Eventually you get used to how adults stare at you. Time to leave. He placed Blind Charlie's fish bag on the counter. He muttered something in a secret language. You always took this to be like some fucked up welcome mat to lap up after each order was filled — the god's will — and also like some insult that the gods had even put him in this position from the start. What it meant — as he held out the bag out at arm's length — his eyes curled with weariness — was that it was time to take our fish order and leave and our soulless asses be gone.

Maybe you stay in the neighborhood forever — stepping over fault lines — the avenues at war -- watch the spray paint walls for directions — fetch information — make yourself welcome…

*

Blind Charlie was pleased as ever when we arrived back with his dinner. He took the bag into the back room for a second. It didn't take the Hardy Boys to figure that out.

And it certainly wasn't like he was getting extra ketchup or anything. The Friday night package — where did he store it?

When he returned we had the big Friday night plate all ready for him. He gave us the bag and so we took out everything from the paper containers and greasy wrappers — the fish coleslaw fries and rolls — and laid it out banquet style. And really- it wasn't that hard to serve someone a meal. Blind Charlie took a moment and savored what he smelled before he sat down to eat.

Maybe you should stay in the neighborhood forever — learn to cook fish — make yourself valuable.

Blind Charlie's attitude toward the neighborhood was like free will. You had free will to choose whatever you wanted. But you had to choose right with your free will –and if you didn't choose right well that was the wrong thing to do. Not choosing right meant dissent. And the only way to solve dissent was to snuff it out. No baggage attached. You'd need some crazy quilt of thoughts mashed up in your head to cross Blind Charlie. Someone eventually would though — that's how the whole thing works — way of the world and all that — power made its own equation — power equaled the desire to steal that power — so we end up eating our own.

Blind Charlie liked to taste the coleslaw first. It was like that first act set up the rest of the meal. And no doubt Links made good coleslaw. And the fish always carried its own weight. But sometimes you wished the sacramental approach to how things were conducted were different...

Maybe if you stayed in the neighborhood forever — your work went underground — and helped gut the fish law...

Satisfied with his first tastes — was he ever not — the package secured — Blind Charlie poured us all more wine.

He told Reds to go and order any pie on the menu. In fact he said- holding his glass aloft in a toast- where it caught a strange hankered dust broadcast in the slow light below the dim lampshades that cornered the room- in fact he said again — serious and righteous and emphatic — there was no compromise here — as long as Da Vinci Pizza stayed in business he said you boys have a home.

And in true tone we tossed down our wine in a gulp.

Reds asked if he could order extra pies and then later on tonight sell them on the street?

Blind Charlie stared at Reds. That enough was spooky- to have Blind Charlie stare at you was spooky — but it was the way Blind Charlie held his shoulders — laid back against his chair — weighing them up and down like a scale that had nothing in it for balance.

Mister Reds he said- if you want to have three pies in here by yourself there's no problem. But you have to know how it would hurt me to see my pies sold second hand.

Cripple was famished. But that's the way it always was with him — easy enough to shovel a slice of pie into his face with one bite. And he barely stopped to breathe when he ate- like oxygen was just another item on the menu- and he had to get as much food into his body in as short a time possible — keep that old developing digestive system moving before he passed out. Cripple might have made a great pack animal if he was born that way. Cheese bits stuck in the tinsel as he smiled — odd ends of crust flew off his braces as he chowed through a second slice and laughed.

Whereas Blind Charlie was a very neat eater — napkin at the ready like an old gent — someone who took slow meaningful bites — pausing with the time of his meal like there was neither reward nor problem — just wine and conversation and life while it lasted.

Cripple was a savage compared to what? He lived to eat. To hold some fat pizza meat up to his eyes — inspect it — passing it through his fingers like a rare coin — and finally in a snapping bite made it gone like sweet justice. Maybe in a past life Cripple was a gravedigger. Maybe in a future life he sold popcorn or hot dogs hawking the aisles at professional sporting events.

Blind Charlie asked was there more trouble tonight?

You wondered what happened to the world if there was no trouble?

Reds laid odds somebody got hurt tonight and he also wanted Cleveland and seven on Sunday.

You boys make me laugh Blind Charlie said.

He finished his roll and ran a hand through this thick brown hair-beginning to gray in streaks and receding at those delicate points on the temples. Still Blind Charlie had great hair.

You thought maybe Blind Charlie's hair was like how the body made it up to him for having no eyes? How many guys did you think Blind Charlie's age wish they had his hair? What were their solitary hours like? Did they regret needing something that was not their own — like always wearing a hat as though you needed a disguise — like fearing the dreaded comb-over each morning as your wife watched you behind your back in the mirror?

A problem in fact was if you stayed in the neighborhood the future was built on places where you can't hide...

And the way Reds ate food — suspicious because he didn't own it — problematic because a meal had no added value — a no win solution because his food was gone the moment he saw it and that put him in a bad mood.

It's a hard fall — that's how the spiritual chants on the gospel stations put it.

We've been doing this since the sixth grade. Meeting at the shop and going out and bringing the fish back to Da Vinci Pizza. You figured — it was better being here than holed up inside your home — watching television and looking around at your family –separate and bubble-like — alone and crashed together under the same roof with not much sense why we were there together other than the shows we were watching. Evidence maybe to a long birthing accident and some weird scene of investigation into the whereabouts of a void ...

You figured Blind Charlie had his world and you had yours. No big deal. We met at some intersection where crime and food did business. And this was an employment option — that once offered and if you accepted — followed you through life. Unless of course you took it on your own and crossed Blind Charlie. There were stories about guys missing fingers. And stories about fingers missing guys... That's why it made sense. You fetched the bag. In exchange you got pizza. And that was the equation — even if you made it crudely — down and dirty it was like a rudder that kept slipping out of your hands and you kept grabbing after it.

Friday night pizza in Jersey-land– when you think — when you think like that — it's not difficult to imagine and take a leap and say fuck it whether it was true or not — when you think like that you wanted to cry out and let the world know — Da Vinci made tasty and genius pies.

Problem was — when you thought about it — you were only a kid — a drifty adolescent because the sky hadn't screwed your head on yet.

Maybe you left Jersey-land. Maybe you walked around the world and searched out pizza shops. Taste different pies — sit in different back rooms — drink different wines — meet distant and starved kids and listen to local wit...

Maybe Eden traveled with you — that was an idea.

But think — pizza shop to pizza shop — like some fucking cosmic dude dropped from the sky and you walking around and grabbing a slice. That was the ticket. You needed to convince Eden to go

Suddenly Cripple jumped off his chair. He spun around the room — well as much as someone can spin with a bad leg — a fucking lounge leg Reds said — and he yelled which way we go... what we do? With eyeballs large as paper plates and grinning with an erector set bolted across his mouth — Cripple threw his body about the room yelling duck mother-fuckers duck!

Blind Charlie shook his head. He rapped his knuckles twice on the table. That meant displeasure with Cripple's mouth.

But when you looked at Cripple — you understood — well — you had insight or some shit like that — this was a reasonable calling for him. Baggy pants handed off from his older brother who went by the tag Bongo Gland — discard clothes that were now wearable clothes and held in place with a clothesline scrap for a belt and they hung upon his skinny waist like sacks walking in the air. He was like some hopped up prophet — Ezekiel in the wild — naming tribes and throwing others out of camp.

You said it yourself Cripple said- looking back over at Blind Charlie-who said nothing but just kept staring- looking back over at Cripple and waiting- and Cripple said crazy people throw fire on gasoline!

Cripple flew over to the door and opened it and stood looking out at the restaurant.

The paper cloth tables were filled — ghosts from Friday gone and heroes from Friday tomorrow — they all looked like they wanted to be forgotten for a moment. Scratchy opera music played breadstick and garlic and tragedy love songs from old 78 vinyl.

We stood beside the big ovens and waited against the pizza heat and the aromas that killed us. If we needed a way to be alive this was a close enough fit. If we needed a condition to tell us where we stood — as pies left the ovens in waves and addictions were unstoppable — a line of naked dough balls were prepared by hand — to be invented as more hot pies and cooked with a sweet fucking know how. Dreams and death — hunger and hopes — were the same — the same radiant tab paid in full until the following week brought us out.

See Cripple yelled! Hey he said everything cool! How yawl doing! And I know you wanna be inside here on Friday — that shit's a given... yea that's what I'm saying! And you know outside them boys will hit you and steal from you — but god damn this is Blind Charlie's house! And that ain't working you over once you get something fresh in your minds — fuck no! — No — you don't do that in between shit...!

Blind Charlie went to the door and rapped his knuckles three times on the jamb.

Within a moment — hearing that sound — a cousin near the cash register stood before Cripple. To say this guy was big and meaningful — blunt and diplomatic and not to be fucked with — really missed the point. With a few easy steps he herded Cripple back into his chair.

Thank you Blind Charlie said.

The cousin quietly shut the door behind him. And that meant the door stayed closed.

*

Cripple asked for more wine.

Blind Charlie poured us all another glass.

Maybe Blind Charlie's generosity would do us in. Maybe that generosity was a force put on hold. You understood you didn't have the brains to figure this out — because you kept feeding your ideas into a pencil sharpener and the more they turned the shorter they became. Or if you were drunk enough how do you image your surroundings without asking where was the end of the story?

Blind Charlie asked what Cripple meant when he yelled at the restaurant?

The worst of it Cripple said. But seriously Mister Charlie no disrespect but go outside.

Thieves were all over Cripple said. But inside here things were cool and looked after. You see what I'm saying?

Yes Blind Charlie said. I do see what you're saying.

Blind Charlie exhaled — like an old man in dreams — fighting the show of intended consequence — exhaled in sanctuary to the back room. A ring of cousins watched over him — armed and ready to push back against the end of Friday night — making pizza and protecting Da Vinci against — existential threats — you heard that phrase on television the other night — existential threats — and you liked it so you kept on using it.

Don't all saints need acolytes? Didn't every power require the possibility of betrayal?

Blind Charlie looked Cripple in the eye and said- but Joseph- you're the thief that you're talking about.

Yea Cripple said. But not like that. Outside those boys steal from me! What I'm saying is a warning. Mister Charlie — with all them fires you talking about — this shit gets bigger and bigger.

And Blind Charlie asked?

Man I don't know Cripple said- another slice waving in his hand. It's fucked up.

Blind Charlie rapped a number of times on the table and smiled like he knew exactly what he knew.

Yea got it Cripple said. Sorry.

Joseph — Blind Charlie said. Just what was it that you're saying?

I'll tell you what Reds said. Nobody's happy just to get along like that — know what I mean? And so they say — like wow I'm happy — because people need to be happy and all that — but you know — so what?

Go on Blind Charlie said. He cracked a piece of flounder between his old teeth.

Let me ask he said: What? We're not happy this evening? Smell the sauce out there…. Was there somewhere you know better? Somewhere else you'd rather be? Hear the customers? Don't they sound happy? Don't we have the rewards that today required we have. Are the pies good? Am I satisfied with my fish? And those people outside this room — seated — eating and drinking –afforded a quality service — were they not happy?

Beyond tonight there's another day. More problems… get on with it…

Reds nodded but you could tell he wasn't hearing this for shit.

So what did Reds know that he wasn't telling the rest of us?

*

Reds was all mannerisms about it like he was being fucking polite. Like yea it was good… and yea I'm into it — here's the glass — hoisting the glass — when someone toasted — to a relative who done a good thing recently like bring home money for the clan — or a dead ancestor — whose eyeballs were third rate and taken for granted while alive but in death his words were enshrined like cosmic spray paint on a long and sturdy family wall no more no less in the big dark night … but in that scant heart that operated beneath his chubby ribs — it was a heart where valentines went to die — Reds figured he'd been there — seen that — drank that wine and still wanted more — not for the big dark night with wine and memories — but a fucking payoff. How many Friday nights did it take to get ahead? How much wind did you need to put up with? How many people did it take — stepping into the back room — and asking hey what's new?

Cripple swirled his wine around in the glass — what did that mean — some movie action shit like he just saw a James Bond flick at the Band Box — and then tossed it back and dropped the glass on the table for more. All right he said and pushed his chair out and got up from the table and dusted off what might have been his lapels if he wore a suit or even knew what a suit was. He grabbed a broom from a corner.

How did Blind Charlie see what to sweep? Was dirt the same for those with eyes as it was for unsighted guys?

And holding the broom like a stand up microphone Cripple said good evening. And welcome to the back room. His MC voice was corn syrup enough that some day it might land him employment — working a club on the boardwalk — introducing washed up ladies in G-strings doing titty fan dances and showing ass for senseless money changers.

Friday night calling Cripple said. Outside: what we got was like this — simple enough to get a handle on — young boys with heart for show and no money for proof. It's not your old man's world anymore — that's a quote from my father straight up from the news couch.

And to quote — uncle demon — you know who that was — he's the pigeon head from the Daily News — yea you know who that was. That dude with the awful clothes — the shinny Mustang — and that hair- damn that hair — that hair needs to be arrested — that hair needs put away- that hair in the open was an invite for someone to come up and scalp that shit — and who said quote ..."this neighborhood not only fails but seems to act on cue and deliver itself into more home-bred cycles of poverty and generations of hopelessness. But more to the point this neighborhood gives us another dim infested scene. This is the challenge before us. And a duty we must recognize and a responsibility we shoulder. We must- as a moral people- stand against- and defend ourselves against- these erosions of principles and this decay as the root cause. What I've seen here — and what we must share and fear- this is a place where values mean little. Because this neighborhood- like others I've reported upon in my columns- happens to exist and in a very odd way — almost like a weed in a lawn- a place where dishonestly lies and criminal action take center stage. And need we even begin to understand as the murder rate climbs each year?

Why do not these people living in this place ask themselves questions? Questions you edit with pride- as you're your children grow each year – you thank god for mercy — you thank god for the police commissioner — those are examples where growth and care deliver a future. But this murder rate- what are we to do? Worry about directions and expectations that exceed us? And as lawful citizens- those who resist lawlessness- those who refuse to tolerate a lackey attitude toward civic responsibility- those who favor safety work and prayer: we also need to ask ourselves a question: Should we even care about a few worthless streets…?"

Ever seen that motherfucker's hair Cripple asked?

Blind Charlie laughed. But he still rapped his knuckles on the table and smiled.

Cripple excused himself. Sorry he said — got carried away.

You memorized that Reds asked?

Cripple said my dad worked in the print shop so I'm used to it.

But let's shake things up Cripple said.

He stood tall on that bad leg and held his broom.

And it was a bag leg — deformed and buckled like an odd twig.

When he was a child Cripple was taken aside by god's front men one day in church and told — the reasons why anything happened were mysterious.

What was the advice there? Sorry about that? We'll get back to you?

The doctors told Cripple: his leg had probable cause to be the way it was. Nobody at Jersey-land General knew what happened… Might be a rogue protein feeding on Cripple's cellular makeup... Or maybe he ate lead paint while hanging in the womb… The closest guess it seemed was that Cripple was infected with some kind of postal virus… Pen pal kids around the globe were writing to strangers to queue their loneliness but were also sending pathogens to other kids they hoped and wanted to befriend. So it was like — sorry kid. No cure. Expect fever motor paralysis atrophy on down the line.

What Cripple got for his early troubles in life was this: a big fuck you from all sides — and was told that he would never have a normal life — and he was told — never give up the hope.

Whatever the truth was about Cripple's leg it didn't add up to fucking gruel. Because Cripple couldn't walk right he was already in the grave? No big shot involved came out and said it — but what was unspoken was what they viewed as Cripple and his doomed identity — scraping a sneaker toe on the pavement as he walked — the lame unfit kid using up prayers and medical resources — to no benefit — no matter where the money goes.

*

What we feature tonight Cripple said to the broom — and god knows what god does — along with the usual suspects — what we'll be looking at tonight will be freedoms and all that other shit — namely death éclat and funk.

What the fuck's that Red's asked?

By this time Blind Charlie was tired rapping his knuckles.

What Cripple said?

Éclair or whatever Reds said.

Éclat Cripple said.

It means brilliance Blind Charlie said

Geez Reds said

As I was saying Cripple said — staring at Reds — his braces picking up the tarnished back room light — old world floor lamps with tasseled shades — chain pull switches that frightened the dog when they went on and off — we got the man himself tonight — Mister Blind Charlie.

And what he says tonight is about fire. Maybe the big one — was that what you think?

But you don't know that or not — now do you? Maybe it roars from tomorrow like a crack in the street. Right outside your door and you too dumb to notice it- burning and lighting the sky up and all them ashes falling down and getting blown through your windows. Yea you — sitting on your fucked up couch all night and you believe in one thing — that you in command because you got the remote for the night. But this fire was high stepping on the ground because it got impulse — and it don't matter what we think.

And over there- sitting in the corner- like he won't be seen- we got the holy ghost- the original spook himself- before god ever spoke a word there was the spook filling in the shadows and thinking about it. So worried he goes nuts like a car wreck that hasn't made the papers yet. Worried — yea that's the spook — his MOA — worried one day and making tracks the

128

next- rolling it back and forth in his head like a cue ball on the table that can't proper be set up — what I'm saying is the spook can't measure the shot — so worried in fact this dude carries extra sneakers in his back pockets just in case he needs to run further away than he figured.

People are nuts Cripple said.

Zombie heads — yea you know them — they live in your house. You got families loaded on greenie in the morning because last night now they hung over and need a short Ballantine at daybreak with sloppy eggs and skinny bullshit bacon off the lesser butt of the hog that frying in the pan it shrinks down twice less its size more grease than meat. Then your toast dies.

That's how a day gets started.

Then getting home after lousy jobs — hold on that's what families need — it's the same old you — but hey come on it's reversed to disguise the bullshit you woke up with this morning. You ain't starting the day anymore because that's over but what you do know is to slow it down now. So a little barbital on the bus and a little nod behind the newspaper and a stop at the tavern and have a few to take off the breaks — and you walk in the door and then put the big blinders on and reach for heaven's whiskey and grab some dead toast nobody ate from that pearly white scum formed on the pan that nobody bothered to clean.

But let me tell y'all a story about Reds. Reds is so tight with his cash. Yea like nobody don't know that right? But at Christmas time- when things are all homey- and like yea it's a time while colored porch lights holds court — what Reds does is pays somebody to steal his money — the cash he was gonna use to buy presents.

Then he tells the family shit I been robbed!

Ain't nobody in that family believe him. But so what — everybody used to Reds spilling his mouth and nobody getting anything from it.

A day later he meets the guy behind the grocery store and spreads him a few bills and they do a bag of glue together. Reds calls it pocket sharing. Man there was one time Reds was so high — he was able to put a spitfire airplane and a thunderbird model together with all the goo and cement dripping from his nose. Hold on now Reds — you know what's so...

But while we here lets look on. What about the holy ghost Cripple said? See? See how he holds himself in a corner? And hold on now yea sure he talks trouble. Talks it like he lives it… but my main boy here lives in his head and so forgets — what — there's all this shit outside? But how can that be? How does he know? Oh yea mistakes be made and we ain't walking away from that. But here's what — And why should I lie? What the spook thinks about — and what he wants — that ain't no secret — but it makes the spook a little scared — to be found out- is he wants this girlfriend. And what this girlfriend –well there's nothing there yet but some girlfriend in mind — nothing but radio songs he dials up to the dj and asks for — and don't give no name but says hey play this with like a fake voice on the telephone — and I give him credit for his thoughts — because she looks like she invented nakedness! That girl's like a prayer that got answered! Might be one day god questioned her and she said hey here's the bus schedule and I'm finding a stop to get off. And there's the spook — in a vision — kneeling in a dark room — hoping and wishing and praying… except the spook don't kneel. He fakes it at mass and keeps his butt on the pew. But hold on that's brave. Not kneeling –and trying to figure it — here comes the red knuckles! — Getting small how's it like beaten in public …

*

Jersey-land dreamer
game changer
how far can you run you asked

The more you looked at something the more you wanted it — and who didn't know that? And the more you looked at what you desired — the simpler it was. What you looked at and what you desired lied back to you — too much to take in and feel okay about.

There was a back room behind the back room — tucked of to the right behind the soda and beer cases and with a folding iron grate that locked in front of the door. And there was always a cousin standing there and guarding the room off the back room. And two more cousins outside in the alley flanked the back door — old school assault weapons beneath their coats.

And another cousin was at the cash register where there was a shotgun under the counter. And another cousin kept an eye on the front door and carried automatic pistols and stun grenades for support.

And you were sitting only a few feet away from the back room off the back room.

Wasn't money the lure — money enough to bleed you out?

You didn't want to be a fireman. You didn't want to be a milk delivery guy or follow your grandfather into public transportation.

You never liked decisions to begin with. Mostly you avoided making them. Decisions loaded you into the future — for anything out of order — too much to take in and feel okay about it. But your blood had thoughts pumped up — hot and animal — from your ass crack up to your brain stem — the mechanical whoosh-slush-whoosh-slush-whoosh-slush from the heart echoed between your ears.

How do you decide to become a thief?

Did you have the necessary sourness to carry this out?

*

Yes Blind Charlie said — some nights you boys take me right down to the bone — like I'm having my fortune told.

You guys are young he said … you earned your meal… now it's yours alone — at this table. This time was good what you did. You boys did well. You have a position. Salute.

When Blind Charlie offered a toast no one refused. It wasn't simply the wine but the larger problem that enveloped you.

Yea for sure you earned a meal. And Blind Charlie made you family. And your obedience pleased the cousins to no end — the one guarding the back door to the back door — and the other one standing and grinning slightly between the back room and the pizza shop. You were in. Everyone sensed that and everyone flexed that. You had a ken for loyalty. You had a good taste for pie.

What was worse — being a twelve year old?

What was better — being a twelve year old?

*

...maybe that was only a guess... Later tonight night you'd meet Eden and lie together on a flat tar roof and watch the sky. Tell lies to one another until we fell in love with our words ... hold hands and remained forever close until we said words again and were scared about the adult anxieties about to replace our own. Beneath stars we couldn't see but we knew they lived on — different and rare — a place where no oxygen existed but where light stilled burned.

Blind Charlie knew about it. So far — you hadn't fucked up was your only guess — because the cousins followed where you went — because nobody yet stepped from the shadows and broke your head. Blind Charlie knew — he knew about you and Eden and he knew about you and Eden and the sky. But he never mentioned anything on a Friday night. Blind Charlie owned Jersey-land and ran the future through his wrinkled fingers and sensitive reading hands. We were impossible to meter. We lost curfews. We split dimensions and lived for a chance to live. We rested on rooftops. Down below the rules never changed. Strangers continued to fight strangers with their teeth.

But you had to play it small and then play it even smaller... Can't be afraid no can't be afraid even though you were afraid... just make it smaller...to deal with... easy doses... grab it...shrink it where no one else followed... make it small enough to hide.

In that back room off the back room there was something more valuable than your dreams. Must be straight up cash — that's what you pictured — rolls of hundreds and hundreds of those rolls- and then packages filled with those rolls — hundreds and hundreds of those packages — just start adding zeros and it's not long after that you saw a fortune.

Payday was like ten feet away.

Blind Charlie asked us all to hold hands around the table. He wanted to pray. It was Friday evening. He had the world on his mind. He always did. You hoped somewhere down the line his soul was blessed for the effort. Friday was the day for Blind Charlie to voice his heart. No problem there. Prayer wasn't the problem. Playing small ball wasn't the problem. Being part of an instant- that was the problem.

Blind Charlie led us in prayer. And for moment — just a moment — that moment demanded too much attention. It was hard to clear your head with prayer. It was real hard to clear your head — prayer was mossy headed and fixated on edges you could not cross — but you knew the drill. Why blame anyone else? So when Blind Charlie's words spread across the table you listened.

Was it Blind Charlie you heard? Or was it his words? You dug inside-sidestepped around- and hoped there was only a message here to abandon.

You were someplace else. And that someplace else mattered for the world.

And yea it was hard to understand. So on Friday night you listened to Blind Charlie and his heart. But there was a mash up in those prayers — something that was as hidden as much as it stared you in the face. The words of prayer were slippery. On one end it might kill you. And on the other end prayer might fill you. So you learned — a prayer in the night — and so fuck it — because you owed Blind Charlie a lot and you loved him — his companionship was money sunshine and a good word — you listened in silence even though you wanted to scream.

Maybe prayer worked. Maybe with no questions asked the hands of prayer rolled you over sweetly like a massage and come what may had your back against trouble.

But really you had no faith. That's what it took. And really you were scared like everyone else. What if all that shit in the sky suddenly gave way and fell and there was no oxygen left? What if the landlord got a better deal and threw you out overnight and the family and the rent were optioned out and there was no home any more?

Prayer was like going nuts when finally you kissed a girl for the first time at a Saturday matinee. Prayer was Captain Nemo and the giant octopus twenty thousand leagues under the sea.

Prayer was Blind Charlie's soothing voice in the back room — lonely tales and dreaded back windows — the cards were on the table because you had to have vision straight ahead — squeezing our palms — cash boys he said — promises to set forth our dreams — no mouth shall go unheard nor unfed as long as Blind Charlie held a breath in his body — the family's body — once he was gone — squeezing our palms — looking up and saying ha-ha –ha with his empty eyes.

Prayer was shade — a deposit — a place that wasn't thought — but a different kind of ground to lay your head upon — once the brilliance of god sent the angels flocking around your head like spook detectives to interrogate and translate whatever hooks you needed in the world and whether or not you got the favor you wanted.

Prayer was a scheme- that's what it felt like. Feelings made from themselves overnight and just as soon forgot about it and got on with the next day.

But the question that scratched your back was: how come it was put together? Did it exist by itself by itself like darkness? Or was there like a starting point like sunlight?

Bug-eyed ancestors eating worms in the dirt... because there was fear in the dirt... and that's where you thought to start...

*

We prayed. And then we went back to Friday night... eating and talking and drinking wine...

Blind Charlie asked if death was getting serious. And that worried him ...the younger they were... the younger they became...

Reds said give it up.

Blind Charlie said that was hard- there was hard labor to think about...

Cripple shoveled pie- scooping at our plates for grease and cheese-scavenging whatever leftovers we left behind.

But you weren't really listening. On television there were deodorant commercials and tin foil advertisements. Did we really smell that bad to get on prime time? How to wrap leftovers properly? Would somebody left in charge please give me a fucking break...

And in a small pop up box on the left side of the screen was the daily body count from the latest Asian war. And that little pop up box ran all day- and in ran in parallel- with the lottery results on the right hand side of the screen that posted rewards as quickly as they came in.

*

Maybe it came as no big surprise- but the last correspondence from your brother was simply that: the last one. Then we got some fucked up explanation letter from the government. Then some uniformed guy came around to the door expressing condolence for our loss. It was kind of okay. It was like personal. But personal in the ways that drive through food was personal or getting a soda from a machine was personal.

The whole fucking thing was weird. Your brother dies. A uniformed guy you never met rang the doorbell. And while you felt sorrow — for your brother — you also felt like sorry for this other poor bastard and what a stupid fucking job he had. What was this? A transition for pain — a form letter — a rehearsed speech from a wee private when it mattered the most?

You looked at this guy and felt like even the sky was sorry for him. This was like his job. And looking at that fucked you over like belief just sucker punched you. And you saw — how this was — like maybe this was his pretend death brought before him in a flash… standing in a neighborhood he had no idea about — and this was what it meant — this message to strangers — when he got to combat. Maybe next month he'd be overseas — and then in a gun sight he was gone. And then afterward some other unnamed and uniformed kid showed up at his parent's door. And because it was his job — wait — fucking wait — just fucking wait because no one was answering — whose fucking job was it? They just kept coming — these messengers — you saw them walking around the neighborhood — afraid and unsure like the rest of us — straight back and proper behind a dark uniform. You couldn't figure it. The same old sad news — that was their job to spread — like they had ancestors employed in the business since time stopped eating dirt.

Your brother didn't even have the sense to butter his corn.

He ate it naked.

Who the fuck ever heard about eating naked corn? But that's the way he ate it. Why? Why didn't he butter his corn? Everybody else you knew ate buttered corn. Wasn't that why corn was there to begin with — to be buttered and twirled and eaten quickly?

Tell me if I'm wrong but isn't death the same as death no matter where it happens?

One day your family gets the official greeting that's like hey with all respect but your kin has been blown up in some shit hole government fight? And a few days later on the evening news a young boy gets beaten to death on a neighborhood street in a gang war.

Somebody please explain- how the difference was — how the dead sorted it? Did it matter? Which gang was which? What war had what gangs working for it? And wasn't all war fought between gangs?

You thought- yea for sure- but fuck it. The circumstances were the zeros- the body counts in war and the losers in a lottery. But it was still fucked us up. What you knew or thought you knew was confused from the beginning till something like a lie you were told was the end. Prayer? Yea prayer was cool. But it was just another thing to fall into and drown in limits. Where did that get us? It was like a formal fuck off. Maybe something happened but who knew really what happened? Who was there? Who was there when the dead happened? And your brother and the poor kid in the street went away — who was there — or what was there — or damn it how was anything there — with them — where the dead go and we don't know shit about it? Prayer was not going to get us out of this one.

What your brother wanted — the sum of fucking totality — how lame that sounds but you will back it up ... despite the image of truth — and where does that come from anyway- what fucking source made off with all the profit ... all your brother wanted... All he lived for was to go fishing on a day in the world and then to be left alone... to walk along a bank... sit on a rock and toss away a line. How many strangers around the world did he have that in common with? Future citizen one day and then boy in arms ... gone before the date you could even vote?

Why even go back to another war in Asia? What ever happened to a history...lessons that said learn your lessons?

Yea that was still an old question- pressed down- and no one you knew was there to answer it.

A question made stupid by just speaking it out loud- yea — if you took the possible answers in stride and accepted them — And if you did that — because the answers were made up and friendly to begin with — it made you stupid — listening to answers that weren't — like you were some sawed-off cats paw and balanced and a sinister ramble pitched to assholes were finger tales from the start that kept you stupid and suffered the fright and ramble over the networks and the neighborhood gossip that made a sinister balance among the working rise to patriotism and how that scared you. But at the end of the news hour you're willing to shit your pants and sacrifice another day. Everyday kids were flown back... And the next day other kids were flown out...

And dying like that was like a ready-made answer — right. Like a fucking artwork down at the museum that you admired — when St. Sebastian got punctured with arrows as he's like tied to a post way up on a rock...the expression on his face as he stared big eyed around his fucked up world — watching the arrows fill his body cavity with sad holy card pictures like the early flip book movies — but the point you had — the bone that came to you for to pick at — what did god get from these brutal situations?

Listen you assholes — at least that's what you heard — and you hated if you hated listening even if it was god- what you heard — guess what... count yourself lucky... and then when the real shit gets here--because this was just fucking around... and so you said tell me god said who cared about Sebastian? Like you were a curlicue dope — and here were some words jumped out of a book that said get on the stick — like you didn't already have a library card right — but you read them and remembered them. But the truth was for the simple fact. St. Sebastian was there and you were told to believe these were just words- and within those words- glued to the text- there were lies- just as easy to believe as though those words were truth.

And the more as you went along- the more it seemed that lies equaled the truth.

Like death in war it was easy to fuck yourself over and believe the truths. Not only because it was so but it was also noble to do so. But what the fuck was that about? What did that mean? Even if you tried to believe- and looked for a hook to place you nowhere in some place where you might believe and go on from there- there was always some other shit — to dirty your home — to scare you to death because someone might come knocking around and tell you there was a score to settle.

There was like some fucking formal relationship with process — and as with words there was a spelling question here — like whoever bleeds out on a jungle floor created depth and that formal relationship with process. As though moving backwards in time made our sacrifices worth the goddamn photo you had — your brother and his mates in the company smiling back at the guy who took the photo back at the base before going out into the boonies with a full load and starting the shit all over again — but at the same time the death war and stale egg breath photo family was an invitation: to pause: to contemplate the heat and the pale faces behind the jungle burn that were death from those you know today — when the face in the photograph was alive — and you recognized — despite the official guy who showed up on the doorstep holding a photo belonging to someone you once knew — and despite the official bullshit — you still loved.

And you know- what stands apart- in the funny sad crafty words from your own mind — as much as that was reliable — was this batch of images that either held you or you were afraid to let go of.

When you thought about how dead your brother really was — an abandoned house on some creek we used to fish at came to mind. It was pure to the ruins now. But in its day it was easy to see what was there — a place that took up fairness and nested on the land where it was built — no distinction — simply material — the creek narrowed and cloistered by woods went by and gave the place a signature.

Old stonework walls splayed away from an eternal plumb line where years freezing with no heat gave the mortar away to a slow explosion outward. Window trim that scratched your head because you needed a reference to take it in and made you question the afternoons fishing there but that made you cry and ask who the fuck needed more questions when your brother had ben cut in half by Russian made machine guns? Who the fuck had the hands to make that time… shape that trim…make it fit according to rafts of arithmetic… turn precision into the workable … the way an old map showed a road — now they all bugged bug-eaten and mildewed and soon forgotten — delicate inlaid floors that had the same window trim fingerprints all over them — and too bad because shit in spades always happens to floors in abandoned buildings.

The last time we were there — like the first time when we found it — sad rundown and perfect in the trees — that was just a month before the latest war in Asia became personal. What did we know as we walked the stream south toward the reservoir- casting in pools- listening to birds we didn't know whose calls did not exist back in the neighborhood. Walking together and weaving the stream looking for a hit like a spare Mark Twain moment — young guys light out for territories — but that was your own fucked over imagination. For your brother it was more like a paragraph from Fishing Stories magazine about a few bass in the lily pads. He knew. He knew where he was headed.

And there was nothing separating us from the millions of families we were connected to — that were not only lost in history — but were making history — adding another death and another vacant place onto the world to be filled in the cycle.

But how could anyplace- anywhere — anywhere in the fucking world — who gets it — was a place where we just had lunch — and that was lunch together for years — and now it was no more. It was like a fucking Jeopardy question: what is war? You got some news one evening. It was like death was on the horn and wouldn't stop calling until you picked up.

And it wasn't the existential threat calling- you know- that type of death- where everyone believed they die and were down with it and accepted the offhand careless everyday death like sharing a seat on the bus might turn into a murder. So the next day — when death was starting to become a memory and there was a fucking date with the casket inventory to recognize — was that how soon it took? You got the letter and then you got a sad ass soldier with beret in hand and then you got a flight schedule home but where that flight landed was hundreds of miles away from where we lived. It was gaining a voice — pissed off — real pissed and you listened to it — like bread from heaven. So the next day you fingered off school once the bell rang and walked out because if school mattered or not you were just going off to die later after class and why be concerned about verbs and tenses and what's known.

God's finger Blind Charlie said sympathetically.

Cripple wanted to know what was left. Was there anything left in the kitchen….

*

You came to these reasons as a way out — out for sure — but you did not want the weight and that crushed you for being a chump — regrettable though you felt it was necessary — on a Friday night even — suddenly what you wanted to needle you out — you wanted something so desperate — but imagination left for a minute and you had a lurch to hold onto if not to believe in — why you didn't know? But not for long — what was reliable returned like a season — a matter of time till the good side brought you back into play — so meantime you were left with the odd thinking side where the brain sounds like an add-on television for the Pompeii pocket fisherman — whose tag line was — and boy does it catch fish! What it left you with was a dead body to figure out. What the fuck? Who was ready for this? He was already dead and already gone and already in the ground with a cheap little flag on his grave-head so why launch an investigation into your head over how people got forgotten?

*

Your brother was an altar boy. A good altar boy — by standards — but how was that– you were never there — but everyone's older brother was an altar boy. What did that mean? He never explained. Only thing you saw was a ritual with a stomachache because in some way or other every altar boy you ever came across feared a priest. It was like so much fucking else. Intentions tore you down…and trashed talked the good sons of the neighborhood into a judgment — and this one that swallowed its own head off.

Yea there was reasoning…so fucking what…

And coming up was Father Grababoy…

And what did you say?

To yourself- you said better to say nothing now- and then scream again about it later to the sky…

Better to brood… well maybe… but certainly hold a stiff tongue… than to have the fray jump your ass like a chump. Because you were smart. Right? Men like Father Grababoy were imaginary creatures — part angel thoughtless part demon chortle — strange fucked up dudes

140

dressed in black — holding onto the ghost inside their body for dear life — because dear life in the fucking end of things betrayed them as much as they disappointed it by grabbing the fucking life they lived. All this shit was complicated. They worked a good anger and a honeyed lashing service against the fucking servile sitting dumb assed in our pews while crimes were committed on our dimes behind our backs. A Halloween scare mask and then a hug to say hey it's just me — or the unwanted Christmas gift that said creep all over it — or the chewy disgusting yellow colored marshmallow chicks at Easter whose chemical texture had to shorten your life when you were invited to feast on some and other treats while Father Grababoy held open house.

At least that's what you heard.

How do you deal with something wrong before you get there?

You thought about Paladin. Have gun will travel.... Maybe that was god... They way the work universally found Richard Boone and then at first he heisted and said no in that craggy face behind a whisky- but after listening to the tale at hand pushed the table back in the saloon- had some mind transfer- rode off with retainer in hand- and went to find out who to kill or who bring back and throw on the docks for justice.

Can't you get it right just once Father Grababoy asked?

Strange thing was you couldn't handle the Latin. And so naturally you screwed up the Latin. When it was your turn to recite all the dead verbs- the dead language you tried to understand- the whole fucking mess was unable to reveal itself unto a world of transistor radios and hot cars. Why even think about the demands studying made if there were no questions to the answers? Latin was like a way carved into your head to go backwards but without time travel. And time travel was cool. At birth you were baptized before the heavens by the cloistered. A few weeks later you were given a shot from the science gods. Together- it was rumored- this made you ready for life. To understand and go back and forth and make connections to impartial truths as you grew up was like a demonstration. But learning Latin had zippo movement. It was like talking to the sidewalk. Nobody asked if you cared. Nobody asked about nothing...

Fucking dead Latin — what was there to get here except another schoolhouse lobotomy?

No you said but I'm trying.

Father Grababoy held the hurt inside. It was like he could not believe this was happening again. This time around would be like my third flunk out. Hey you need to chalk up something. More to the question the eyes in his head went huge. His face was the color oxygen left off when the tallow in a candle finally went out. A steady yellow flickering went bright... flamed with scale... generally mortified itself with passion... then went out... thin trails of smoke lost themselves in the air ... a seeping waxy smell filled the room... a tissue death screech that never left my ears... and a spleeny grin from the man in black... with no help in sight...

Father Grababoy twitched in the limbs- like a puppet whose strings paid no attention- like he had no midsection for support. The guy had bad electricity — several grandparents you knew in the neighborhood also had it in the spine- the television said it was in other places across the globe — and the result trespassed across his body like he was starved into existence by the shaking. Give me what I know! What I know I had! But when you looked- you saw- and decided -it was too late for him. There had to be dying but who was paying for it? And what was Father Grababoy's grand fault? What ran him over and did him in? Was it not seeing eyeball to eyeball — because he was on his god's ticket and god left him out? Was there no gratification in being a servant anymore for the heavens even if there was a bad day on the ground? Did he want something more? How did he figure what's left being a trivial howler and a hidebound sod at Sunday mass?

So how was it possible for someone to be wrong all the time? Wasn't that like physically impossible?

Both of us... no quarter... no inch given... just like that mournful trumpet the night before the final charge at The Alamo — at the Renal Theater- with Eden beside you holding hands- when John Wayne and Fess Parker and company knew beyond the ass in their pants they were outnumbered to no good. And come morning- when it was over- history walked away tired and sympathetic and left the dead on screen- but down in our seats our nerves were scratched. In the end the ushers tossed us out before the next show...

What did silence mean? Go fuck off? Were you living the way you were as a matter of poor taste and doom? Was there a trumpet? Did you hope for one? A song that jumped into heaven or hell by the deaths of famous movie actors and you were just a kid on the way? There were also sloths and finches… the windows had to be open and if not they got broken from rocks down below… did you have to jump when you did jump… but when pressed it was everyone's rubbish to pile through…played against the likes of Father Grababoy… his survival- as well as your own listening… A slow maneuver… and to your understanding so far what you heard was a mournful note…how many over time and so in that fucked up space between man and boy you listened… and you wanted… the big matter was a laugh because you had nerves and they had boundaries as much as they were limitless… sympathetic as much as things were lonesome… truth… when pushed power was maintenance — hold the day — against the swag — Father Grababoy — what the fuck? Because he was ordained that made him like a door prize shrew at a fucking bingo game on Friday night… with a terrible smile … a bogus light weight finger touch on the back… ladies first of course… and then such a faithless grab on the husband's shoulder…. All you saw was a guy… nobody special in decline… on earth… there was nobody special on earth… you either earned the words or your failed the words… and what was left over was your love and that was the sky…

So when you failed the Latin words — again — it was almost a kick — a life you owned and a reverie you felt for loss and sorrow– an eyeball to eyeball that fucked some trivial mission to speak clearly about the dead and the dim lights afterwards where you lost a life… You thought may your brother rest in peace… May Lenny Marks rest in peace — although there was nothing much left from Lenny Marks but a red stain on a bandanna mailed home — but fuck it — that bandana was human and that was the neighborhood — and anyone else in the latest Asian war they were altar boys once and dead soldiers thence — so how do you put up resistance… someone please let me know how to do it — please let me know how to put some muscle on — so that you're not a chump in a cage that on occasion gets attention brought toward you through homilies and dead words.

But nobody's wrong all the time… are they? Was that possible? Were there really demons on one side and angels on the other?

And what happened if nothing made a sound...

Then it hit you. It was like the flip side... a record ... a chart breaking song on the radio... everybody bought it for that song ... but on the flip side was a lesser song... not a hit ... and so a kind of emptiness pressed upon you... and then there it was... the lesser song...

But nobody's wrong all the time are they? Did that seem like it flew in the face of the impossible?

The problem wasn't some back and forth between angels and demons and who gets the spoils as much as it was you were desperate to even things out — all your friends were desperate — all your enemies were desperate — and we came up against sadness and a fucking zero too narrow to escape through.

Suddenly — you could almost predict the hoary monologue and the volcanic backfire that was Father Grababoy's voice when he was pissed- a bit of a sadistic talk down with ten thousand splinters of broken glass thrown your way — and by now it was no use ducking — no use imagining getting out of the way — so you asked him just where were angels? Where were the demons? Who the fuck helps out?

Then he hit you for real. That stupid red mark left on your cheekbone and hurt your eye was like an unholy cloth germinated across your face. And that wasn't the first time a man of god backhanded you. Just how in hell did Father Grababoy exist?

Faith duty and obedience he yelled and raised his hand again. But this time he didn't strike. He held his hand mid-air and it was like light years or inches away from your head. Was that an angel hand or was that a demon hand helping you out?

You have no attention he said!

His hand restricted — whatever the reason — fuck him — you planned to kick him in the balls anyway... A half-witted hand palsied or a second thought in his head shook in the air — like he saw something in his hand — evil's message — or like he might die before he had enough enjoyment hurting kids...

What's the point you spat back...a little blood shot out from your mouth and landed on his dark cassock.

Yea you thought — you were the monkeyshines — neither happy nor sad about it — but that's where you got the hit and that's where you shook the loss. But what mattered was standing — standing alongside the smack. Yea you thought and you hoped what you thought was right. Standing among multitudes — scared and charmed — like how many juveniles got smacked in the face from the likes of Father Grababoy — kids whose clutch was way too short to burn — hungry and alive and needing some different sense to be alive and to be set loose upon worlds and worlds beyond our dreams. To live forever- like those fucking loaves and fishes from old times and you thought it was so fucked up you might as well try crying and dissolve your life from there and crap your fears and begin again.

Father Grababoy went at it again — the mad immigrant priest crashing into a world he hated. Another scream without the story of the bones — a second tier howl — yea this time around it lost something. And what was missing was that animal's howl: that sound which poached your face pale enough to halt the sunlight on an autumn leaf and stopped your breath in a corporeal heap and drew blood from your ears and you kept hearing it over and over again like a nightmare only awake and walking around you.

You will get this right he said.

And so you thought no. You never would get this right. And that was enough to live by.

Years ago Father Grababoy said — and his voice closed upon your ear and was tiled with hot lead — I offered a plea to god he whispered...

*

Really what you needed was to listen to the silence. That was clear as you fell against a dumb hardback chair left over from the 1920's or some shit when your grandparents grew up in the neighborhood. Just listen and let the sting pass over. There was a ringing in your ears. But that wasn't the silence. There was a level below hurt where no calculations mattered. Nothing meant anything. From the corner of your eye where your eye wasn't swollen you saw a door. The classroom door ... aint that a shit you thought ... right over there was a door ... You might get there if you worried enough about it- but fuck it. Might as well chalk up

145

a failure on the blackboard and leave it there signed sealed and delivered as it was to try and move.

Why bother? Why save your ass? Why save your ass if there were nothing but demons and angels on the sidelines?

Father Grababoy moved on and handled the next classmate.

He left you slacked in the chair. That last smack was enough to put you down. It was too bad that it was your life and not some fabrication from Father Grababoy that knocked you silly.

But hey — now was the silence. Here you had a point. Silence — bloodied — fucking mordant — pointless — eternity — embargo on inches to get away — first hand know how — but you couldn't think that well so you gave it up and it was like floating on a breach of consciousness. You saw the sky against the ceiling in the room without moving. Fucking invisible — yea sky — so you said nothing and passed off your attention and once again wished Santa Claus brought you a gun… On your face — if you had a mirror — stupidity ran your nerves down a lank passage to slander and phlegm and was jacked against them in your body. Your breathing came in heaves and gagged. You felt — and knew again — this history — taking another shit upon you — taking a shit for us all if one of us gets beaten — and left a rouse for you to come around to — a deep bruised eye developing again — a mutiny one day — a vis-a-vis to spit blood natural as rain.

Time was to play the nearest card and you had to an ace to get out that door. You ran your mouth. Father Grababoy hated it. He was already turning his socket into the next kid.

The average parishioner goes to mass each week you said — running your tongue across your teeth. Thankfully there were still all there- and so you said they go from habit and generation- and are mostly cowered into the pews- indifferent to the time except they're afraid — and that's why they show up…

…You wobbled in the chair with a fat lip and a myopic viewpoint with one eye swollen shut… and it was nearly funny enough for belief…

… And who doesn't give two shits about what you do…

…You said to Father Grababoy: you're some fucking guy: from out of town: gussied up in faded and left over vestments with egg stains from the last guy who ran out of Jersey-land and so you're sent here as fucking god's replacement? Your only hope was that we're all still blind from the last one and nobody notices you cross-dressing over on 65th Avenue at the Liberty Belle.

Can't do a fucking thing about it. You calculate the penalty and pull apart small weavings of memory for any clue sitting in the middle of the third row… and then flip him the bird with both hands.

Got hit again.

*

…If only the angels helped out.

…Or maybe even the demons lend a hand.

*

Your arm twitched at your sides. Bad electricity set spasms through your fingers. This was bad. But this was the way out.

No doubt you knew Father Grababoy. Religious people had second natures like everyone else. He stood at the front of the room and blocked the door. His arms were folded across his chest. No doubt he was a mean prick to deal with. But his anger was all authority. Yea you knew Father Grababoy: a sad cheeked guy — thick brown hair that usually fell across his murky face like he was a duffer after a drink and had to keep pushing it back off his forehead like that was a way for him to speak and be heard — he was past his youth but not yet a dolt despite the nervous tics — he was someone you wouldn't want to sit next to in a movie theater — he tried to fake himself into eternity with some tough guy middleman act: and while it was plain he had the stomach for the job, down below — deep in the true belly of life — it just seemed to you he forgot he forgot and he forgot…

And so you were given another chance to recite the Latin.

Did anyone else in the neighborhood but you appreciate this guy?

He couldn't play basketball worth a damn. And only volunteered for coaching because afterwards his permit and claim on the parish was as loose as his smile was liable- and he was able took a boy aside after the game and play his tricky stuff on the kid like his holy Johnson wanted corked and then went gossamer…

He snuck cigarettes in the alley behind the rectory.

He busted boys for doing the same and lectured them — hard — behind the dumpster. But when girls were caught smoking Father Grababoy was all counsel- with an arm across a girl's shoulders- like his touch was delivery and his fingers said no worry no guilt. Behind the dumpster his hand reclined across a winsome girl's bones. His fingers worked the girl and pulled her flash hair toward him.

The guy was sent into the neighborhood with a review and an edit from god?

How sweet was that.

Maybe the option was sadness… forget proper response and the catchy inflections….

Pain had a beautiful sideways dialect that contaminated your thoughts and at once contemplated their outcome. Pain raised your voice even as it lowered your outcome.

Father Grababoy stared over our heads. The class cringed in their seats. He shouted us down. He forgot about that last kid and his Latin lesson and returned his crackbrained attention back toward you.

It's always the same you said lisping through your bad lip. It's always the same.

Nobody bothers with the Latin. Except maybe the oldsters you said because they love the sound and find that sound beautiful. But even then- they fade off it. They know the sound of those words were as dead as the old country.

What do you think Father? Are you content with the lifestyle you lead?

Hit again.

Damn you said holding your eye.

Father Grababoy said recite the verbs. Again…

You said ordinary people wouldn't do this. There's too much else in-volved… If you want it in plain words you said the link between heaven and earth does not need a priest.

Father Grababoy: said recite the verbs… Begin…

Here you were close. You not only saw the door across the room but also felt that door. And that fucked up but hopeful spectacle made the door an illusion- a fellowship. What was the worst that might happen? That you got caught again walking out the door and were collared? But at this moment- three years into this- this- like you thought it might be- would top you off and finally leave you be and on your own. Without suspicions- you would be a flunked out altar boy- and wasn't that glorious? Neither god nor the inverse of the spelling — dog — without a land you called home — yes — all that you saw was out that door. And that door opened onto a corridor. And down that hall- through two flights of stairs- were the six big doors leading out of the school. Beyond the doors was the street- and above the street- once you reached it sweetness and promise was the sky where you belonged. The blood in your mouth told you so…

People need a priest you said to Father Grababoy — like a television audience can't do without cue cards from some guy off stage -when it's time to laugh or strain their eyes. People need you because you're the cue card guy. So go fuck yourself. And you know the reason why. You the priest say blah blah blah in Latin. And the altar boys in return at the bottom of the altar say blah blah blah in return. But it's nothing but mumbles and shams — distrust that sounds like Latin at the correct intervals but what I'm saying was the Latin — the fucking verbs — was never really what you said at Mass. Even the drunks understand that. That any Mass you attend was nothing but a speed ticket you said. Get it over with and then it's done… and do you think ordinary parishioners care?

Father Grababoy said I know my congregation.

Well they know you also you said. But they don't know Latin from the moon. Maybe the old people know about what they once knew. It was a different ticket for them coming across the sea. Blind Charlie and his people know that tongue you said. But it's a cruel fucking joke played on the rest of us. How to believe inside — you can't answer that can you — how to imagine a soul — you can't answer that either can you big daddy…where does grace point toward…

But what happens here is where I'm stuck- not only with you — but also with the words and sounds. We're chickens roosting in the pews. And fuck off if you think I'm gonna be stewed.

You pictured him open mouthed and silent and veins vibrating in his neck. You closed your eyes — like ever — before you and after everything that happened next you got screwed. And he was screaming at you — doing his best — as an agent of god — but that was as flimsy a ruse as taking the Packers with two on Sunday.

He said one day you will regret that.

Maybe so you thought.

You're a benchwarmer you said. Nothing this side of church could ever help you so shut up.

You just another lost fuck- but you wear a collar.

Recite the verbs he said again- like in his mind were the big old sounds from a heavy organ behind his voice.

What are you kidding you said?

Church service lasted as to be like the cliff notes to spiritual experience?

How do you square that you asked?

Why memorize some language centuries old? And when it comes to the theater and the day to do it nobody lives it. You know this you said. I've seen you. Don't you hate saying Mass? Go on you demanded — admit it…

What's the first thing you asked? What's the thing you think about? What topped your list? Was it poor god — looking down at the heap and the hue — and could stand only so much before superior numbers brought him down? Was it poor Father Grababoy and his flat gelded mist of a man and his gloomy beatific cry for time — oh for time — oh for only more time — and leave it to god to not only bail you out but for also to give you up?

What is the matter with you? That god took you on as a spiritual consul as you asked and then you fucked up? Where's that big deal now? That you're a cheap warranty dealing heaven's goods but behind the clouds you know the score and give blowjobs in back seats to the heathen and so you ask — how did it become that way while you shake in your own head against your own observance?

150

What you asked?

Please recite the verbs Father Grababoy said.

Why?

Did you ever stop and think about poor people you asked? Each week in the neighborhood they appeared like fixtures — lighting candles on the side altars and praying to saints that were marble statues — whose features never changed — but the idea — that ace was everlasting. And dropping nickels they can't afford to into the poor box with a sad metal on metal echo throughout the high dome of a silent church hall– the candles flickering off the alcoves and stained glass windows at dusk and the common side pews where prayer was the most natural word to live by — and by doing so they hoped for a miracle?

You got an answer for that you asked?

You were getting closer. The words had their mark like a dog's teeth hooked onto a fleshy arm. And that meant the door was coming sooner.

Why do you imagine he asked? That the lord and his instruments and his instructions were given to this world? Was it made to be a playpen for you? Is that what you imagine? No he said. We have this world to make it so. Do you think about it — do you think — oh dear — I'm a fuck up and that somehow makes you grand? No he said. That's not it. And that's not how it goes.

Now he said… Recite the verbs… Now.

What was so pesky about Latin verbs anyway you thought?

Agicacola present tense– Agricalala past tense — Agricahumdum-bum future tense

And that was enough- finally — to get you finally thrown out of the room. Another swat to the head but hey just a little more blood leaked from your left eye. And a dull black shoe tip put up your ass and then you were gone — so gone — giddy in the ether — finally done with it — after three years and flunking each year — to be an altar boy that you never wanted to be — but now you were officially flunked out hallelujah — you would never be back again — age and graduation saw to that — finally so gone — you were gone — so gone and so thankful like some ransom had been paid — walking away bloodied and stupid and feeling like some incoherent prudence covered you with the wrong skin — but gone was the sound — gone was the sound listening to the sky and its charmless laughingstock clouds.

*

It was sad. And that counter point you needed to keep walking around the neighborhood before dark. Then you had to report back home. For the solitary meal left on the stove to warm up — and read the sports section at the empty table while you ate — and tackle the occasional offhand adult questions like how was your life going etc. Well maybe not sad like that — you know — like how human sad was like how autumn leaves were sad and had a miscellany to fool with. Like when you looked at the trees — the leaves before they fell held up a candor to laugh at — a color deep in the heart to get on board with — and a terror that refused to give up a lie. And the sky was home. We came from the sky. And sometimes — what you demanded from the leaves — was could they tell you what comes from all this because it's so short?

But this business with Father Grababoy was screwed up.

At least this fight was the last tussle over fucking Latin.

Next year you were off to the big high school world...

It was likely to be another place where some other head talked you down... That's what the older guys said... but they were talking you down also...

As you walked to get away from things — Father Grababoy flapjacked across your memory. Things were sad. You felt like a cartoon figure draw across panels where not much happened. At 20th & 66th you watched a squirrel chewing away on yesterday's stinky cheese condom.

Your own footsteps soon caught up with themselves. And that was funny. This happened again and again... so damn it you had to laugh again and again. Like there was some discredit in the pavement and that reached out and caught you by the ankles and held you solid in the air and prevented you from pressing on your Chuck Taylors.

Eventually your footsteps let go. Whatever it was that held resistance let go. Whatever it was you were let go. You walked in spheres. Jersey-land was your birthplace. You were checked out as its own terrain. From Father

152

Grababoy — to the next asshole on down that line — it was against your own loadstar you lived — being young — what the fuck else was there because you were treated like some fucking rat that needed to be caught on the floor. The brood of your imagination needed to be skinned out.

So you walked… incomplete…insulted… unprotected the whole fucking thing… But fuck it. You were happy… well happy in that defeated sense that made you stupid again and fed up.

But you had a body and a field inside you. You had a name that fit your skin.

Walking across Jersey-land and then back across Jersey-land again — walking below the city glister of drunken streetlights and the chemical bursts from the scratch lands — clouds that failed then sky — sheeny wicked tasting yellows — harsh brindled reds — gruff orange — poison greens.

And at the bottom of the sky to the west — above Cheapy King's Used Car lot — there was a blue like a tease from old world light — polaroid light — manufactured camera light and maybe you faked it and tried to admit to something that was not really there — it was a light that waved your eyeballs — light that killed years — light that belonged to the dead — to Jersey-land ancestors finished in the sky — gone beautiful light — the sky was yours and continued throughout before god was even born. Light was together.

There were blues we associate with crayon names — blues on guitar strings — a blue above Cheapy King's Used Car lot that made you feel tomorrow around your head nymph-like and skin deep — billions of years of starlight dropped antiquity on a dime and turned blue now once all that speeding light reached the sky and illuminated a sidewalk you were standing on.

The daylight slowly went blank… you walked for ages…. night where it was hard to see…

scatterbrained
layered
a flunky aviator
slinky flipping down a stairs

Until Cheapy King's neon lettering started blinking and scratching in tubes above the worst cars in the world for sale.

*

That's what made it sad. Grababoy was just bigger than you were. And naturally had the velocity of papal history behind him — and you — waiting to break frankly — to escape hellfire and its agents — you had thin time for false idols.

Yea. That was it. You stand in a room and talk each way out your mouth like your swag was super dilated — you stand on a sidewalk and wonder and try and invigorate and amplify the shit from existence — or have a world to yourself at face level and outlast free thought for as long as we were able to choose our exits — before superior numbers took you down.

That seemed the way. Did it matter where you stood? Did it matter if you were standing at Avenue C and Wister Street in the last stretch of thoughts before you went home and were shut in for the night? Did it matter if you were on the moon or in Asia or in the back of the class?

Harm was forever like a hymn. It all came from the sky and we got caught running away on the ground on the ground on the ground. Did it matter — how many assholes there were and how they ran your life? Did it matter –did it matter — and was it funny enough to kill you? If Father Grababoy beat you in the classroom then it was okay to swat a kid — because everyone in the neighborhood understood the reasons why. Because the neighborhood knew you were wrong — as soon as Sunday mass came up and the altar boys names were announced — you were wrong and would never get right. In the long view of the streets from Avenue C in the east to Tulpehocken Street in the west Grababoy was right — the size of the crime didn't matter. If you were ordained and embraced god then that was the ticket that made you go. And yet what you failed to be — year after year — what you failed to be was an altar boy — year after year you fought the good fight — you tried for all your heart not to get caught in church business. To do so made you a menial darling — for one thing there was no immunity — and yea you got paid well if you agreed to gull-trap the young ones — but what was the price? How much do history's crimes cost?

You had this mule-like sense that these things kept you going. Refusal equaled strength but after a while watch out and protect yourself etc.

Just what was it? What was it we already knew?

But sometimes — more times than you had senses — like the sky above gave you times on the ground — to have that ground clutch your feet — and that clutch lifted up your feet past your heart and past fear — namely to have the times — from the sky — to have the fear — to fear the times you had and you walked down below Ogontz Avenue and dodged the trolley where if times were right you waved to your grandfather driving the trolley on his last run and he shook his head when he saw you which was the same message as saying I'll see you at home later– But the reason below Ogontz at Waverly Street was where Eden and where her family lived…

The corner boys knew you. Avenue C… a gang-network… on each corners a branch…. Each corner with a dozen young boys…. holy fucking branch-works like nerves in a body… connecting like they all had head parleys… they would torch the blue if you ever mentioned it… they were heavy enough to turn you into an obit without even your cash to pocket … they laughed at that … called you skin names… and laughed at that and let you pass — with a few indignities — they laughed at you and slapped you on the back…

Because… and they laughed and tossed you around… you did no bad against them. Because you were in love … and that was fucking crazy… and if you were that crazy enough they'd let you walk though the grounds…

But Grababoy was older. And adult anger was fucking creepy.

Stress levels — we learned about that in physical education class. How to spot it when someone older than you went into numbers and turned crimson faced like getting caught about some fucking booty they stole. As though life were a thieving operation. How much farther might it go until his head burst into a scarlet fountain of blood and his heart came out his throat and his neck veins went blue as the old sky and he flipped out and tore his vestments off because they burned his skin and he cried he was losing his soul and losing his wings and crying out protect me I am love protect me oh shit I belong to the sacraments oh help me oh protect me...

Adult anger was creepy.

*

To paraphrase an early scene from Doctor Zhivago in the movie — it was a date with Eden — a night holding hands in the sky — we walked to the Esquire Theater over at Broad and Olney and Ocean — a bit of a hike but we were cool with it — dark jiffy streets to skip over — insults from shadows — we left cash on the sidewalks because we weren't amateurs but we also stepped faster to get away — the shit to pay was bold indoctrinated and stupidly forthright in its breach- and with an unsound head –wise — but fuck it — we had our parents' money and we didn't care...

...Where the Russian commandant on patrol one night stands at the wire and watches what was his to control like a machine and overlooks some dreary peasant stealing wood off the sides of a wasted war building for his home fire. In the over-voice the commandant says: one man stealing wood is a pity. However- two men stealing wood made for a counter-revolution...

Even if that's not for word when will we leave one another alone? Who else that day flunked altar boy? Did the world even need altar boys? Sometimes things were made small by thoughts of failure. Other times those thoughts — like you were squeezed and disfigured — made things less deadening and left you relieved in the drift of your own accountability.

You walked Eden home. It was tough to let go from her hands in the sky.

Before you went home you hit a little whiskey that was hidden in the bushes. You sat on top of the mailbox at Avenue C and Garnett Street and drank. You didn't like whisky. It burned and felt stupid in your throat but fuck it what mattered was the job that it did on your head. Other nights it might be rum hidden in the bushes. Or vodka. Didn't matter. It was the head that counted. We just paid the money and an old head left the liquor in the bushes outside the rectory. Judging by what was left in the bottle tonight not too many people had been by. And it was bad form to drain the bottle. There was always someone. Someone coming up behind… someone later than you…which meant there was always someone ahead of you… no matter what bottle you drank from you were always caught in the middle of time… and unless you saw an old head — like Ace MacDonald passed by and you flagged him down and you gave him money for another order to be stashed later and fixed in the bushes — it was best to take just what you needed off the bottle and leave something for the rest…

You sat on the mailbox. You drained the bottle. Some fucking old head replaced it the next day no matter what the day so fuck that. When you heard a siren you slipped off the mailbox. Lost- wanting to be sharp and faded- biting and thin- critically violent and fettered- like getting on a subway car when there are too many people- somebody has to go before you crack and go sheer inside and yell get out of my way…

Altar boys fail all the time. It's the beauty and the passion… You fail… you are the ardor and the rage… the fervor and the transport and the document….

You walked around the block a final time. Then let yourself in the front door.

You ate grapefruit halves that were left in the kitchen.

You watched the midnight horror movie with your father. He'd just gotten off his shift. And this was like how and this was this where we knew one another over the years… a half grapefruit with a teaspoon sugar and a horror movie before bedtime…

*

And thinking about it- while you dozed in bed and spun and were uncomfortable lying still- nightly and meditative- and put your ear plugs into the transistor for late radio songs and reached down between the mattress springs for the chill pills stashed there- you couldn't fault Reds-but it did scratch your head why. Reds was an altar boy. Three years running and that felt like there was something crooked going on. You asked him about it once like a month ago before you were up again for review. But like most things he blew it off. He screwed up his eyes. He hit you backside the head and told you wise up. But over the years you get to know a kid. You get to know someone. And it's not all wise up and being told to fuck off- what it was was that it's not that hard to recognize a lie.

Mostly Reds wanted to be Cousin Jimmy.

Cousin Jimmy was neither a lie nor was he ever an altar boy. And that was funny — like the way everything was funny — because everything was funny — and because it held a place in the world you could lie awake forever in the night and not figure that one out and be funny about it.

Cousin Jimmy was cool beyond a day in January — a fucking surge when he was stoned that made him a figurehead among the wasted. Oh yea that was Cousin Jimmy — a purgatory folk song might be sung around his head — or a cop's hands around his throat and down his wallet. But fuck it. He had dash — that was his life and he lit that up like moonlight on a clear mean night. Every sorry ass — everyone in the shadows with hands out who wanted shit from Cousin Jimmy — they looked at him and what they wanted was that dead gleam in their eye that he perfected looking back at. And that was the story on that. No more questions...

With his mouth working like a carnival barker he owned the corner at Avenue S and Wyncote. And we nodded standing around like an audience waiting for a taste. He was the host of the night like he was some fucking Johnny Carson- But underneath the streetlights we were all the same. We were jumpy. We glowed in the dark. And we were rich with what was practical if we got it.

But in turn we all held onto what we needed — namely it was the defect of the day. To eat or die — to charm or go dim — and what spelled those directions was a split head. To believe Cousin Jimmy and pay his price — copious with fancy karmic names like petal battlewagon that you understood was so false — both the price and the name were beyond intellect and dollars — or to believe Cousin Jimmy and fork over what he wanted.

The cops said he had personality. But they laughed that away because he was a junkie and a wanted man. But they also had the fear. And that fear was Cousin Jimmy let loose. Cousin Jimmy crusading the streets with his bags of heaven or hell — it was your decision and it was your bag to have or to have not — and the cops were excited — to catch him like a trophy — but they feared his influence as a kind of fucked up aristocrat on the streets — Cousin Jimmy wasn't anything that you might say was so-called —

But when he talked his shit this made you and the other corner dwellers in a way turn into Cousin Jimmy's shadows. And that mark…it cast a long one…

Mostly Cousin Jimmy got high… got high… got high again…. from the spooks that surprised his head each time he did and then rejected him each time after…he got high… off the crows of romance that waited in the trees for him until one night he sang on some dark factory street — got high like a grave robber… got high… because in this life he played his music from a killer eight track that he ripped out from underneath the dashboard of a neighbor's car and that fit him like a new tailored suit worn to a party.

Cousin Jimmy had outrageous long red hair that grew from his scalp like flames in the wind. As an ID police blotter he wasn't hard to miss. And with the hair went flashy downtown clothes. Super wide bellbottoms from the military surplus store — crazy stripped English mod shirts from old YouTube videos — the ones with the high collars like starch incarnate and had bola waists to show off a tight famished ass.

He drove a hot convertible that was modified to not only look old but to sound old. What more can be said for tragedy? The car was like a midnight blue or some illegal color for a car to have. And if you looked close enough — it was a real chronic almost sincere blue. A dark streak across the night-lights — idling at the corner like defiance -where if the girls wanted a ride they got their wishes — and where the boys cried out and were tossed their bags into the wind as he drove away.

What the who — or what the what — or what the hell — or just fuck it — because thinking about it you went through the route because you thought about it — and so you thought what if there were no more questions anymore but only answers that fucked themselves over.

Did it matter what you thought? Reds wanted a model.

But what could you do? Far in the head — like a haunted future that studied your own face — you saw Cousin Jimmy years later in the view you had now lying awake in be now.

Not much was to say about a junkie on the run. The heroin trade... the girls girls girls...suddenly his car was fucked to no end and he had no stereo because he sold it to get high ...bruised dented and scraped just like his car... a cheap wire antennae taped on the hood fed a him dumb radio because he needed to get high ... like never getting the songs he wanted ... like he had no more passengers anymore ... always looking over his shoulder at the cops whenever he parked at the corner. His nickel was way over. No more feminine laundry to play with... no more young boys listening to his back seat poetry... Cousin Jimmy cashed it all in — he had to — you saw that — like it was a fucking gift you had and that was to understand the dead while they stilled walked.

Old warehouse clothes — forlorn and weak-kneed jumpsuits from the pie factory where a younger brother worked — bellicose in a cool poverty because Cousin Jimmy did not wear out — he was weal and wax and supernatural and believed he had no mind in this world that might be caught up in the every day thing- but he was wrong and his skinny bones and hair gone flat and dull not only vexed him with the life he lead — not vicious because it's a life we all lead — but he was shaking- an echo of chemical joy — sinful if you believed in that — and in a kind of venial sense he was vast in his crimes ablaze and unpardonable.

He died before it was even noticed that he was even gone. Slumped against a steering wheel... at least this was his ride... what was left of it anyway ... parked under a stone bridge in the northwest... autumn tress grabbed the canary sick streetlight and tossed a harlequin –like shape down below and made bordello-like heart sore shadows on a broken up Godfrey Street... a needle stuck into his left forearm... sad and wobbly... both Cousin Jimmy and the needle... hanging like an ornament from a fallen vein...

Too bad you weren't believed.

You might have saved Reds some trouble.

*

160

The good we find in ourselves we may find in others was Blind Charlie's reply.

Reds was having none of it. Nobody's happy getting along he said. Tell me who pays a goddamn to thinking there ain't something to get over on he said.

Mister Reds Blind Charlie said- you know the rules in the house. Not that language if you'd please. Blind Charlie stared at him- as though to remind Reds where he was. In fact- despite being sightless- Blind Charlie edged forward in his chair and looked at Reds like he might say just who do you image was the fool here.

Such a bright one Mister Reds he said to his face. What do you plan on doing? Hang onto that street corner forever? Is that what's that I see? Do I see something other? You like the Friday noodle run- am I right?

Reds nodded that he did. It wasn't anything heavy or deep- but it was artful in its own way. And mostly- and because there was no way otherwise for him- it paid dividends- and that's what mattered. That's why you do things.

Reds said no. He'd get off the corner soon enough. He needed some time though.

My god Blind Charlie said. What are you telling me?

Reds stammered some lame ass answer about getting his shit — uh stuff together. He'd blow off school in a fucking –uh-fringing — minute if he had the chance to make real money.

Blind Charlie tipped a sip of wine from his glass to his mouth- like a gentleman in the movies without even seeming to drink it. He looked around at us all. Those burned out eyes said get ready — get ready — entanglements confusion and danger — get ready...

So he said. First thing he said was you earn real money. Second thing he said was that the real money you earned well that money had a price on it. Third thing he said was don't be stupid enough to believe that you don't have to earn real money.

Cripple emptied the bottle. He was enough into it to be soiled well past the Friday noodle run. He said let's gets serious. All that pizza he'd bitten hung onto his braces like calcium formations backing up on a wall underground.

Suddenly you were worried. What if we were offered jobs — the kind of work that went serious and held you with money but with little exit if you fucked up? Would you be clear enough to do the job? Absorbed by it and screwed by it but enough to kick it off and not think about it — careful steps in Blind Charlie's world — steps you haven't lived — but they seemed to be so and so they scared you — because one side of your head looked deficient and failing –like confusion — but on the other side your head was a shield and there was a shelter and a fortification that buried up under things. If your ass didn't run scared then you made money. That was the lesson. And that's the answer Blind Charlie wanted.

Trust he said.

Without that he said- you boys just grow up. And you learn nothing.

You believed it.

You feared it.

And you felt your heart bounce on the earth.

But where were you?

*

The sunlight — oh — to be outside — and not sealed indoors — like a moldy sponge underneath a sink — like a puppet head in school — like a Spartan head in church — pay attention — that's what the dirty air said. There were powers to believe in and there were powers to reject. Everyday was snippy crusty and insolent and other days put a heel to your throat — well that meant others put heels to all our throats. The sunlight was warm and unsympathetic to begin with — because that was a power nobody put a hand upon because the sunlight rose from the sky and the sky told all.

But it was a visible sky. Well partially visible through the usual chromium haze...

And when you saw that– a visible sky — that meant it was imagined to begin with.

What it was — the imagination — was the story un-curtained and babble-mouthed and spray-painted on the walls like prophecy. It was told in videos on street corners by sad devices and their dying batteries. In the alleys the imagination was written on the air by the old heads talking and passing bottles in brown bags. Young boys opened their thin glassy enve-lopes and went deep- peaching themselves and decanting into the night with the story on the nod. But it was a story despite time trying to kill it.

A visible sky meant beware. It told how good fortune was there just above out heads.

It was practically against the law to look at a visible sky for more than a sly passing moment. Because you might locate what was out there…

But fuck that… And what that meant. The sky told all. Uniformed officers told us not to be scared and so please move along.

A hard yellow light made the asphalt gleam in the afternoon. The sky was harsh and well off. A blunt milky blue kept itself heavy through the bleached clouds like an eyeball eventually going blind without getting its drops.

All lawful borders were fables anyway. But why ask a stupid question to an answer you already knew? Was that because you also were stupid?

There were credits here but there were no charms. It was just another visible sky.

Once every month maybe it happened. And so you told yourself like anything you get used to stuff happening.

But that was another lie. But lies were beautiful weren't they? Not being factual and getting away with it — looking someone in the eyes and getting away with it — looking into the sky and getting away with it — looking inside and looking outside — and feeling like you pressed it home and kept it.

A lie — oh a lie — beautiful furnished and sweating lower house company — it gave you cover. And a grin that followed you and let you fool people. At least for now it worked like a trust. But time was short. If you were good at anything- it was to worry about what was about to happen next.

But when it happened — and if you were lucky enough to be outside and see it — when the streets were hit with visible sky and it whisked through the avenues and the clamor on earth — Stoplights stared you down from high wires… stop signs said don't linger… Nervous gasoline fumes blew in your face… A trashcan rolled across 21st Street blowing out cellophane papers like it was preoccupied … All you wanted was to hold that minute... To fill your lungs... the air you knew... your fidelity... your horror...

Pressed. You were pressed — like a mixed up bad preserve and a confederate desire you were pressed against the atoms in the air — the stuff that made us die- the stuff that made you an inkling and pressed you therefore to be alive... you stood above the weeds fading in scale from old sidewalk cracks at 20th Street and Wyncote Avenue — ventilation... being in concord... ferment... lively... a sweep and a daunting...

Fuck that Reds said. Stop thinking! And he slapped you backside across the head...

*

We cut up the alley.

We ran across the Lot behind the Leeche Brothers Automotive Shop. They fixed cars for honest people. They fucked up stolen cars for dishonest people so they would never be seen again. You had to keep that money coming in and ride the string while it lasted. No magic bus for the Leeche Brothers... just cars... broken or fingered.

We missed the exodus was sprayed on the block walls... but we'll be back it said...

Not again it said in crazy white and black script... you almost heard the drumming behind the letters.

Lecche Brothers building was falling apart one concrete block at a time.

Like it was an open season on the rear of an automotive shop — a concrete page where the neighborhood writers filled a wall with thoughts made worldly through the commercial nozzles of spray paint cans.

Gang slogans — sweet dumb but overdone genitals — big-toothed clowns — monster guys in top hats — titty gals with twin-fisted pistols– more gang slogans — grinning faces and militant faces — an erasure then a re-spray then an erasure then a re-spray — the back wall of Leeche Brother's Automotive Shop was beautiful — and it was beautiful because it was made that way.

Leeche Brothers was the shop where our parents took their cars to be fixed if there was trouble.

Police officers parked their cars across the yellow lines and leaned against the hood with a free coffee and a fixed laugh.

Stolen cars came in regular and left with a manifest.

When they left the garage the cars weren't stolen at all.

Blind Charlie and the Leeche Brothers were related.

Everybody in the chase took spirit money.

No trace no harm no accounting it was zero day payday…

The back wall was beautiful. It was made that way.

*

The Lot was a dumping ground- a junkyard behind the Leeche Brothers Automotive Shop. A u-shaped building that fronted Avenue S. and from behind took up some indeterminate tainted ground butting next to the Daily Freeze with its limp soft serve and killer fries and the adjacent alleys off Wyncote Avenue and 66th Street. Brute cars too atomic to be sold because the thieves didn't do their homework and so like they stole the mayor's car or some shit — Blind Charlie would ask on a Friday night: why are there stupid thieves?

And if so — if the cars were too hot — they were stripped for parts and what was left was then packed into the Lots like criminal Legos. Eventually they'd end up at the facility down by the Delaware Bay and were then squashed by a giant machine that reminded you of Blind Charlie himself — and so were transformed into fraud and metal bundles and cash and then taken overseas and sold where no one gave a shit for any less.

Forgotten sidewalk slabs torn from curbs without a glace from the city. And Blind Charlie paid for them to be taken out and replaced because he wanted new sidewalks for the pizza shop. And if the relatives asked- and if they'd done well the past year- then they got new concrete too.

Mostly whatever shit ended up in the Lot was linked up to Blind Charlie.

Crushed beer quarts left over in brown shards — that was some architecture word Eden said meant evidence and maybe she said might be hunted down by future intellectuals looking for trails and order and something lofty this civilization left behind — years in the drink-

ing whose rush in the life went from grandparents to grandchildren —
hoisting bottles and breaking glass — a vex among generations. Maybe
tonight you'd again add to the culture.

Appliances old enough from the Europe wars that were failures in
the new world and that Blind Charlie replaced for the neighbors FOC
because the stores he didn't own were butcher shops skinning people's
money and left them raw one paycheck to another with worry. Blind
Charlie hated worry. If someone in the neighborhood worried then
Blind Charlie worried. He offered a hand to the neighbors affected and
naturally had the money and the spine to back it up.

Other toasted machinery were crammed against the back wall with a
mountain of shit assed car tires and busted transmissions and brittle hydraulic arms leaking oil and mangled shopping carts where the homeless
parked because it was a wary place to hide your ride.

There were rumors also… A grave or two and close-fisted beneath
the petro-soil of The Lot…

Reds put headphones over your ears. He lit up a joint. You clicked
play. Old Who songs…

*

And there was this weird tree growing in the Lot. It twisted away
from the wall and was bent like it was a deformed tree right from the
beginning you know and not like a tree you'd see in a park or something.
It wormed upward past Leeche Brothers flat roof through all the shit
dumped there over the years. For most of your life you watched it grow-
toward whatever light it found- past the tar dripping over the sides of the
roof and the neon sign with a bold Leech Brothers in red script. Guess
it was like most trees other than its fucked up shape. Green leaves in
summer and crisp mustard brown in fall and in winter its branches were
bare and sad. That's about a tree's life right? But it was a good tree you
thought. You had nothing against it. Was it lonely though because there
were no other trees around?

One drunken evening Rhino and the boys tried to set fire to it. But
Eden and the other girls stopped them. No burning down the tree they

said. What's up with that Rhino said? No burning down the tree they said. Seemed like Rhino and the boys didn't know what to do. Who figured on girls showing force? Anyway — it was a standoff. But it didn't matter. There was beer to drink. There were other kinds of hell that needed raised from the night. Why commit violence against a plant? It didn't make sense. Weren't there better things to do with the witching hours?

So we left the tree alone. Blessed be the meek or whatever the fuck that meant. You had trouble with the volume adjustment. But you found it and dialed it while you exhaled the rope Reds usually had to smoke…No one knows what it's like… but then the tape shit the bed before it got to the part behind blue eyes… but shit… it had to change… the method right…?

*

Best thing about The Lot: it was shelter. You disappeared there when you needed to be gone to the world and be forgotten about in your own head.

Worst thing about The Lot: most everybody else knew you were there.

But the best things outdid the worst things.

The Lot was a retreat from whatever you fucking wanted to avoid. You could drink a beer and sit by yourself and wonder …why you were scared… or

you could sit by yourself and wonder why you were brave. You looked at rain colored nudie books. You thought what you wanted was flying away with Eden…

Reds lit up a Kool and took a drag. He smoked the local Asian brands. He leaned against an overwhelmed and quashed milk truck and blew out smoke like he owned the universe. The milk truck was like excommunicated from life.

Maybe our parents understood. But you had your doubts. Not that it was fucking personal against parents but the doubts you had were like words in the air. Having a life was like a skeletal freight to needle you with dying they implied. But like any other birth that dared breach the void maybe you knew what release was but didn't really know it? But mostly their advice was guidance by the rules. You lived by how you were raised etc. And maybe that added up and made sense in the pocket change version of things- but what did they know that somebody else down the street didn't know? Maybe they skipped town on you and were just reading the manuals? Maybe it was natural why they didn't say much about anything.

Once upon a time in the neighborhood — this wrenched milk truck — or some fucking milk truck that looked just like it — laid to waste in The Lot beside the tree — and as crazy as it was beautiful the tree was growing a branch through a torn off door and scraped its sap and DNA against Leeche Brothers filthy back wall. Once upon a time the milk truck was known for hope heart and timely deliveries. You remembered this. It seemed important to know this. But who knew why… Who was it in the back of your head that said your needed this.

The milk truck's driver was a coarse-mouthed white guy with decent aging hair and who never drove too fast on narrow streets and who honked thumb's up at all the kids he knew to be on his route. He dropped off sweet curly rolls and portly sized eggs in unmarked cartons- bacon slabs and sausage links if he had them and orange juice- and grape soda and cans of whipped cream that seemed to have everything to do with breakfast.

Too many others he said were moving into the neighborhood. Ya'll know what I mean… too many others he said were moving in and jacking down house prices and acting out. They ain't us he said. And where there ain't us he said there was problems staring back everywhere you turned. And the more of them he said well that means the less of us. Pretty soon we can't be — if ya'll know what I mean…pretty soon he said them motherfuckers… All them cousin shit you see well that drives us apart because we ain't cousins you see because we're just ya know … we're just here. All that cousin shit gets me mad… know what I mean. We don't need fucking relatives — and I say that word in quotes — know what I mean — it's like a fucking emphasis but you don't mean it — like a fucking joke but you get more worked up over it… that's what I mean. Motherfuckers moving in from the boonies…

How many other milk trucks were there? Did you have to remember them all? If so wasn't that awkward? Where a milk truck comes and goes and wasn't that a laugh… was it too late to say fuck that I got no swag from history….

You think into the future and imagine that milk someday will come in a yellowed powder in sad plastic bags. There will be soapbox instructions on a label on the bags. Get the story it said. Official script. This powder contains at least five nutrients… this powder has undergone rigorous training… this powder may cause cancer but may not… side effects may include but are not limited to: bad breath — eyeball swelling –sweating acne breakout on the forehead — purple sometimes hard toes — and as such seek immediate care at a nearby clinic where three forms of identification and fingerprint scans are required for admittance… do not add chlorinated water to the powder at any time as this consequence may cause an unbearable stink requiring a vacating from the residence…

Yea you could see into future. Someday we were told the cows were gone from the farms outside the city-land. One day we were told there were no more cows anymore. They were needed elsewhere we will be told.

But there were times where you stood invisible witht he familiar — or was it invincible with the familiar? Not to matter. You were confused. The joint was burning. And it wasn't just another stuffed routine with another voice you didn't like ordering you around. But the familiar — the sights smells and actions — the stuff you do and the way you feel about them — It's like a fuse attached to your world- a cherry bomb — what a word to remember — like we used to blow out a tire on a parked car — and when it goes off your head happens instantly with exclamations and wide eyes.

Each day — each portion — each some day — some fraction got reduced — a common denominator tramped onto your day and left you thrilled and wanting for life to do it again. Maybe all the shadows that fell from the sky in strange winsome blues across the neighborhood were really the light all by itself and those shadows braided the streets because things were twisted around the sun…. hydraulic oil wept slowly from metal drums… cancerous lacquers made the dirt greasy around the tree… if not the earth that was leaking through the seams….

Are you ready or what Reds said lifting the headphones off your ears.

He was throwing cement bits at a pigeon picking at the remains from a hoagie wrapper.

He took a long drag from his Kool and let it go- blowing smoke ring where they spun off into the air. His marks missed the pigeon.

You looked at the bird and you thought it said fuck you back at Reds. And you thought back at the bird yea go finish your lunch.

Yea you said you were ready. Gimme those unopened underworlds and astral side streets and highboy utopias. Yea you said ready as ever and stood up and tripped over a broken crate with nails and shit sticking out.

Reds shook his head.

*

We dipped back out of the alley and walked around to the front doors where all three Leeche Brothers were talking to customers and wiping greasy hands on greasy rags or they were shouting out employees hey that this aint paradise so hurry up with Mrs. Kelly's car!

Traffic wheeled by on Avenue S. in flashes and vanishing speeds. A bunch of pigeons flew off the roof against the sky. Oddly shaped like a kite and uniformed in flight like some wind we couldn't see.

Across Avenue S. at 66th was Hartley's Store. A small corner grocery with buckled floors and a dusty tin ceiling and old bored shelves that titled with the flooring. Inside Harley's the air smelled like lunchmeats and cheese just sliced for a sandwich — smelled like sweet onions in bags and smelled like apples in boxes. All those smells came from upstate where they had such things- where they were grown and plentiful from the fat dirt of lonesome fields.

And when you got a sandwich at Harley's you had to pick a dill pickle to go with it. They floated inside a wooden barrel. They floated in something called brine Mister Hartley said. Mister Hartley said brine was part zeal and mystic to imagine and then a skillful job to make. Mister Harley said if the brine worked then what you had was out of this world.

Hartley's Store on the corner was holding out. It was holding on.

Fuck. Somebody in church should make a sermon for Harley's life. But that imagined prayers mattered...

But the big supermarket invasion was launched last year. We fought it. Not because we cared. We weren't any good at that. We fought it because we were good at stealing. A couple times a week we'd go stealing at the big supermarket. We got stoned and marched out like fucking patriot homeboys.

And it was sad to look at where the big supermarket was built.

There were houses — a block of homes — people and families treated like guttersnipes yea they were the usual suspects jagged without money and minus weight — second-rate meager scrubs — bananas gone brown — imitation watermelon slices — and so the block was knocked down. A decent old block was in the way and was removed to make way for the oncoming vanilla traffic and toady sugar pies.

For all the worries the block possessed — like they didn't have enough already to fucking worry about right? Yea things were like a bastard — costly sketchy and a trick sometimes to drop food on the table. Yea no doubt people were no angels. You took what you could. You sold what you could. Everybody made a little gush on the side. Nothing paid better than selling off something you never owned. Times weren't exactly easy nor were they paid off like maybe a fortunate spirit that you wished held your hand. And the finery of soul lacked a decoration it deserved. Mostly you got by and nursed the day. But then some fucking lawsuit uprooted their lives. Some waver in the law made the rents bad. And the hacks signed off. Everybody on the block was tossed into a kind of cosmic dumpster. They were given the last month's rent back. And were told to leave with no questions asked — and no questions would be taken. And if that wasn't shit enough to light the monkey hairs on your ass on fire- two days later the cops banged on doors and slapped abandoned building stickers on the doorjambs –crime scene yellow –fucking human non se-quit-tor imminent domain post-it-notes while people were still inside…

And so — like a bedtime story told to the little ones — the fallow land was transformed. A king capital replaced the old slums with a huge gleaming castle on the asphalt. Sparrow throated workers buzzed at the doors and introduced you to the many and many aisles of goods to have. Inside the light was radiant enough to almost kneel beneath.

So we stole as best as we could. And that was righteous to no end. Sometimes we took a critique that we were too fucking young to get it — but we made good on that by thieving more and made premium by what we spread around. In a sense we took meat off the beast and only charged for cost.

*

Hartley's Store sold jawbreakers and jellybeans and chewing gum by the cent.

Hartley's Store — small peanut butter cupcakes three in a pack and with a grape soda quart they made a perfect doorway breakfast before the school bell rang.

Hartley's Store had these small fruit pies in hand held pie tins and especially the cherry pies did it because the goop in the center had such a starling taste and was so chemically made red like a cherry it was almost real and nearly took your head off.

Harley's Store big chocolate bars cost a quarter and they exceeded your palm and were beautiful to look at — even before you ripped one open and stared at it and then broke off a bite...

Stop it Reds said.

*

How do you hang in there when you're ruined?

You just do Reds said.

It was simple wasn't it you asked?

Simple Reds said not paying attention to you. He looked around for a Lecche Brother.

Guess it didn't matter much either at this end. What Reds thought you meant.

He was too preoccupied. With his own self... forgetting his back. Always combing his thick red hair. Always on display was what he owned. He fingered a bag from Cousin Jimmy. His slow fat fingers worked it over cautiously. He dealt the envelope between his hands and treated like it was a hallmark card from god congratulating him and he couldn't stop reading it.

No Lecche Brother was in sight.

Reds was sure. He had the envelope. And the envelope was certain.

You stood around watching. Watching the Leeche Brothers at work. Regretting we were here again. Because a visit to the Lecche Brothers got you nothing for waiting and got you nothing in your pocket while you stood around and waited for Reds...

...Like a fucking half-witted wonk you listened to the Lecche Brothers gab and waste time like time didn't matter unless that time happened on their own time while they fucking gabbed. Pneumatic noise changed tires. A petro-stink from the cars leaked oil and the leaked oil found its way onto the street gutters. The next rain pushed it toward the sewer grates and dumped the oil into the narrow streams and the quick tide marshes. Then at their mouths and deltas they dumped the oil into the ocean like a curse. From that point the ocean shat out the petro-stink into the air. Oil laced rain then in some future thunderstorm fell down on the fucking Lecche Brother's Automotive Shop.

Tedious — that's what you felt waiting... self- consciousness and tired that's what you felt waiting... but you hung on... because you didn't understand but you scared up a thought that you were boned and tipped from the sky... that's what you felt... happy when money was made and you knew there was no reason for you to wait... but you didn't know like what was exact or dishonored... where there was no cash there was cash hidden from view. Why did Blind Charlie deal with Reds this way?

What was new or what was sturdy or what made the deal prime for needle gravers or thinking about it while you and the fucking waiting made you as senseless as a pointless Hercules, or a library den with volumes of wasted thinking sprinkled with lies and knocked back like a round of drinks in the Lecche Brother's dooryard... You weren't sure why it felt stupid to be ignored. But it did. It was stupid to be ignored and left to wait around. Stuff like that pissed you off. But you weren't sure why.

*

...But you had to hang in there despite the trouble. Right? And for how long would that be just a question? At what moment from the future would Hartley's Store be not worth keeping? And that scared you... the idea... no Hartley's Store....

On hot summer afternoons- when you were a small kid- you made a few bucks running errands at the schoolyard for the older guys playing softball. You had to split time with Reds and Cripple. But those two couldn't move for shit so fuck them. Cripple was slow and down for obvious reasons. Reds was lazy and didn't give a shit when it came to labor. But if you hustled between innings and fetched sodas for the older guys you made a little decent money running back and forth between the schoolyard and Hartley's Store.

*

It was scary to think about- but then- since you were thinking about it anyway- and kept on thinking about- it scared you anyway. What's to be said but to keep thinking about it?

It was like having a weather system settle on your head. You think and you live and you live and then you worry. And so you develop a few necessary moves.

Namely: what the old heads said was this: it does not matter what you think.

But what you thought was this: the simple beauty walking among kin.

But what the old heads said was: there were now others moved in.

So they put the idea into your head: what was the neighborhood they said. And they didn't really want an answer.

Basically what they said was: this: there were differences and you needed to understand them. Otherwise you got no use they said.

And there was no question about what they meant by having — no use.

And the old heads mattered.

They weren't Blind Charlie and the cousins — but the old heads mattered. They were like a self-happy street patrol — ethnic themselves and cock sure — Europeans but they said no Jews. The Jews some said were like the others they said. Mostly they looked for what they didn't want in the neighborhood. And then the old heads grabbed them and beat them and tossed them beyond Broad Street at one boundary and Island Avenue at the other: And don't come the fuck back!

And so that raised the value to the problem to something like to hell with it in the long run.

Throwing people out only succeeded if the others didn't come back. And then — the hell with it right — they come back anyway with more others looking for heads and naturally they wanted a better fight.

This was an old story right? Some fucked up legend that sooner or later had to be booted senseless and ruined.

Hearing it took the wheeze out your lungs every day … and left you face down staring at a curb and thinking about it like you were thinking about it… but what you were thinking was fuck the old heads — and face up — you needed to live with yourself — you thought whoa fuck this old head shit was so tired and so you presented a dodge to fighting — terrible wasn't it to have a life — so in effect you lied. Sure you said to the old heads: I'll fight the bastards. I'm fucking crazy. Protect the neighborhood… But you had to trip carefully with those words. Otherwise you'd get a tattoo across your heart.

Once the old heads drafted you for a fight. The others were coming they said. And since you were now subterfuge you agreed to join the battle. You were given a metal pipe and were told to wait behind the big Sycamore tree at 65th & 20th. Anybody who ran past they said you were told to clock them no questions. Well that was an option you thought.

Well you thought here you were — waiting in the night like a fool with a metal pipe and instructions to bash some unknown fuck's head in…

You ended up with this Nigerian kid… here it was… the fucking standoff scene!

We made hand signals. Your dumb metal pipe versus his scary knife…

You dropped the metal pipe. He didn't understand. He went after you with the knife swinging the blade in close like he knew what he was doing.

You said no — no — no. You threw your hands up. You imitated he might do the same. Guess at that point you surrendered. Wasn't there a better kind of smarts to be had?

Ah his face said. But his eyes were pricked behind his expression. He wouldn't put the knife back in his belt.

The only reason you knew he was Nigerian was because the old heads said so. They said we'd be fighting the Nigerian that night.

So we walked away. Stepping with a crease into the night you motioned and we quickly dived into the alley behind the 20th Century Club. We smoked a joint. The knife was in full view. You thought about the metal pipe...Sometimes in the dumpster there were vodka bottles tossed out with a snort left in them.

He had a lousy Nigerian accent you thought. But he was the first Nigerian you ever met. So how would you know?

And you had this lousy neighborhood accent that didn't speak Nigerian at all.

Take a pill you offered. He was off at first and drew back. But when you tossed one down he nodded ah and did the same. It was screwed enough what the simple drugs did to language...

But anyway you tried to explain...

And so you said to Frank — his old heads told him that Frank was his neighborhood name — because he kept intoning: me Frank me Frank! He held out his hand without a knife. Maybe he was just high. But what the hell!

Well Frank you said look at what we're fighting over. Do you see it?

Frank shrugged.

And so you tried to express to Frank the totality where you and he were. Your hands swept above your head. Like a crude halo or a compass arch on a map in hopes the geography got through to him. In other words here we were you said. Slumped against a dumpster and stoned together and suspicious in the night and together in a way because there was no trust...only a suspicion in trust... Who can trust anybody? We were left with not much of an answer and with the old high eyeballs going over each other in the trenches of our poor humanity...

Europeans you said — okay you said — Europeans that was us you said — and you pointed with your hands inward and backwards at your chest. You thought was this stupid or what? Of course we were Europeans. Didn't we have that on our skin?

Frank understood the sound European. He gave a signal thumbs up.

Yea you said — we're Polish we're Italian we're German we're Irish we're French we're Brits we're Swedish we're Norwegian we're all the Slavs that survived as refugees from the Asian wars and so we grounded here in Jersey-land. We had ancestors years ago that were refugees from all the other fucking wars and they ended here. And so what? That left us with the fucking latest Asian wars — in fact you said to Frank — what the fuck matters?

He nodded like maybe he got it. He did the compass arch thing above his head. Maybe it was mimicry. Maybe it was sympathy. Maybe he thought about that knife...

Who can trust anybody he said in textbook English.

Qui peut faire confiance a persome he said.

Wer kann jemand vertura he said.

Abangakwazi ukwethemba montu he said.

*

Guess it surprised you. Especially when you asked and Frank said that was Zulu. Now you knew somebody who spoke Zulu. Even if he was the other.

But what was a kid who spoke Zulu doing in the neighborhood?

Did his old heads manufacture him from some idea across the sea?

Maybe he was a plant the cops put into the action?

Maybe he wasn't even Frank?

*

Just a minute all right (?) ... But who were you talking to?

You needed time out. You need another pill (!). Another pill to get the former antediluvian head right and no doubt the practiced decayed and shorn out head right but hopefully and thoughtfully the wild green and senseless head needed to be right before the obsolete model of your present own head went south.

Afterwards you were afraid. That was good because that's what always happened. Once the pill took hold — what? There was no fear? Yea there was no fear... But that was a lie. There was always fear. The pills just showed it easy fashion-like. But only for a moment — because that lie was affordable. You knew it. You felt it. You like fucking overture it.

But when the pill did grab hold — many thanks were offered…god must have been a chemist in a former life.

Still it took a moment to get your ass– as you knew it — unscrambled.

Laugh worth the effigy and the breathing…. So you started the clam sauce… before the raven-haired woman got home from the airport… and you got back to the thinking request. But damn there was something else you hadn't taken into account…

You had a meal laid out in mind… and a meal laid out in mind…well that made a lure laid out on a table — a chandelier of feelings…. taking up that minute… following it well it might light up the night… so it takes a minute… to get right…but before you start talking again and the pills explodes in your head and these fragments in thoughts collapse into your head like a framework that's been dynamited and so what's to understand but pieces and getting back on your feet…

…Invested. In order to build certain things other certain things were needed to be knocked down… were invested in truckloads… ass-selling and money …invested to get past tactics… big education and pay it off … naturally… what everybody was involved in… sly and cheating… process… required was a return on efforts across the board.

And so given that — where do you work for but the state?

…And have computer models those fucking stamp heads and pint heads who lived in the fortress lands beyond Exit 17 — and who rode to work each day on the secure outside lane and who were supported by the state…. played combat with the state… but whose office had no guts… and the company — decades upon decades ago they snubbed the neighborhood… even before Blind Charlie was born… gas heads put the design in place and guess what… gave it shape to happen… but who fought the cash… who was the misery in the same breath? Wasn't it simpler? And then let them stew in the wild and have the police force pick them up as vagrants?

Frank had it down after he shook your hand.

He told you he needed to get back into the others before they wondered where he was.

You understood that. You needed to go find the metal pipe.

Ah oui he said.

He slapped you across the back and laughed. He dashed way into the night and turning around to face you and laughing once more. Comic book Frank you thought he was comic book Frank.

You were glad Frank didn't cut you. Because if he did that meant maybe he'd cut you again in the future if he could- and that might depend on so many things beyond you or Frank's control.

But you felt — weirdly — without evidence — and this might be trust — shit what if it was trust — so the pricks on your nerves stood up like a brush scrapped against your arms and you said whoa... a registrar throughout the body — and so you imagined getting cut by Frank — again — even thought getting cut never happened — it was just something that might happen — and you feared getting cut — but fuck it — what do you believe? Your feared that Frank cut you — and you were big on fears — do you believe your eyes seeing Frank's knife being put away?

You were glad you didn't need to demolish Frank's head with the pipe because that meant then you needed to hit him again until Frank was gone to his fucking languages and then there was nothing more to do but to leave him behind and bleeding out on 65th Avenue...

Something Stinks. That tag was painted on the wall and was like a young writer's call to being. When they were just starting out and needed to make a name for Jersey-land to notice grabbed a wall and wrote: Something Stinks.

And once it left the can and the deft hand it was then realized in paint. Something Stinks — painted on a wall — and maybe it was now painted over the years — and over the years other signatures painted over the same message– Something Stinks. Something Stinks — and once it was painted on a wall then it was the world. It was a ticket to recognize. And it was like snapping a playing card down with the last card in a flush and then taking away the pot. Our well being in the world was represented on those walls….

Spray paint the gospels Blind Charlie once said….

We — the neighborhood — Jersey-land young boy writers— we who where our ancestors — they were long gone and buried in the Chestnut Hill Cemetery… but we weren't our ancestors — but we were our ancestors — we fucked up both values because … well — you didn't really know why… but you had some ideas about why that was. But what were your ideas worth? What you figured was: the complaints from the past were some hallucination handed to us like this shit was sacred.

*

You went back to grab the metal pipe. You had to hand it back to the old heads later on because it was their property. What the fuck did you need with a metal pipe? And in that event- meeting them at The Lot and handing it over- you'd make up a story. You'd tell a lie. But it was a lie that held worth and being. And not a lie that made you scared to voice it. It was the good lie and not a fret. The good lie — the personal lie — it was a beautiful lie that only you knew and it was the lie that saved your bacon when an old head looked at you the wrong way.

Yea he had a knife — details like yea he was dark skinned and almost cut you… details like yea you swung but missed… details like he almost cut you and you fought and he ran…

Behind the big Sycamore tree someone tagged the wall recently.

Aliquid habet faetorem

Fucking Latin? What? This had to be bad. Someone tagging in Latin? Was it following you around?

We learned that in school. We learned in school one day that the Jersey-land we knew and the Jersey-land we called home was to be — "removed in situ throughout the neighborhoods as necessary for a positive development in the future for the entire capital."

The neighborhood — enough said — the neighborhood was the heart. The beat developed to survive. We got that habit from birth and truth to power we wont let it go.

But it was also the satellite neighborhoods where the movie theaters and the arcades were — they were gone too.

And the outer limits neighborhoods where cousins rode the trollies of the damned back and worth to work in the capital — they were gone too.

All that you knew — your whole life –the existence that you knew — the past twelve years since you were born — that was gone too.

Some fucking politics — that's what made it gone.

Something called — them — fucking grunts in caves — small fucking Romans in bad haircuts — bishops — slavers — the mega-lien holders from the latest Asian war holding the rent money in Jersey-land — they got the fire and they made the words — and what those words said — and meant — was that the neighborhood was gone.

Somebody you never saw was about to make your home gone in a flash. It only took a signature. And with that fucked up name with an official pen in his greasy hand not only made him a fortune with a stroke of that pen but also the moment when he sold the neighborhoods out then he and that pen signed his own death warrant and made his headstone visible enough in the graveyard to be spat upon and desecrated yearly like a celebration anniversary whose importance as vengeance would be handed down year after year until the grave sank deeper into the ground.

There was desperation going around Jersey-land.

There was beauty.

And if you can't get past either side — without a fight from the middle — that meant you had to reduce it and choose sides.

The down and the dirty side money that everybody made — the families — the crazy homes we lived in to get along — the fights that made families crazy in those homes — the down and dirty side money that made crazy families forget the money and fight to remain and to get along to fight again and love being families in homes — if things were holding then things were tight — and that's what made it gone — it was gone because we couldn't hold it — this development shit was stronger than the rest of us.

So we killed what we could. We blew up the real estate signs. We got tattoos on our butts that said — fools' errand — with a flaming orange dragon and strange blue flowers around the script.

And the problem child for this trouble was the boardwalk.

*

Fuck. The point was there were infinite nights on those rotting planks. Dial it in. Dial in the vim and you forgot the powers at school and the paltry homework — forget the part-time job you had — all that shit was like bran meal to a dog's face — the boardwalk was where you learned to walk with gratitude.

So what else could possibly transcend the boardwalk? What made more difference than the 170 mile walk minus a few from the big river in the south to the big river in the north? All those miles — minus a few — beside the Atlantic — passing through and connecting Jersey-land...

When you were on the boardwalk — above the trashed beaches and the deathless surf — and this might be a stretch to say but you felt the tides — and being on the boardwalk was to walk and to think and to think about walking and to walk about thinking.

All things equal it was a circular nut that pleased you.

On a good night walking in the crowd you felt certain things. It didn't matter if they were good or not. What did matter was to feel them and not to feel like you had to explain them.

*

The shops that came and went like seawee on a wave selling nothing with threads clothing and glued–up ceramics that were like junk from

182

the latest Asian war and Jersey-land was someplace mindless to dump them due to political ends — intoxicating greasy foods with foreign languages and oh it was a wonder eating and trying to talk from stall to stall — sugar sex drinks with grinning prostitutes selling their effects — those over and under games for a quarter that were laid down on a lanky felt mat and that suckered you for every quarter you had — but hey you always had one more quarter somewhere in your pocket- but it was the fray coming apart in everyone's minds — when they saw in those minds what was going to happen... The boardwalk was going to be demolished.

Because it was a picture from the future...

From the ice age where filthy rich soils left in the south grew corn tomatoes and peaches up the world's wazoo ... Up mid-way coast to old shore homes tucked into barrier islands and built from cheap post-war loans... Then farther north up the coast where the biggest city on the planet stood tall and countersigned like a secret housing... And below its nag and the stink from the rivers leaked into the bays and dead long-shoreman's cards ... the boardwalk was continuous...

Continuous... like birth — what did you do when happiness or regret or when any emotions knocked on your back door? But if you walked far enough — from the south and reached the north — river to river — that was like total — 170 miles minus a few river to river — a necromancy took shape down in your bones — occult and friar and mongrel. And then — oh to disappear for days on a time — to walk was to forget and to live — a moment outside the fucked up time you were handed — another day to see and not obey — and another day to forget all the shit ... beside you walked above the tides! ... the nasty purity each Jersey-land neighborhood brought to that naked mile and despite all that you felt sorrowful with each step you walked because each step you walked was not only solid underfoot but also limpid inside your tiny thoughts. And if you walked the whole way back and forth — blowing up the signs when you could and leaving behind spray paint cans and a cache of pills for kids with the talent — you thought damn it was worth it?

Either way it was gamed from afar. It was never too soon to see that early on. Heaven and hell were bought off with cash. Like the bumper sticker said: seagulls and summer people shit all over everything.

The boardwalk running up the spine of Jersey-land's coast was not the mistake that the capital said it was.

Rather the boardwalk was a wonder to behold.

So fuck the pyramids and the camel rides to look at and jerk off the geometry against space... fuck the hanging gardens because those plants might have been nothing more than poetic constructions ... fuck that big warrior statue like some asshole that get felled in an earthquake or that temple swallowed by flood... fuck Zeus on his stupid throne... fuck that lighthouse because it was too tall and that mausoleum built by slaves ... all that shit was tragedy because all we got for it was graffiti from the past ... so if we're were talking about constructed phenomena — well — the boardwalk was now.

*

At First Avenue the boardwalk ended. Scaffolds blocked the way. They were like giant letter X's in the way. Space invader insects the banks installed and were meant to scare everyone away. There were large nails stuck forward a few inches or so through the framing nailed together. Medieval? No further admittance — danger signs and bright yellow tape — and what that said was to turn around and walk away because soon all this would get better. Beyond the X's and the damnation warnings was a signal: money was on the way.

Walk away? Fuck that. You were born here. You lived here before that scaffolding went up.

Little by little in situ Jersey-land was going.

Beyond First Avenue more construction had already begun.

We voted on some fucking referendum. Like that mattered. We already had the word and that was the word we needed. And we used that word with a simple magic marker x on our ballets.

But surprise — the infinite phrase — the world spinner — with a heft like gravity — a law like gravity and holding whatever to the ground — hey — fraud was the word.

You were paid off if you stayed away. And were told if we showed up at polls at St. Benedict's parish hall our ass was in no way guaranteed but we got paid anyway.

Take the money and leave. Yea we all got that. And some of us did. We took the money and ran. But since life was as beautiful as it was devious and energetic when you took the money — and let it be known you voted against the money but took it because what the fuck– you took the money — and around the corner and you gave the money to a cousin. Then you went back to St. Benedict's hall and voted again. And you got the money again. And then voted again against the money.

One time as you walked out the polling place some capital thug in an overbuilt suit questioned you: why you here he asked him in a strange mechanical tongue that pegged. Weren't you were you too young to vote he asked?

Not since the latest Asian war you answered. Everybody votes.

Probably not the best approach to problems at hand but hey who's counting...

You young too much how where you vote so to vote you too young got how question when you vote without question answered.

This guy was as stupid as the meatballs you had for dinner last night.

You wanted yours you said.

Why where you vote for he asked?

The dumb ass monster meatball held rolls of money before your face with a steady hand. He was big. The suit he wore was big. The cash played though his hands was way big. But then you saw something — something fearful — that any size he needed to be he already was — and he took that on like something more than a personal assignment from up high. Maybe you miscalculated. Maybe there was too much trust in your own balls.

But the meatball seemed principled to what he did. And paranoid it seemed that he might crush you and your hubbub act in his hand and judge you- and not in order to prove to his employers he was sacred to their next steps.

But then he slapped money across your face and threw you out the door. You landed seven steps down on the pavement. Looking back up and holding your head you saw money sprinkled down and the big suited meatball laughing at you.

When you were vote you get good vote he said. This lesson-voting it is you asshole. More money where voting lessons you asshole were good. Don't where you were how you did forget. Understand?

Everybody understood. He said so: why when you different when more money do you see where if more money makes everybody look this way and when everybody has same then make you see more money comes the end. Understand? Go now he said. See the stairs again and no more money.

Jersey-land was fucking cribbed.

Everybody took the fight.

The banks wanted the boardwalk extended for those minus few miles. And the capital agreed.

The banks wanted to run the boardwalk down the wetlands to the bay those minus few miles south. Across the bay the lights from the Delaware casinos shone in the night sky and rippled across the fast moving water. Cashed-out badgers under the influence and charmed losers waited for ferry service back to Jersey-land minus the roll they earlier stared out with.

But the wetlands –the wetland were a fellow thing. They belonged in situ to us all.

Jersey-land knew. Its big old nature heart knows what those minus few miles meant.

But how did it matter? That was the question. If the 170 mile board-walk was going to be torn down anyway to make room for the schemes and dreams of profit then why were the minus few miles that were never built in the first place now about to materialize?

But ask anyone — ask anyone except the well stroked bank hands — anyone except the capital — ask anyone working the map lines — brilliant sharpies reimaging geography –ask the oil workers drilling in the swamp — ask the fake Euro- companies where the capital owed money — ask and all they'd say were the wetlands were foul smelling and nothing more than another stock of landscape whose purpose was to be sold and bought.

It didn't really matter what the wetlands really where. What mattered was what the wet lands thought... Flushed in the tidal rush twice a day and the Atlantic breeze. But that flush and that breeze brought us other worlds. Everything that moved and everything that breathed and whatever lived in the atmosphere in Jersey-land belonged to the wetlands. Survey crews from up the turnpike measuring Exit 17 for expansion could not get that.

Only we got that. Only Jersey-land got that.

So fuck the banks — that message got tagged on walls. And was tagged again and again and was written on walls under whatever limits spray paint took on. . It fucked with limo doors. Someone even got under the wings from a private jet and tagged it..

But it was hard to the point where you knew that one day you were going to lose this fight.

Birds and turtles — crabs and fish — ancestors– happiness and fear — they lived in the wetlands for thousands of years. And over those years — where ancestors walked and worked the shore for food to live on — walked and worked the shore for the insight of dying to rely upon — we all came down into being with bird and turtle names — crab names — fish names. Years and years ago it meant a celebration. You were alive in that name. You were born. You were given the end to see. You dug in the muck with the turtle. You first got drunk in the wetlands. You took your first love for an evening in the wetlands. But now those names — centuries old with meanings back toward centuries before — were pressed upon us to be forgotten. Because to fight the banks and the capital and the church that meant the whole idea of contemplation was being crushed from the simple fiber of Jersey-land. And it was said we were insufficient. We were a stress laid on the contemporary politics of being. And the better way to replace us it was said was to be stimulus minded and unyielding and have nerve enough to tell us that the wetlands were not measureless in the sad world of things.

The oil workers drilled in the swamp living out their scanty dreams for more pay from big Asia.

Banks foreclosed getting more booty from human bones.

The capital kept putting up more signs...took out more time on television... fucking creeps in mossy suits handed out toll free numbers for you to call... should you change your mind.

The neighborhood was a dinosaur. Your home was a target. The message was stapled onto telephone poles. Reduced to flyers jammed between windshield wipers. Basically it was a bad xerox copy they wanted stamped onto your head.

But you would not dare forget and give them the game.

Not that there was a winning shot...

But oh when you harvested the crabs in season — it was like you helped put balance into the end of the world. Every year since you were old enough you caught the millennial crustaceans and sold them. That's how the restaurants served them on menus. Millennial crustaceans fresh from the bay — admired and tasty when steamed in the same salt water they lived in. Oh they were good. And Blind Charlie loved them when you stole a batch from your dishwasher job and brought them to him over as a gift ... not like that fact mattered because Blind Charlie owned everything that moved in Jersey-land. But he loved it when you stole something with a purpose.

But through the years you got older and the price of millennial crustaceans followed and that price climbed up above twice what they were worth. Probably it was that way with everybody.

When you pulled a crab out — buried in the muck — and not solely the trusted muck the Atlantic designed — but also there was the cadmium muck that leaked from a paint factory on Bay Shore Boulevard and sank and was not to be moved with its lead properties — and the oil waste muck sloshed on the tides and replaced daily with machines taking mechanical shits — and the death peat from murder victims over the years and whose bodies were dumped in the wetlands for the crabs to devour — so when you held them up against sky to inspect — year after year you balked at what you saw.

These crabs had huge legs like a dog and small-unsettled bodies like vanilla wafers. Their eyes were crossed so they looked like a clown target you shot at for a prize at the Atlantic City fair. The crabs were mutants. Disaster flags. The restaurants sold them as a longstanding species still harvested by hand with famous Jersey-land premium leg meat. And in a sense the more ugly the crab was the more it was paid for in cash.

And were then Blind Charlie's trucks in fat tubs of ice headed to seaboard towns and driven by felons without a driver's license but felons everyone knew as cousin. The arcades when you needed a place to hide — the radio music and pin ball machines that made the arcades a safe place where you could hide… the trashed up neighborhood parks where you got stoned… where you hung out with Eden … where the dope was good and we were good — and good enough to know better … All this would be gone…

All this was going to be ripped from Jersey-land.

Jersey-land was your body.

Some fucked up dinosaur had better odds with that asteroid than we did.

It was hard and hard again to be looked at by social engineers and then be recommended we were ready to go and so in consequence the neighborhood was tossed on the heap. And the answers to the neighborhood's questions were our own problems thrown back in our face. The neighborhood was since called a slum. And as such was numbered on a list of other neighborhoods to be eradicated for positive development.

Thanks for the heritage and all that.

*

When we filled out the necessary census forms for capital assistance-we gathered them up together and then set them on fire on the corner. Afterwards the ashes were placed into the return envelopes — with of course the postage guaranteed by the capital.

Jersey-land. Home. Ancestors.

We were weary hungry and drunk. But that's how we arrived. Did it matter who we were any longer?

We were sad.

We were graceful.

We were common.

We were fucking angry.

We inherited genial slurs and the bland slap on the back.

We had someone else's troubles shape our directions.

But what we had — what we have to shape today — in opposition to today as then — our hearts — what we had — in opposition to going forward — going forward in opposition to shape a future day: what we had — within the hives of families — were language and dreams.

Shaky ancestor rents — homes that had no reliable locks on the doors and on the fireplace mantles of living rooms where the fireplaces long ago stopped working were statue saints whose images were dear and bruised and deeply worshipped. Each statue — each family rent — was a compatriot in its own native way to the good of Jersey-land. Some statues were polished marble antiquities and some statues were plastic repeats machine stamped by the thousands. But all families had this in common — wherever they came from — the statues had meaning. And whatever that meaning was didn't really matter. What mattered were the statue saints — the birthdays — the sacred feasts — markets on neighborhood streets — queer tasty foods and strange book sellers from worlds across the ocean — once you had your fortune told and the old lady in some kebab hair gear wept when she saw the lines on your palms were crossed over heaven and hell and kept doing it the more she stared.

Hey. Jersey-land.

It was written on the walls. Spray-painted on the walls against boom box sounds and the image and the text and the guts to live for an idea — to capture us today — small ordinary and loud like the saint statues did for the ancestors — Jersey-land was a fucking holistic tag where gravity and difference brought to life fear and its opposite. Jersey-land was our fucking DNA — the way some tags appeared forecast — like some alley painting and the way in which it stood in for images on old chapel walls and who was left to decide what was divine looking.

*

Everybody's ancestors came from someplace else. Duh…. Like we didn't understand that. Duh… all you needed was to look around you one day and that was enough to get it. We were Euros. But we were second generation Euros. But there it was — the guiding principle in block letters above the blackboards in school… always a Euro…

Beside that was an embossed copy of the original pledge: Euros made the world in god's image.

It was written in that ancient script with all those curly-cues at the ends of words that seemed to commemorate weapons and suggested violent sexual behavior. We were taught that in school that being Euros was a fucking revelation.

Jersey-land was indeed founded upon a Euro beginning. That left the ancestors with a kind of clockwork to understand but at the same time they needed to deny it. Others would follow. What to do about them? And once upon a time whoever else followed and landed on shore would then be tagged forever and classified as third generation and beyond — they were the others. And the more the others followed and landed on shore the darker their skin was. This was clear. And clearly it violated the original pledge.

Mister Armstrong managed the little league team and drank iced cola by the quarts and loved his cap that said coach in Cedar Park red.

Mister Crane had the big green pickup truck with tool cases and ladder racks and he drove everybody to the games and then he drove everybody back home for nothing.

Larry Seabury — the belly rubber –Seven-up by the quarts — gin by the sneak — a figure know in the parish. He drove this little foreign station wagon that was dented on both sides from DUI crashes. He went to mass every day. He helped out where he could for the church. He was devout. He lived with his elderly mother. He loved her. If you spied on him during Saturday afternoon confessions he spent ponderous time on his knees praying and tossing quarters into the metal box and lighting candles below the statue of Mary. Sometimes if Mister Crane's pickup truck was full — then Larry — the belly rubber known for what he did — was always there to help and ferry a kid back home. Larry prayed to god. He insisted he wasn't a villain but just a guy who liked to smile. Larry went to church each day. In the police report he said he was certain god understood. He was confident. Larry said god answered his hope. Larry said he placed his offerings upon the altar in exchange for luck with a kid. The monsignor showed up at the ball games mid-innings and after glad-handing the parents through a few strikeouts and base hits he easily vanished off the field with his chauffeur. But sad to say — sooner or later — we all took rides home with Larry. We answered his prayers. We sat on Larry's lap. When he parked underneath the railroad bridge at Crescent Street with some old trees making dreamy and creepy shadows beneath the streetlights — or when he bought ice cream at the take out window on Broadway and then quickly ducked off onto a sand road in the wetlands that end in cattails and weeds — we were alive — we took in his ugly breath with the Seven-up chaser — his cursed face and crying red stained eyes — we sat on his lap — we felt his essence — Larry the belly rubber — and then we stabbed him in the hand with a Bick pen.

George the cop got free hamburgers from the Frosty Top takeout window.

The president was always believed.

Fathers went to work. Mothers made babies. Kids sat in church pews.

God jerked a manifold hand inside the cat's cradle strings of government.

Euro life was heartbreaking simple and dutiful and was considered a privilege.

Until the new faces of the others arrived...

*

When was that moment?

*

It started out with small things. Name-calling: small events: that's how it started: that's where it started. Because Euro thinking was an everyday privilege and there were no lines to cross that weren't already defended before hand. Euro thinking said three boats came across the Atlantic and made life new here. But life was already here. Is that what we forget? Do we dare forget Euro thinking? And what it made us?

The slave ships only made it later...

Blind Charlie's relatives — the ancestors — they made land. They came over on those three ships. It was said in legend that the earth moved in the right direction once they arrived on shore. Legend said the ancestors spoke in the necessary tongue and were understood despite their swords that in effect spoke universally. Legend said the ancestors built the first communities in Jersey-land. They took over what were heedless and scatter-brained living hells — the camps — the pointed wooden fences around each camp — the sad fires cooking a rotten deer — the camps that had not yet imprisoned other camps — other camps stalking them — Blind Charlie's ancestors landed on shore and made this trouble their own. The ancestors fucked up the camps. Tore them up and tore up their ideas. They introduced a new word: crime. The ancestors — if you believe the legend — made this clear. What was wrong was a crime. And crime was not a sin. Because sin was hitched to a plow no one could handle… and the ancestors made this clear: they fucking plowed any field on the planet they wanted to…

*

But that was fucking history.

The ancestors knew it. Taking over real estate was their school in trade. And with cash and big hands they made communities.

By the time you were born — odd and city bred — you were a row house indifferent descendant called a Euro — neither visible nor vigilant — at home with allegiance inside shadows.

But there were lines to be crossed- and if you were careful- you crossed them. The scag money you made from the sad jobs you did was just another cover for heartbreaks. Any disrespect to the contrary was like an explanation spelled out for you that you sucked.

It was other people's money that mattered.

Why not if they had more money than you?

Columbus set sail upon a new ocean now didn't he?

*

You needed to originate somewhere but that was impossible — make yourself over but that was a laugh — you needed somewhere else other than the small believable street lines in the neighborhood.

You needed to go further than otherwise being a Euro.

It was especially easy to see that once the others moved in.

But this was the neighborhood. Row house after row house after row house built on tiny streets down to the sea and were plied atop each other like cracked ill-fitting puzzle pieces with bad foundations on one block and lousy roofs on another. This was the only home you knew. You came from the stars. Until that fabled day in ancestor prophecy — when the Atlantic was due.

*

Like the night Thaddeus — after an argument in the parking lot — was thrown into the plate glass window at the Ogontz Dinner. He landed on a table where a couple was enjoying a early breakfast after the bar hours closed. He took a sip of their coffee and looked at their plates and said he wished he had scrambled eggs earlier instead of eggs over easy. He then went back out into the parking lot to fight.

Like Bootsie one evening — waiting at the corner for the crowd to show — and was sitting in his tricked out convertible Ford with the radio loud and smoking a joint — hanging out doing nothing getting high — then he was sneaked. He got hit in the face with a radio antenna. And before he knew it the car of his life — his tricked out Ford- was stomped to death by others with hammers and tire irons. Before it was done he got off a few shots. He hit a few others. He needed seventeen stitches. Two days later he was back standing on the corner.

Like Bobby Alfredo — he ruled 66th and 20^{h} — this was just another foolish angle that made concrete neighborhoods linked to one another. Not much to brag about. But 66th and 20th was run by Bobbie. Bart's Radioactive Sandwich Shop made killer cheesesteaks with soda refills and sponsored a decent softball team over at the schoolyard. When he woke up in the hospital — after a fractured eye socket and a broken collarbone — the first thing Bobbie Alfredo asked was: did I take one with me?

*

Trouble started so easily that you couldn't hold it down. You said that with imagination and imagination was the scatter from the sky — the marshal in mind — the ally you had. You told Blind Charlie so and said you did not like it. Trouble made running the errands difficult you said. Everybody sees... everybody wants... everybody touches you ...

Blind Charlie said relax and forget it. Life was simple. You want a crowd? We have the best cousins. They watch your back. And anyone was watching them ... well like I said that's a simple matter.

No you said. You don't understand. I hear footsteps. On every street there's an echo and that becomes more and more... and whatever that is — no matter where I'm walking I feel that. And that echo... it scares hell out of me.

You want a ride then Blind Charlie asked?

No it's not that you said. I'm feeling like a window about to get broken.

No Blind Charlie said that's not it. His old guy smile was tough to resist. You're just starting out he said. You need some time to figure a few things.

What things you asked?

The kinds of things Blind Charlie said that make you smart. We like smart he said reaching forward and grasping your wrist.

Blind Charlie was an intimate man. He grabbed you strong enough to shrink your face and bring your expressions close up in a room. His creaky eyes — dead since birth — shy and native and calling out — tore down the darkness — between a sightless condition he owned and a crazy insight that spelled out and mapped the shadows — his eyes never let you go. When you were in Blind Charlie's eyes you were the vinegar and he was the olive oil.

Better to have a salad than not you thought.

Blind Charlie's eyes made DNA work like a troop. A hot mix — his eyes were performance-enhancing drugs and the terror of a song you heard in a language beyond your own strut and cram.

We like a guy who knows how to bargain with a double-headed nickel.

What's that you asked?

It's a deal we like to make he said. Depending on who the client is or course he responded. So here's the skinny. We turn over the pocket and get paid for our stuff. The deal goes well. Nobody got hurt. What's better? Happiness is in the air. But then you turn around and rob the other bastard you just made the deal with. Whatever that takes to make it happen — that's was what you need to do. There's your answer. No more footsteps. No windows broken. Easy right?

*

Mister Butler saw it different. He lived on lower Avenue S toward Broadway near exit 89. From his third story attic window he watched the AC Parkway travel night and day north and south.

Mister Butler blamed everyone.

He blamed the Euros for fleeing the neighborhood.

He blamed the doom beards. He blamed religion books for importing a thousand-year-old feud to Jersey-land land. And then setting up shop next to one another in the neighborhood as though they came across wide ocean travels for no other plausible reason than to continue a thousand-year-old feud in a different place.

Mister Butler blamed god-fearing people.

Mister Butler blamed himself for fighting in that war.

He blamed the lost refugees for not staying with the fight after he left.

Mister Butler was shot a few times and he killed a few times. He was a natural fuck and blessed by a soul he briefly knew but that effect was now gone and walked out the door a longtime ago.

Mister Butler worked for Blind Charlie.

Explain liberty to me he asked the paperboy every day. And then without getting a satisfied answer he pressed a dollar in the kid's palm every day.

*

It's a head thing Reds said.

A Leeche brother — maybe it was Howard or Manny or the shoe

man — or any of the others brothers whose appearances were remarkably similar — similar to themselves as family resemblance can be — they also took on a certain look-a-like quality as to the car accidents they pounded and sanded back into road shape. It said Manny on his overalls and he wanted to know what we wanted.

Constant greasy noise and pneumatic whirring floated out of the garage. A monster tow truck wrecker was parked outside on the titled driveway: the words Collision Specialists and a phone number were painted on the cab doors with swirling flames for emphasis. A car honked and car brakes followed on Avenue S. Manny the Leeche Brother looked up from his carbon monoxide reverie like a surgeon responding to a hospital code. Painted in oil- resting his chin on the palm of his hand- elbow waiting on a stack of tires- smoking a cigarette and getting some fresh air- serenely inspecting the harvest of junks and mishaps that were all his- Manny the Leeche Brother had the look of a man with money in the bank and an everyday case of beer waiting for him at home

Hey man excuse me Reds said.

Manny turned patiently around and faced Reds. Do something for you he asked?

Yea Red's said. My father's car died last night. Maybe the battery or the starter I don't know… The old man wants you to haul it down here and take a look.

Want it done today Manny asked? He couldn't look more annoyed at having something else to do and needing to do it late in the day.

Fuck yes Reds said.

Manny turned his eyes all over Reds. I know you he said. Don't you ever curse me again Manny said. You learn some manners. You follow me. Boy.

Yea Reds said. I follow. It's on Tulpohocken. White Oldsmobile. Think you can do it today Reds asked? His tone was suddenly less demanding now that the Leeche Brother stared him in two.

We'll get it this evening Manny said. What's the name this time?

Terry Baker. Number's in the book Reds said.

Somebody yelled from inside the garage- and Manny nodded and faded away back to work where a smashed Buick Skylark required his transforming touch.

You laughed to yourself. It was the name — Terry Baker that was funny.

Terry Baker was the name everybody used when they found themselves in a situation where giving out their real name was highly inappropriate. Like if the police stopped you after curfew- then you were Terry Baker. If you were caught shoplifting- then you were Terry Baker. Anyone asking question about who threw the eggs at the trolley — well you said Terry Baker did it. And this was quite unfair since Terry Baker was an actual kid in the eighth grade and not just an alias a dozen other kids used to cover their butts. You're not sure how Terry Baker got into all this trouble that he never created. But somehow it became an established practice. And therefore it was gospel because everybody did it.

Terry Baker was known as chicken chest. That was because Terry had a collapsed sternum or some shit. It was like a birth defect — and birth defects were big — they were the ultimate excuse for the family if a kid ended up being ugly. Kids came up to Terry Baker and hit him in the chest with a backhand slap and yelled chicken chest in his face.

It was like there was a hole where his chest should have been.

Every time he got hit in the chest you tried to imagine Terry Baker and his looking at his x-rays for the first time. A doctor even- once told him- you have a chicken chest.

Terry Baker said it didn't worry him. What he said was the whole fucking chicken chest thing made him mad. Like he said I got no personal view and got robbed out of that he said with the fucking chicken chest thing when I was born…

 Yea it was strange you once said.

And the fucked thing was — that when you took time aside with Terry Baker and hung out with him — he started to giggle no matter what and would not stop — until he was smacked in the chest.

Terry Baker smoked cigarettes by the plantation.

He was fucking his older sister Ronnie.

He said he longed for cancer because at least the packages were cool.

Terry decided one day he and Ronnie would get married.

What happens when there's no white Oldsmobile you asked?

There is Reds replied pointing his cigarette at you and using it as an exclamation point.

Whose is it?

How the hell should I know?

Reds had a habit when he was impatient. Not only would he snort some crystal to exaggerate the point but also he'd look at you like you were the stupidest participant on earth. His eyes got dark while he stared you over and then got excited while he shook his head. Look he said I already stole the radio. I got it last night. These fucks are just taking it off the street. And removing it — he said –from the scene of the crime.

That's stupid you said mostly because you didn't like crystal. What does it matter where the car was?

There are things you will never understand Reds said. But you are right– one thing that does not matter is this: where the car was.

The crystal made your eyeballs funny. What's up then with it you asked?

What's up Reds said lighting another smoke — what's up was that I got these guys to do what I told them to do.

Just to steal a radio you asked?

Yea he said. His eyes were blazing. And to a degree they shut you off from looking back at him. You imagined lightning on the ocean. How that flash shocked the water and you then saw ghost shapes reaching beyond the horizon line. You saw campfires lost in the early morning before the cops drove up a wetland road to scatter the party and then big criminal flashlights digging for kids in the rustle and weeds– yea he said just to steal a radio.

Reds you said how much did you get for that radio?

What does that matter for he asked?

Well you said — there's trouble — but for what?

Cousin Jimmy tightens me up.

You tried to calculate the value from a stolen car radio in the neighborhood — ten bucks?

Listen drifty he said — indicating we split Leceche Brothers Automotive Shop — what was it you need to get?

*

the coffee meditations

That was true.

You didn't know what it was to get what it was that you wanted.

You go with what you know Cousin Jimmy knows Reds said.

That was true. But regardless you had to wonder.

*

Reds had pressures. He lived in a big Euro family and was the eldest son. They settled in Jersey-land and were expected to ape the old country onto a new address. The ancestors loved to talk. That was expected in a way to settle in. You talked and therefore you made a lousy apartment building a home. And being young- it was our job to listen. The ancestors coaxed stories from history and made bread rise from the jive pulled from memory. If Pi and it's repeating answer/non -answer number was a science way to look at infinity then the ancestors on feast days told their stories across neighborhood parties.

But talk stood in the years without a chance- because nobody young shouldered what that talk meant and so in consequence that talk stood lonely as an old man at the trolley stop while the years went on behind him.

Reds was expected to provide.

Not his job he once said confidentially to a priest. And after confession he left the booth and forgot penance and robbed the poor box for whatever sad holy change had settled there.

Three brothers — at least they learned to steal and brought something home before they blew it away on candy or skin books — a young sister growing up nicely — well nobody talked about that yet — and Cousin Jimmy taking up bed space and bad nods — he knew he was a bastard — But he was a head before his time — and so knowing he was a trickle of water in the blood of family Cousin Jimmy had skills — good cash — meat — cigarettes. Reds said family was like you smiled while you lied...

*

Later on you'll understand: That's what the parents said: when they got drunk together and alcohol content was passed on as wisdom to the kids.

*

But behind the grins of family were the tight lips of family. And behind those tight lips there was the William Abbey family. What they held common was a simple notion — dead on the ground as it was in the sky. There was something to desire. Why settle for less?

And what you desired might not be there a minute later after you wanted it. Like a peanut butter jelly sandwich — as soon as Reds made one — if he blinked and looked at the television — that sandwich was gone — and a blessed sibling was eating it. Or there was no bread left... or the peanut butter was scraped to the end... Or there was no respect left because a filthy knife was left in the grape jelly and that jar sat on the kitchen counter for days without anyone paying it a mind...

*

Cousin Jimmy asked what do you want for the radio?

Reds had his ten bucks and his invisible smile.

Cousin Jimmy was stuck. Because the radio was shit — impractically dented from impatient prying — shredded wires from impatience — but because Reds was water in his veins — because decent money was hard to come by he paid decent money for shit. Cousin Jimmy took the radio and paid Reds the cash. They were both down the yellow brick road together — delusional — fools — and strange kin.

201

Reds' old man was a long-haul driver. He drove trucks since he was a boy. And he paid his money upward. Any truck that was built then William drove it. Violent to the cause and loyal to the union — he once broke a cop's knee with his sawed-off Louisville Slugger during a riot over wages.

He made money. Good money for the years he put in. William took home a healthy check for his runs and his back-hauls. But William Abbey also sought opportunities. Who didn't want to make a little strange? Because he loved money… that's why…didn't matter if the money was crisp or wrinkled- just as long as Mr. Washington's portrait was printed on the bills.

So he back-hauled freight for cash on the side.

That was stupid business. Crossing the bosses was hands down dumb. But William Abbey loved money.

On the legit he was already hauling wire rope spools. But those spools were special. They belonged. And were built to conceal thousands of pounds of dope on each run.

William did not care for dope. William loved money. Dope was crass. Dope was useful in bargains when you did not have money and was an excellent solution for moving assholes away. Money was like digging all the radio stations William found while driving. A big country meant a lot of radio stations. That was money. Dope was like being fixated on a song you heard in Ohio and then being lonely for a couple days before you found it again on the airwaves in Utah. Or not.

What mattered — what created endeavors from shit-headed mistakes — was honesty.

William loved money.

The bosses knew that.

So that day when William was called into Blind Charlie's back room

— William Abbey was lined with money. Money to kingdom come — money left in the sallow rings of business where life crossed over a line and met death in a fact of manners — or it was just money — a money that looked sadly like someone who looked like William Abbey.

What the fuck do you think this is Bobby Alfredo asked?

William politely set bands of thousands and thousands on the table and stepped away.

The beefy cousins were silent against the walls. They grinned though their stiff held teeth like a holy order of reptiles about to feed. The beefy cousins — decent ordinary guys on the softball diamond — but when they were in Blind Charlie's back room they came into that back room with a single mind and a purpose and no funny business.

What Bobby Alfredo asked again. This is what — stealing you dumb fuck he said and shook his head side to side in cigar smoke and bewilderment.

No you're right William Abbey said.

I'm right? — I'm right? — Bobby Alfredo asked. Then tell me what the fuck is wrong with what the fuck I'm seeing here?

Another cousin raised his fingers. He wiggled them like he scratched the air and wanted his fingers inside somebody's ass.

The beefy cousins took a step forward.

William Abbey put out his arms against the beefy cousins and asked — what does happen when you lie? Do you say sorry? Do you try and talk your sorry way out of it? Well no then. I'm not sorry William Abbey said. The money — any money — was there because it had to be there. I took the money. Anybody in this room admit otherwise?

We don't address that Bobby Alfredo said.

Yea William thought.

Enough! Blind Charlie pounded a single fist on the table. The back room sucked itself into a silence that made a monastery seem like a mosh pit.

He reached over to the table. He picked up the thousands that William Abbey left. Blind Charlie weighed the money in his palms and nodded. It's money he said. A beefy cousin stepped forward but Blind Charlie waved him back.

However Blind Charlie said — and while I have my opinions he mused — let me ask you this William — and take your time — consider your answer carefully — we never know what's in the cards do we– so tell me — why is this money on the table?

William nodded toward Blind Charlie.

*

Forget the cousins he thought. The bosses were false magnitudes. They lacked posture. Except for Bobby Alfredo. Because it was common cause that Bobby Alfredo was dangerous. He was a guy to avoid. But Bobby Alfredo was also someone who carried friends and enemies alike and so Bobby Alfredo was like a psycho and so you had to catch Bobby Alfredo on a good day to insure that time was not wasted.

William held up his open left hand as a gesture of peace.

But Blind Charlie was the odd infinitum — to infinity or forever more — and to William Abbey that meant Blind Charlie begged no questions and held business to no steady answers. And to William that was why Blind Charlie was more than somebody's escort showing them to an alley where they were about to be killed.

Why — Blind Charlie asked again — is this money on the table? We can all be patient here. If you look out that small window he said that's the night. But really William — let's move on. People have families. People have obligations. Damn it Blind Charlie said! I got pizza orders backed up in the front… I only got two guys on the door… but what I don't have from you William is your explanation.

Blind Charlie took a stack of thousands and tossed it over his shoulder.

Because I stole it William said. He felt great. William loved money.

William — Blind Charlie said — his false eyes shadowed the room — honesty and the dammed Blind Charlie thought — his eyes said William — everybody Blind Charlie knew always needed a little extra — William he said loudly — Blind Charlie's voice rose in octaves — like those opera records he loved — so William he said: why is this money on my table?

Well William said I stole it.

Blind Charlie was disgusted. You might as well praise the thief as to stab him in the back.

That's been established he noted with his thick dark glasses. Being sightless — fuck you William Blind Charlie thought — it was first choice or last resort…. We need to know why you stole it William.

William I understand the difficulty Blind Charlie said. I understand. But explain to me — William you listen to me and you explain to me … William you listen to me and explain to me… and don't give me big questions to a small answer … don't tell me you wanted a little strange… don't tell me William — this was money — and that's why.

William Abbey looked Blind Charlie in his dark glasses and said: I wanted to be satisfied.

Fuck this Bobby Alfredo said. There's a shit can outside with William's name on it.

Blind Charlie sliced the air at table level and the back room went silent again. Bobby has a legit point he said to William.

William smiled. He asked for a drink. Was there any pizza he wondered?

You know he said there's a lot of side money being made in the shadows. But yea he said who in this room doesn't know that? When's the last time you never scammed a driver? And there's a shit can outside with my name on it? William downed his drink and wanted another. Blind Charlie poured him three fingers and then added a fourth and said go on William.

Honesty. That's what William Abbey said. He looked around the table and crossed eyes with everyone there. For emphasis — for backbone — for William himself and his love for drinking — he knocked back his drink and slammed the glass on the table. He indicated he wanted another.

And so what Bobby Alfredo asked?

What matters? What matters? Don't you have any idea? Any idea how fucking nuts you sound? Do you know how many drivers you have? You don't even know the fucking answer do you? Do you? You can't even begin the count. Employee's right? Your minds are so fucked up…

Blind Charlie interrupted. He said — my mind William — is hardly fucked up.

What matters are these William said. He laid a hatch of paperwork on the table. He finished up his last slice and felt immediately like heaven.

The cousins gathered around.

This is not good Blind Charlie said.

What these are William Abbey said are fucking evidence. By now he was drunk. He loved that. And he loved money. He also loved to stagger when he was drunk. William Abbey knew love.

Go on Bobby Alfredo said. He was a little testy because William was one of his drivers. He thought — what — twenty-five fucking years? He thought you accumulate a lot of shit over that length of time. He thought if there was anything bad then he'd shoot him in the head and presto no more William Abbey. That was easy. And Bobby Alfredo liked easy.

How much side money can you imagine? Think about a figure. All right you got one? Well you're wrong. You're so fucking wrong William said. How the fuck do you know what's going on? You're a bunch of table-siting assholes. Been out on the road lately? And guess how much money in a day gets dealt behind your back? So that's why the cash is there. Hey can I get three more fingers? Thank you. And yea I took dark money for bogus back hauls. But that's how fucking stupid you are. What you got on the table are the profits I took in. Cash in hand and no questions. I paid my expenses.

Blind Charlie told a beefy cousin to count the money. And then have somebody else count it again. The beefy cousins weren't exactly scholars but they knew how to count money.

Eighty nine thousand seven hundred and forty eight dollars was the reply.

Verified was the other reply.

So Bobby Alfredo said what you're feeling guilty? Maybe you skimmed double that and now you're all confessional because you want off and need to stay alive?

William Abbey laughed. He was drunk. He loved money.

So what do we have here Blind Charlie asked?

Numbers William said. And that here — was the money you never got to see. So what you got were fake invoices and bad runs. Yea I did the runs. And yea I put the money in my pocket. What I got you though were cell numbers and warehouse addresses and guys' faces. Whoa don't you see what you should see? What you're looking at on the table are your total losses the past three months.

Blind Charlie had a beefy cousin scan the papers.

And so Blind Charlie asked…. The unfinished thought stuck in the air like a dart…

Yea Bobby Alfredo said what the fuck is it that you want?

Honesty William Abbey answered.

Blind Charlie was puzzled. He looked at William as though… He cocked his head as though… He kept thinking as though… and kept looking over William as though… Why not keep the money he asked? You keep your mouth shut and stay out of trouble and you have a payday on us. And how do we know? A beefy cousin was now standing behind Blind Charlie.

You want honesty? That's fucking absurd Bobby Alfredo said and laughed himself into a fit chocking on the question.

On Blind Charlie's nod another beefy cousin placed a light hand on Bobby Alfredo's shoulder.

Yea honesty William answered again wiping tomato sauce from his mouth with a fine paper napkin.

He stared across the table at Bobby Alfredo and understood — from the beginning of time he got — when William first began driving long haul to satisfy someone else and bring home somebody else's money — that Bobby and his clam's linguine grin was not a person you picked on to fuck with.

He turned his gaze toward Blind Charlie and met him in the eyes.

William took another slice. Best fucking pizza he said — now here you got honesty — honesty in a slice — what's more simple — best fucking pizza he said again. And not a shit can with a hole in my head.

William Abbey loved money.

And he especially loved three more fingers.

William Abbey loved it when he was drunk. He loved to stagger out a door and try and negotiate the way home with the pavement rolling beneath his feet.

He loved it when he was right.

William looked to Blind Charlie. A good man he thought is hard to find.

I stole the money. I stole the money because I could. Because I fucked over those other guys I stole the money because I like stealing. I stole the money because I like how money feels. I stole the money to give it back. I don't steal from you. I don't steal from Bobby. I don't steal from any guy here. I stole the money because it was like a fucking trance. I stole the money to be fatal and see what that was like. I stole the money because I knew we all would have this conversation. That's why you steal. To have money is why you steal. Is there another reason? I stole the money to be a big shot. I stole the money because I wouldn't spend it. I stole the money because one day my kid asked: what's a quandary? I stole the money...

Other than that William Abbey loved driving. He loved gears that worked. He loved weather conditions. He loved those beautiful truck stop breakfasts where after driving through the night he pulled the rig into some fucked up place in the desert and relaxed in strange landscapes and local accents that he feared. Skinny lonely waitresses brought him coffee eggs bacon and a toasted English muffin with salted butter and white cheese slices on the side. Didn't matter to William. He was where he was because he loved to drive.

William Abbey loved money.

*

Making ends meet was like double clutching a tired rig up a hill William Abbey said to Eleanor.

No other family you knew had the wants that the Abbey Kids wanted.

You're no fool for Shakespeare pops Edsel the youngest in the brood said.

*

Eleanor Abbey loved detective magazines. She subscribed to Real True Felony and Naked Rough Life. During the daytime she positioned her chair to face the front windows and look over 65th St. Entertaining herself with the skillful details over unsolved rape cases and intriguing double murders- Eleanor dropped her focus from anything complicated. And so allowed only a single weightless vision of herself that was measured by one page at a time. One page at a time — that was all she needed. All she needed for herself was one page at a time. And by then

— one page at a time — a page in time — that was who Eleanor was she thought. She blow out smoke rings and nibbled on Tasty-Cakes. The living room ceiling was cracked and started to fall in small plaster droppings across the living room floor. Eleanor flipped a page. She couldn't be more happy. Like when the investigators in the June issue found the head in question floating down river toward the falls before it went over and was spun beneath the churn and whatever was left the fish picked the skull clean etc. Eleanor Abbey had a sense for these kinds of things — like where a severed head goes etc.

*

No cleaning the house. No making food. No common language used in big family habits. No religious unit. No dumb thought-out knots about growing old. No geometry of feelings to sort through. No exponential change in awareness. Eleanor Abbey lost track. Some mayor in Toledo was gone. The Tasty-Cakes were gone. Eleanor saw how perfect her smoke rings were formed. It was a fistfight that did the mayor in… a domestic argument that turned bad… his lover broke the Mayor's jaw… but what happened to the lover… To be continued…

*

Eleanor still wore the alligator slippers. William bought them for her. And ever since he always felt good about doing that and smiled when she wore them at home.

They were driving down Florida and were on their way back north to pick up the back haul when Eleanor suddenly said stop. William pulled the rig over. Nothing but fucking swamp he thought. She jumped out of the truck and ran back to a native flea market. William Abbey bought alligator slippers and an alligator ashtray and a cheap print with an alligator's large nasty jaw set against a golden Everglades sunset. Eleanor was happy.

William freaked with the landscape. It covered too much ground he thought. There was no space between for anything he could see. The deep swamp green vegetation grew out against his vision. If he looked at it in one place for too long it began to grow further. Mossy fingers fell from trees and grabbed below for anything that was lost. William Abbey was overwhelmed. There was no green like that on earth he thought.

*

William drove as an independent trucker back then. He ran the east coast with the sweetest rig a guy ever laid hands on. He proposed to Eleanor much the same way. A sweet rig she asked? When she was nineteen William flattered her with candy bars and diner food meals and that special soap that he got in tiny samples from motels along 95 in South Carolina. Things took awhile — but then Eleanor never hesitated once she got her bearing. A guy's attention... a guy's rig... a guy's good money... Everything in Eleanor's mind said climb aboard... imagine a poor gal from Stenton Avenue and 21ˢᵗ Street ... and now she was driving through Gettysburg and Richmond and Atlanta... blowing the air horn and laying it thick against passenger cars travelling below them and she was married with no real home but the truck ... William Abbey drove for hours at a time but he always took the time to look across the cab at Eleanor with a dog lust in his eyes... she laughed when she saw it and when she saw that look she cracked him across his face. William Abbey was in love. Eleanor knew that. She loved William. And she knew... she was a cut above the rest. And that William deserved that sweet point of being. Savannah. Air horn... Eleanor loved that...

*

Daytona was a favorite spot for her on the runs. Eleanor thought Daytona was like a person. Yea it was a speed car race. But what happened she thought was hidden. Like a center inside yourself? But one that placed anxieties elsewhere? Like who explains themselves proper? Daytona was a human being she said.

And so she said to herself that's not a problem — pulling a deep one off the flask — leaning against the shiny chrome fender and rolling a joint — pulling another deep one off the flask.

Daytona she thought spelled out drunks who danced for days. Daytona spoke confederate whispers in a girl's ear. And a girl might be a fool if she if didn't listen to the twang and bang coming on in a different language than back home up north. One evening they pulled up to the Alabama coast. William said c'mon and jumped down from the cab. He ran down to the water's edge and rolled his pants up to the knee and waded in the low surf. He splashed gulf water into the air bathing himself after a fucked and grueling run from Vegas. He yelled c'mon c'mon c'mon! But Eleanor didn't want to go up to her knees and stop there. So she got out the big knife from under the seat and cut her jeans into shorts. Soon she was overwhelmed and floated in the warm salt water off some place she didn't know called Mobile. She remembered William Abbey and how delightful he was when finally the rig was parked. You want crab legs or oysters he called?

*

Eleanor loved those shorts.

She loved the gals in the midway. Without even understanding it- her shorts were almost marks for theirs.

But those gals were professionals. They got paid to hold advertising signs and wiggle their tops. And after each lap was finished the gals exhibited hot crotch gestures to suggest this race ain't over yet...

Her frayed shorts were a touch away from reaching her hips... Just like them professional gals... She imagined what it must be like...standing in the midway with thousands in the stands cheering and watching her ass...

*

The funny business... the monkey grin before sleep assimilated you into your husband's arms... the morning dove's coo if no one bailed but she knew... despite the pleasures and the madness and the long swim back from blankness ...the purpose to hold onto love and what your own instincts were within another's body once daylight warmed the cab… and she feared to let that someone go… But Eleanor woke up and went out and got coffee.

Sex was like being left outin salt water then afterwards taking a fresh water indoor shower… the cosmic afterword felt clean … you flew in the stars… drank whiskey in old familiar alleys… ducked beneath the long waterfall back in northwest Jersey-land … smoked beneath the covers… hit it big in a card game… traded jokes with obvious criminal elements on a shady dock in Delaware… made money like sex made love … ate Chinese take-out food on the road… listened to barbeque music on the pod with sweet and separate headphones… had no fear of hell… at least that's what she called in during a radio preacher's show and for her effort the preacher told here Eleanor was forgiven and was allowed god's grace in return… no turning back Eleanor said to William…let's get north.

*

Eleanor met a pit crew guy the night before the 500. He was decent enough and somewhat good looking and seemed like he had a kind head. And so underneath the stands they made racetrack angels together again and again until daylight when the wheeze and purr from rhythm and fucking spoke out against them.

Cousin Jimmy then floated back in time from the bardo to catch a ride north.

*

William didn't much matter about it. But he was empathic about one thing: he told Eleanor: Cousin Jimmy would never be called son.

*

William and Eleanor were married outside Baltimore on a freeway overpass. The reverend was a trucker/justice of the peace whom William knew and who happened to be only a few miles south on the radio. They stood against the guardrails holding hands. Cars zipped by above the speed limit like cartoons and gunned against competitors for a lane close to their exit. Below them a freight train rattled. A giant excavator was busy tearing into a row house block and exterminating old brick houses. Eleanor and William stood against the guardrails holding hands. The reverend asked if they wanted a bible? If not he said- it didn't matter. Whether or not if you invoked the divine or not he said the service was the same price for both. He looked at William and said no discounts for the secular. They all shared a flask. Before the ceremony they all stood as one and watched over themselves as one and drained another flask as one. Eleanor said I need to cry. William said I need to pee. The reverend said I need to get back on the road. William and Eleanor stood against the guardrails holding hands. The reverend said you both hold the future in your hands. Eleanor and William looked at each other and floated on their wedding kiss. Then turning around to the reverend they both gave him the finger. Bless you all the reverend said laughing. He climbed into his rig and hauled off. Miles up the highway — toward the way home — on the radio — just before cutting off Philadelphia and crashing the bad bridges over to Jersey-land — William and Eleanor heard the reverend on the radio — and whatever he said they hauled on north.

*

faster than gravity

Reds laughed. It was crazy and high pitched like his younger brother Edsel. When the time comes it'll be me that fills in the blanks he said.

Yea Cripple said its cash makes the most

Ain't that right Mister Charlie — you banking on us right — I mean to get outright?

Reds said I don't have to pimp no ride because I got my own. I see it written he said. All I gotta do is step in and the rest is mine.

Blind Charlie sat listening and smiling. Outwardly he possessed a quality of patience. He never raised his shoulders. Nor did he ever cock his head. If he didn't have people killed for a living — and if he didn't run cash past local state and the feds — you imagined Blind Charlie to be some usual second-rate guy. A guy you hung with for an afternoon and shot the breeze. All day he sat in an old chair and read. All day he spoke to his old dog and the old dog nodded. And all day constant deals passed through his say-so…

There's too many things for certain he said. But before they happen — that requires a skill. You boys ready for that?

Cripple wrinkled up his acne. He scowled at the air he was breathing.

Good thing you were in a corner because you started to fall away into the soft distance. Who cared? And if so why care about who cared? Wasn't this all just a tangle to fuck you up and leave you twisted and frightened in the spider webs of the world?

Outside the back room in the pizza shop a radio played music while the ovens were turned down and the floor was mopped up after the dinner crowd left…

Maybe you should stay in the neighborhood forever and bring people music from unexpected places... music and pizza and golden fried fish and clean their windows each day... Maybe you see Eden tonight but you know that's a mistake but maybe that's what makes it right... a breakdown of nature... all that stuff of truth and that's what you want but it makes you see and hear things slightly false... Maybe there was nothing more real than Eden... and thinking about Eden made your insides feel like untied shoelaces... Maybe if you stayed in the neighborhood forever Eden will be the girl in the music... and while you liked the idea that you vanished without notice there will also be a tomorrow in the neighborhood... Fuck this growing up. It ghosted you.

You went over to another bottle and uncorked it. The radio music played on.

*

the coffee meditations

In the dream a woman wades into the surf with all her clothes on. She looks back at you and the raven- haired woman and says — her words are not voiced but spelled out and rise against the horizon in text in cartoon bubbles — it's not the question and it's not the answer. There's something in between...we look at one another and our voices become the same cartoon bubbles. Nothing could be better. Daylight fading. You look at the raven -haired woman and the cartoon above you says you driving me delightfully mad with love. Planets appear in the evening sky. Her cartoon says is time an orbit? We eat fish from the sea. Drink wine pressed from the earth. Stars rush from the darkness. Our breathing stops together at exactly the same moment. Crickets come alive in the dunes nocturnal and intimate with the darkness gathering about an orbit.

*

We claimed a favorite spot in the dunes where we were born. Beside the Atlantic was a place and that was embryonic to our brains. Calm warm morning in late summer... we watched a lone guy swimming in the low tides. The cold water got the better of him and he gave up and went for a towel.

We had the requisite large coffee bringing our tired muscles around to face the day. The sun rose bright red once more in perfect equilibrium-with you to see it and the Atlantic to hold it with us together. A thought settled in your head — you loved the Atlantic Ocean.

Why? Why not? You searched the memory banks. Why the word

Atlantic had standing. Not that you come up empty but the favorable response was haven't we lived here before? What slice of all the days was present when we sat in the dunes? A dark glossy seal floated lazily over small waves and soothing star drenched waters. The raven-haired woman kept her best face into the wind. This was her birthright also. Together we own this you said. She nodded and pulled closer inside her hoodie.

But something beyond — beyond you — beyond you and beyond her — beyond our years with our backs leaned into the newly planted sand grass — beyond the slap of the tides we felt some elementary thing — centuries that were elements and why those centuries captured us as elements and brought us together like a chemistry experiment. Like love came from nowhere and that blindside always killed you.

Was that because you were born? Born at the ocean? Born at a time? There was no answer.

But for now the Atlantic was enough. The Atlantic took our breath away. We held on together despite the warp of the years.

Wordless understanding passed between us. Gulls fought over a dead crab. The swimmer left. The beach was deserted.

Atmospheres overwhelmed you.

There must be music or a breeze or a condition to make this moment come from nowhere. We were lost in curiosity. Had been all our lives. Why was lovemaking like a candle?

*

faster than gravity

You rushed out the house after breakfast. You waved goodbye to your mother. She sat in her everyday chair. She read the newspaper. She listened to dead news on an old transistor radio before afternoon at the opera began. And then she stayed transfixed for two hours without worry — without concentration — she sat and listened without interference — it was sweet she said — the opera she said emptied her brain.

Would we ever buy a new one? Or would that be the only radio we ever had?

In the sky above Avenue C. a cloud floated in October blue.

Across Avenue C. Father Grababoy was opening the church. You slid past trying to be unnoticed. The church was always locked up. Sad wasn't it? The church had been robbed so many times that it now was only open at dedicated hours. How much money was there to steal from the poor box anyway? And what about somebody who needed a church but couldn't get in because it was locked?

But today Father Grababoy was out early.

And you lived across Avenue C from the church. Your house fronted the rectory across Avenue C. You looked across Avenue C onto Father Grababoy's window.

How bad was that?

Honestly you knew how bad it was. It was like living across the street form a nightmare.

Father Grababoy had no magic. He went through puzzle marks in his sermons like he couldn't handle the words without dropping them. He stumbled into infinity like a goddamn rookie that couldn't pull it home.

And all those questions from the faithful — whatever faithful was left — and those were mostly the real old Euros who still prayed together in common — but their age and the new world added up — and in a manner of speaking they might be dead following the service. Father Grababoy feared those questions. He had no answers. So he double-talked then off with god-saying things. God saying bromides that meant nothing but they were reliable with old people. Faith took more effort than the day's walk etc. Father Grababoy ended his sermon especially lost and disconnected from the pews. Because he knew what it was and how it was done. But he did not know what it was really… And what he did not know — that was exactly what he needed.

Who the fuck were these people?

Each Sunday — each sermon — Farther Grababoy — stage fright — fucking please — he balked — fucking please — he searched his passion — fucking please — Father Grababoy trembled at the altar — he had nothing to say — no belief — each Sunday — his head was low and cradled among his colorless protracted fingers — each Sunday — fucking please he prayed but how was he praying he thought it was a fake he thought it was fake it till you make an offer — I have nothing to say fronted his mind…

Back in the pews the old Euros watched — crippled by silence — and they fingered rosary beads like money clips — a devotion and a longing for a touch of the divine to finally steady their lives.

What was real he thought but he understood how bogus that thought was — then — each Sunday — fucking please — I heard a voice crying in the wilderness — each Sunday — then it was up to him fucking please …

Father Grababoy tossed the microphone over his shoulder. When it hit the cold stone floor noisy feedback jumped out and wailed electronically. Then Father Grababoy turned and faced the congregation. He kicked the microphone. More noise and feedback filled another church gathering he thought. Maybe he thought it was nothing other than just fucking please — some — some each Sunday to come — no belief — he searched his passion and fucking please — he stomped the microphone

into parts. Very polished marble and anodyne statues that were important enough to be murdered and transformed into saints lined the sanctuary like eyeless dins on some cultish yellow brick road. The old Euros
never understood this. What was with the microphone? But they were
told it was his way. Father Grababoy's way to chase away new demons.
The church bells always rang on the hour.

I heard a voice crying in the wilderness. I am that voice he said. And
you are that wilderness he said… fucking please he thought… but it was
each Sunday he thought and fucking please he thought… but it was his
job to need that trouble each Sunday.

Who can tell me what sin is he shouted!

*

But today he was early opening the church doors.

You wondered maybe Father Grababoy had something to get off
his chest? Did he need some confessional time for himself? So that was
puzzling. Why go through the trouble? Why become a priest? Why join
up with the legions of god when inside you had a knack for sin anyway?

And did those sins — a priest's sins — what did they have in common
with the rest of us?

Did sin happen on a different level for a priest? Wouldn't the order of
things be screwed up?

Confessing sin was built firmly into our logic. Confessing sin was like
taking a good shit: you needed to do it and then get on with the rest of
the day. Twice a month we all went. Fuck we all shit more that that! But
we herded by god's fear into the confessional booths — to wipe the slate
clean — and in doing so were rewarded — for dumping sin –from first
dumping sin and then as you went further into the confessional process
to express sorrow — and from there — if the digital altered image on
the screen between you and god's stand in — if the priest with his phone
connection to the heavens — with your own heart felt declarations of
shame — then you got goodness in kind for a bargain — you were dealt
a handful of prayers to say out loud in public — and while kneeling in
public then everyone in the church knew you had dirt on your soul —

and it was only afterwards — rising off your knees -- walking down the main aisle like you were pious — inside you were conflicted like why did it matter — did it mean something — that through all this slight of hand and traditional folly — it seemed like you played the fool — and the shadow puppet in the confessional booth had all the say so…

It was so convoluted that it threw you for a laugh. Confessing sin was like watching bad wrestling on television before your father got home. After the day and humping the second shift when he caught the K-bus and rode home in his neuron-silence and three word crossword puzzles and with no peripheral looks he was enveloped by the scant hours of the morning where thieves worked and where whores were not yet satisfied. The moment you heard his key in the lock you disappeared. So before you confessed your sins you got stoned. At least that made sense. And waiting in the alley beside the church you thought it over. You pondered sin. But it didn't add up. You tried it but it didn't work. You smoked two joints. But still it did not work out. Confessing sin solved no x. And you wanted that x solved. You looked deep into the sky. And then you walked though the big wheezing doors of the church...

*

Reds looked back from the confessional altar. He stared at the parishioners. He flipped the bird.

*

Cripple dragged his bad leg from the confession booth up to the marble rail. Maybe his prayers might help augment his redemption once he got there. Who knew?

Hey yo Cripple yelled to the big statue … can I get a miracle down here!

*

Beyond the heavy polished balusters made from imported Italian marble — Blind Charlie made sure the church got a good deal — was the altar.

And the altar was like the street corner where god hung out. And it was there — at the marble rail — where the separation began. There were only manifests about god you thought. Exploits and protractions and quenched out explorations... giving you the business... getting your money's worth... And it all crammed your head like a suspect caught breaking and entering... Why didn't anybody jump the marble rail? Just get on the other side — take it in like some newbie wanna-be — hang out with god on his corner — and see if that felt crude or like illegal. Why didn't anybody jump that shit like we did the subway turnstile to get a free ride on the train?

*

And sinning was — mostly to get the point — sinning was what you believed in. Sinning was all the wonders you thought about in the future. Sinning was getting your hands buried in the warm dirt of experience. And the best part was — you didn't believe in sin.

Sin was another fucking identity- that somebody else- somebody else — somebody else away from you — somebody else gave you the model and the belief and the sign. It was like getting a cub scout uniform or getting a report card or getting a part time job bagging groceries...

Your suspicions were that sin was manufactured for many an alternate reason. But mostly your suspicions came down to a singular divide and that was the reason and that was a diversion for us to lose track of the marks of the sky.

*

All the punishments for sin that were handed out like candy only turned you around and left you inside out. And that was a cool feeling and never to be replaced. Frightening you with somebody else's demons- Father Grababoy to be exact — was a weak proof that the folly you knew refused to look tired and be dulled with life. How you gonna act? Maybe you wanted to believe? But probably not since belief required an equal merit in the art of how to be disillusioned and there was already enough of that by the time you reached twelve years old in that time...

(...There were demons sitting on car fenders on Avenue C that would stab you in the back for a dime and demons teaching geography in classrooms that cracked your skull for a wrong answer like Brazil's big export and demons making anti-cognition noises sitting across the aisles on the K-bus while you rode the line in silence and daydreams...) Ah...

And so what was the question?

Where you supposed to feel guilty?
There ain't no truck in that Reds said.
Anyone said different was looking to get paid Cripple said.

And since your brother was shipping out toward the latest Asian war in a few days did there seem no difference between the big statue and wanton killing? Wasn't that the biggie in play across thousands of years... not to kill? And so the message was die like me?
Trying to frighten your demons was useless.
There were too many loose ends.
But it hurt bring yelled at.
And when you looked at the question — where your own name made its own way —and you understood a dilettante like Father Grababoy needed likewise to hold his own — but his act was all big daddy thuggish and lost in the stars and was there just for show — like parsley on a plate of spaghetti at Da Vinci's pizza — as ever there was never a fucking answer to questions — only the dirty bliss — the rare dole — the jealousy — the spiritual pants — the god damn ramparts daring you to cross over — but in all that belief — you finally got it — there was no belief — there were no fucking answers you saw.
So why make the effort to save an illusion?

*

And so you wondered how lost was Father Grababoy?
He stepped into the church. From across Avenue C he looked weary

and drawn out. The heavy wooden door with its opaque glass blocks and barricaded air swung closed behind him. You really needed some muscle to open that door. Why was it so heavy? You really had to pull at the thing to get it to open. Sometimes the older Euros in the parish barely had the arm strength to budge the damn thing. The door would open only so far — one arm pulling and the other arm braced against the wall in opposition — then both arms weakened and the door and its inertia took over and closed in their face. They had to let it go. Or else the door dragged them along to where it rested back against its casing with a soft thud. Wasn't it strange that a church door into the house of god required such force to enter?

Maybe heavy doors were holdovers from medieval times....

Dark age time... barbarian tribes tearing ancestors into pulp... gangs ignorance disorder stealing and killing... much like the streets today!

Heavy doors... necessity against invasion... disorder and stealing...

But there was something sad about it all. And that you didn't get.

You got the sadness and that was easy. But you did not get the door.

What was the door?

Was it an entrance for the faithful to become hidden against popular knowledge?

Was it a construction to worry about later when it was broken down by hidden magic?

Was it a point of being?

Or was it just a door?

It meant something universal for what it was you looked for. But it also meant nothing. Because what you looked for was usually taken by the time you got there.

Across the blue sky at Avenue C and 20th St. you stopped and watched birds. What did watching birds mean? Hundreds of birds — maybe thousands of birds — Hundreds maybe thousands of birds streamed past in the sky. Birds were cool. And what they were doing in the sky was called migration. And so you thought was it possible to know a bird?

*

You stared at those closed doors.

And you imagined Father Grababoy walking — slowly walking — up the side aisle toward the altar and tucking himself into a pew...

...He knelt alone... big empty church... morning sunlight falling down through stained glass windows high on the walls... slanting into a matrix of shadows... onto dark corners on the side aisles... where marble saints rose above small prayer candle flickers in tinted glass holders... where Father Grababoy was caught... suspended among the marble saints... stuck inside time... what was sacred and what was profane... did he know ... did he know Father Grababoy... that he no longer had existence... thoughts to be and unanswered prayers... the church silence and its haunting echo... those thoughts and those prayers guided him and bullied him and broke him down to a reflection...

And at some level — some odd perception — you got Father Grababoy. He made attempts. There was a great disorder in this world ... and he missioned himself to strike it down... he wanted to stand tall at the end of the world... but he was discovering what a comic hero he truly was.

The power invested in him might be ordained... but his muscles shook beneath the long black cassock... when he spoke power his face let loose with blue veins... they rose above his eyeballs... crashed one another almost symmetrically across his forehead... a voice with total heat ...the octaves of his throat almost fried for the trying... hoarse and coughing... distorted...he knew the game was rigged... but he tried... namely Father Grababoy wanted love... but the love he wanted was impossible for him... namely it was his job to love everyone... but that's a tall order... you imagined Father Grababoy felt cheated... it was his job to fight... translate misery down... open the gates for others to witness the beautiful... but when did the battle stop... the pretty boy emotion side... the epic curse... clans destroyed clans over fucking claims... the ideas...the arbitrary beginning... people's heads... what was so necessary about all-powerful beings anyway...go watch the advertised faces of god lit to the heavens above the boardwalk on the billboards along Ocean Avenue...

*

You might be imperfect and maybe incapable for any deeper thought other than wanting to save your own ass — but you always felt you did nothing wrong. All you ever did was to be born. There was no choice in that. And somewhere inside this split screen image how were you supposed to find out what was yours? Or what was ours?

What might we all want? And was it possible to have that delivered?

*

However — on the other side of things — the monkey coin — on some other level — some other level — you thought — you were reminded — there was little for you to get about Farther Grababoy.

For one thing don't interfere with my death.

Don't place words between my teeth.

Allow love how to figure out its own revenge.

And fugue your battles… why neighbor defined neighbor as a forfeit … why do ideas talk only to be told well they have a short memory … why did our backbones rise…why did our flattening feet cause suspicion…who were the demons… what were the angels… why cover over the fixations with god… with some kind of Beau Brummel pop and flop algebra…many x's to solve… what solution you saw was to fail miserably… match Elysium … forget pang… forget free loader… forget credentials… forget foolscap…

Forget quack… forget the therapist… forget lurid and qualm… forget push-over and reservations… Forget the thin abstractions… forget the second thoughts…. forget your breath… forget how suddenly it takes away reasoning and dreams… forget the bandits … forget the tightrope… forget the weatherglass and a swan song…remember to buy god a drink the next time we met… a double for us both…

*

The demons were pissed off. The sat on your left shoulder and yapped. Imagine an agitated subway rider sitting next to you — five

226

stops to go — and who wanted your attention and whose attention you wanted to blow off- what you wanted to be left alone to finish the ride in silence… but demons only listened so far.…

Yea they were pissed off — because if you didn't listen — without your service — that shot another hole into their collective worth… if you didn't listen … they guaranteed it to pieces… if they died then you were taken with them forever after…

The other comic heroes owned super cool lives as angels… feast days and celebrations named after them…tombstones with their names carved into granite aka eternity-wise… tall muscular animals in play… brilliant swords …prime teeth… dressed for a broadside in gossamer steel… owning the sky… arrogant as their cousins who rose from the ground during a storm on lightning bolts…

And the demons — their comic hero status — ridiculed by consensus — who got to the microphone first — they were in the tank — like sorrowful dogs left tied to parking meters that no one stopped to chat with because they looked so bad — therefore abandoned on first glance…

The angels sported soft linen wings and they never got dirty.

The demons humped the ground with stupid broken feet and bones filed with garbage.

And these were our choices?

The demons waited in the shadows. Once they grabbed your shoulder fuck you was what they said. Stop killing yourself.

The angels illuminated your footsteps like the streetlight above 20th Street and said stop killing yourself.

And for sure it was a heavy business. But what was Father Grababoy doing in it?

He had all the wrong moves. He had no idea how to make anything form to what he had. He was lost at running a gang and he hid from retribution. But it was his job. He was entrusted. The big heavy doors of the church… they were hard to open… they slammed behind him …

The angels never said much.

The demons wrecked your eyeballs.

Why bother getting involved?

For all you knew Father Grababoy was the kid who never got invited to a birthday party. And to fuck over matters he sat on the curb wondering whether to be sad or not and was it strange and unsettling to be forgotten? He was a Norman Bates type escaped from a Psycho movie screen. Just waiting to do the shower scene?

With his Listerine breath and Winston cough and his red-eyed trance Father Grababoy held onto his life as it were threadbare act in a carnival. A ridiculous player… out of position… he tried to bring things homeward and make peace unto the house of the soul of all things… but he failed and he realized that … marrow deep… that was his failure… what he felt you imagined was like his spiritual quality hit skeletal and lost soft tissues and nerves… drove into the bones like a cancer… afterwards… or whatever… he followed… the nights began like fucking taxi cabs downtown chasing fares and asses on the night his own dead soul began to prowl…

The angels said a small frond of an idea about how you remain was still there for the taking.

The demons said oh for sure let's have moral lessons and a quality type world to accommodate the complicated sensory multiple heart.

The angels said what happens if you tossed the world into the air? What was the chance it would come back together as before?

The demons laughed and said forget it he's superstitious about death.

The angels said the saints constantly moved.

Why be saved the demons said. When the abstract theories of salvation only serve to dismantle you…what was there to be saved in the first place?

The angels said what you do with your heart each day?

The demons said it might come down as other than what it was and was now fully disordered?

The angels said there were many scripts… many natural inventories… multiple testaments…a concrete meaningful heart …you stay in the world… find a proper order… how you reach time… how do you count time… when you dress time how does that affect you…

The demons said hey you its Saturday. Tonight you hitch up Eden over at the Lot. Hey you — those watery green eyes aren't cheap… and this is no world for you to be ever saved... it was good a night as any to go... don't make a tradition though about setting yourself up...

*

You looked back across the street. The church did a strange thing. It became smaller and smaller... and smaller... like a slow motion fade out ... pushed into the distance... a blurry frame... the church it physically moved in time... shrank before your eyes... folded upon itself... and collapsed on the street ... a cardboard pop-up house... a picture book page ... you kept seeing a building fading... a zero point... where no things and where all things existed in one shot... and then the building fell over ... and you froze and then you ran ... you never moved but you moved... into a far distance... a few blocks down 20th Street you caught a breath... shaking... grabbing your hands...

*

Suddenly you were late. Late... late...ulcers in your mind... your mind in your stomach... and if you were late... isolated... you might not die on time...

*

Dr. Cambodia called it a phobia. Basically you mucked yourself over to reactions or something like that and from there you got shitless.

*

Several people waited at the corner like a niche — waiting for the K-bus to show face. You ran past them — tossed a wave to someone you might know- but you had to run and this was no time for genialities.
All week long we waited.
How to lose track about today?
How to miss today entirely?

And how to forward a vision into impossible days to come since those days were in the future and were not available today?

It was a simple tide-over answer. We waited now to enjoy later and were lost.

We waited for the school week to end. We waited for the workweek to end.

We waited for the weekend to come.

Maybe we waited far too long to see how god forgot our lives.

We waited for the weekend. We bought our troubles in kind and paid for them.

How the air opened differently on a Saturday than say it did on a Monday.

But wasn't it still the same fucking air?

You ran past. You were late.

Traffic either side Avenue S...traffic antics... witless shortsighted V-8 folk tales ... handy grace... carry on... blockhead bonehead noodle head ... no matter what they called you... you made it... ducked through the contortions between cars... the long trailing sound... car horns yelling behind you... like you sped across a void and faced yourself looking aback ... but you only made it across Avenue S... the old close call... one car missing one way... the other car missing opposite... you ran because you were late... might have been a stupid and sandwich death... times were like that... but how many times... were there... like that... the accidental death ...screw your exit...

*

Meanwhile the schoolyard kids from one side and kids from other sides were throwing footballs around and getting ready for the game. We played one another on Saturday afternoons — the tournament of champions — winner stays on the concrete and losers go away. Losing was nowhere but it was important to understand. It was like a title game each afternoon we played. We packed our identities onto a touch football universe. The winners held face... but face was difficult... you had bragging rights... if you got through the schoolyard with a win somebody might tag the score on a wall… face was difficult… but bragging rights… until the following week you got like a hall pass from being fucked with…

Running into the J.L. Spider schoolyard was a relief. To see everybody was like you and were inhaled by the sky and floated weightless for an instant and then you were released into shouting and grab ass and strutting around the theatrics of boy mechanisms — all of it was clay — wet material — hands and voices — partisan strikes beyond ideas … trouble spots — all our own to nag the soul out from behind the title characters of legend — who won today and who better get out of the way — who was the chump and no good and who failed today…

*

The hoops court was also in session. Tall sleek magicians roamed the air. You stood and watched the play — a sweet agility — kinda mean — respect that flies — like there was no difference between the figure and the ground about being scored on. Head fakes… pure fakes… body fakes… language rising and double clutching and suspended about fucking gravity for a clean and geometric bank shot against a twisted iron backboard.

Two points … count it… the old swoon feeling… the ransacked dead spot on that backboard…

Like the way Junior Clifton got up for a rebound — everybody left on the deck checked out his shoe size on the bottom of his chucks and had one option to play and that was they looked at Junior Clifton and wondered how was that shit possible.

Or the way Curtis Moe saw the court all at once… all confused … science eyeballs adjusting figures in dimensions … shifting fingers like they were hidden fingers not doubting the ball … the spin of the earth … the pass that never broke time… defenders wiped off the planet and sad… another two… Curtis Moe was the smartest guy you ever seen play.

When Junior Clifton got off his feet he determined what instantly happened next…

When Curtis Moe took the ball in his hands the sidelines took up a chant that likewise synched his play: I believe! I believe! …Dunk that shit!…

231

At the far end of the J. L. Spider schoolyard — by the swings and the monkey bars — a man showed a young girl how to ride a bicycle on trainer wheels. There was something about this sloppy and erratic act that nearly burst you in two. The little girl falls over several times. And it's kind of apparent that falling over doesn't matter. Not to her and not to the guy you take to be her father.

Dad lets loose. Pride yell... dad pride yell go baby go!

Finally she gets it. She's off on her bicycle... without anyone holding onto the seat...finally she gets it... alone and peddling and young kid madness... some touched new world she made and a manic world mirrored right back at her... that she's not experienced until now... but now she finally gets it... and now she finally gets it... finally she gets it and shrieks delight... You imagine milkshakes and French fries at the Dairy Rabbit ... she peddles them both back home...

*

You looked around but didn't locate him yet. Cripple was the team manager and our general mouthpiece. If we had something to say we said it through Cripple.

Some team managers tried to boom box you off your feet. Super heavy bass lines and super heavy radiation lyrics and super heavy crews and super heavy gals and super heavy water bottles and super heavy sandwiches and super heavy parties and super heavy nights and super heavy booty and super heavy taxi rides and super heavy dope and super heavy cool...

Other mangers showed videos all time. Hey asshole they yelled! This was you last week! What a fucked up play!

Cripple laughed and folded his arms across his chest. He tipped his Vince Lombardi hat down across his brushy eyebrows.

Broadway Jack and the Coin brothers and Edie the Chevy and Rhino the Bob were all in the house and getting ready. Somebody threw a football toward you. How would it be? How would it be if everything were as simple as looking up one afternoon and catching a football out of the sky?

Good one today Rhino said.

Watch out for Richard White. He's mad at you for last week Cripple said.

Rhino looked back at Cripple and said Richard White can't run.

Hell yea Cripple said. But that's because you took him out last week.

Richard White goes down Rhino said.

He's not as dumb as you think Cripple said. Preliminary SAT's say he topped 1200.

How do you know that Rhino asked?

I stole the test scores Cripple said.

How you do that?

What do you need to know?

Light skin Billy?

Around 1100.

And Marshall Tate? Don't tell me he's a genius.

No he's not Cripple said.

So what's that mean Rhino asked?

Marshall Tate never took the test.

Hey throw back the ball a Coin brother yelled at you.

But instead you punted it back.

Jerk off the Coin brother said.

*

the coffee meditations

As you fell asleep — nodded off really — light from the passing lunar eclipse fell through the skylights — at like 196,000 mph — was eclipse light the same as ordinary light — and made the floorboards glow.

The feeling was forced cool and relaxed. Small mind bending pills worked into your bloodstream. A toast to chemistry filled up the holes in your body — and much akin to down-shifting the truck — speed drifted away and you slowed — you stared through the roof at the cold excellent light banked off the moon.

Things — what were things — without really knowing — what were things — whatever things were they were frightening and a pleasure to mess with. Tumblers in a lock were set. Old boyhood angels floated up. The raven-haired woman called from her sat phone.

Fact was: what did happen?

Mostly questions like this bored the urine bag right off your Mister Ed.

But let's give it a time and ask: what did happen?

Back then in the day — and now suddenly it was today — credits before your eyes — and then tomorrow was like having your own being disconnected and bent underneath a crude flame that early humans made ten thousand years ago — cooking predators — watching for predators — were they scared while they ate beneath the shadows on a cave wall?

No matter really... But what was the best guess?

The questions remained generous throughout the years. And that was as good a sign as ever. They held more promise than certainty ever did anyway. Because you had no answers. And was that enough? Was that enough for you to get on? Was that enough... getting tangled in the alba-

tross of words across years and beer bottle explanations across tables ...
What was the guess... how many pizzas did it take to settle an argument
into the deep night?

Getting high before you die was like a stigma these days.

The trades that ruled — the new-inspired medicine — docs on the
federal dole to relieve student debts — they were anti-dope and more
likely to proscribe a natural manner of suffering to end your time. The
gospel among new docs was to use your brain against pain. However
who had the time when your days had a calendar super-imposed on
them like those old thin tracing papers that you drew through to outline a map for a geography class. Who had the time to think about your
brain to help your time end suffering? Lucky though you had an old
school doc for an old school dying. And the cousins had your back for
your needs bless us all. But the feds watched everybody. If you went to
the pharmacy then red lights flashed over computer networks across
the entire country. Ending suffering was a big thing. It was an issue
on blog-ports. Televised multiples on the networks wanted to know
why was there suffering and what was the government doing about it?
But why you asked — fucking wheeze that report — but asking the
question why was prosaic — without character — flat earthed pointless half-witted and stony — just keep asking the question why — and
soon you discovered the question why had nothing to do with inquiry
nor reflection nor any library abstractions to dive into for help. For
such a temporal dash across the horizon — life no matter how fine it
was — no matter the love you shared — no matter what transcendence
you stumbled across — those fine white pills drilled the ass from your
soul — before the horizon ended and shut your eyes — suffering was
not some medical knock-knock joke.

After the fifth inning you stepped outside on the deck to watch the
eclipse. You looked into the big starry night. The fuzzy imprint of the
Milky Way stretched across the houses and trees in the neighborhood
like a single bone of the skeleton of the universe. A slow moving shadow
crawled across the ghostly white globe of the moon.

Back inside on television the same eclipse was broadcast live on cable.

You alternated between the methods of watching.

The moon show outside on the sky and its illusion and the revenue cousin inside captured live on television…

Seemed like workable dichotomy… nostalgia for catchwords to talk about the moon… prime time technical astronomy complete with expert advice… how to watch the moon…its instant themes… Was it too late to act?

Might as well down some wine. Pain never left anybody alone. A commercial between innings with a smiling Asian doc who said when you're healthy then you're in control. Was that comforting? The wine was better. The pills were better. Designated chemistry — enter the land — yes it was there to be high — the land between doubts laughing in the wilderness and honey in the morning tea — signal twines — greeting card amnesia — the pills … your insides…

So yea. There were graveyard shovels in the breeze.

Why was it we had to say goodbye? Who the fuck made up that rule?

So you stood on the deck and watched the eclipse and caught the innings throughout the evening.

Fucking great to be alive.

All the layers of hell: war poverty hunger disillusionment greed jealousy anger: they weren't going to disappear overnight. Simply because it was you — the non- you — hey it's always been a fucking lottery — tickets punched no tickets punched — simply because you floated on a wave — warm and narcotic simply because you were flushed — because the moon was changing and that left you with a non-you — a weightless romantic — a kind of upside down satori — the moon shimmered — a light underneath under water — it was more than you were ever able to generate — hell could not find you at the moment. You were both light and dark — quivered optical hypnotic — pulling both shadows and brightness apart without design — seeped in eroticism — retrofitted onto the night — like a dance or a wheel or breathing outdoors — hell had no chance at the moment. Little back and forth — bare and sensual like wet paint — an everyday feeling like a slice of bread — hell couldn't find you even if it was too much to ask. Moonlight fell across the skyline of autumn. You wore some old hat against the chill. Sixth inning and the guy on the mound threw sliders and K's. Gray-faced wooden fences — slates peeled off the frame hung on thin rotten nails — not much fence left — silver boards like an old man's whiskers — nobody was ever around to mend this fence — it wasn't yours — the fence wasn't yours in the meets and bounds of the property deed — the fence belonged somewhere else — so you waited until a day came where the fence dropped onto the ground — slat by slat — gradual and unraveled — what then would come from our separate yards — for decades an old rotting fence was a reliable buffer — business on this side of the fence and business on the other side of the fence and no quandary held in between — the other side of the fence was a home owned by two Jersey-land cops — perfect the raven-haired woman said. Seventh inning and the guy still had something left but he got clocked for a run that tied the game. Signs appeared everywhere along both benches– what's the strategy — if the guy was off balance and if so could he regain it tonight and not some other day. Prayer flags were stretched between the forgotten limbs of a tree beside the fence –a broad tree — entropy undressing from the stars into a tree — a settler's tree — it didn't belong in Jersey-land any more than we did — the prayer flags made you fly — measure it one way — measure what's the same way another way — primitive lonely divine — a conversation stopper — if it's not too much to ask — something other than a scorecard — what the hell — the raven-haired woman called again and wanted to talk about pain — you said let's talk about the seventh inning and the moon and the garden blooms this year and canning red sauce and pickles that kicked ass. Chaotic expanded motion — you read about chaotic expanded motion in a book this year while hiding out in never-never land. You thought a lot about whatever it takes to make a state of mind. You remember a meal you made after we were married — a meal for your in-laws — fish tacos on a physically implausible crisp shell with sesame oil and lime juice mint cilantro and hot pepper flakes — bean corn cheddar and roasted peppers quesadillas that cracked with Tabasco and a maple sour cream japolte — and hold on we got hot soft burritos coming — wrapped around marinated grilled pork and pineapple and fresh mustard greens and slices of dried figs with fresh squeezed lemon juice and a crumbling goat cheese — and salsa — and guacamole — chips and tequila — a chocolate mole sauce to go with waffles and ice cream — what's up with the south of the border routines a cousin asked — you smiled and didn't explain and he understood. No one in the family expected a firm answer — especially to say if that answer went in the wrong direction from the question asked. But the southwest fare was due to our hiding out for a year — it was a pattern to fear — we caused trouble — then we vanished — so we spent a year in Mexico living on the cheap and paying our bribes for us to get back stateside. Blind Charlie had a full plate and two shot glasses — the clan was chowing down — wiping plates clean — looking for seconds — Blind Charlie motioned for you to join him — great food he said and he reached over and held your hand. Blind Charlie asked you a strange question. It was late in life for Blind Charlie — the cousins were after him — they wanted his blessing — they wanted Jersey-land. You thought about the back room –now that you were married into the family. Blind Charlie said to you what ever happened to good old onion dip? The raven-haired woman called again and said what happened in the eighth? And for the first time in years you thought about the guy behind the newspaper waiting to get his scan. Nothing you said to Blind Charlie nothing you said ever happened to good old onion dip…

*

Do you think anybody cares? The demons were yelling. Fuck you was the obvious answer to the question they asked. Without negation they're just B-side creatures waiting in alleyways and streetlight shadows. But like hell always happened you kept on negated the demons over time and so brought them continually to life.

Fuck you!

Yea you got used to that. You got used to their awful smelling breath and stooped bony claws hanging on your shoulder.

Pain and dementia they said with a screed ha-ha-ha you asshole.

But what the hell you thought only the peculiars move around enough to matter. And it's not clear just what makes a difference.

Oh fuck you!

Just might be true you rationalized. But it's October and we're still pulling tomatoes from the garden. Do you account for that?

Account for what they said. You base your life because you suck they said.

In fact you told them — when coolness forms in the evening after a warm Jersey-land day — something outside the lines of memory taps you sitting on the beach — staring at the dolphins — sea water salt air figures curving before a flat horizon –there's a change in the weather they say- the tides will shift — the margins of betrayal — a cool evening — sunlight fading and brought indoors for memory — a fresh ripe tomato — bitten — juice sprayed across your face — nothing quite like it ... enjoyed... bite again...

It makes you stupid they said. Stupid! Stupid with clocks... stupid with the sky... Fuck you !

There was this one time you said to them. Late into a Friday evening — some unfortunate somebody was pounding nails... Wham — wham — wham — and then again with the hammering... Wham wham wham — and then again... Each time the hammer hit the sound became heavier... And heavier... till there was no sound left on the air but wham wham wham... And so your thoughts were about wine and love and percussive Brazilian music... how the sound became sensual — that hammer spiked those nails... And so what happened... you downed a glass... downed another glass for the imaginary laborer... opened the boom box... hit play... minutes later the hammering stopped...

No fucking way they said. The guy fell off the ladder! He probably broke his neck!

No you said. He just wanted to stop. He wanted a meal.

Kiss ass they said!

No you said. No was the preferred word they wanted. If a season comes to an end that doesn't mean it's the end of the season.

What the fuck they said.

He wanted a meal.

And you knew that?

Yea you said. He wanted a meal.

Well that's just special they said. Here's a plain old trajectory. You hop on board and take the ride and at some point you're delivered a result. But whoa hold the fucking land line because suddenly everyone gets it in their head that it's not a linear world. What a genius! And so

on that if life was time — and time was a clock — then life never repeats itself exactly.

But it goes around you said. There's the motion of light and also
there's the notion of right.

Wham wham wham the demons said. Why not tell us about circles
and waves and particles…

The guy wanted a meal and I helped him out.

The guy fell off the ladder and died they said. And don't tell us about
wishful thinking. Don't say if only this weather could last… And please
don't tell us this argument has gone on for thousands of years…

But it has you said.

Unfastened and spoiled and brisk and looted…

Fuck you!

Check you said.

Incubus give an ear lend an ear undo unbind unlock untie…

Checkmate you asshole.

Craving intention store...

*

This morning you sat on a boardwalk bench to kill some time and
grab sunlight and got lost looking across the Atlantic. How should you
feel? Another surgery another year was common ass fodder to play the
fool… But your phone reminded you to ask — how do you feel today?

*

Wobbly physically — cold internally- but really it was the light and
the ocean and that made you inbred and quiet and a shade-off loner.

The sunlight fractured the water. Because you were overdressed with
a few extra layers topped with a rough thermal hoodie — a hoodie you
picked up at a funeral auction from a dead clam fisherman — and the
hoodie kept you wicked insulated — you started out from the bench
thankful for the hoodie but felt sorrowful over death.

But once you found Jersey-land — sitting on the boardwalk — seated

240

on a bench in heaven beneath sugary pagan skies — then Jersey-land found you again. An overzealous heat rose with the day. You bought a black coffee and star fruit muffin from a millennial skateboard kiosk.

Fifteen minutes later you bought another coffee from a bicycle taxi.

But the bicycle taxi ride came with a sweet tight bag of dope.

So there was a ride up the boardwalk and back and that was par. Avoidance was part of the deal. Curtains were drawn around the cab. You wanted to feel at home — in time in boardwalk in Atlantic — in the empty bag. Soon there was a modulating cushion — a head for you to get more feeling it seemed — and maybe overcome some guidelines for the day and give your head a much needed place to land.

On the ride up the boardwalk the boss cabbie knocked on the window behind him and suggested we stop at Tomorrow's Nut House. Sounded total. You wanted burnt sugar cashews over-fried in cheap dark rum. You wanted unsalted almonds frozen in hot Viet rooster sauce. You wanted a plain bag of popcorn. You wanted those gummy creatures but only in a small bag.

*

You thought about a scene from the Wild Bunch. William Holden says to Ernest Borgnine — after like a half-century being shot up — William Holden can barely climb onto his horse from all his wounds — not to mention they got shagged earlier that day — all the gold pieces from the bank heist turned out false and were nickel plugs instead — things went to hell — they shot up the town and the town shot back — nobody was having a good day — And finally when William Holden finally gets his ass up in the saddle he turns to Ernest Borgnine and says we gotta start thinking beyond our guns.

*

Two handsome buffs spun before you — wearing themselves out — like two guys hustling instagram specimens — they spun before you and did variation 360"s on roller blades while hugging and grab-assing. Definitely a nooner you thought. The physical business the spandex climax the smiling whistles and call emergency lettering on the crotch and the aches and perfected skin lines. According to their artful ball caps pulled ever so to the right side they played softball for the Transition Bar on Washington Street. They looked as though they knew one another for much longer than this life seemed to allow.

*

You needed breads crumbs. Something to feed the pigeons and seagulls and rats — even though you know better than to never to feed pigeons and seagulls and rats — you needed bread crumbs or fucking peanuts to fulfill this anti-social act. You asked the millennial skateboard kiosk to go and fetch you some peanuts. Maybe he said but you know that shit's illegal.

Just the freebies — like well-being — sitting comfortably — pain was a token and bugged you in the first place — because the sky was a place you needed — it was outer space that hurt your eyes — and thinking what you know now you'd eat the peanuts and not give them to the birds — not because it was illegal but you were hungry and if you had peanuts well fuck then they'd fit the bill all right. Where were you in all this? You had friends and birds. Money fell out of the sky. Too much to collect...

*

Well fuck you the demons said. The riches...your health — what bullshit was that?

Well you said that served you better than the wheelchair dreams lately that chased around your sleep.

What's the matter they said don't you like people in wheelchairs?

Leave other people out of this.

What else was there they said? You and your habits make us ill. We try with you. We give you attention. We call you one of our own. And what do we get for our troubles? You pretend. You speculate. For you coincidence was never enough. Why not give it up? Why not admit it?

You considered it... why bother indeed? But you laughed it off. You repeated the explanations.

No news that you repeat yourself they said.

True. No avoiding it. Each day we end up repeating ourselves... it's like in the morning you ask — wasn't that you last night?

Fuck you.

Ah...when the demons crowd your head...when they insulted you with ancient blasphemy...when it's bad enough to have demons in your head... when they get nasty and turn disrespectful... you mess things up to understand them later on... wasn't all this funny you said... wasn't this something you never imagined to know anything better about...

Bastard they screamed! You know better than that.! Ejaculatory dumb-bell merriment bullshit!

Time to drain the head you said. Want a fortune cookie?

Bastard.

You promised to send the demons a valentine come winter. A hill-top scene when you felt better... bendable... the haul for now... the quiet on the other side of windows of naked evergreens... chickadees grabbed and called for the silver air... how snowflakes fell... how snowflakes were falling... white carnations nobody asked for...

*

Make a note: understand park benches.

Make a note: pain removal was strange.

You wonder: was being alive the body's request to get high?

Why don't we have bodies that won't fail?

Make a note: a conspiracy exists: melancholy atomic memories: muscle groups fade from working systems into bone cracks and damaged tissue networks ... why don't we have different bodies that stand up and forget time... a nice piece of hitting in the sixth last night...

*

Geese paddled the bay near the mouth of a polluted inlet. A small hawk hunted the brush.

Tasty three legged rodents — ill mercury fish — and who knew what sort of freakish bivalve burrowed into the sandy bottom — the sad fertile marshlands of yesterday — where all the shit we threw away accumulated sooner or later in the muck — and the feeding chain started a toxic advent toward extinction... a pinch hit rocket double...

A gnarly bearded man with a large weathered backpack walked past. Steady navigational footsteps and then he stopped and looked back at you. He wanted money.

Who doesn't you asked?

I'm walking around the world he said.

Fucked up place to start from you said.

I just need a little for tonight he said.

Where do you go from here you asked?

Up north. Maybe see the great lakes... maybe see Canada... the plan is to hit the west coast and then walk to Mexico and see what happens...

There's a straighter way to Mexico you know.

I'm out for a walk he said.

Right you said.

So you reached into a false pocket in your pants pockets and handed the guy a hundred dollar bill. To be understood — mostly not to be misunderstood — when the money left your hand and passed into his — you made certain he noticed the machine pistol you wore that the raven-haired woman left you — a sublime indicator but hey –but what it said was that you and he were not cousins — and that he should move on and disappear but not into any air nearby. Was there was a reason the guy was traded four times. He was a catcher when he was a kid.

*

Later you stopped by the video store and made sure the money was right. Not that you had anything over on the cousins but you were expected to show. Plus for stopping by on time you got a free movie and a bag of popcorn.

*

But pain led everything … like the bunt in the eighth… but the raven-haired woman said no no no — So fuck it — for right now- all that mattered was that it was beautiful and October and never would it ever show up this way again.

Sky and geese — sight and sound — if only this weather lasted — lasted to screw the demons — lefty and right pitchers and then a switch was that it? Or was it nineteen games? Anyway it was blue sky warm with white wash clouds and fugitive tides and the plain word gorgeous — on the whole it was like being kidnapped and held captive inside a landscape painting that sold for millions.

The sky formed and never refused its grip.

It's a sensual world — if we live in it then why not die for it.

Zinnias still bloomed on cracked browning stems.

You even listened to the post-game show.

A link to the same time — the same time floating — the same time floats — as though the scenery were moving and you were still — where an image you passed suddenly passed through you — and that mix up stop-gapped you — what you needed was not so much a first step but a vacant empty step that lead you back home.

Pain was all in your brain right? Or was it your brain was all in the pain?

So you walked — over to the video store — pulled around blue corners — walking into warm shadows — creased over the sides of buildings and spilling on sidewalks — the incessant barking from the market stalls on Winchester Street — chlorinated sea turtle broths available in pints and quarts with free oyster flavored crackers — imported faux leather shirt collars made from plastic garbage — a poor cousin — he was far down the line from Da Vinci's pizza — sold reclaimed chickens from Iowa and he guaranteed these birds knew no range at all… and so you walked — like a set of numbers pulled toward an equation — a musical collage — people smoked and dropped onto the heavens — a millennial kiosk handed out odd tourist maps — little girls flew away on

bicycles all hair in a streak — a kind of purple grace — at some crossed
eyed intersection: red lights green lights yellow lights all going nuts —
the timer shit the bed — nobody knew what to do — seated gleaming
and material — but you've been here before — passing among the same
common physicality — burning sunlight –geese with blue overhead — a
house you recognized — dense street foliage — climbing before a porch
where empty chairs sat — if chairs can even sit or be empty — an open
upstairs window — a voice called out and vibrated the afternoon : I'll be
right there — it was a voice you'll never see.

*

In the dream you were sketching Venus and Jupiter with a cheap-
ly made ballpoint pen on the branches of some trees in the backyard.
A UFO flew overhead and stopped. A piece of toast floated down on
a beam of light from the ship. You accepted it and biting into it you
thought- this would go well with coffee. Before you moved the planets disappeared. A light pulled the toast away. Inside the UFO the alien
crew undressed you and probed your body. Lights waved across you like
strobes. Large metal bells echoed off the stars. They notice your scar
and reject you as a specimen. You tell them no really. The aliens stared
at your penis. The aliens dropped you back in the yard and flew away.
They looked back at you from narrow rectangular windows and waved
goodbye.

*

loose change

You were floating. Without giving it a thought. You floated across a warm honey colored pool way in the mountains. You floated on a barstool and watched Fast Eddie and admired his solitary thoughts. After last call — finally he thought — he cleaned off the bar and tossed the last glasses into the last soapy tub of the night. The he sprayed the spar varnished bar top with a disinfectant that smelled like a girl's junior prom corsage.

You floated and you enjoyed the floating. You watched Fast Eddie and you enjoyed watching Fast Eddie. You enjoyed the honey colored pool and you enjoyed the mountains and you enjoyed the barstool and you enjoyed a cloud of narcotics.

Eden Jones sat beside you. She chain-smoked and laughed. Last call unraveled around wearisome tables. A web-like assumption pooled outward from the bar where Fast Eddie leaned and administered last call. A soft innocence — the regular names — a pickpocket's intent to jade money — fast Eddie looked over it all and said life was Okay…

On his business cards it said: Fast Eddie — Proprietor — Music — BMF — Cards — 20th Century Club.

Lonesome rodeo songs wrecked around low conversations. That's the way it was. Fast Eddie didn't put no funk on while he cleaned the night's mess… twang and forgetful loss… those were the songs he played… songs that made you feel like the quarter in the jukebox was being fed upon.

And it was delightful — sitting next to her again. It made you feel vaguely in love with someone — a shiny new day feeling — a fabulous rolling over in the middle of the night and there she was naked feeling.

The cigarette burns in the carpet looked like craters on the moon — blank traces like asteroid holes falling in from gravity and hitting objects carelessly. Once a year Fast Eddie replaced the carpet. It was simpler he explained to have this planned demise than it was to horde and pester the drunks to use the ashtrays. Definitely it was the more expensive way to go. But it was easier on his nerves. Over the years he developed his doubts. He saw the regulars each night come in and contribute to destroying something innocent that he paid for. What the hell he thought.

These were silent times for Fast Eddie. A kind of retreat where he put things back in order — the stale odors — beer whisky and smoke — soggy cocktail fruit — Eddie picked up a quiet and a strength -a place where he surrendered to the time of day. A place that was low and less favored and unbothered and where he didn't have to be Fast Eddie: the bartender: smooth and loose and filling glasses. You get to be too important for people he thought. You get trembles and a little paranoid. Everybody shouts at you: need this: need that... Fuck it man. I'm just doing my job ...each brief glass he sold added layers to confusion — the worldly alcoholic pressures — pouring drinks all night for the children of the earth — ghosts in residence looking back from the bar mirror — take a step ahead and not two behind — the fool and his serial identities — glorious painted lipstick smiles — don't interfere with slumped bodies if they haven't dropped on the floor — Fast Eddie thought this was my job — to hustle life...

*

You looked at Fast Eddie. It was easy to read his mind behind last call.

*

Most people drink but was it his job to act like a cosmic lifeguard?

Most people drank he reasoned because drinking was a problem and they went through the motions and got past the obvious.

Some people act like the almighty tornado itself.

248

Wasn't his job to wear them down.

Wasn't his job to get them free drinks either.

Fast Eddie was content. Peaceful. Content and at peace — Fast Eddie hummed a tune and vacuumed the room. He was the lord of nothing. The night was nearly over. Then he and Salem were free — free to be alone and hit a club or free to be alone and go home.

Fast Eddie thought what do bar owners do?

You thought what kind of sex they would have in the morning?

You starred at Eden Jones. Everything was unknowable. You caught glimpses — picked up feelings. And given that Eden Jones was more prone to being out of your life rather than in it — you decided long ago — oh yea it was long ago — that if you were going to have this vague love sensation then it might as well be something like floating.

Fuck ownership Fast Eddie thought. But you know you might as well be in charge...

And if you had the money — Fast Eddie knew how to straighten you up and sell you the means to tinker with your brain chemistry.

Don't think the old Greeks enjoyed their wine?

You think those Silk Road travelers didn't get stoned along the way?

Fast Eddie said as long as people have heads they can't control they will ingest digest inhale inject the substance at hand.

Yea you said. It was a marketplace of sorts. You know you said you take a testy circumstance — and that was bugging you — and that put you behind a mask — and then you drive it deep where no one else gets it. You own it. The beauty. The absurdity. The reason for being optimal was watching everything in sight. Because you knew... you said to Fast Eddie... because each night wears off...

*

Reefer Madness had it wrong. Great working title but all it wanted was to mess with the odds and ends of the sub-plots. Using a drug will make you crazy and angry and lazy.

So what? Don't be angry. Do your schoolwork. What's any of that got to do with how we perform in the clutch?

We were dissatisfied. And we couldn't find the way out. We can't find the way out.

Been that way for years in the thousands. What was the thread? What was its name?

You knew the sky. Was it inside there? What sends those cool messages of wonderment along the spine?

*

Fast Eddie was cool — hip motherfucker dude he thought. He looked good in classy sharkskin suits with a dark vest. He looked good in hats — perched forward or tiled back or sky piece down — he wore them neat against his clipped balding and graying Afro. Fast Eddie looked good in shoes. Each day before he opened the bar he stopped over on 5th avenue at this old guy's stand and had his kicks polished and shined.

Hell was what we know the shoeshine man thought aloud- far as we saw it was like going only one way — and that was around the block enough times to makes us all have a double history you see: trouble and blessings — and neither had shit to do with tomorrow.

*

21st and Norris stole a car one night. They crashed it about two blocks away on 66th Avenue. They were all drunk and dusted on cheap wine and powdered horse tranquillizers. On any night 21st and Norris was famous. Plus they had guns to make the fight seem spiritual…

And quite naturally — seeking greater density — they gravitated toward the corner. Fast Eddie and friends stood outside the bar talking and singing and passing skinny reefers around and drinking pints — bottom shelf gin and whiskey — the top of the night times.

It's a shame people can't think clearly when they carry a gun.

And drinking and guns and big mouths were a total lost algebra where nothing anyone did equaled x.

One young boy ran his mouth. Bitches he said I'm on your corner.

And the young boy kept at it. What happened next was unavoidable. He pulled his gun. 21st and Norris pulled their guns.

And before the young boy ever had the time to realize what his last thoughts might be Fast Eddie shot him in the head.

Fast Eddie shot 21st and Norris and emptied one gun and then emptied another.

Bodies exploded.

By morning 21st and Norris were long gone out to sea on fishing boats as chum for shark bait.

But he also thought: what the fuck: what has brought us to this?

*

Freddie Noel — he had this thing about his identity — that was his filter to sift out worldly debris — he added names and he changed names — and he swore off settling for a final name — he sat at last call between you and Eden Jones at the table. Seated there- beneath the glare and 2AM lights that Fast Eddie turned up as the nightly signal to empty the bar — you were closed in by nomadic beings. Like being the valley between highlands — the unsettled trough between high waves — you were the odd epicenter to measure motion against — you lived between the rush — the dash off — a quest to go — acknowledge the terrain — throw away the map and report back later... in effect Eden Jones and Morgan Everest Noel were rigged by nature to never stay and cunning to happen elsewhere while you were left behind...

Who assigned identities? And were they supposed to comfort or discomfort?

Maybe it didn't matter. Maybe all that mattered was to have common souls flanked on either shoulder... But that was a question — and who answers the questions?

Underneath the table Eden Jones held your hand. Misty electricity from first grade on reached out and touché — your sad neurons were bare-assed signal flares for your brain to see.

Whenever the time was ripe you never doubted it. And when that time was ripe you held onto Eden Jones while you could. Ah. Maybe last call never ended... right?

251

You first met Morgan Everest Noel — at the time his name was Mickey Emerson — one Sunday evening — an evening to remember — because each year there was an evening like this to remember — because winter had faded off the gallows and springtime took over the air on different winds from the southwest. People gathered pagan style to celebrate and filled the wrap-a-round of an old Victorian house veranda. You needed a ride so you took a bicycle that leaned against the house. The bicycle was there and you needed it.

You remember the look on his face when you pulled up to the house with two cases of beer balanced like infatuation odds on the handlebars.

That's my bike he said. Like the bicycle was a secret mechanics or something magic.

Well you said you figured it belong to somebody.

Have a beer you said. Nice ride too.

Mickey Emerson– Morgan Everest — Freddie Noel — he was a wanderer by trade. You don't know where he came from because he wouldn't say. Didn't matter Mickey said. I'm not there now am I?

He had long straight blond hair. It dropped past his shoulders down to his waist. He was a natural — tranquil radiant and careless blond — he beat the Clairol commercials to the punch line — you only have one life so why not live it as a blond — but despite his natural roots he showered with peroxide anyway. Keep it sunny and second hand.

Turned out that Morgan was living in the basement of the house at St. Anne Street where the springtime party was going on.

Yo coincidence you said.

No it wasn't he said but some things do happen.

After two beers someone behind you reached around and put a drop of springtime acid in your mouth while you were talking you said no way.

Okay Mickey/Morgan/Freddie said and took a hit of springtime. Maybe. But. What we have here was a random event — explained by multiple scriptures — backed up by physics.

No no you said. Have another beer. You want some springtime? Then you realized that had already happened…. Or was about to happen… or you needed to catch up but whatever… when the springtime hit surfer waves formed in your brain… when the springtime hit you gained the old ways… the time… fractured futures… the past in an ice block… but mostly surfer waves and a crowd paddling out…

We lived in multiple generations you said — suddenly feeling the springtime hit and took you onto an ocean night — a realm being the perfect bait — with a strange cheese and oven bread and pickles the size of your thumb — you never asked for it someone just gave it to you on a plate — keg beer was now served — with multiple factors you told Emerson that fucked up multiple discrepancies and bent time and where suddenly one day you're old enough to fight war with its mother lode like allegiance murder and sinister love whose broad stokes covered up the dents in our make up with a formless dickhead with whatever came up and what was the exact opposite of war and was now suddenly at odds with the late re-runs of the country's institutions twisting themselves psychotic and into bad jokes stuck into late tube monologue what the fuck were we even anti-war and didn't that seem like an interference with life and so what happened when we reached the moon for the eighth time and landed there with another no grand overall belief supposed to be guiding us as we watched back on earth we were watching another step in humanity's progress but how many steps would it take how much scientific work bench and deep mathematical motes and a longing to try and circle around just what have we done which was nothing more than to try and understand the nature of a place and the next thing you know the Pentagon wants to install a space cannon in space and the White House wants to install a GPS tracker in our heads oh yea it was for safety taxes and thoughts where's the disconnect no doubt it was going on around us like beliefs in whatever but had started to wither like arthritic hands with tattoos of Jersey-land on our arms and everyone searching for a cheap wage…

What are you talking about Freddie said?

We were the drifted generation. Pushed into places that never lasted in one place for long. Like sand dunes — the visible things keep shifting — and I'm like the guy with the fucking broom you know pushing the dunes back into place.

*

253

Occasionally he was your roommate

Occasionally he lived in a stolen van with stolen tags that he stole regularly.

Occasionally he was a pizza delivery guy but he bugged the cousins.

Or he worked on a garbage truck and did what Blind Charlie's minions told him to do.

No matter what — Freddie Noel was the perfect anecdote — bound for a method where he got glory in the end — a name in lights — to prove he belonged — Freddie needed to be the angle guide — on a fishing rod trying to hook the Atlantic — on a telescope looking for the small mystery of Pluto — even a bicycle a rowboat a surfboard what Freddie Noel wanted was to steal time away from the things you wanted.

*

When you saw the basement where he set up housekeeping — things rotting — the atmosphere of a dungeon — peculiar dirt everything like finely worked dust — moldy household items — cans leaking varnish — mice living inside a lawnmower — you asked Morgan how long you been down here?

Two three months he said.

Rents affordable he said.

Do you want to get out of here you asked?

It was a simple matter. Freddie Noel — or whoever he was at the time — packed up what belongings he had and left. He had books and a knapsack and a violin and the idea that it did not matter where you lived. So he exchanged a basement room with a dirt floor and crawling bugs and big fucking cancer rats for the third floor of a condemned building where no one belonged but the whole floor had a view of the ocean from every window.

Mickey Emerson was the the apparition he constructed about himself. Morgan was solid and fixed — even as he fought otherwise. He said things. He did things. Algorithms placed them on a record. He turned over rocks to study and make notes like what life was under there. Mickey climbed trees and slept in the branches because he imagined that he was a poet. Morgan took apart the van's transmission to find out if that make and model and year's transmission did have a crack in the block like it was said it did in Consumer Reports.

Some nights we cooked a meal on the beach. We had a mirror in the sand and a tiny solar engine that Mickey found one day on a police car and we focused that power onto a heavy metal pot cooking the stew filled with the day's findings.

And after doing so we toasted the big sister Atlantic with a conceit for history and bottles from our own time. We stayed up all night on the acid of the season and hung out underneath the boardwalk construction with its hurricane aggregate cement foundations and deep plastic imitation tar infused planks above.

We placed questions marks against the sky. Morgan Everest played his violin. Until the shifts among the night got testy with the overall darkness and even the last stars went underground. And that meant the sunlight — and sunlight meant the next morning and that drove us back to our strange molecular jobs that kept us away from the Welfare Office on Rose Street.

Some nights we'd walk up boardwalk to Zachariahs Thousand Foods. The owner insisted he had a dog and that dog was a remote grand-cousin to the movie dog in Zachariah — the first electronic western to hit distribution cinema.

Jamie the soft-eyed angel worked the takeout widow. She rehearsed rhymes between customers and waited for the girl of her dreams to walk by. Each shift she looked out onto the pier and tourists and old Jersey-land boards with the surf splashed up the gaps.

Jamie was a small beautiful kid whose elbows propped her up on the gnarly wooden take out window. Other places had cool vinyl is final but not Zechariahs.

To call her just a teenager with faint curly brown hair and a twist in her thin darkly painted lips was to miss a calling. Jamie was already on bicycle tracks in her head when a customer asked her the question: Yea she said it's true. These aren't implants. I was born with Disney eyes.

And how many tips did that generate you asked?

Can you believe that she said?

Someday when the sky comes back — thousand of photo discographies will show Jamie and strange families underneath the Zechariah sign.

Anyway

Freddie Noel had a number of talents as well. He was good with other people. He understood their affairs. He listened. He was Mickey Emerson. He was Morgan Everest. Or whomever next was in line... He offered himself- the generous PHD candidate and his thesis on catastrophic memory events in bio economic psychology — the guy on foot going around the world but still with one foot on the platform — a casual stare that was as much invite as it was listed above a sliver tongue and a romantic touch...

What it really came down to was that Jamie — the soft-eyed angel — gave us free food at the take out window while she chatted up Freddie.

One night you remembered. You tried to imagine why you remembered this peculiar night but you didn't find anything and so came up empty. You and Mantis sat on another sagging gray bench outside the stinky public toilets while Morgan fetched dinner for us.

Garbage cans from a nearby restaurant lined a wall behind us. And before us the Atlantic tide rushed against the pier and tide hitting the wooden pier made sounds like explosions — which to no fucking end unnerved Mantis: sounds like broken hands he said.

In the restaurant the tourists clapped with drunken glee and paid with robotic credit cards as the waves slammed against the protective plate glass windows.

Freddie returned with our food nestled in three greasy white paper sacks.

Mantis ripped open a bag. A treasure chest fell onto his lap. There were dozens of slim hamburgers all neatly wrapped in greasy white paper. Lettuce tomato onion and mustard and ketchup and relish were already on Mantis saw. Mantis held them tight against his body like he would a dead buddy. Times were tough he said. Hell don't matter.

Freddie's bag had the milkshakes. Rumor had it that if you let a milkshake from Zacharias sit out all night then the following day the milkshake lost its glory and was now solid enough to be used as a lobster buoy.

And your bag — nobody takes that away — but what you had was a feeling — that you were quick and wealthy — because your bag had all the golden luscious smelling French Fries the free world had to offer.

Mantis was gone. It was like he ate a hamburger with each breath he took.

Can't get enough of these he said. But really thinking about it he said we should be eating plants and shit like that he said. You know for fucking health... But these are damn fucking good he said!

You admitted that free food made dinning out especially satisfactory. The prime sense of instincts came about because we were stealing. Nothing you saw took the thrill out — nor the thrifty out — when looking at how pale each situation becomes when you're high young and foolish — sitting on a bench outside Zechariahs Thousand Foods — why pay — when there was no mechanism collecting the fee?

Yea Mantis said there can't be no economic theory trumping this shit.

Freddie said what he feared was payday. What he feared he said was riches.

That's bullshit in the first-degree Mantis said slurping a plastic multi-berry milkshake to the end until the straw imploded up his windpipe and his cup was empty and he reached for another.

No Freddie Noel said. It's not like that.

Hamburger Mantis said wiping his mouth on a paper napkin.

No what scares me Freddie said was the crisp excitement from clean money. When the money in question leaves the bank teller's hands and then it's yours each Friday evening before the bank closes. With each crisp twenty there's another crisp twenty and so on until your whole makeup starts to rotate.

Fries Mantis said.

And what happens Freddie said was that each crisp twenty hooked you onto another and you end up putting in years you can't imagine....

Fries Mantis said.

Trade you for a milkshake you said.

Deal.

And for that sequence of twenty dollars Freddie said — if the muddle of retirement doesn't get you — a photograph on the mantle like another link in the family shrine — then the cemetery plot turns your ass into the past and maybe somebody else you never knew starts looking you up for clues because they get paid to catalogue the dead and wipe your benefits off the dole.

It fucking ends Mantis said shoveling fries into his mouth — nodding around for emphasis it ends he said... But you know he said I'm grateful to goose around and be at ease and fuck all else... it's not like happiness

257

goes anywhere Mantis said… stories about your life and the fucking holidays… but if you fucking get to think like well shit there's a morning you don't want to see then that shit is definitely fucked up then you got to cease and desist and start the bombing run all over again and hope the fucking targets never cry out loud enough for you to hear.

*

Freddie said the present was too weird a time he said like he had doubts not only about time but he also had doubts about his talking about time. If things come in faster does that make them better he asked?

Not really you said. But the sky wants us back.

*

Other nights you'd looked around the room. Mickey Emerson was not sleeping on the couch where Morgan Everest camped out.

Sometimes he left money for the rent.

Sometimes he didn't.

Sometimes he washed the dishes.

Sometimes dirty plates were left in the sink demonstrating seismic patterns for days.

Sometimes Freddie was vague and emblematic and not much more than a shell in a gift shop.

Sometimes it appeared you knew him for your entire life.

Sometimes he volunteered at the hospital and sat with the terminal old men just to seem like an unaffected presence.

Sometimes he was the cosmic boy scout. Working the soup lines — helping kids learn to read — running errands for old ladies —sometimes he walked around Jersey-land and was primed for a good deed…

*

Or sometimes Mickey Emerson was so stoned he forget everything and easily disappeared from wherever he was to the thin air beside him. Freddie plied no reference. Morgan played that in spades. Or sometimes he got so stoned in the evening that he couldn't dig the sand pit for the bonfire: aka- squid Italian in good bread crumbs and light red sauce — aka: clams in chowder and muscles steamed and the iced tea with lemon juice and salsa and roasted corn and was done for eating when the dregs of the fire were almost out –aka: hotdogs with a seaweed and a sweet onion and potatoes stabbed many times over with fork twines and rolled up in foil with rosemary butter and salt and then laid beside the corn in the fire… Or sometimes Freddie was so stoned he roasted the squid first thing before anything else had a chance to cook …

*

Morgan was chatting up a couple of neat freaks at the bar. They were transitional genders: identity creatures when all else failed their lives. Both enlisted in the coast guard and wound up with primo records of service. Medals and honors and shit like that. One male turned female/ one female turned male. They lobbied the feds to have a cutter christened with their hyphenated name…

Eden Jones was dancing.

You were floating on like a barstool in the mountains.

Mantis was openly and quietly rolling joints on the table.

Fast Eddie walked by and shook his head politely no — no he said.

But Mantis said this is illegal and its everyday and its beginnings date back to the snap of human consciousness so that means we're totally on the same page as was every other human consciousness to date.

Now doesn't that fuck you up he asked Fast Eddie?

When he finished rolling Mantis offered Fast Eddie a joint. And with the sly nod that made him a successful businessman and knowing that saying thanks to his regulars gave him maneuvers down the line Fast Eddie pocketed the joint.

And Mantis — after he returned from the other side of the world — his aim was to try and shape one single day in his life from where he felt better than the previous day. Then he'd take it from there and try and build something. And what was that? Mantis didn't know. But what he did know was how to try.

Currently he was years behind the target.

Currently Mantis was walking alone in a valley of big forces. And they would not leave him be. Yea the big forces he said but they were not the special forces he said.

Mantis you understood and his aim he said were to avoid the ghosts rising from the mud floor of that valley and reaching the sky.

No big deal he thought. Push comes to shove — truth be told to power — all that shit he said like you're only as good as your next shot — it was no big deal he said. He'd just go into the bathroom and roll more joints for later.

Wild snake-like hair grew out from his skull in dark crawling and heavy thickets that seemed to drag his skull along with it as the hair grew outside his body. Think — maybe someone took a curling iron and let it heat a mop sized pad of steel wool until near combustion and then dumped a can of black paint over it — what you might come up with was some wet dream bozo the clown's evil twin looked like. Mantis and his hair frightened normality. Like how do you stuff all that into a hat if you're not a Rasta? His hair was an emotional explosion. Think electric wires broken off a utility pole and jumping and sparking around the street. Every Sunday since Mantis came back he visited his grandmother on Poplar Street for Sunday gravy. Every Sunday when his grandmother looked at Mantis she got them both a beer — and then fell she back on the sofa and put a ball game on and said one day you will give me a heart attack.

Mantis downed his beer in a one thirsty gulp. And he said to his grandmother — looking at you each time I see you well that time I see you — that time gives me a heart attack he said and sat beside her and together they watched the game of the week and split a twelve pack and dinned on home made pasta and gravy until they burped and then they both went back for seconds.

*

Mantis was a damaged packaged of goods and despite his shortcomings and mistakes with regard to his military life he shall be treated with the respect and dignity due him and to his service. However Mantis was not to be reclaimed.

The Strike Report said Mantis was unable to restrict himself in order for himself to be controlled. He should be contained The Report continued and questioned according to standards and in situ shall be relived of his duties in the infantry. And if according to standards if the questions were met with satisfactory answers and with a sufficient maintenance to the answers and were credited with due process and corroborating sources then it is recommend that Mantis be let go and left go fallow.

And should the answers which Mantis offered as answers were then determined not to be satisfactory answers within the department's wishes then Mantis shall be allocated to the lowest pay grade possible. Obviously within that lowest pay grade addendum — since by then it was to be determined that Mantis was not at all plausible in the field but also all records of Mantis as existing in the armed forces shall be adjudicated and applied to all inquiries aka — Mantis — therefore it should be noted on the public available Stone Cold site that in the course of the war Mantis was a common name and so due to the outmost security concerns — aka — Mantis — and the charge we have to be open to the citizen public — therefore on the Stone Cold public site it has been recommended and approved that multiples of the name Mantis complete with bio and last known correspondence shall be published on the Stone Cold site with the appropriate links — real or otherwise — but Mantis as we speak does not own his own living presence. Given his violent history — and let this rejoinder be forceful- ultimately — once Mantis checked into the clinic once a month for his money — the necessary therapies shall include injections and interrogations but understand there was to be no physical harm mentioned upon Mantis.

That said it is our belief that it was in all our best interest to encourage Mantis at all times that he recall the guidelines he signed and that he understand the consequence for gross negligence. Because either way he imagines — he's playing it — shall be made clear to him that we have more than enough hell-fire ways to bury him away and gone.

And that was from a CIA report the cousins stole one evening off a secure government computer.

Blind Charlie didn't like it. Did not like it one bit and he said so.

Do we know anybody in the CIA he asked with disgust?

Not really Bobby Alfredo said.

What does — not really — really mean these days Blind Charlie asked?

What it means Bobby Alfredo said was that no we don't have no guy in the CIA. What we do have however was that we got a bug in the CIA.

Why are we in the CIA? Blind Charlie was a little stuck on the question.

Bobby Alfredo said — trying his best not to upset Blind Charlie — well you know one day we was snooping around and then you know we got like this toehold on a site. We kept it you know and being curious we dug deeper and soon that toehold was a footprint.

A footprint Blind Charlie said. From what I know you can follow a footprint. You can spray footprints and see them in the dark. You cast footprints in plaster and match that against a guy's shoes.

A cousin said the CIA thing well it just happened…

Nothing just happens Blind Charlie reminded him.

Well yea the cousin said scratching his ear. But once we were in we decided to keep looking. Maybe we haul in something big… who knows…?

That's favorable Blind Charlie said. But who else has seen this?

That's the strange part Bobby Alfredo said.

The strange part Blind Charlie nodded and bit his lips in thought.

Yea Bobby Alfredo said. Somebody else — somebody we don't know — they sent that report.

Tell me Blind Charlie wanted to know. Have we ever — taken — anything from the CIA?

Well a cousin said — he was in charge of the backroom computers — he said once we took the firing pin sequences for car bombs. And once we stole some airline reservations. And once we stole photos but we made that work. Once we stole a birthday clown. Once we stopped a train. Once we billed an underling at a DC party for 300 pies and we got the money but we routed all the concerns away from anything Da Vinci's.

Blind Charlie liked the cousin. And like every cousin Blind Charlie was there at his birth. Stai attento. Mai fidarsi. ma si scopre deve fidare.

Blind Charlie was tired. Another cousin got him another wine.

Blind Charlie flashed his hands across the air and the cousins in the room got it and they put the computers to sleep and listened up.

Have we ever taken money from the CIA?

Have we ever stolen money from the CIA?

Have we ever been bookended by the CIA?

You have tonight he said to figure out whether this is a blessing or whether this is a curse. Whether this works Blind Charlie said — or whether or not we're a rabbit in their pot.

It was true: Da Vinci's made the best-cooked rabbit in the neighborhood.

＊

The military escorts pushed Mantis through another foreign land once his plane set down in Germany. Bad orange jump suit — shackles no less — shades on his face because he asked for them — wild blackberry hair no authority wished to cut without the authority to cut it — maybe that was bad news — a grin for the press — there was no welcome band for the latest Asian war veteran trying to return home

＊

When Cripple graduated high school he took the government up on their offer: if the government fixed his leg then Cripple owed the government two years labor. And it was plain on the contract that if the government fixed his leg then Cripple was free to fight in the latest Asian war.

Once Cripple had the operation — once his future was set — he changed his name to Mantis.

＊

What was worse?

Automatic weapons fire from a tree line that hid the enemy like hallucinations but you kept firing at them day after day? Or were they the phantom weasels you made up in your mind keeping you awake all night and they chewed through your shorts with bone sharp needle teeth?

War was a very uncomfortable place Mantis said. Sadly he went on. He owed years. What was in common anymore?

*

Mantis was walking patrol in the highlands. He was not supposed to be where he was at the time. There were lines on a map — and he had the map — and every minute he needed Mantis had his boss phone with music and photos and satellite updates — so he kept walking — alone but not really lonely — he was cool in country — but fuck them he knew that — but he was told not to cross the map — under no circumstance should he go beyond neither parallel nor meridian as this was tantamount to crossing state lines.

Mantis took a minute and sat on the foreign earth. Time to water up… time to take a break… but you never took a break when you engaged and eliminated… because time decoded things that mattered … you got up off your ass… kept walking in the highlands thirsty and spooked…

…. Keep walking shithead. Just kidding the boss phone said. But not about the walking part Mantis said to the crazy monkeys overhead. His orders were: If need be engage what you see and eliminate. Otherwise — in some 0-hour from today — you need to eliminate yourself: ha ha just kidding the orders said in code– so keep your phone charged and your make your pisses short — we make contact not you. Repeat: engage what you see and eliminate. And remember don't eat a snake you don't know ha ha.

Mantis packed the phone away and thought what the fuck? What else was there? Was there anything different?

Engage and eliminate: the Sunshine Ops Corp… how could he forget? How could he not to recognize it? Mantis owed his first shot to something like the Rosetta Stone phrase he lived with day and night during training: engage and eliminate. Engage. Eliminate. Move on. Check your phone.

How could he plan anything in advance? If it moves then you kill it right? One day in or ten thousand days in — time was all the same. But somewhere it mattered he thought. Yea he had the big doubts but you don't let doubts stand in the way when you're staying alive. That was righteous. Staying alive was righteous. Engage and eliminate well that was righteousness doubled over down with a good hand. Mantis thought — getting up on his feet — the rifle he held pointed throughout the highland path — yea somewhere he thought — engage — eliminate — do the job — Mantis he thought… you were a fucking exterminator. Somewhere all this mattered.

*

Mantis came out from the bush and onto a clearing. He killed somebody along the way. Wasn't a corpse what he had to do? If you can't be sure to fire then your target was sure to fire at you… But what happens when everybody's dead? I mean anyway and who am I supposed to be the dutiful soldier or an assassin? Best eye in the jungle that left what it saw to be flat and dead?

In the clearing Mantis found the remains from some old outpost overgrown with vines. Fucking people he thought… they always built shit that never lasted. But this was odd. This was oddball and this was not on his phone.

Mantis starred at what he saw… stared into what he saw… fucking walls he thought. It was like he received a picture in his head and what that picture showed him was the outline where walls were built. He saw broad flat stones. They were scattered on the floor of the highland earth forgotten and carved.

He knew it — somewhere in the highlands — coming out of the jungle — not even checking his phone and his grids — Mantis knew. He knew. He knew from his sad feet upward. These stones he saw were the remains from like an ancient temple. Fucking amazing shit he thought. I knew he said I saw it.

There were hours left in the daylight to walk. Really his phone said — another piece of cake. Three hours past nightfall he'd locate the target and set his options and turn the phone off. He'd bury himself until morning. Then the little fuck gets it in the back of the neck. Then his head started rolling. It's so clean Mantis thought. We have damn good weapons. And the dude doesn't suffer. He just gets his head blown off. Like fucking wham — and then there's only the next different thing for him...

As he left — as he considered leaving — as he went one way out and then another back inward — Mantis suffered what he referenced to be a change of mind. He stopped and took off his gear and pulled his ass onto the dirt. He looked toward the temple. And it wasn't on his watch and wasn't on his phone.

I know this he said. I know this was what was happening he thought. Like I know there's weirdness and I guess on it and you can't do without it.

Mantis found a stone that suited him and sat down inside. He quietly pretended and removed his helmet. Mantis kept the rifle strapped across his chest but he was pretending that also. You have to give up something he observed. That's how he saw it.

But Mantis had suspicion built into him. What if you gave up a helmet? Wasn't there a fucking chance in the universe you got shot in the head?

He still had his head he thought?

Mantis was walked along that stone. He was lifted physically by what he did not know. He walked arm in arm with the highland air. He got that. But he felt stupid. Like what he did he did it all wrong.

Fucked up feeling Mantis thought.

So he walked away back into the jungle. Nothing lasts long right? Then he wouldn't go any further into the trees. He turned around and walked back. Fucking maneuvers he thought because he duplicated this maneuver several times. Several times he thought? What does that mean?

He sat down inside again. Mantis removed nothing from his gear. Fucking soldier he thought. You're a fucking assassin his brain said. And don't forget you be the best.

Time here was lost from what he thought. That's how Mantis saw it anyway. No fucking time here and what a perfect time he thought for his last ration of acid.

After walking alone for seven months straight in the theater of operations in the highlands where he killed people in places where he shouldn't have been anyway... No voices... Only phone messages... No human contact... Only contact... Might as well walk among the dead he thought... Mantis ate a candy bar to calm his nerves.

He didn't worry about that because candy bars were not to worry about candy bars calmed his nerves and to shoot straight you needed calm nerves and candy bars along with a wee brace of native poppy.

Whoa Mantis thought. Time began to move in such a way he couldn't expect. But he saw it even before he entered the clearing. And now he thought I'm sitting on a temple stone.

Heavy moist air like a jungle fever wrapped Mantis from tree to tree. He sat in the ruins and wondered: Mantis wondered if he fucked up the ruins by sitting there? After considerations — after watching his tattooed hands fold — the left hand said Mantis gives — the right hand said Mantis gives... it was a confusion thing he explained to the crew that owned his phone... Mantis felt no reason to be on the move. Three hours past nightfall and seated on an old temple stone — Mantis turned off the phone as he was instructed to do.

*

White lights left imprints on the dirt floor. Mantis saw it moving around — not like he pictured it as being broken — but it was more fluid — Mantis watched time until he laughed and coughed up air — nothing dull he thought but what does nothing dull mean he thought? Domestic he came up with. That was a word time gave him. Mantis dug time. He liked looking at time. Mantis saw it moving around him. People walked past on the temple floor. Mantis dug them — clothes and ornaments and tools. There was a tall girl making dumplings from boiling water. Some real old guy repaired a sandal tread on his right foot. Young boys ran past with dead birds and green onions.

Fucking A Mantis said. This was way off the calendar.

Normally Mantis was the ghost.

Normally Mantis walked around a village.

Normally he then buried himself.

And when time was right he got up and fired off the necessary shots.

But this wasn't normal. But what the fuck did normal mean? But Mantis dug this business living with people.

Whoa he thought. Easy soldier. Other lives stepped right through him. Mantis ate another candy bar. But really — with the phone off that meant he was off the grid — not operational in a way — normally Mantis was the way- he got in and he got out and everybody got paid — but this temple shit stopped him — these people lived out of time — ancient motherfuckers wasn't that right? They didn't exist and he knew that but what did that mean — Mantis did not exist — they were ghosts like him… and they grabbed his heart and nearly stopped his breath with their lives.

There was this one time he was shot in the ribs and so reached into his kit and stabbed his ass with morphine to shut down the pain in his voice. Big rule: never give yourself away.

Did he learn that? Who taught him?

Was it something he remembered? Where was that from?

By now — am I in time — am I out of time — Mantis stripped his shirt off and lost his boots. Mantis dug the highland dirt. A fucking temple from the past he thought and how fucking cool was that to be sitting among ancients and their hometown. There was no one around to understand him when Mantis stood and spoke.

I'm from Jersey-land he said. He grabbed his rifle with both hands and held it over his head against the lowering red ball sunlight in the high-lands like this was some triumphant movie gesture he imitated. Whoa. Easy soldier. Why do that? But there wasn't anyone other than Mantis in the theater of operations. Fucking bullets he thought. Were bullets more common than words? And having that thought made him sad. Sad like where was the end? Sad wasn't it because Mantis was in the middle of the shit and nowhere near the end. Mantis spoke bullets in many languages.

I'm from Jersey-land he said. He lowered his rifle. Whoa. Easy soldier. His training to be a crack shot in blind alley circumstance included Mantis taking acid. Taking acid and drowning in a mud puddle. Taking acid and having sex and doing something stupid like not coming. Taking acid and decided among what berry leaf or root to eat because two out three killed you. Mantis dug taking acid. Taking acid and emptying a clip into a target's head before his wires and the electro-shock got him. No harm he said to the ancients and laid his rifle down beside his boots.

But — what the fuck — was he crossbred in time — because he knew everyone in the temple.

Mantis stared at the stones because he dug them like kin. Was it okay for him to see into dirt without like a fucking microscope to help him out?

They moved. The stones and the dirt only moved because he was stoned… But the stones moved and the dirt moved. At times the stone and the dirt moved together.

No fucking mistake about that soldier. Mantis laughed till it hurt.

He wished for a drink. He thought the jungle had just about fucked itself out of being.

Mantis wanted to die in the night. But why and what was the opinion?

In his head he saw a floating bar in the South China Sea… he wished for a table in whatever that fucking garden room was called and a table underneath that big skylight where we watched the saucer pans take off and land… he wanted the best crossword puzzle they had and hands down Mantis wanted the time to work on it… Mantis wished for a noodle bowl like he once saw on R&R video about floating bars in the South China Sea… yea a noodle bowl he thought and a noodle bowl topped with those cracked fiery prawns and fresh lime and mint and kick-ass tamari soaked peanuts…

However — through it all — till the next helio-drop — and that meant no drop until the next shot was judicated — however — Mantis — upon curiosity and dead order need — found two irradiated whiskey foils in his sack. Cryogenic-fried Kentucky mash that tasted nothing like whiskey from the home planet but a drink that made wonders in return for stressed out bones. Yes he thought. Wasn't it common sense to order quarts and not shots? Mantis thought they both weigh the same. So you might as well pack artillery.

Mantis found the temple stream and mixing things up went directly to a cocktail hour for one.

But the stones moved. This was better he thought. Everyone was here.

Like he had just pulled up the temple personal file. Linked up bios and associate contacts and family payoffs and goods traded by tribes and goods received by tribes and goods stolen by tribes –and the small wars… everything was here. Mantis wished he had a plate of crab cakes from a shady take-out window in Belmar. Did fucking crabs even grow in Jersey-land?

*

Mantis remembered something — about a time in the fourth grade. It was a class trip near the end of the school year. The class went to middle Jersey-land to visit a farm.

Mantis remembered the trip as going to a place where there were no cites. He remembered tractors and vegetables in neat straight rows. The red dirt he was told was god's own clay. There were houses with crude antennas titled on rooftops and only four television channels to watch.

Cripple was amazed when some big white kid took him along to see the peach trees.

What the fuck — where did peaches come from anyway? Cripple could not believe it. Fucking peach trees. He couldn't believe it.

*

It was the best trip. That's what Mantis said. But he understood that it was probably not true after all. After so many shots — after so many freeze dried liquors from the plantations — even after eating peaches in his memory — Mantis sat back down — like he had found a peculiar stone to rest upon — and realized that he hated using the word lie.

But while that was the point he was getting at — it was also beyond the point he looked for. How many nights — when he was first in the war — did he walk point? Yea he was shot a few times but that wasn't the point. But he couldn't finger it: just what was the point?

Meanwhile — Mantis loved that word — meanwhile — the temple unfolded in time.

Meanwhile there was always this lonesomeness he envied around strangers.

Meanwhile he thought Mantis kicked ass.

Didn't he have a tattoo or something?

That wasn't it.

What if there was someone smarter than Mantis?

Confused he said. Talents thrown in reverse…

*

A walk in the boonies — slang for the mission — and then an old temple showed up.

Figure. Define. Enhance. Repeat sequence if necessary. Figure. Define. Enhance.

*

Mantis lay on the dirt like a captive spread eagled in a game of war and listened to his chest machinations going off for the second day in repeat. No fucking way. His heart was beating. No fucking way that he was not alive. Yea Mantis said. All the wallops maul and drub that was inside and was crapping and was horny and scared and Mantis thought: this was a setup. His thoughts were lost the moment he had one. And on his phone Mantis passed the technical definition what it meant to be alive: to state the obvious and then get out of the way.

Fucking ops manual Mantis said.

Mantis denied he had a job and canceled the report.

Investigating a possible hostile site he typed.

The temple dilated his being.

Must be words Mantis thought.

Somebody on the other end of the phone fucked with him again — did not answer his inquiries directly but instead sent Mantis more of the same broken sentences he'd gotten from the phone for the past twenty-two months.

Words like bemoan and bewail and words like gruff and grandiloquent and words like hitch and hole… a phrase like a hardon state of mind… a phrase like the magic he worked cautiously back storied him entirely…

Mantis got the tactical point of worry. He was trained. Shoot the targets and plot the kills on Quick Time Player. Tag the enemy was the punch line — eternity was the joke… but meanwhile when he shot them he also shot their ancestors… their ghosts…

*

Mantis thought about it. He thought about it and gave it more thinking and thinking about it his thoughts lead him nowhere particular.

Maybe when the phone answered it was nothing to even think about. Maybe it was just a fucking phone dude.

But those phone guys — they were military personal — Mantis needed them — he collaborated with them — he never met them — they were the phone — and when the phone spoke Mantis talked with strangers — fucking strangers — but Mantis had a mission and success depended on them for information… But the phone didn't care — actually the phone laughed… Mantis shot someone and needed coordinates… the territory beneath the map… fucking scenery vend augury he called in… paint me away high-priced secondary holy greed he called in… And from there Mantis needed the way out.

The phone said: squeeze it poltroon squeeze it lukewarm…

But that meant nothing: nothing in code to Mantis. And getting nothing back in code meant the phone laughed: and when the phone laughed that meant Mantis was hung out.

Same side Mantis typed back?

Same side the phone replied. That's what makes us great.

*

Weren't there tears when things broke down?

It was hard to understand that's all.

This meant he was still unemployed.

If you control your breathing then you pull the trigger.

If you took a life that meant you kept your own.

That was it.

272

Mantis wished for green onions. He knew shit about green onions. But what he knew was that he wanted green onions. He tried dumplings once — a long tine ago — during a weekend R and R he took in the north suburbs near the big line with China — he remembered small cracked plates — French signatures on the back — small bowls of thin fiery ginger sauce for dipping... big American beer was everywhere he looked... women sold themselves wherever he looked... Mantis enjoyed the dumplings... did likewise by the big American beer... tried a woman before daybreak whose relative he may have shot a few days earlier...

Proof was Mantis knew the answer. He had to. If he didn't know the answer then the helicopter left him outside. And the helicopter wasn't the phone. The helicopter flew inside the war. Mantis had an alt-code. In a perverse way having an alt-code gave him a dry spirited chuckle over the phone. If you called the helicopter direct — within an hour the whoomp whoomp whoomp rotor sounds where in the neighborhood — searching above — looking for a way to grab your sorry ass out of trouble.

The helicopter always asked how long you been in country?

As long as it takes Mantis said.

Out you the helicopter said.

Got scope Mantis asked?

Out you copy spirit boy... Landing zone several minutes your north... Willow Grove Park / Frankford El / Frosty Top... over... you be gone spirit boy...

But he didn't believe it.

He knew the helicopter was true. Many times the fucking helicopter was like god. Mantis prayed to the helicopter to deliver him from shit and had the faith to be afraid that the assembly line back home got the nuts and bolts straight when they built the helicopter. But unless the helicopter was shot from the sky by some vintage rocket launcher then god the helicopter showed face. Mantis was harnessed from above and hoisted skyward. Bye-bye danger land Mantis said to the pilot.

The pilot always laughed like he was stoned and said glad you're back. The pilot said — like he was always stoned and had everything to give — watch this. Here's a round for the bad guys. The highlands below their climbing arc into the sky were toasted indiscriminately with rockets. The trees burst on fire. Only the rats survive the pilot said like he was always stoned. Mantis watched the landscape below catch fire as the helicopter sped off below the clouds. The temple was a piece of work he thought. He wished everyone well.

*

One night Mantis went crazy in the jungle.

It's a rain forest asshole the phone said. Nobody calls it a jungle any more.

Waiting meant he was buried that much longer... waiting... for patrols to appear on his jungle — fuck me learning — rain forest radar... and that meant several things... Mantis had to work primo to stay ready and be still because the intelligence on enemy movement was off... and second he brought up a phrase to court... and last he wondered if time played favorites.

The phrase he brought up was in code but he sent it anyway: keep cleft blackjack 9 mercy cudgel clumsy repeat clumsy dictums amass repeat clumsy bluff acknowledge flatter garb shade informal clever dark golden rule dictum fuck dictum fuck dictum solid dear.

The phone replied: baby line 9 homely score.

At least the helicopter pilot laughed when he laughed at his job.

*

Transgressions against military discipline grew weekly on Mantis and his file.

Once he called the forward enemy dispatch — along the big line with China — fuck he knew those guys — and ordered communist noodle keep out. Dumpling great he added in his crappy Asian war accent. He knew those fucking guys.

Once Mantis radioed in the wrong match for an artillery strike. The suspected village wasn't blown up. Rather he pointed the mortars at his hilltop position.

He took his dog tags off one day and placed then around a water buffalo's horn. Send the beast plowing he thought. With identity...

274

Mantis phoned a major one night in a command zone in the south and called the major a dim puttied shit. Where was his request Mantis demanded? Did he not call for and ask explicitly for a download of Axis Bold As Love be web lifted to his unofficial phone?

Well the major said I'd take being called a dim puttied shit as a confidence these days. But no go on the download he said. The major could not requisition the file — Hendrix no less — did he think the army was made of money? For someone who did not exist in protocol and someone whose base camp was never on the map how was the major to reply and where was the major to send this download?

By then Mantis refused all specified code words with regard to person.

Meanwhile he continued. He shot people. He walked in the highlands like a free soul.

*

It began where it began to fall apart Mantis thought. That's a great thought Mantis thought. He got shifted down from the hills. Code translated said: useful elsewhere respond ass. Even as he regretted it — Mantis went back to code. Maybe for the first time in the war he was afraid.

And for Mantis the word elsewhere was a word with similarities to the word meanwhile. He dug them both.

Meanwhile elsewhere he did not like this. Being shifted meant losing cover. Being shifted meant descent onto the hot trails and the dead helicopter paddies. Fuck. Dying was part of it he thought.

But he dug the hills. He taught Jersey-land to the natives in exchange for their tongue. Mantis wore the ceremonial necklace from each place where he worked and was buried. Each tribe he fought with: hunting bad guys with the elders.... Mantis gained cred and that meant popularity and recognition meant a necklace. Funny he never imagined how death equaled prized jewelry.

Nobody ever — from the phone — nobody ever from the phone they never gave him nothing except the point where he was walking... they never air lifted dope– they never air lifted the extra-ammo on time — the never lifted a hand to get him toothpaste — yea that's great Mantis said

275

ever see a white guy trying to hide in the jungle without the right cameo grease... or shoelaces for fucks sake!

So what did that mean?

Each village wherever Mantis stayed he got a necklace. He killed — many people — that killing — what everyone else called it — many people — the many people the villagers wanted dead.

And it was said to Mantis by the villages — through translations — whoever wears the necklace rises up and takes the world as a motherfucker.

Walking down from the highlands Mantis sported six different necklaces. Teeth from kills and stones from mountains and animal fur and bird feathers and lizard tails and assorted junk from the latest Asian war like ancient flip top rings from beer cans and metal dog tags identifying soldiers from days way past before today's soldiers were bar-coded on their necks. They lassoed around his shirtless neck and were valued where he walked in the highlands. Mantis understood that. He dug each necklace and dug each village.

*

But now he was going where? The god-fucked north and some stationary and fortified hole in the ground and defending the lousy western flank?

Everything west this side of hades-town belonged to the enemy. From old Burma gone through ten thousand names trying to identify a country — to creepy Bangladesh with its streets blocked with movie assassins and wonderful goods for sale — to Bhutan up in the cloudless clouds — you'd be lucky to find a friendly face or a bowl of soup that didn't blow up in your face.

We gave up the west a long time ago Mantis thought. Didn't we give up the west a long time ago?

And coming off the highlands Mantis checked his phone and his satellite position.

He answered the phone: lust rude sumptuous honey limpid unreasonable sconce.

The phone answered back and it sounded like a helicopter pilot was laughing at the other end. You are employed baby 9. Repeat: you are employed. Baby 9 cleared pert flippant goad spasmodic. Even happens dude the phone said out of code and so good luck and we've loved fucking with you. Been a pleasure sir. Don't call us. We'll call you back.

*

Mantis snaked in behind the lines. Shit was everywhere he thought. The phone sent him a text with a smiley face attached: eight thousand and counting. That meant the enemy. Eight thousand fighters gathering outside this ridiculous compound meant there were another eighty thousand behind them in place and another eighty thousand behind them like in situ of the mind — the fucking west was lost so what the fuck was he doing here?

Mantis came down slow on the trail and hid for a while — and then advanced — and then hid again. This was fucked he thought. He watched the enemy materialize in numbers. Numbers frightened Mantis anyway. But he personally had never seen anything like this. He hit the delete app on his phone. That action took him one step away from ever being seen again. He called the helicopter. Fuck code he said which really was the last ditch code to send.

Request: spring daisy. Repeat. Request: spring daisy. Wildflower no care no care fable business no flash immediate and hear this mother-fuckers we request support spring daisy filthy we go you gone they pious.

Mantis then dismantled his phone. It was now an armed weapon. Ready to toss. Fuck.

Before he committed to a position though Mantis had to think. Outside the wire or inside the wire or did it even matter? From his sights this was a forgotten piece of real estate. A strategic firebase — but in what eternity was this decided?

West of the wire — and forget the fighters — there were millions beyond who hated Mantis. Little kids hated Mantis. Great uncles hated Mantis. Entire boundaries hated Mantis.

Strange thing he thought. To be hated was like applause.

Mantis decided the better chance was inside the wire. And fuck Mantis he thought.

*

When he got inside — Mantis literally got inside under the wire without a security breach — he walked through a nether land below ground in trenches. Gun posts every sixteen inches on center — mortar launches the ones that fired cascading grenades and sent off maximum shredded metal per grenade once detonated below ten feet this atmosphere — bulldozers fitted with old school howitzers that had wicked long sharps of barbed Lucy wire in the shells — and behind all that was Bennie Han Na. And Bennie Han Na was the most desperate counter-measure in the field. Bennie Hah Na avoided strategic impulses as programmed to get around Geneva and the fair game mindset. Nobody knew what Bennie Han Na knew. But let's just say Mantis thought the fucking dude was totally equipped.

Some bikini atoll newbie — about to get shot though the ear anyway — Mantis saw it like seven seconds before it happened — while he saluted Mantis and pointed out to Mantis that Bennie Han Na was a computer the newbie then dropped flat and lay in his own blood like he might need a refreshing nap.

Welcome to the front lines a chaplain said.

Seems like ashes and entrails and not a whole lovely chorus if you know what I mean Mantis said.

And what are you doing here spirit boy the chaplain asked?

Passing through Mantis joked. I was told I was employed.

Yes the chaplain said I saw your rifle.

Mantis looked the chaplain and asked — so what's up…I don't have a fucking clue so what's up padre?

Are you here to save us the chaplain asked? Pick them off — one by one — until you have them all and none are left? And we walk away from here? But son — bless you my son — but those were fucked up rumors. Unbelievable expectations. Drain and rinse bullshit…

Padre what are you talking about Mantis asked?

The chaplain sighed. Mantis thought he was okay on first recon. But Mantis held deep suspicions. By nature he thought do you trust what you don't kill?

278

February the chaplain said: 543 dead. And that's not even a leap year he said.

Mantis guessed that was supposed to be a joke. Jokes were good. Mantis dug jokes. Jokes were like tickets to bullet wounds... But jokes don't get your question...

Yes the chaplain said I could see it on your face. Son he said you stand among countless believers. And you — I'm afraid — to quandary — you are not a believer.

Fine enough padre Mantis said. But then why am I here?

You're asking me why the chaplain said? Do I suggest that I have answers? No. I do not. Basically son the chaplain said why I'm here is to be the welcome committee and bless the goodbye ordinance that hence has blown you apart. You are here because we need every last son of a bitch we have our hands on — I know what you do and I know how you've done it. Do you think that bothers me? Do you think that bothers me here?

Well yea Mantis said. I do think it bothers you padre. We're about to get our assholes shoved backwards.

But son the chaplain replied we are being shoved backwards. But the only direction we shall go shall be toward god.

By tradition the chaplain outranked Mantis.

By tradition chaplains worried about their job and smoked too many cigarettes.

Got the picture padre Mantis said.

No I'm afraid not the chaplain said. You got the picture? When the fuck did that arrive? So you listen to me —

Beg your pardon sir but I don't exist sir Mantis interrupted. Never have. But I'm employed now. When this gets done I still won't exist. Been that way padre.

Oh I get it the chaplain said — so he went on and took Mantis by the ear —

You listen to me you spook-punk dispatch I know you and I know this was how you cover. This here shall be a real go-figure moment for the record books. Human fucking confusion at its peak... artillery hellfire for days... not to mention supportive air strikes... every five minutes...

who the fuck was who… Operation Niagara it's called so what was the purpose holding the hills Operation Viagra it was called every five minutes they changed it so you tell me soldier what was the purpose holding the hills when every five minutes and now we're dug into this shit hole the ground shakes beneath your feet and you wanna know why you're here well I will tell you why you are here you are here because every fucking five minutes we're getting blown up that's why you're here all those explosions they blew apart the hills into craters back into asteroid time and everyone waited for a decent roll of the dice but do you think that happened no it did not and that was just the dead on our side yes you dumb fuck that's why you are here shit man at night you hear the other side digging toward us and digging toward us who was the ass that put us in trenches the other side was still digging toward us after five thousand bombs they dig toward us tonight and they move about wordlessly…

Copy that padre Mantis said. And then he walked away. People with faith always lose it Mantis said to a corpse. It was bad he thought when you can't commission the dead and get them away proper.

*

But it was just like the padre said: fucked. But Mantis did his job. He snuck outside the wire at night. He waited and he shot people. And then Mantis snuck back inside the wire. He felt like a factory worker on a damn time clock.

But in the month that followed — the words — effective kills — had so little giz that in the end — like everything else — they were meaningless. And if words were meaningless Mantis thought what was next? And so for the fist time in the war Mantis occupied a single place to fight from. Fucked. Behind the wire and sandbags — ten thousand friendlies at his side — behind Benny Han Na — behind this elaborately staged set piece made to order for everyone to die — Mantis felt a loneliness and a coldness that blinded him. Dying was part of it. He looked around saw all these guys scraping bar codes off their necks. There was more going on here than just numbers he thought. How much personal and weaponry and canned beans were at stake? And without getting too deep into it weren't there like entire hostile countries camped around them? What kind of fucked up stagecoach movie was this?

One night Mantis shot an older guy in the trench wearing classic black silks. By tradition someone wearing black silks was venerable and was called ancestor wherever he traveled.

When he went to check the guy's belongings Mantis found a post card on a string around the guy's neck. It read: Mot Frechman chet. Nguoi Trung Quoc da chet. Tieng Nhat qua doi. Big My da chet. Ban cung se chet o day.

Positive that ancestor Mantis said reading Silk's postcard for a second time. Then he slung the card around his own neck and was gone in the trenches below the darkness below the tracers.

A night later Mantis barely ducked away in time. He crawled against the trench floor and rolled over on some guy the whole time breathing dirt shit and matchsticks. Random fire hit from everywhere Mantis looked... the loud jam of explosives... pieces splinters and bones shot upward in the gunfire and then fell back down into the same gunfire and were hit again... almost nothing physical... the quick big nil... things shot up once and then shot up again... what was left? The trenches were hammered... a wind driven storm pounding on an exposed house... shredding material acquisitions... shredded infantrymen... like there was no plan A... not to even bring up a plan B... at the bottom of the trench Mantis felt the sky... the sky was calm... at the bottom of the trench Mantis thought about the universe... but that was too strange to consider under the circumstance and so he left it alone... above his head the trench was shredded into binary moments like here or not here for long war-like minutes before the bullets and rockets and flaming air let up. It was probably a Tuesday he thought because that was the day the other side got resupplied.

Dude you all right Mantis asked?

The sergeant was hit bad. There was more air moving out the sergeant's chest holes than there was air passing into his nostrils. Bloody fucking holes but Mantis understood what they meant.

Mantis injected the sergeant with morphine. He sat down beside the sergeant. Who needs the pain more Mantis asked?

The sergeant gurgled. You're dying dude Mantis said.

Copy that. The sergeant tried to move. He tried to but he couldn't.

Easy Mantis said. Copy that.

I don't mind dying the sergeant said.

You're a liar Mantis told him. Mantis wanted a shot of morphine for himself.

Haven't always been so the sergeant laughed. It's bad huh?

Afraid so.

Appreciate what you're doing.

I don't Mantis said.

Copy.

Understand I can't help you.

Understood. Don't leave till it's over okay?

I won't Mantis said.

And while the sergeant wheezed for life as a kind of principled unity — Mantis drove a needle into his arm and needed to forget that life ever happened.

Do you think this a private moment the sergeant asked?

No Mantis said reaching for his rifle I don't. You know — it's like private — when — suddenly you notice there's no color left in the sky. You're just dying dude. Go easy.

Right.

*

A month later Mantis shot his last target. He took the tires off the lead jeep carrying a congressional delegation sent over to inspect the war. What's the plan Mantis yelled?

When nobody answered he shot the next jeep in line. Next time I shoot the civilians.

*

At the court marshal proceedings Mantis tried to explain. Fuck conduct he thought. Imagine how difficult he said and imagine what it takes to un-locate yourself in time?

Mantis told the court he believed that he was genetically malfunctioned. Sitting in the jungles all that time messed up his DNA he said. It was too easy to hide in the vegetation. He became a living and breathing part of it. The jungle challenged his mind he said until the jungle got his mind. It became natural to shoot people. Fighting a war from an invisible position was a piece of fucking cake — it was a fucking walk in the park — a day at the fucking beach — like an over/under dice game on the boardwalk that the elders taught you how to beat — I set my phone to timer and reminder — timer and reminder — shooting people was like having a fucking privileged lifestyle — I was word — I shot my target and slid back into the jungle — I was the jungle — I ate bugs — I fucked a snake —

*

Two military policemen — big silent guys with truncheons and side arms and an overall square-ness — bracketed Mantis on either side of his chair.

The charges against Mantis were beaucoup serious.

Yes Mantis said he understood them.

Insubordination... attempted murder... willfully damaging government property... failure to identify yourself to a superior officer... failing too heed a superior officer's command to lay down your weapon... failure to act in a manner benefitting a member of this nation's armed forces... failure to comply with military discipline... failure to comply with a way of life... failure from thinking... failure at birth... failure to sit and not question... And so on.

*

Mantis pictured himself in an air-conditioned hut in the rear with the gear at the bottom of Asia before a tribunal of clean smelling men about to judge him. He imagined how a grenade worked. What day was it?

Hey he said to the cops look outside. It's snowing! It's like the first snowflakes in town and that's like something to remember and you're walking beneath them trying to catch one on your tongue and you're so unprepared for them. Do you think this has anything to do with the traditions we have? That we always believe in no matter what the fuck crosses our paths? We need to live in a constant state of excitement don't you think? But what happens? What happened to me? Do you care? Do you figure this at all? What the fuck happened — when that constant state and that belief in a constant state and the excitement happened but I'm dead in the skin and wearisome in the head? With the courts permission- do you have answers sirs?

Some middle-aged officer stared at Mantis and said yes.

Mantis looked back at this straight edge colonel and met his eyes — one eye for another- like a showdown…

Baby fat Mantis thought… a fucking goo-goo officer… cute and righteous… no action in the field for years… pocketing taxpayer money… retirement brain … not upsetting a thing… the wolves and jail and history can have everyone else… but all that Mantis said in his chair — shackles around his wrists and ankles — big square MP's loaded on either side of the chair — what Mantis said about the colonel never touched the colonel because Mantis said the dude was an officer and had his rank and he was connected in time.

Connected in time… far from Mantis… But fuck it… this colonel he said was another forgotten guy… that happened in military taxonomy… the colonel was skank… never was a warrior… career man… impotent Mantis said… however for pension and truth and consolidations before the colonel walked away to gravy-land he was chosen to be a judge and certainly he needed to be a prick as a judge… money rides your back not justice Mantis said … a guy whose family owned a grocery store in Iowa and that's all he thought about … getting back … a grocery store clerk… soft like pudding… hot for his wife… damn good father for the kids… fly fishing on a Tuesday afternoon… but until then… those Iowa reveries had to hold….

Mantis — as he understood himself to be — was armed forces. Shoot. No questions. His back was safe. But that was yesterday. Right Mantis said.

What was that soldier?

Nothing sir.

Fine then the colonel said. But we are not here to talk about me. So tell me this: do you believe — facing quite serious and substantial charges — that you are making things better for yourself here in this room?

*

Mantis asked if he might have a can of soda? He said as far as military justice goes it's a hard business. Three hundred plus known kills sir and twenty-nine prisoners taken and handed over. Year's sir — no common humanity for years sir — jungle fatigues that rotted off my skin like I was a snake — no one called sir — for years — no one called to ask how you doing or to say happy new year — I've been outside for years sir — I did my job — I shot the target — I wanted new boots but it took months and begging to get a pair dropped to me — I needed a new scope but my phone did not have an up to date weapon's acquisition app...

About that phone the colonel interrupted — was it true that you threw your phone at the jeeps?

Copy that sir Mantis said.

And why was that?

No choice sir.

And what does that mean the colonel asked?

It was set to detonate sir.

And so you threw it at the jeeps?

Yes sir.

Maybe it begs the question for this courtroom the colonel asked but why did you throw your phone at the jeeps?

Mantis replied I didn't want to be blown up sir. I dismantled my app. And so by taking that action in the field my phone was a now a weapon....

Yes the colonel said and with a timer...

Copy that sir.

Why not use it elsewhere soldier?

Mantis answered the jeeps were a good target. Sir. Can I get that soda?

A good target you said? The colonel admitted he was puzzled by the prisoner's response.

Prisoner Mantis said Prisoner? Weren't we in court he asked? Don't we take into account — like — fucking jurisprudence? No way sir — no way — no fucking prisoner here sir and let the record be clear.

Let me ask you a question sir — if it pleased the court: have you ever-called in a napalm 3 strike on the other guy's position? Have you ever seen what that does? Have you ever sprayed Agent Orange 7 in rice paddies just for the fuck of it? Have you ever seen what that does? And then you think: does the place where you live interfere with the social life you wish to enjoy? Were you ever bothered by the feeling other people were reading your thoughts? In fact it's snowing today. Look outside! Nothing comes from it. Nothing accumulates. In fact it snows most of the day. Then it's heavy. Then it might drift. There's a squirrel sitting on a fence as winter begins. He jumps off the fence. He goes mental sir. You know? He's looking for food. But the squirrel's got this underdeveloped brain where he can't remember what he stashed. Have you ever felt that colonel? Don't answer sir because I know you have. You're able to walk underneath the snow like you're in the future all light-hearted and shit. Impossible beauty in snowflakes passed over you. Suddenly you stop on a dime you don't own. Suddenly this dime you don't own flipped you over. Elemental forces in the worlds collide — do you think sir? Or maybe some lost part that went out heads? And where we once remembered the world by no longer existed?

Soldier — what does this train of thought have to do with us — today — being in this room the colonel asked? Let me remind you: you are under oath.

*

I can't fight Mantis answered. It's like I get daydreams or some shit. Fuck sir it's easy to shoot people. But I can't fight. Have you ever shot somebody? Sir.

Yes. Yes I have the colonel replied soberly. But my record is not questioned here.... and furthermore...

Furthermore wasn't a word Mantis dug... Not like meanwhile or elsewhere... Mantis dug those words... Everyone's record is being questioned he said!

Here's the problem. What we have was an army in the field who does not daydream. Because they're scared to death they're going to lose their life. Sir. So they fight. And not daydream. Big problem you have sir. And what's worrisome was that sooner or later command started pulling deities out of air just to prove we were still on the ground and shooting. Copy that sir? Are you ever bothered by feelings that things are not quite real? Do ideas run through your head for no good reason? Do you frequently have spells of the blues? Have you wound up thinking something turned me around and made me act against my will?

Staying alive was part of the job a major said.

What's next Mantis asked? Are you telling me it's my job to stay alive and not be alive?

It is your job the major said.

No Mantis said. I am no longer employed. Sir. I have never existed.

What a nut case the major thought.

Look at this guy's eyes Mantis thought. It's like he's trying to get something fierce out of dishwater. The whole fucking array was sad...

Nut case the major thought.

The major needed to be on a plane soon. He missed Korean food. He missed his shirts ironed by pretty girls. He missed roll call ironed by pretty girls...

Mantis thought this was one damn good cigarette. Permission was authorized for another soda. Mantis stood from his chair — this had an immediate effect on the military policeman. They each placed a large suggestive hand on Mantis' shoulders and forced him back into his seat. Rank was some dinky side street along a vast marketplace of avenues to travel Mantis imagined.

*

Since we disagree that means we can't agree and that makes it ironic since we seek agreement within our differing points of view to argue for... don't you agree sir?

Explain that the colonel asked?

When you shot someone Mantis asked the colonel did it make you

287

feel- like — social? Like a real lampshade on the head type of guy at the party — the type of guy you always see — telling jokes — pouring drinks — slapping everyone else on the back — but truly inside had nothing worthwhile to say. Was that you sir?

I honesty tell you soldier I have not experienced anything like that the colonel said.

Well then — you haven't lived much have you sir?

Another major interrupted and said this all makes for nice small talk — if we were in the mess hall for god's sake!

Soldier — you are charged with serious breaches that weakened us all as a nation at a time of war– and these charges demand military discipline. Attempted murder of civilians — a disgrace to the uniform — giving comfort and aid to the enemy...

Whoa Mantis said. What the fuck was this treason shit about?

Did you not dismantle your app the major asked?

You show me yours — and I show you mine Mantis said.

This is not a game soldier.

Agreed Mantis said — but what I want to know is: what was the fight in the west about? Explain the buildup sir? Explain the trenches sir? Explain why we lost thousands sir? Your kin and mine...

Tactical field operations are not the reason why we are here –

Why are we here then?

You are out of order the major said.

Tell me why Mantis asked?

The major looked at Mantis — he was like a guy who needed a beer and couldn't get one and was now faced with a closed barroom door. A shuffleboard guy Mantis thought once he leaves the military for the sunny kingdom of Florida. High pants marlin-fishing drinks at noon etc.

Hell major Mantis said the only thing I feel bad for were the jeeps. They had a purpose.

And what about the congressmen some other major asked?

Fuck them Mantis said. They don't sign my checks.

Who does then the colonel asked?

Good question sir. My money gets sent home.

Where's home?

Jersey-land sir.

Never heard of it a major sneered.

Never heard of Jersey-land Mantis laughed… You never heard of Jersey-land? You never heard of Jersey-land Mantis yelled you dim wit with no balls!

*

That's what I'm trying to explain. You're sitting on that side of the room because someone like me sits on this side of the room. Without that line — down the middle — we don't exist!

Here's what I see gentlemen.

A middle-age weariness that starts as a bad thought that you dismiss but that bad thought kept growing and soon if filled your eyes. Bad thoughts gentlemen Mantis said. You got the family mortgage. How do you play that against your pension? Thoughts keep you awake at night a little longer than you'd like them to. But you're back in the world. You don't have cheap government booze and the best native dope. Gentlemen here's what I see. You're sitting in a fake wood paneled den in the basement. You're staring at an overdue auto payment and sighing. You never questioned your service. Never doubted the uniform. You're proud because all that was real. But this happens beyond that sir. It's late at night. You pour another drink. Work through the bottle. You're down in the basement with photos from your tours hanging on the walls to keep you company — an entire floor below your family — rubbing your eyes because they're tired — and this is such a batch of shit you're not used to. But you consider yourself a religious man. You fear god — at least you believe you fear god — but you're confused. And praying was not really what you were about. What do you do sir? You're living on something like easy street. However — you are no longer in charge. You question your heart. Do you miss giving orders? Or would you accept instructions given by civilian life?

Another colonel spoke up.

Everyone makes an ass of themselves. Would you deny that soldier?

Affirmative sir. Everyone is an ass.

289

Just a way of the world the colonel asked?

More than conversation sir — it's the words that I dig.

Let's say we equal one another out the colonel said. The point to make here is not what you think — but what you did. You opened fire on non-combatants. You opened on your own army. And let's say I understand the congressmen being targets. Personal statements justify the myth right? But firing on your own troops...? That — soldier — shall be a charge ratcheted up the line. You dig words? Then dig this: treason: giving aid and comfort to the enemy. Your ass is pinned soldier. Hello?

*

Mantis thought this was all so amazing. He looked back at the colonel with a tilt of his head. Incredible it was he thought how it was to be alive. The colonel had a long boney nose and the standard receding hairline that was wicked popular on past shows on television. Wonder if you can still download that shit? If he wasn't careful the colonel would be absorbed into a void: a murder of aging officers. Mantis finished his cigarette. And with a heartfelt nod to his own fucked up being he decided it was time. Let's cut to the chase he said. I plead guilty to everything. Being guilty was just as good as being innocent. Doesn't matter to me. Send me to jail but that won't change a thing. Send me back out to the boonies hunting bad guys. What's the difference? It's a trap and I'm the bait. But if you put me back out in the field — if you give me another fucking rifle — then sooner or later I promise you I will shoot the jeeps again. And from there I can't guarantee anything else. High velocity well timed shots. Just right now sir someone just got it in the throat. Fuck it Mantis said I cop the plea.

*

The officers conferred among themselves — lots of hushed voices and uneasy glances thrown periodically at Mantis.

*

You make up sets of rules that govern people Mantis said. And then you make up another set of rules that everyone uses for who they are. How do you act when they collide?

You're a soldier a major said. And that's how you act.

But how do you explain that Mantis asked?

You don't the major said.

Soldier the colonel said — for the record — you have denied counsel and have chosen to represent yourself. Am I correct? Otherwise — should you request counsel — the appropriate legal representation shall be provided for you. Do you understand?

Copy sir. If it pleases the court I wish no counsel. In addition — for the record — I stand satisfactory with my conduct.

*

Mantis remembered those lines from a movie he watched with the helicopter pilots. Before his first drop into the highlands — while the borders between countries shifted in war-time — his map was useless — good fucking luck the pilot said and lifted off out of sight into a gray and rose colored twilight sky — and then the helicopter and all sanity Mantis thought disappeared around the hills.

*

Mantis quickly stood and elbowed one military policeman just below the boney part of the breastplate. There was a spectacular nerve at that spot. Hit it right — no breath — momentary paralysis — a stupid collapse but no real harm done. The other MP — Mantis spun to gain momentum and then kicked him hard in the knee. Damage there Mantis imagined. Can't say I'm sorry but I'll say sorry. Sorry asshole. The MP went down cursing — son of a bitch motherfucker and all that. By then his mind was on his pain and not his job. Geese Mantis said. Who are you people?

Mantis stepped over the fallen MP — clutching and searching for his breath like an overdose hit him — and grabbed his weapon. Lucky shot Mantis said.

Luck has nothing to do with it you bastard the other MP said.

291

Mantis released the safety. Big fucking plus sign he said.

Give it over. And Mantis got the other MP's gun.

What we have witnessed here was a simple lesson in disarmament Mantis said. He pointed the business ends of the guns at the officers in charge seated behind a large wooden conference table. Tape recorders spun. Cigarettes burned in ashtrays. Several drinks were spilled. A major called for Mantis to stand down.

Mantis fired a bullet into the wall above the major's head.

This action gets you nowhere soldier. Understand?

Mantis fired another bullet into the wall. If it pleases the court — Mantis said — I have enough shots left to kill you all. Sir — I will ask you once — and only once — do not move from your seats. Do not pick up the phone. You are permitted to suck air. Understand?

Put the guns down soldier... Please... this is a request... this is not an order the colonel said in a wheezy voice.

I copy if you copy sir.

Copy that soldier.

However sir — thinking about it — guns are all I have sir.

Enough with it then the colonel said.

Always open to possibility sir.

What is our next move?

Sir Mantis said — if you keep your ear to the ground and you listen for what the real shit is — you will find we are entering an era where spare parts will be hard to come by. And hasn't this happened already? War-time and its outcome decided by mechanical failures? How many spare parts? Was that what this was all about? Do you think things often go wrong for you through no fault of your own? Do you cross the street to avoid meeting someone? Do thoughts frighten you — like earthquakes or fire? Do you sometimes have difficulty getting to sleep even thought no one else is around and there are no noises to bother you? Does the place where you live interfere with your obtaining the social life you'd like to enjoy? Do you have shooting pains in your head? Are you bothered by thoughts like people are watching you?

Revenge dawned on Mantis. Sweet revenge...or was it served cold... he didn't remember...

But that wasn't it.

He had the guns but that wasn't it.

No officer moved but that wasn't it.

Earth was calling. Maybe that was it. Mantis just wanted to go somewhere different. That made sense. But there were five scared men sitting across the room and blocking his way out.

Hell it all ends in tears anyway doesn't it sir Mantis asked? There's some kind of midnight in here don't you think sir? Political fucking irony my ass: you think you run me? Well you do. You know it and I know it. The thing about it was I liked the job. But it was like the job started to hate me. Oh I know sir — we don't explain that. Fuck you people... Hey — look outside — it's stopped snowing!

Nobody moved.

If you stare into it — the snow melts away.

The neighbor across the street — she waves hello and says — can't you just wait until the summer's over? What's up with that? I see a day where it's hot and sunny — a beach weather day and it's kinda glorious or some shit like that. You don't need a lot of clothes. And you eat salad food after you swim. Maybe you got a garden back at the house and in the evening you can weed that. Maybe you cut some flowers if you have a girlfriend. Shit I haven't had a girlfriend in what — five years? There are bicycles and birds because they like summer and all that. It's August. Yea. It's August. Back home. I can see it. Fuck I can smell it! Peaches tomatoes and corn — the fucking saviors — growing in my grandparent's fields — the fields that haven't gone under yet for tax delinquency — barely holding onto the real estate sir — before they're raped — the investment jackals show face about once a month and offer to buy but offer cash-less shit in return — deep glacial Jersey-land till is what we're talking about sir... So where's my money? This amounts to a simple question sir. While employed — hunting your bad guys sir and with all respect to you spineless motherfuckers — my agreement with this nation's army said — hunt the bad guys — and your pay and your bonus pay per kill automatically goes home to a chosen account — Sir that account was my grandparent's peaches corn and tomatoes. Sir why was it — that for over two years no cash of mine went toward peaches tomatoes and corn? Where did my money go?

We can look into your claim a major said.

Wow that's great sir. Thank you. But let me assist my claim sir. Three hundred plus kills at $1589.67 per head. Twenty-nine prisoners taken and delivered at $1943.98 per head. My rough calculations — give or take a few heads — was this nation's army owes me $533-276.42.

Are you mad a major asked?

Sir I am a little angry. That money was agreed on and so was fair trade. I care nothing for your tactical operations process. I have killed. I have done so in good faith. Now it's time for you assholes to pony up. Where is my fucking money! This moment here just might be your last breath sirs. But you know… what I'm thinking about… and don't fucking move dickhead major sir… I will clock you between the eyes and put you back into yesterday… you sir are beneath my contempt — I will kill you and the last thing you remember will be peaches tomatoes and corn… I've done your shit work but now what I'm thinking about are breezes off the ocean… I'm thinking about Jersey-land… I'm thinking about pollutants in the food chain but it's a way of life…fuck you major… Boardwalk clams and clam shots… Clam juice and ice cold alcohol… I'm thinking about deep fried battered shrimp with a fresh made red sauce … I'm thinking about a girlfriend to walk on the breeze with… A girlfriend who loves beer… Loves big popcorn barrels and fucking matinees… Loves salted peanuts and sitting at the end of a pier and tossing shells into the tides… A girlfriend who loves pizza as much as a goodnight kiss… And that gentlemen — when you're a teenager — when you have the sum-mertime blues — it makes you feel things you don't know — like maybe I'll just fuck off for the rest of my life… find some shade and roll a joint and read a book… later you walk over to Frank's Play Land By The Sea and hang out with your mates and watch the sunset… The Atlantic is what I'm talking about motherfuckers — and when you're there you forget and get grateful… Yea. That was it. I'm grateful to be standing on the pier at Frank's Playland By The Sea and smelling the air. It's like you've been imaged in a dream. You can't sleep so you walk around all night. You see memories. And you think no place else. No place else even comes close. In the morning there's a faint smell of rain. The first day-light is silvery. It's too fucking beautiful to be believed. No other time in the world ever held you like this. Sirs — it's like thinking and being stupid at the same time... maybe you've never experienced this but you're like some cartoon guy who's in love...

No officer spoke. Nobody spoke to answer Mantis. An awful silence followed.

Mantis looked at a colonel and looked across majors and looked at another colonel.

An awful silence continued.

Fuck it sirs — you win. Mantis cocked both hammers and then opened fire. He shot until he ran out which was a funny thing to think about he thought. What a fucking excellent result handguns made he thought. The east wall of the hut and all it's windows were shot to hell. Mantis looked at the colonel and laughed. He had two clips left. Mantis lined the officers against the shot up east wall. And you know what else — Mantis said: I miss a couple of dirty water dogs from that guy with the hot dog cart at Bien Ha Avenue and Ocean Drive — I gotta have onion mustard and relish untoasted bun — that would taste great now... if I were back in Jersey-land. But Fuck it sirs. See yawl somewhere around. Dig the noise he said.

*

When the smoke cleared Mantis said you fucking assholes — you're still alive. It must be lucky bastard day he said. Mantis shot nobody. He just fired around outlines.

And since he just thought about it — Mantis walked over to the table — laid the guns down — and went back to his chair where he set down and waited.

*

Mantis did six months in a hospital in Germany. Or at least his body was there. The doctors fed him enough drugs to render and sedate him comatose. Wasn't that bad Mantis said — you learned when to expect getting conked out of your mind and laid up on your ass.

Then he did time in prison-time back in the nation. But that was fucked up royally. So he went back into a hospital and did more hospital-time.

Mantis was judged to be occupationally insane.

He was unfit to withstand casualty acclimation.

Mantis was a burden on the taxpayers.

So a year after his crack-up Mantis was dishonorably discharged from the nation's armed forces. He was sent home to his last know address — even if that was a doorway to an abandoned building about to be knocked down for an urban renewal scheme.

Mantis tried to enlist in the Peace Corps. But from the start that idea was a lost one due to organizational standpoints and Mantis' repeated drug test failures.

Mantis tried the CIA and the FBI and the DEA and he even went to AA because he thought that might help him with his drinking.

He drove a cab for a while but got fed up with all the white people riding in back and giving him directions in his hometown.

*

Early one morning you saw Mantis. He was holding onto the back of a garbage truck.

You hadn't seen Mantis in years. You hadn't seen him since Cripple's going away party out in the trash lands. By then — after various operations — Cripple's leg was finally straight. And his limp by then was nothing more than a quotation. More words. Mantis dug words. What else happened? Mantis' last words that night were: fuck me. Last-time we saw him the last-time words ran away with him. He left the party. He ripped into the bay. The last we heard was laughter. The last we saw was kicked-up water. We imagined Cripple swam toward Baltimore with the incoming tide but we never heard otherwise.

Where you going Mantis asked?

Going to work you answered.

Cool. I'll go with you. What do you do?

Paint churches you said.

Cool Mantis said. So you're like the guy who needs to paint churches?

Not really. It's a living. It pays money. Not much more to it than that.

Okay I got it Mantis said. You're a workingman.

Guess so you said…

Fuck it man. You're a census figure. Every morning you get on the bus — the same bus as the day before. You take the same seat on the same bus as you did the day before. Fuck it man. You got the same hopes and dreams as everyone else. You carry a brown bag lunch.

Actually you said you walked to work each day. And you never took lunch.

Fuck it man — that's makes you good and lucky!

So you work on a garbage truck you asked?

No man I just like riding on a garbage truck. Gives me a specialized world view…

So what you asked?

I work on a golf course — on the driving range — handing out golf balls to people who amount to no more than business deals. Everybody dies to be in the country club. And I'm somebody's idea of a servant. What church you painting?

St. Anne the Inviolate you said.

Fuck man I went to school there

Occasionally Cripple was your roommate.

*

Eden Jones finished her beer. She then drank yours. How good was that? She danced around the tables and played that song again. When the quarter hit the slot — lonesome rodeo heartbreak music came waling back to life. That was the song Eden Jones played.

She wore her hair long this time — straight back and knotted in a dark ponytail. A deep red t-shirt with the words — out for trout — rose delightfully on her breast. Her denim skirt was way too short — not for you — but looking at Eden Jones her mother would say: oh honey why not just get married…

And yea Mantis said — somebody gets their sorry ass out a motel room and they head on down the road in a truck with some sad memories that might not make as far away as they need to be — oh yea I love that song Mantis said.

Here's a question you asked: if it weren't for love would physical attraction be possible as a magnetic force — and — if it weren't for physical attraction would there ever be love?

It's too early to think Eden Jones said.

You were glad for the simple motion when she sat down. Like it meant something you thought. You and Eden Jones — admit it — the sky knew it — you and Eden Jones were quilted together seam by seam — the fucked up borrowed moments — we culled out together — a band of thieves — your eyes — her hijacked sex — not limited...

Everybody try this Mister Drifty said.

Morgan swallowed the first pill. Followed by Mantis and Crystal Bill and Mister Jimmy and then you and Eden Jones.

Mantis kept rolling joints and asked: what are we doing here? Which way are we going?

However our obsessions come packaged- they are here — mind you — to stimulate an evolutionary pattern: namely to keep going. Morgan said — or Emerson said — and took rounds for last call.

You need a counter-act for all the weirdness Eden said — her hands touching the air as she spoke like water drops popping on a hot skillet.

We will be travelling sideways Mister Drifty said.

Hate that Mister Jimmy said.

Its all right Crystal Bill said.

Sure but does that make the laws of creation meaningless?

Didn't know creation had laws.

What about Adam and Steve?

One hair-brained scheme isn't as good as the next

Are you saying there were no Adam and Steve?

What I saying was there were a lot of Adams and Steve. That's all.

Creation. Impossible. No way. No way something gets made from nothing.

That's a point but it's more spiritual than what we need.

Yea –but what about all that small talk? Don't everyone parlay like they're making shit richer just by opening their mouths?

It's called happiness dude. And all that small talk is like some fortune.

The more you say the more think you know — and the more necessary it becomes for you to pass mustard...

Muster you idiot — you pass muster... not mustard.

Happiness — last time I saw happiness... that was a tough league.

You need some shit like a belief.

Oh not that!

Something that — I don't know — something that makes happiness cool — but keeps it marginal and anyway from messing with you.

So yea. Take each day. Something happened that made you wish you had a lobotomy scheduled for that evening — after drinks and dinner naturally...

Yea. Some stupid accident wrecks the morning...

Yea. Some stupid person tap-dances across your head because they have these obnoxious ways about doing things...

Oh Yea it's like it's built in that people have no brains...

Ah where does that leave us since we're the sorta people we're talking about...

And if it fucks up then it was just an excuse...

Yea and that's when you don't decide and you go boo-hoo...

We live for what we don't remember...

Personal feelings are a game among unequals...

Our fantasies provide us with straightforward answers....

What could be simple?

*

Back in the day I killed the other guy Mantis said. Just shot him — while he prayed to his deity...

Even shot a woman Eden Jones asked?

Twice Mantis said. Years with training had taught him to speak without hesitation. But while answering his mouth cracked when he answered Eden Jones...

Clean kills he said ... I was employed.

And that made what...?

No. That made it one more stop on the end of the line.

Yea. Does it come down to this? Like you're mission impossible and you want to fuck Barbara Bain — but you know you're not starring in this production?

You try and make things happen...

Basically it won't work out...

Does nothing work out?

Didn't say that...

One night I was sitting in the back booth...

Which one?

There are only two booths back there so it's the one on the right...

Copy that. I like the details.

So this guy comes over. And it was a night where I felt spectacular. Damn — I was spectacular! So this guy comes over and starts buying drinks... alluding to he and me and what might happen. Of course I said! Until my eyes pop out!

There's pleasure without responsibility you know...

A puff of smoke...

Yea like feeling drab afterwards...

Or housekeeping arrangements...

Quality of fucking life huh Mantis said. He looked around for Fast Eddie. When he didn't see him Mantis started rolling more joints.

When did this start to catch your attention?

Remember that soap opera?

Which one...

Junior high...

When did you start fucking Eden Jones asked?

Yea let's talk about obsessions...

Well if I fucked Billy then Sue had to fuck Billy because I did and that meant I had to fuck Patrick because Sue was interested in him and Cathy also liked Patrick so she went and fucked Billy and that meant I had to go and fuck Jefferson because he liked Cathy....

A broken hearted game Mantis said... And mathematics... And who the fuck was good at that...

A wig then for every night Mister Jimmy said.

Best to keep one another qualified...

All the other worlds we get to see... all the local environments we trip over... it's like a privilege to be knocked dead...

Yea. Think about it. We take great portions out of our waking time and spend that time trying to fuck one another. Searching for the great fuck... that great primal ... And knowing you will not be satisfied with only a single human fuck — it's time to leave and look beyond the grunting — sand crabs crawling over our legs ... poison ivy in the weeds... those polluted gulls pecking at your ass ... And now it's time to make time with the sky... Unfortunately that's been bastardized... Don't seem like we look for the time or the sky... Nothing but rebound fucks. Hop over fucks. Slip away fucks. Argue fucks. Mature fucks. Civilized fucks. What really happened fucks? Interlude fucks. I gotta go fucks. Periphery fucks. Cold fucks. But what proof? We think it lasts. And it does. You need to be fucked but there's no place like home Dorothy and what I think is you click your shoes....

That's crazy. But I like the ways you put it. ... And what are you doing later tonight...

That's not the point. And I'm busy.

The last time I remember fucking —

Yea and that would be when creatures reproduced asexually in salt muck ...

The last time I remember fucking I felt glossy three-dimensional and flatter than a picture...

What happened after all that frantic mesmerizing was done with?

You're able to go anywhere...

But there's a hitch...and in the other person's eyes... What then?

Then you feel like a ghost...

I see that Uncle Pin said.

Mantis asked Eden if she wanted to start dating...nothing big... maybe they just start and you know take it from there...

*

All this talk removed you from the night.

The table continued to talk about sex and lunacy and compliance and excess and more pills and whether or not to have convictions and sneak another round when Fast Eddie wasn't watching but he was and whether or not to have opposition to those convictions if you had those convictions in the first place.

Mantis rolled up a bag of dope and handed out joints with each passing remark.

Inside you felt the sky calling.

You looked across the table at Eden Jones. What proof indeed...

You looked across the table at your friends. Great warmth took over your mind.

You looked across the table again at Eden Jones. More than warmth took over your mind... you always did like to spy on her...in grade school you wrote her mysterious 007 surveillance poems and left them inside her desk... in high school you lost track of Eden Jones ... just the person mind you but never the inventoried memory...because her parents sent her away to be finished... she went to a boarding school in some snot laced town ... yea and that was never Jersey-land... and yea that was an institution with cred but with little meaning... You looked across the table at Eden Jones and remembered a time in a time far away... Your mother said oh my god it's only love so get over it... from day one until the sky ... we answered to something... your head was twisted over in some other direction when you first saw her... and that still happens today whenever you see her... first thought best thought... they say it's a fabulous sky... and you met Eden Jones in that sky...

So we both agreed: we don't need baby-hood.

Parents we asked? Us we asked one another? That had no chance to work.

But you said to her we need each other. We can't find better opposites.

And she said there's more to think about than that... than before...

Oh — but where was the deep felt heart in all this? The frantic mesmerizing... the eyes that were never ghosts...

It's not only about that Eden Jones said.

Let's get married then and fuck the world.

We can't get married because we had an abortion! We can't get married because we had a baby! Those reasons are way out of time. And they have no sky.

We need the sky. The sky will help us.

Do you not understand what a mess this is?

Everything was a mess you thought.

But you did not consider Eden Jones a mess.

I want my own say in my own life. Damn-it!

You felt like a balloon slowly leaking helium.

You felt like someone first going to high school.

You told Eden Jones: you would walk to China and back to bring her a spring blossom for the wedding.

China she said. What's up with China she asked? And what am I supposed to do in the meantime- wait for you to get back?

Well you said I was born there. The second time around... And you said walking to China might prove something.

Like what?

Do you remember the second time around?

No I don't Eden Jones said.

Perfect. When I bring the blossom back — that means us.

What?

Like in the songs. Where the song sings he was in love with her forever...

Idiot boy she said.

Yea you said — just like a weed in broken concrete — underneath sunlight and rainwater... growing and fuck the odds...

I got that Eden Jones said. But I'm eighteen and I'm going away to college. On the west coast — as in the west coast — as in three thousand miles from here — if you remember geography...

You told Eden Jones you did remember geography. From the sixth grade when she was sick and the whole class made her a map of the world with get-well quotations in various languages and foreign countries. And there was a small x that was the neighborhood and a cartoon caption saying you are here.

Hello?

Your parents don't need to know.

First she stiff-armed you in the middle of the forehead. And that hurt. Then she took your head in her hands and kissed that life long indentation she just made there.

Then she kissed you. Which — belatedly — you remembered as this strange erotic vacancy in time — and that — coupled with beaucoup kisses back — that started the ball rolling and lead up the way to someone in your arms who once was pregnant.

What heart? No worries right? I'll just pick up a new one tomorrow...

We'll be in touch she said.

And for the moment you brought your head up off the pavement and screwed it back onto your shoulders. You looked back into Eden Jones ... that was probably the easiest thing you ever did... into her eyes... yea they changed color and yea they changed shape.

Having a track record helps she said.

You know that doesn't matter to me.

You're wrong. It does matter to you. And it matters to me. You have it. I got trust in you.

You're not even going to say: don't let me down?

No she said because you won't let me down. You want those kisses from a girl. What you wanted was maybe different from what those kisses meant... Ooh it's the funny business — am I right?

All it means is I gotta go. And no you don't come and visit me. We're three thousand miles apart and it stays that way.

Says who?

The cousins. Watch them. Watch them very close.

I eat pie with those guys every Friday night!

That makes sense. They don't suspect you. Yet. It's early and the cousins are looking around at the cousins and everybody's wondering and everybody's got their thinking caps on... But if they do get wind that something's rotten: first the cousins talk to the obvious pick... and that's you.... the cousins speak with you in a frugal rough cousin manner — and then they haul you before my grandfather where you have another conversation... and if your talk displeased my grandfather then the cousins take you back for another kind of vocabulary lesson. Believe me — you don't want to lose your tongue.

You kept imaging Eden Jones — she just can't walk away. Not like this. Not that quick.

But she did. Silent and elegant — a creature from outer space- passing

304

through dimensions that earthlings joked about- and never seemed to have the time to follow through when there was such a question as why...?

*

Eden Jones left on a bus.

Your eyes were tombstones. You felt like shit. You said you would hide for days and you did. You felt like your life was ruined. Even the sky pressed down clouds on the neighborhood. She can't walk away.... But she did. Eden Jones walked into some vista-cruiser... joked with the driver... stored her gear over and found a seat... the automatic doors hissed closed behind her.

*

You remember the Ocean Avenue Movie House. And its shining marquee that showed movie times and coming attractions. The neon tubing glowed and wrapped around the theater front in horizontal bands of blazing color.

Next-door was a miniature golf course. You wondered: how many inane putt-putt hours you spent were spent knocking a ball through the rocks around the lighthouse...then down through a skull and bones ship with the crazy pirate voice that laughed said welcome to Davey Jones' locker... and from there the ball played back up from the ocean bottom to some fucking racetrack where if you hit a horse your putt dribbled through to green lawns and houses and an easy ninth hole... And don't believe anybody when they ask what ever happened to Laugh-In?

Curious vacationers strolled along the boardwalk. Strange people's shoes were orchestrated around you. They had so much time. It seemed pretty obvious. A car horn backed you away toward the curb.

Pretty obvious it was to your slapped brain — that in the months to come what you anticipated from Eden Jones were notes from Eden Jones and those notes were to be highly classified. You tried match your thoughts. Were you a slut? Yes you were. Were you an easy mark? Case closed. You were in love. You had a teenage brain. You were fucked up

305

and passionate and unable to process what this was. You might as well choke on your own breath as to understand that you were in love.

But then evening fell on you.

Eden Jones was just a girl — no — that was like a sleight of hand definition and no take to accept that.

Eden Jones was just a girl you met — closer but no money to bet with.

Eden Jones was just a girl whose walk and smile and manner of speaking fleshed out in you some kind of old pond attachment like peepers calling out in the springtime night.

Eden Jones was a girl whose touch allowed you to be otherwise thoughtful.

But she was right. This was unfair to her. And you were right because it was difficult to forget someone who you had eyeball-to-eyeball sex with...

Before she left for college — yea you got it — she was three thousand mile away — Eden Jones said: how do you feel about gardens?

Gardens? Fucking gardens you thought?

Suddenly you did not understand much... did you belong to some guy hooked up to a feeding tube...were you something thin and rusty left in a salt marsh... the gargoyle from the Hunchback of Notre Dame that Charles Laughton asks: why I not made from stone like thee...?

Eden Jones asked: do you think you can grow enough tomatoes to last for a year?

Yea you said. You'd grow enough tomatoes to feed you for a year.

Eden Jones looked at you with green eyes that seemed distilled from seawater... eyes that oftentimes cut you in half...the eyes that made your dick fly with the birds... Eden Jones looked at you and said: let's make it a pint of sauce for each week in the year. So now you're working against time. You don't have a year to grow. But you do have to can fifty-two pints of tomato sauce in that year.

And where do these tomatoes get grown you asked?

I know some land Eden Jones said.

Where?

That little community space past Broadway where you turn left at Radio Shack.

And that's where you want me to grow tomatoes?

Yes. And if the cousins ask you: what do you think you are doing: here is your answer: Nipote Blind Charlie.

But everybody in Jersey-land has tomatoes!

And that's why you need to grow tomatoes she said.

*

How come Fast Eddie had that country music song? What ever happened to the Mad Lads covering by the time I get to Phoenix?

Fast Eddie said: I like cowboys. Besides he said — that song was on the box when I bought the club. And I decided to keep it.

*

The former owner of the 20th Century Club — back in the bay it was simply known as BAR — a dumb single light bulb hanging over shaky wooden letters — always fretted how things turned out. He didn't want to sell. He liked owning BAR. It was a damn good business he thought.

But he was about to die from a brain cancer that ultimately went from his skull back down the spine and raced around inside his body until at the end he blew up like some tank with a bad pressure valve. And so before he died — he recognized a deal when he saw it. The price was good. The former owner sold BAR to Fast Eddie. But he never got over he was going to die and that soured the deal.

And so the 20th Century Club was born.

*

The toilets were easy and they were all that remained for Fast Eddie. The rest of the night were some dirty glasses and the odd paperwork he'd fudge whatever way was needed and however it added up in his favor.

Fast Eddie's dream — and he had them — no question — Fast Eddie got things — was to own a small cozy place maybe a block from the board-walk with like seating for a hundred — live music — good food — a place with influence — but a place a little lost — a place maybe hard to find.

Fast Eddie said man this was sweet. Fast Eddie said this was happening.

He said all right — picture this... you're walking along the beach... early morning... fucking gulls talking their heads off... the beach sweepers riding their machines picking up yesterdays trash and getting the beach clean... today's trash won't show for hours yet ... so what you got was clean white sand... a take-out coffee and a damn fucking tasty breakfast sandwich... blue ocean waves... and fucking dolphins man swimming off the coast — did you know dolphins are smart — maybe smarter than you... just kidding man... that's on me... But as I walk on the beach — wearing a new suit but barefoot you know — you gotta do the thing right — every see some dumb ass on the beach wearing shoes — that shit's pitiful — you gotta do the thing right — But here's the real time thing — while I'm walking barefoot on the beach money was changing hands and minute by minute it was built taller than it was before.

Fast Eddie told you he saw this happen in his mind.

You told Fast Eddie you came from the sky.

Fast Eddie love to hear that. Anytime you need a job he said...

But he saw it. That was important. Cash from the club made his head serious — dead houses to buy made his head imagine — entertainment arcades on the boardwalk and juice carts and a fish and chips franchise on a pier ... And for all Fast Eddie heard the horizon line was infinity so we might as well go there too..

So you don't worry about dreams Mantis asked?

Don't do that shit Fast Eddie said.

What Mantis asked?

You know what I mean.

Don't get vibrations on what I see Fast Eddie said.

Can't help it Mantis said.

I know that Fast Eddie said. But damn it dude I did some numbers-

Yea Mantis said. And a lot of them were mine...

Damn it Mantis. This is the perfect place to make money. I got the sight. Think about it: gin and beach sands...

I don't entirely enjoy gin Mantis said.

... Vodka and beach sands...

Better Mantis said.

Vodka and beach sands... a hot pale city an hour away ... they pull into town and see endless waves... that makes them thirsty...some capillary action that happens between the brain and some fucking glands...

You know that Mantis asked?

I did some research on the phone Fast Eddie said. A little beach space... you put a raft in the water and float on the waves.... It's all good the guy on the raft thinks... And that's where the juice carts come in — they sell beverages and they give away motherfucking coupons for that night's special at the fish and chips place...

*

Fast Eddie held a tumbler up to the bar light. He inspected a lipstick stain on its rim and so rewashed it. He was it in the remains of the soapy bar tub water- checking around — were there any other glasses that need his attention –

What we need were dumplings Pun Chow Elliot Chung said. He went over and spoke to Fast Eddie. Pun Chow Elliot Chung and Fast Eddie cracked up beneath a fake nautilus wall light above the kitchen door.

*

Salem sat down beside Fast Eddie. She took the glass from his hand and rewashed it.

Any fool can do that you know?

Yea but it ain't every fool that stays around.

*

The night Fast Eddie met Salem they were aboard a party barge on a Booze and Cruise trip up the Delaware. She was standing at the far end of the boat- sipping her gin — quietly watching and passing the warehouse skylines on both sides of the river.

Fast Eddie left a card game below deck — told the table he'd be back and left some winnings on the table as good faith — plus the dealer was Fast Eddie's uncle — and uncle Fred had Fast Eddie's back — had his back so Fast Eddie stepped away — from that moment in the family when someone popped a cork and cheered birth on! — If you were in that family then somebody in that family had your back. Damn positive feeling he thought. He went up top to grab some air. Best if he got away from the chain smoking nervous motherfuckers at the table.

Nervous guys made Fast Eddie's brain dance wicked in his head. They acted bad and they smelled bad... and that was the clue he said.

And yea there was a reason why they didn't use deodorant... because they were stupid. And they needed to telegraph it... like they weren't stupid... Who the fuck did they think they were playing with? Mister fucking loser... some jolly rube from out of town...?

And what was that fucking word he read about on his phone — fairnomes? And because these three guys at the table stunk he looked it up again with more diligence this time: three guy stinking was suspicious: he found it: pheromone: a chemical secreted by animals that conveys airborne signals etc. Three guys at the table and they stunk and they were dumb as shit and Fast opinioned that meant they were playing together as a single ignorant mind.

So Fast Eddie grabbed some air.

Cadmium factories and glue factories and plastic bristle factories drifted past the party barge on the shorelines. Hillocks filled with old car batteries and bald tires and chopped up cars were sunk into the river's edge at the low breached end of a dirt road. Four gents in lawn chairs fished off the road... a boom box played radio songs... another box played the news... a third played a baseball game... Fast Eddie waved... they opened a cooler and toasted him back with four cans of ice cold beer...

He noticed her and tried to make it cool but a knock from outside went off inside his head. Good beginning Fast Eddie thought.

She leaned against the rail and watched the river below. Chopped inky water foamed and swelled out from the party barge's wake. Salem threw her drink overboard. The evening sky was humid sticky and congested — red weather report air hung on her once fresh clothes and crept onto her skin — sweat and grime — you can't escape it she said out loud.

You hoping for a breeze Fast Eddie asked?

I'm hoping to get away Salem said.

I'm hoping to stay Fast Eddie said.

Salem laughed and kicked a sandal off her right foot in Fast Eddie's direction.

Another good sign he thought.

Can I get you a drink Salem asked?

You just now threw a glass overboard.

That was empty.

You sure have a strange way calling for another Fast Eddie said.

Now if I get you a drink you will be standing here when I get back Salem wanted to know?

How about I get you a drink and you be standing there?

I promise you I will be here.

And I promise you I will be here.

That's makes us both curious.

Nothing wrong with that.

Fast Eddie knew she was wanting for him to turn over his hand and show what he had. He looked at her and thought maybe he should just walk away and not think about it. This was either a train wreck or this was as smooth as it got. And Fast Eddie led what he assumed to be an uncomplicated life. There was sex and there was money — and there was money and there was sex. Pretty easy shit to deal with. Nobody gets hurt in the long run and everybody's fine.

All he wanted was some air. And now — he's got this dilemma- who goes and gets the drinks? But damn she was good looking on the eyes. What options here? Name the odds? Nudity was one. Craziness was another. Or if you flat lined the whole thing it wasn't more than two gins.

Are you going to stand there all night fool? Slack jawed and rag faced — all thumbs and nothing to hold onto — stuck because you can't move because you stuck in one place?

Go on fool! Get us some drinks!

Fast Eddie was back at her side and grinning. Ask me a question baby and anything's a possibility. And two limes just like you asked for... got you some fish sticks too... and plums... I got us some plums...you like plums baby...

What was Fast Eddie thinking when he put away the adding machine for the night...

What dollar amount was he out of balance...

Fast Eddie was a constant deep in the angles all his bones had...

It was lonesome work behind an empty bar...

And Fast Eddie was always the last man out. ...

Dumplings are good Pun Chow Elliot Chung yelled! He kicked open the kitchen door and stood there with steaming platters in each hand above his head.

the coffee meditations

With the raven-haired woman away on business you had the entire house-time to yourself. The days fell into ratios. Equations. Reveries. A nonpareil living minus the weak promise being a changeling. Relax she said it's just an old bullet wound.

Reasonable evidence suggested you were splitting infinities.

Relax... just an old...bullet wound...

If you were in love did it mean that more bullet wounds were here to come?

How was it the sky mattered throughout the years even as you've put your ear to the sky all those years?

You and the raven-haired woman were married in the sky. A great blue day to get hitched... untroubled whims falling upon us and devoted like singing and getting drunk with the justice of the peace... the loops of events... solitude and love...

Why do things matter do you think the JP asked?

Why be troubled over natural things the raven-haired woman said. She filled the JP's glass again.

Maybe there's a benchmark the JP said.

Just a normal wedding — right — another day in the life — strange days ahead — two creatures under the influence —

Oh absolutely. It's normal when you worry. The JP asked for another glass.

Well you civil servants sure know how to do it up the raven-haired said.

Goes with the contract the JP said.

It's a pleasure to know you sir.

All mine the JP said.

What's your thought about dice you asked?

Personally I stay away from them the JP said. For me it's tough to be in two places at once.

How so?

Damn good question. I guess I'm not comfortable with it.

So you'd rather: like win — or lose — outright and be done with it. And not be between the frames so to speak — where you lose lose/then win then lose/ then you win and win/then you lose — and then you look to get back to winning.

Something like that the JP said.

How do you decide?

I don't believe I do the JP said.

Reasonable evidence suggests everything matters.

You've done more homework than me the JP said. But anyway — dice — one-way or another — however they land — don't interest me. Can't say I'm not drawn to numbers though.

Not to mention those numbers mean money.

Well played the JP said. He grabbed his pork pie hat off the couch. The JP thanked us for having the courage to get married despite the government warnings. He shook our hands and left out the front door on champagne wingtips.

*

Relax. She said over the phone. Every day we lose our marbles.

*

You still had the postcard. And what she said: Everyday we lose our marbles. On the front half of the postcard was a giant Indian head wooden nickel on a pedestal in a parking lot rest area. And there were buffalo some-where behind a fence across the highway — tourist material — like the buffalo were employed by the state. Visit South Dakota soon was the tag line. And reading it again it was remarkably like staring directly into the past — and seeing your life back then — on a wrinkled 3x5 paper card.

Nothing happens when everything was on the move. No chance to be solid she said.

Which turns out to be the future? Was that a surprise? If not that must be the beauty.

*

And nothing really moves at this hour. Where do thoughts go? When your mind wanders off while preparing coffee? No sound from outside the house like big mouth adults jogging before daybreak and letting the streets know they had jobs to attend to later after the sweat and consciousness and the spandex wore off. No sound from inside the house either like plumbing pipes knocked silly by mysterious gases. Do those thoughts drift toward love? Do those thoughts drift toward solitude? Taking in the air? Doing as little as possible before you give-up the thoughts and before you wonder what was that about? And don't disturb where the buffalo roam....

But not matter what else happens — in whatever world we came from — from whatever world we choose to inhabit — you looked at a postcard — and from there — deep in the fields of your marrow — a hand written note pulled upon you and wouldn't let you go and it seemed there was a course in mind — not only for you — but also for the words as you translated them — from her to you: touch pass through and remember...

You take appreciation from the quiet morning.

Sitting down before dawn let the night sky go with a large coffee with cream and an old bullet hole in your chest. And what that meant.

To be left alone was cool — without the noise in the fields — your bones made nervous by the make-believe face you saw each morning — the need for patience — relax she said but never forget who it was that was hunting you down...

Then the refrigerator made its loud mysterious noise.

There was an airplane in the sky and it was propeller driven and that made you envious.

And the sudden wham against the front door that was the morning paper shot from the cannon arm of some guy earning extra income. It

315

was always the same. Wham. Then a car door slammed. And then a car drove away.

And just as forever the bone noise faded and there it was: the quiet waiting.

You set the coffee cup down on the counter. You wanted more: More caffeine: More sensual early morning. More syncopated neurons. More toast. Was it precious or foolish she wrote?

*

When was the last time you heard anything about Jill Deals? Was she out of jail?

But there it was on the counter. The obituary arrived yesterday. You printed it out.

Maybe you wanted more evidence than electronics permitted. Maybe you wanted to hold onto it and let it be and let the print out crinkle and scratch from you handling it.

How odd. How odd was it to get the news months later after her death? Not that it mattered in one peculiar sense: when you're dead that's all for the moment. And it didn't fit anyone's life to say that death was a tragedy. Or to quote: a tragic ending. What the fuck did that mean? What tragic ending was that? Do you track it? Do you wish it away? Was this samsara in your bones? You didn't know how to act. Maybe that was the best way.

Someone's death was not a tragedy just because they were once alive. But all that obituary name-calling made echoes in the stillness. Another coffee and another toast and something material made from nothing? Was that elliptical thinking or was a dead exit visited upon you or was the obituary page a typo error flying past your eyes?

Who sent the message?

Mister Drifty could puzzle the encryption. His heads-up work provided valuable cover-time for the raven-haired woman in the past. But regardless about calling in the dogs — it was nervy to find the obituary popped on all your screens. Many states of mind were out loose in the world and they were willing to do you in and collect ... but who was it this time? And how much were you worth this time?

316

*

The image you lifted off the printout was this: a smiling young woman with a chipped front tooth: a sailing ship tattoo on her high left cheek: artificial golden hair like shiny new Camaro paint: weird clam-shell necklaces that rattled on her tank tops: seaweed tattoos around her ankles: lacquered toenails: evenings together: walking the dogs in the park and buying peanuts: then taking the dogs down to the beach to let them run riots and crash into the surf: good dogs off the leash behaved that way: we believed that every step we took and every word we said might alter the world.

Back in the foolish and delightful young-time we squatted together for a year with third floor ocean front living on some bombed out in-surance claim on Neptune Avenue and Tree Street. Not a bad place to start... but sadly there also had to be another way around: when you begin to think about someone's end... any circumstance became what you wished to remember and then usually you fucked up the memory by overplaying it.

When it came down: when time felt drawn time was sad: was that her ending stared back at you from the obit page: no photo: just a cool phan-tom: made you inside out to speak her name and that was a gift you got from time: moist clay on a potter's wheel: overcooked chicken wings she ate by the plateful: the flat spot in her voice: her first arrest: your first bail money: apocalyptic eye make up: rumors to build: a love affair the state police investigated: you remember her: now: but that was confusing be-cause you never knew her as a middle aged woman: you knew her: another best teenager in the world: maybe in respects we never exist until we die...

*

Quantum light memes build over neighborhood yards and silent wood frame houses against half empty October trees.

Quantum light memes... Orpheum mediums... Jill Deals... and what to do with her and what that had to do with you... memory patterned memory living... blues like the sky... blues like melancholy lank... tuneful sugar... Jill Deals... once again... it was necessary... to step away from your own sorry ass and mollify with time... quantum light memes you had those bookmarked on your phone... Patterned speed dominoes over complex reflective surfaces clear as glass and environments or behaviors and — totally cool — gets to be in more than one place at one time and beyond the lines of spontaneity finds chance locations to gather in one place or move to another place because it was all the same — and totally cool — it depended on how you looked at it — because this quantum light meme needed no outward decisions to come through the windows as morning — it just did — as a matter where everything material was solid in name and everything material buzzed in questions about being a solid — or not.

What were the odds that you made the oatmeal at a time when you thought you did?

Did you make many oatmeal breakfasts in many different locations simultaneously?

Did that oatmeal taste differently?

*

Something's been circling the house lately. Maybe it was the encryption fog...

*

Maybe you pretended you were house cleaning.

Maybe what you found were simply endless obits still circling over the years.

Maybe you had an idea this personal stuff hit the trash on Monday.

First thing you found were the generic stuff. Metal ticket cuffs from a concert with our PIN numbers on them. We watched the hologram on an inflated zeppelin screen in the empty lot where the Wind Hammer Hotel used to be. Nobody played live anymore.

And vinyl exchange notes from ten thousand movies in the world that we watched.

Then there were the postcards from friends in arms. Handwritten retro-letters. Back then it was a craze to actually use a pen and send a note forward in the day and back from a place in real-time without a streaming field to capture the immediate reason and include several links to the occasion and explanations why you did so.

Morgan said — from Gibraltar — you never went anywhere did you?

Mantis said — from the stockade — hey great news! I'm allergic to lithium!

Uncle Pin said — from Sao Paulo — I'm wearing a bikini no way I'm homesick.

Pun Chow Elliot Chung said — from a food truck in Nevada — just ketchup please.

But what you looked for were the pizza boxes.

*

You found them in a plumbing chase. They were hidden behind a false wall. You built that false wall — and who knows maybe you built all the walls in your life? Behind that wall were the pizza boxes. No better pie to be had in Jersey-land! And inside the boxes were memories: from those great pies — meals in solitude — funny meals on many turnpike beaches — and what you kept: her photos: her correspondence: her quirks: her night sky.

When a pie was eaten and another pizza box was empty from there you filled another empty pizza box...

*

Occasionally she hung around somewhere long enough and rented a post office box.

Then it was your time to mail her something.

She had two sat phones. One was a direct line to her grandfather that she never called. Only warnings came in on that line.

The other line was her lonesome drunk connection: midnight barroom pool tables… eggs and potatoes followed at some neon dawn diner sinking into a least highway booth with a cigarette she never wanted to smoke… talking to immortal truckers with killer road tales… turning down offers from an immortal horny truckers… driving off and shaking her head behind the wheel of a crusty red pickup truck… she had over four dozen different sets of license plates for the truck should she find trouble and had to leave trouble behind with only a glance backward in the side mirrors…

*

You had an old answering machine tape. Where a physical line recorded someone's voice off a grid. And then fed that voice onto a tape. And you then played it back into a room standing alone and listening… Hi it's me. I just got in and I'm leaving you a message. I'm hopping in the shower now and I have to hurry out again. If you call back in the next fifteen minutes then go ahead because I'll be here. It's funny. When I was little I thought how cool would it be to be a taxi driver. Last night I went to a party and didn't get home until late and so had to leave again early this morning without much sleep. Tonight I'm going out with some people I met. It was supposed to be last week but they cancelled. And tomorrow I have a class but I know that's supposed to be cancelled too. All these things are like that. So if you call and I don't answer call again because I'm in the shower and I'll wait for you to call. Bye.

So. There were ninety-six segments that broke up a day into equal fifteen-minute lengths. Which fifteen minutes was she in? She couldn't stay in fifteen minutes for even the clock to see it through. If you did call back — on a motel line — she would be gone. Or she would be just about out the door when the phone rang. Looking back took a second and then she was out and flipped the lockset.

So. You'd leave a message on the lonesome drunk connection… And then it would happen like time. The lonesome drunk connection buzzed — you were in the past and she was off looking for the future- you thought about her eyes — an apple green color with the lashes furled purple-black and shaded like wildflowers on the side of the road… you

320

said everything that was on your mind: the lonesome drunk connection buzzed again and said don't worry... before you had the opportunity to reply — your voice and your position went through mindful clicks and beeps... you were transferred like a song... and shuttled onto her grandfather's doorstep — where her cousins kept an eye on you.

*

One postcard arrived from a coastal town in Georgia. A black and white shot — a tiny old building near a wharf — a paint peeling sign on the roof said Bait Shack — seating limited live crustaceans.

Parked outside were big finned Cuban cars. In one car were Einstein and Marilyn. He was holding the wheel with a brilliant white scarf around his neck and smiling like a boxing champ. She wrapped her arms around his shoulders all breezy blond visions and looking suggestive in a low strap dress.

A day can be anything she said. Take things in days. That way nothing was really set but twenty-four hours. You lose things by being all about them you know? Hey the earth was just a day in the beginning and still was today right? But what happens when things start pulling on your strings? I lose concentration — that's what happens. It almost makes me feel involuntary. Do you see what I mean? And I have to wonder was this how I want it?

Here the postcard ended.

Several days later an Identical Einstein and Marilyn reached you.

Do you believe we need to think out loud she asked? I wonder sometimes. I think out loud. If I couldn't do that I'd get afraid. Do you ever think if you couldn't think out loud where would everything go? I get confused because I want to make a perfect statement. There's a car horn behind me and I don't like that. But here it is. Maybe you should date other girls. I think I might mean it.

Here the second postcard ended.

Several days later Einstein and Marilyn arrived.

Funny how this works she said. I remember you telling me: my face was always changing. And how you liked that. What if that was true? But what if it's not just my facing changing but me? I remember sex underneath the boardwalk for the first time and hearing the crowds above us walking like meth clowns and the tides rushing in against those smelly wooden piers and we're fucking each other to be alive. But what else do you think you might want to say out loud? How was it that you're certain? Why don't you get premonitions? What if this screenplay does not work out?

What was the question you thought? This thing worked from the moment you first saw her you thought? That's what you thought.

Needless you took a bullet to the heart. And there was no room for thinking...only bleeding out...

But we were always around one another — like from the beginning of time — since when we first met up in the first grade.... you were always around her... How can she ask how can I be certain?

*

loose change

How do you get a date? What do you say? Do you just announce hey I'm available?

You tried online dating skills. But that was fucked and doomed to start: too many people asking too many questions that made no sense. Where was the nonsense you typed in? You got a number of hits. But you felt like they were just another suspicious act worse off than your own.

So you went to the best place imaginable: that you knew: the 20th Century Club.

Her name was Claire. You met her one happy hour on a Thursday after work.

You were paint splattered and looking like you lost the day after rolling out a church ceiling. Head to sneaker toe your whole being was spotted with rose-colored dots off the roller head. You looked like you might have a disease. And you were sweated to a fault. Your body odor might drive a hungry shark away.

Get a swim she said.

Fast Eddie nodded and indicated the door while laughing.

Nobody leave you said.

Claire and Fast Eddie and a few other patrons looked at you and said okay.

You ran off to the beach and swam out to the lifeguard buoy and back and threw your dirty clothes back on and then ran back to the 20th Century Club.

Claire was sill where she was which amazed you.

Fast Eddie served you a tall cold beer and vodka to freeze your life and slid you a pill to slow down. And that was good because you needed some momentum.

Claire had long curly brown hair with a pleasant face and a broad nose and soft foggy eyes. She wore denim overalls with little else underneath them. The overalls did her well. A testament to worn-in baggy cotton Claire slid around in those denims and you said wow in your head.

Sweet you said in your head.

Oh yea you said in your head.

Float in my mind you said in your head.

Claire was studying to be a nurse at a small two-year college inland up northwest Jersey-land toward the water gap.

That's my practical side she said.

Fast Eddie bought a round. He poured himself a short one and raised a quiet glass to the house — and the house shouted back — because that's the place Fast Eddie ran.

And so you have an un-practical side you asked?

Not just like that she said.

How so?

I draw portraits Claire said. Ink and charcoal and this oil wash I cook up back at the apartment. Mulberry Street's about to be demolished in a year — and by then I should have a degree — so I'm working it while I can.

How so you said?

On the boardwalk in the evening I find a bench uptown and set up an easel with a sign out: portraits: $50 a face. I might have to move once a night because I don't have a permit to operate a transient business one hundred yards from the ocean — but really it's no big hassle — because when I'm told to move I do so — and I find another bench — and when I leave — I leave behind some cash on the bench where I was — a payment for the creepy boardwalk cops who told me to move — but long as I move on that first warning then everything's okay.

Ever draw the cops you asked?

Off limits she laughed.

You make money then you asked?

Finish your beer and let's go she said.

Before you dared move you watched her body slide underneath those overalls... like she was a tide to finish upon... on the way out/on the way in... and you were flotsam/jetsam overboard washed-up and abundant...

Claire had amazing wrists. You saw the evidence — maybe tempo was a word you thought as you watched her draw like a gunslinger: her hands were connected to her eyesight.

Vacationers trolled by uptown — eating bags of peanuts after dinner like they were sophisticated and cared less about where they were — kids waving Jersey-land pennants went sugar wild with double dip ice cream cones — oh for sure Claire said... and in five minutes Claire altered a radon curiosity like a tourist opinion — a strange face — into a seductive walk-away memory — as thought she were a human Polaroid and for fifty bucks you got your ego laid.

That night Claire took in $500 in six hours.

Later that night we went back to Claire's apartment on Mulberry Street — a tiny dense attic space — two little windows in the airshaft that faced a heap of invasive vines crawling up the forgotten block walls from a garment shop next door in the alley

She wanted you to pose for her. That was cool because you got undressed without a worry. And it made you both classical and pornographic in an instant — being nude with a purpose — and maybe even transcending a century's worth of naked guys — sluts that we were — posing in a dark room with skimpy back-light — maybe you got to be a famous pose in history — maybe even books were written — who was that guy — some low rent David — the new David although Claire put a hat with a veil on your head...

And you wanted to punch a ticket — for you and for Claire — sans charcoal and ink — the boardwalk and painting churches. It was hard to put together a hierarchy about what you meant ... was it true ocean affections ... was it anatomical equations... whatever obscene and newfound dating game we might turn this into...

When she finished drawing — and you were stretched on the floor naked — you realized– but it was more dreamy that that — this wasn't a question to an answer you wanted: weightless disembodied and rambled: spring flowers and skinny-dipping: but she wasn't naked: she took the sketch pad off the easel and set it on a desk. By now you were straight out permanent and smiled at her from the floor.

What was the best way to give out without coming up short?

How did it sound when you asked her: lie down here? You still had the silly hat with the veil on.

Claire said of course and then left the room without another word to go and have a bath

Did — of course — that mean you were invited into the tub?

Did — of course — that mean all this was working proper like take-out for two?

What kind of trouble have we backed into you asked while she was gone to her bath?

You were quiet... because that's how Claire liked it: not much extra talk... she explained — while you were on the floor hard as a burnt summer sky — turning the ideal of pleasure over and over –just once you thought — caught up in a pocket of time — just once with Claire you thought — how we might understand it — a simple head — you thought because half of us were already naked — how it would be to close that gap — gain our flaws and startle the deities....

I have a trigger finger she said. Don't disturb it.

You listened on the other side of the door from her bath.

The water running and filling a tub... Claire adding bath salts or soap powder... you were dying to know which... how she stepped over the rim of the tub...did she hold onto the tiles to steady her and lift her legs... did she just step in and settled down as the bath water cloaked her shoulders... you liked to think — once there — in the water — yes you wanted to be right there — just once — naked in a tub with Claire — together we lost and together we forgot the dim anxieties and bothers of the day — together we might have a sight — a wet dream — any happiness — enlarged hearts...

But you didn't open the bathroom door. That way Claire existed. Without being real you were able to hold her. But that wasn't lasted...

Some playback in memory-time told you no and let go and don't touch that door handle...

Not that it was a bad thing to imagine: but please you thought... please open the door...

But that wasn't going to happen

You sensed her eyes filled sideways ... matted hair with streaked blond ringlets reaching below her shoulder blades... that way she exists... you reached to hold her ass curves... the bathroom door handle was hot... tender procedures duplicating themselves... that way she exists... don't touch the metal latch... please open the door... brightly stirred loose breasts... you felt so very light ...standing behind a door... jumping... longing... a spectacle of human estrangement... you weren't in the picture at all... in your head you heard the word ouch several times... before eventually you left and walked home ... thinking this was all so strange... with nothing but bath water on your mind...

*

But there was another woman. Claire introduced you to her. She was also a Claire model.

Her name was Emily.

She was rep for a seafood processing company. She had territories she maintained along the whole eastern seaboard — Down East to Key West — that was the hologram logo on her business card.

Here's how it's done...

Emily said face was the selling point.

The right face she said disordered the client just enough...

You have a good one you told her.

What you need she said was to walk into a room and pull true north off the compass needle and keep the magnetics spinning while you pitched.

You have a good one you told her.

She wore glasses as a disguise. Ordinary window glass — that set her eyeballs within slim tortoise frames she had special built by her brother. Her vision was fine. She didn't need glasses. However — by wearing fake

327

glasses — Emily set herself up behind them as though she were only accessible if she removed them.

Emily changed her hair twice a season for business reasons. She followed what her favorite character did in a spy novel series. You cut your hair different and colored it different.

Then you showed your fish and chip statistics — and cheap ocean foods for the future launch charts- to a bored group-set of managers.

You smiled deeply. Gentlemen she said. She let her glasses down on the table. Emily turned on the face and walked out with a sale.

Emily also put lifter cushions in her shoes to make herself taller.

*

Emily was also an after hours vulture. We didn't spend much late nighttime in clubs. We didn't hang out on the pier. And that made for strange midnight pickings around town with you in tow. You need to be the witness she said.

Why not just be in bed you thought?

Because Freud didn't shoot she laughed.

So what happened to the photos?

*

Emily set her telephoto lens with a scope and tripod like a sniper's rifle. She robbed people. Emily shot away their privacy.

Might be families fighting at a bus stop… or she caught a pair fucking with only their pants down behind a dumpster in the park near the band shell… lonely figures behind apartment windows reading to themselves — talking to themselves — drinking themselves into any small measures they found in any small happiness that was given up for them to behold…

Whatever her sights — Emily was drawn to a spectacles: like watching paper airplanes sail that collapsed and died because the folds in their wings weren't made right for flying.

Guess I have a question you said.

What do you think she asked?

You thought a lot you answered.

Think about the big overseas market for old syndicated television series... sitcom reruns beamed into communist villages ... all those people so removed from where a sitcom was shot they start to watch these images as a kind of kinetic therapy — their lives are moved — they begin to imagine beyond their small market channels and they begin to want — as - you know — well they know — you know — and for them suddenly watching becomes an art form they perform wherever they are- at home or down at the bar or crowded around some kids phone screen... watching is an art form. And this is where — I believe — love comes out and captures our hidden spiritual lives. If no one sees me taking their photo that's what defines me.

That still didn't answer your question.

That's what I do Emily said.

But what about the people you look at you asked. Are they having a spiritual experience caught with their pants down?

Emily flipped up her dress and dropped a string –like garment that was more appetizer than it was underwear and bent over — across her ass cheeks was a tattoo in plain red letters that read: the observer changes everything. That's what lets me out she said.

Maybe you're question didn't matter.

And getting that Emily said — I'm removed — I go second hand — go from nature — go from looks — I don't care what — pure defeat or universal elation. I'm let go so I'm not there. What I do is what the shutter does when it falls.

Was this coincidence? There's a guy sitting on the boardwalk and eating noodles — was it a coincidence I found him — was it a coincidence he found me — was he waiting to be discovered — did I track him down — I don't think so to any of it.

So what do you find out?

Emily grinned and tracked the camera across the landscape. We were stationed up on the top fifth floor of The Anchor to the Sea Hotel. She bought a condo room there a decade ago. Real estate prices were cheap after another crash. Too good a deal not to get into the owner told her.

Private bath and room service and windows looking on the Atlantic that actually worked: too easy to pass this one up he said. Can't see making the price Emily said. When the owner balked at her counter-offer — all she did was lay down several photos before him. Deal she asked?

She passed the flask and lit a joint. I find whatever wants to be discovered.

Isn't that a little heady?

I don't think so Emily said.

I love satellites in orbits high above the earth. They have such definition they record you eating French fries from thirty miles away.

And that doesn't worry you?

If I worried about that — I'd have to worry about myself Emily said. What's your point she asked? She found something on the boardwalk and clicked off several frames and stored them in digital memory.

It's just seems — confused — to spy on people you said.

Confusion becomes attraction very simply Emily replied. Why see things only one way?

Probably not... or probably... it's just hard to think that you think that you're discovering people....

At their worst — is that what you're saying? It's a keyhole she went on. Pantheisms — free associations — the irresistible peek toward what's normally forbidden — suddenly it takes over... and I need to have it. I love those bad focus shots where Jackie Onassis takes off her bikini top and the shot goes tabloid. I need to put doubting Thomas to rest. I love ancient levels. I love opportunity knocking. Now- stand against the window — that's good there — but tilt more left — yep — there's a guy walking up the beach dragging a chain of fish and wearing rubberized waders...

*

Should you be surprised? Wasn't doubting Thomas a hallucination anyway? Where do you put faith once your instincts come along?

Whatever it was you took a slice and went off with it.

You fell over and that was cool.

Emily was patchworked in nature. She made herself from innuendos assumptions and puzzles. And that was what she was — and she wrapped herself around you for comfort.

The sex was good. Emily was vivid. We set the ideas.

You lived out a splash dash eternity for as long as you could — the love equals sadness affair. Suddenly you were opened to how quick it ends. And just as suddenly — upon having Emily's missionary touch — your senses went down the rabbit hole — your up-tick and your downdraft and your results — had you walking on air. The sex was good. Emily was vivid. We set the ideas.

*

Love equaled feelings?

Yes she said.

Was it that obvious?

Yes she said. Wasn't this what you had in mind?

Well it's not exactly the dating game!

Do you need the cure this morning?

Yea you said.

Just wait till I play the remote.

Hurry you laughed. We're losing inches.

*

Where was Doubting Thomas? Did he have his say? Other than sticking his fingers in god — was it possible for him — Doubting Thomas — to be in one world and was it possible for him to be in another world at the same time?

Was Doubting Thomas a setup do you think?

Should you be surprised if he wasn't?

Emily loved to make photographs.

Emily obliged a balance in time and it showed why she ruled...

Love moves — doesn't it?

No she said it doesn't. But it does help the shoot… to be at either end for as long you can… what I want was to take emotions away from strangers.

Think about it like this: having a credit card you can't pay off… the more purchases you have the deeper you go into debt … and that — she said — was when the freeze happened… and when the freeze happened that was simply a chance you missed if the shoot didn't happen…

Confused you said

Think forefinger she said.

Think waiting to show she said.

Think shutter button she said.

Then you're gone.

*

And you weren't that difficult to be immune to Emily's missionary touch. Emily was forever there. Even if you did not know — where she was — Emily was somewhere in the ether. Somewhere around and you knew that and you sensed that Emily was around. She was around the corner behind a cabstand. She was underneath a parked car. She once climbed a crane's derrick at a worksite to shoot the mayor grabbing some ass at a high school graduation ceremony on the boardwalk. And it got to be so you felt the air move when Emily was watching.

Photo: you at work rolling out pale pink church walls in near darkness while the sunlight passed the vaulted stained glass windows at the end of the day and you thought you were alone so you hummed old church hymns in tune with the silence.

Photo: you down at Second Avenue feeding a stray dog a slice of pizza and it was as though the dog was sitting Buddha pose and you were some acolyte distributing favors.

Photo: you and Morgan one December evening jumping off the pier together at Congress St. into the surf against a blowing Northeastern Jersey-land snow.

I thought you both were committing suicide she said. Because at the time we were both in love with Emily at the same time…

Great idea you said but no — that wasn't it.

Happiness was a hangman's game anyway wasn't it you asked?

Don't be like that she said... searching for several apps on her camera... and finding the drawstring knot that undid your shorts.

*

Thoughts like that made happiness a hangman's game anyway...

Thoughts like that drove you mad with happiness ...

Thoughts like happiness landed you where nothing else mattered but the thoughts of happiness...

*

One morning outside the room the birds whispered first — outside the room window and above our protoplasmic heads the birds sat in branches — they sang — we made question marks around one another in bed — the moon was gone — gone back into the vineyards beyond the sky — gone to where the fruits of the day got made — a second in time and repeat that time and then the moon was sent back from the empty soil of the universe and its peculiar yards — Emily asked — do you think about me like me being a girl force?

*

Emily loved the shadows the world provided.

She hid in landscapes.

She hid in faces.

Each morning you brought her the crossword puzzle in bed — along with black coffee and a fried egg sandwich with cheese and salsa — before she showered and launched herself out the door wearing fashionable shoes and an eye popping blouse to peddle seafood to mostly old guy losers who were in the business too long to understand what the deals meant anymore. It was here where she shined.

Being in love — it was so simple — that it stupefied attempts at being grandiose and kind and neatly tying up the loose ends between two people who were fucking.

So one day you begin to imagine this was cool. This whole thing had standing.

*

But Emily — you soon found out — how often does fucking last – and how sad was that gem you believed you owned before the personals you knew turned sour — Emily forgot what you saw. And this — you found out — was where she shined best… Emily used what she saw to better her favor. And for a while that was great — great to be around — things were beautiful when they were new and alive and she pulled your pants down and the sex was knockdown crazy in the body and light bulbs went off in the head and there was ice cold red watermelon afterwards — it was being in the sky again and asking the way out silence and far-out light if was there was a soul — like you remembered — before you arrived and called Jersey-land hometown. Emily loved watermelon.

Yea shit happens. That much you learned. But was there a word — was there a phrase — was there something to figure — something to figure that you already knew?

One evening Emily said — You're an everyday Eddie. You're the guy who rakes the infield before a ballgame. And what I got is you're satisfied with that — no — in fact — you are ecstatic about that.

You told Emily you didn't really know who raked the infield.

What happened to the dating experience? How do you get to be who you think you want to be you asked?

It's just this –Emily said — I'm making a case.

How so you asked?

I need a shoot that's — like — theatrical. I need something real-time but not something reality bound.

Why were there red flags all over this you asked?

Because you need to do this before it's too late she said?

Why was it too late you asked? Who ever said it was too late.

Because she said… the old dry fishing hole….

Wait you said…

334

Wait for what Emily said?

The details you said.

Do you mean — feelings — she asked? How queer. Why do you think that way?

Don't know you said. Maybe I have to...

What she interrupted — what do you need to know?

By then — life — for the moment — was the big zilch. Staring nobody. Screenplay by nobody.... directed by nobody... appealing to an audience that was nobody...

Emily shook her hair –lovely enough — hard enough — to whiplash you and recall her auburn streaks — as though all extraneous matter went flying off with her loose ends — a bad sign for sure...

*

Last photo: Emily tossed her head back on a self-timer app and when that was good she checked her watch. She took a shot and left. Next you went out onto the fire escape and waited below an old electric light above the door. Down below the fire escape was a parking lot and street lamps hanging on forgotten telephone poles lit that up like a level of hell in the comic books. Hidden down there in the parking lot — in the gut fish shadows and sick oil pans leaking gold crude onto a sad gravel lot — there were possessed junk cars and warehouse stuff marked blank in big green letters on crates and people living in Jersey-land owned junk cars and people living like warehouse stuff in crates.

Emily waited for her image.

She waited for you to walk out the door — stand beneath the electric light — look inland at Jersey-land and understand where you got your comfort and hide.

Emily waited for you.

She wanted to flesh you out onto Jersey-land.

You are now a soul losing its body she said pointing a camera with a laser at you.

Tell me it's kindness she yelled from the parking lot.

When she was finished — Emily drove away slow down the alley and onto Wyncote Avenue — where then she hit near sixty — tires singing on the crummy blacktop into the night.

That was part of it.

You had to watch.

You had to watch her leave.

*

One Friday evening you were downtown outside the movie house — waiting for the middle show to begin and undecided — killing time in the ocean air. You almost forgot. How simple life was.

Across Ocean Avenue high tide flashed in the summertime like a crazy recall that you saw and hit the beach with small but solid breakers. Warm sea breezes kicked ass in your mind.

Kids on boogie boards hit the surf screaming.

Muscled lifeguards packed up their gear in hip synthetic packs. Trimmed out bikini girls stood nearby eyeballing the lifesaver guys. Sentient bar dates were about to be set.

Vacation acolytes walked past and poured wine over their heads.

Parent hordes chewed nervous ice cream cones and bitched about restaurants and families.

It suddenly came upon you — this was where you belonged. This was sky in miniature.

Fucked up people to forget — ocean landscape — rebuild a lost self — how long had you been away- how do you account time in a strange land — no long goodbyes...

But you needed to get back home and since they couldn't take you back not yet — Jersey-land was home.

You missed the sky.

The sky wanted you back.

But not yet.

*

So Emily never showed for the movie. No surprise — just a reasonable assumption you understood that she wouldn't show. Emily didn't care for the movies. Not even an old Cinemascope thriller with Spencer Tracy as the mysterious stranger nobody in town trusted in Bad Day at Black Rock. Plus they showed cartoons and ninja shorts and offered free candy.

And you're mostly directionless watching the crowd walk past.

Odd mandolin music floated one story above street level from the Ugly Mug Bar and Grill.

It was too bad really.

*

But love was flexible. That's what you were told. The sky looked after the details.

*

Then Tara George Sands walked up to you.

You said hello and asked -what are you doing and welcomed her to another fictional evening uptown.

What to see a movie you asked?

Tara George Sands was the gal who cut Emily's hair.

What's up with that she asked?

Yea you said. What do you think?

I think I'm puzzled she said.

Another sign you thought.

What did you say she asked?

You had this attraction to follow — like a puppet laughing in gravity you tried to get by while you still could.

Tara George Sands thought about your offers and said okay — but you buy the popcorn.

Deal you said. But you get the pizza later.

*

Tara George Sands — she insisted you say her full name — had reddish blond hair worn short in the back like an athlete — long streaked bangs in the front — pinned with a brass comb but fell down over her left eye. Over pizza she fretted about her hair. It's not the hair really I worry about she said. But I cut hair. So I have to have a decent cut. My hair is business. My hair needs to be about what's been left out from someone's else's life.

Does it matter as long as it works you asked?

Color was so totally important she said. I dye my hair like three times a week. If not where else were my customers be looking?

Tara George Sands took her middle name from her father: Tommy Apple George. He was a man who made his money the old fashioned way: he stole it.

He started out on convenience stores and food carts but soon hit the hard stuff she joked.

Like what?

Banks. Home invasion. A little fraud but he preferred working with a gun. Then Dad got addicted to supermarkets for some race-track money. Late morning stuff when the cash draws were shuffled and the clerks were in a daze like sleepy teenagers. Don't get me wrong — Dad made good living. And he was a single parent raising two kids! But — at some point — at somewhere in some day — I have a memory of time then but not a thought about numbers — Dad left. He left the same day before he died.

Wow you said.

Yea she said. The body was never found...

Dad you said... That was a good one.

*

What journey you asked?

Well — to begin with I was born in Katmandu and on the streets...

Huh?

Just kidding she said. You want that last slice?

*

338

All things that mattered aside — questions with sky — personal simplified equations — walking around — talking around — fucking around — a dusted-off self — prone to forget as much as you remembered — what purpose was there opening your mouth if you can't lie to yourself?

But what else was new?

Touching someone new and stepping off everyday sets of circumstance made you feel a little better — illusive or not — crazy and sparkling — the green lights like the stars — the gears of human hands — one body a beach the other body a wave — a breath spoken that said yes and hitched the imagination — the crystal ping in the brain pan whereby anxiety becomes flat-lined as though you were dead but your senses and your dreams know more than you figured out and they tell you so in recoils while you slept — in spades together in the silence afterwards together while you slept together — in curves — with words — let's get naked — like we'd each tossed a rock and each made ripples onto each other's shallow pond in the salt of the night.

*

She'd been to Nepal several times. Once on a trek — she heard a rumor that her father was alive and was living outside Katmandu. Tara George Sands disliked yak butter but loved the local kick ass beer. The people were beautiful in so many giving ways. They were climate. They were poor. They were a neighborhood that was as close to the universe as possible given their altitude. But she never found her dad in suburban Nepal. Rumors do that to you she said. Try India the locals said.

On a walkabout across the high hills one summer — big cloudy mountains in the distance that were forever storm covered — don't go there she was advised unless you want to meet the gods and the wind — she thought this was a good place. Hang below the gods and end the wind... she walked into a village one day and nearly married a sherpa... quite a man she said... the prayer flags as they fluttered were said to be a blessing... but she knew and fought the prayer flags. She had to get back.

339

Sad she said really.

What you said?

Why people get so touchy about their hair.

But you make good money cutting hair.

For certain she said. Brings home the bacon and the bacon buys the catch of the day off the docks

Well you said people were vain and they have like this built in need -

What need she asked?

To look good or else you said. They want something to cry about when it rains. They want a reason to stare at the mirror other than to brush their teeth.

Back up she said. What's with the — or else?

What do you think people fear most?

I don't know Tara George Sands said. Death maybe?

No you said. That wasn't what I was thinking. But death was always a good choice. Everybody makes funnies about death you said. Look good or die. Like two prongs on an electric plug: looking older but feeling like you still got something left: whether it's a choice between sadness or loneliness: or what seems weird if they got religion and believe they know the score but go powerless but hold on just in case: someone's head was just someone else's head: or should you tell them the truth and break their hearts: that no matter you did to their hair they were still going to die? And not tip as well? No that wasn't it you said.

What she said?

Critical interference…

What?

Standard judgments…

What?

The beautiful indifference…

What?

People fear those more than dying.

I give back what people ask for she said.

No doubt. You have finesse.

I like to think — when somebody walks into my shop — by the time they walk back out the door — they feel better. I'm good at it Tara George Sands said.

No doubt. A good pair of scissors in your hands was like a good drawing pencil. You transform perspective.

Look — I'm a mechanic she said. Good will. Well-being. Fantasy lives matter. And I'm not breaking anybody's heart with my work.

No doubt. You're the goddess of the tune-up.

Tara George Sands smiled. And that was a good thing to have come back your way.

*

Her smile was shy — holding her lips together — acme lipped under the radar — happily lewd — and rested toward the left side of her face when she turned it on — like her mouth and her thin unsettled jaw lines held a secret that might fly out before she was asked to tell something else...

*

Strange coal dark eyes...they didn't move around much — warning against affinities basically made from her observations. Wishful old cotton pants... walk-ins were welcome... do you think it's worthwhile to do this...

*

The lilt her breathing sent across a sheet — fine moist clouds — fluctuating pitches you inhaled — kept going — a deep sea oxygen device — a drowsy Jersey-land night — what were hips — what were shoulder blades — what were eyelids — the act gazing vacantly into the distance without thinking — once upon a storm — you were in — a few billion years to fuck off — but what were hips and shoulders blades and eyelids when they held you contrary to the evidence we all die... But what she said in the morning.

341

Eggs scrambled with onions cheese tomato and hearty shakes of black pepper with light toasted English muffin buttered and several coffees cream and sugar.

Got it.

*

What's the sense getting worked up she asked?

How do I know which stress was right for me!

Yea you said. Saw that commercial.

Those are my haircuts! And so what do I do?

High tech and high style you said. That's what you do.

Tara George Sands said people walk into my shop and they want the best deal.

So what happens — when they want the best deal — and in that best deal you're made to rob these limitations on their heads? But what happens? What happens when I can't do that?

But you always do that you said. You always get clear and get your money. And someone else gets the new head there're willing to pay for. It's a deal. What else was there to be in business for? And don't tell me you're an amateur — the root word meaning — for the love of...

I don't know she said.

Alright you said. Let's take this: some mousy corporate brown hair parted down the middle and pulled back severe and painful looking behind the ears wants you to turn that into a spiky red mullet because she's tired with her way of life. How do you know what to do?

I don't know she said.

So you just guess?

No. Not especially.

You do it well though.

Well she said when people walk in — nervous and complained — we talk it out and then we get stoned. When that's all settled I fix them a boardwalk rain.

What's that?

Several nods with frozen vodka — squid water — clam juice and

tomato juice — a hearty lemon slice — a brown sugar cube — a quart
canning jar filled with ice and a mint sprig.

*

Tara George Sands was at the end of reasons for a latch phase in her
life: human potential workshops.

She tried discovering peak consciousness during a weekend long sem-
inar with a group holed up in something that looked like a bomb shelter.

She took courses in mapping out body techniques for conditional
completion and what was left for potential energies.

There were lectures and political overnights with campfire songs and
covered topics like centering the narcissus or primitive emotional capital-
ism and the sublime new vote.

Mostly she was paying money to gather with other like-minded souls
how to homage the new age. But mostly the process ran out of steam.
Mostly nobody figured who did the service in the bright new village.
Nobody figured who plumbed the walls in the bright new village. Mostly
everybody in the worships clapped in the new morning sun. They held
effigies up on poles and lit fire to the old ways that were the wrong ways.
Then there were chants to rid the human chain that bound us together in
cosmic wonder from anymore chains that might lead us wrong. Coffee
and berries and a last fuck behind the tents before the tent company
piled their stuff away.

Mostly though the process ran out of steam she said.

Was there really such a topic as evolutionary structural opposition
integration to talk about you asked?

It was like a t-ball game she said. Everybody gets a guaranteed hit and
subsequently everybody feels the sanctioned cheers as they take their base.

What was wrong with t-ball?

But for adults she said? Besides she said — changing the world was
just not practical.

In the end you go on record opposing foreign intervention and wanting to end hunger and pledge cash in namesakes of enlightenment.

But in the end we drive away in Volvos and vote Democratic and still prefer to get laid the old fashioned way — way horny and in private after drinks at a local bar.

Where do you think potential energy ends up?

Things go back to sky you said. There's a roadway — we can't see. But it's there.

Yea she said. The calendar rocks — with our hopes — and hope can't wait.

Maybe you said. Hopes were fragile anyway.

Fragile she said? Hopes were solid she said. When they break they get smashed from outside. Something from behind you hits them with a hammer. No she said I got hopes. I fight the outside.

So you said was it like a merry-go-round where you pick off the ring as you pass and the ring was like the best deal you made?

No she said. It was more like an aura you find one day hanging out and you grow into. Or utility bills you pay and practice writing that check out to faceless entities. Spiritual bingo and hey — C9 — that's me! I have it! Then you think: what are the methods? Do they set us up for failure? What are the odds you get C9? What are the odds the game was rigged and C9 was never in play? What were the odds you get paid even if you had C9? Were you a Jungian trying to knead the lumps out of memory? Did you believe religion was going to be there for you? Or talking acid freed us from the minimum wage? What about sex? Now there's a brain wave manipulator -the existential light if there ever was one — and suddenly you receive this go-ahead — a radical idea over fucking a common body until you pass out in someone's armpits — until you woke up the next day and ask do we forget the acrobatics until it's time to roll? And what about a young girl's adolescence jumping rope?

*

She didn't chase after her clients.

She filled in the blanks — with her own walk-a-bout- between necessary whims over haircuts and demands to please scheduled appointments.

She didn't chase uninsurable love despite a star that might rise in her favor one day.

344

Tara George Sands grew plants.

We're not called the Garden State for nothing you know she said.

Glacial till!

That was something else you heard about in school…

Massive ice rivers going backwards as they melt — receding like a hairline and the dome was the arctic circle — what she said… you didn't learn this shit in school…?

Maybe you said…

Maybe?

School wasn't a strong point you said.

She gave you a cross-eyed look — part wonderment and part anchors away.

Glacial till. Fertile deposits — Jersey-land! — the beautiful material left behind — soil made from action and millenniums of action and what happened with all that? You sink your teeth into the results and that's what you get. . Think about this month: what do you like… who do you love. August was blessed that's what because August was the best month in the world.

We're living on the reach — off the cuff — living on a ball in the middle of nowhere…and having a ball for what it's worth…. from like thirteen billion years ago… and so get it -August was the birth of the universe… and it translates down to this: tomatoes peaches and corn… tomatoes peaches and corn…. come on — say it — until they roll off your tongue and you're ready for it because that's all you want…

Yea you said. The Garden State… for sure… tomatoes peaches and corn…

That's it she said. You got it. You said it. You own it.

Been here all your life you thought. You grew up here. The sky dropped you off.

*

Jersey-land was between your shoulder blades. There was ink to prove it so. Nobody's future held anything but that tattoo. There was a day back in school where all the boys checked each other. We all had the Jersey-land flag. A blue shield with three plows embedded in a deep azure color field and framing the shield were two goddesses: Liberty and Prosperity. But after that the image got suspicious. We compared it with the older guys on the corner. Their ink was different. Our Latin motto and the older guys' Latin were different. Same place between the shoulder blades — same allegiance to geography- same benefits being a native son — but it was fucked up. Our Latin said: fuit mentis extra corruption.

But it was Jersey-land. And that was enough to call it home.

*

Tara George — you got tired calling her by that full name — the dead missing father meant little — sorry you said but that was how you felt — she lived in some old shack — a small cramped building about five feet from the railroad line that at one time was a station master's quarters. You remembered the freights that rumbled past day and night — shaking old terra-glass windows in moldy wooden frames and vibrating the walls. When a train passed her house was stupid with energy. Brute railroad waves jumped the needles on the feeding tubes of young cannabis and tore monster scratches across the vinyl on the turntable.

When you saw where she lived — a beat old building next to the rails — and that was surrounded by desolate and undeveloped yards — ghost fields where unsolved bodies might suddenly pop up out of the muck — tide zones that were nature's washing machine — nightmare oil lands that the tide zones flushed — the wildlife sanctuary — the smelly crabs and one-winged sea birds — you were blinded by a solitary thought: and that was staying warm next to Tara George in winter.

*

What a winter. Mirrored. Romance novels.

*

The fallow months. Empty. Taking walks together.

346

Our brains went silly merry and wild. Our bodies doubled down like casino talk on the over and under chance at some rigged table

*

She said — one morning- in a whisper — we were only around — springtime meant we were now patterned like fingerprints in a line-up and what that meant she said was that together we had no excuses and so together we turned light into oxygen. And from there you can't turn back she said. We're a living machine she said. Get used to it. Unlock it.

*

Every conceivable overgrown weed in North America thrived in spades and went crazy around Tara George and her homey shack.

And surrounding this manic carbon vegetation — spreading high — unchecked and invasive — wild to the sky — going defiance — bleeding out from helicopter sprays of old Asian war agent orange — beyond the weeds were like an acre of old shipping containers.

Some with their sides torn open. They leaked bad rain and forgotten rusty chemicals.

They smelled worse that gutted bait fish tossed from the decks of wealthy charter boats... trying to fool the last sad sharks of the ocean to their deaths by cash only... top money... old schools lines if the client wanted... but mostly these days the trophies were caught by automatic rifles...

Don't go so imaginative on the weeds Tara George said.

Yea?

Yea she said. I got neighbors living over there.

Yea you said?

Yea she said. Before they get found...Before Colonel Shots and Detective Shade and their minions swept Jersey-land and they got bum-rushed out of town... I support the weeds she said. Night soil and seaweed and the drainage ditch from the casino. No trespassing signs I stole from the railroad and put all over the place.

Yea it seemed hard you said. Where are your neighbors from?

You name it Tara George said. Across that yard — in there — we got a global sample. And bless them all... Fugitives... Illegals... Skilled unemployed... Little kids and grandparents... Bright Yellow Lovers... Dreadful Criminals... Cottage Families... Fiddle Peg Musicians... Lonesome Drug Mules... Wind and rain souls who never sank in the ocean trying and then finally got here... those are my neighbors.

*

There were roses — cream orange red yellow a weird hybrid blue — they sparkled like Peter Pan dust — the dreamy roll — movie impressions — there were roses growing on salvaged metal pipes — hand stitched trellises — bad welding — spot on rope knots — roses up the sides of that old faded clapboard building — there were roses reaching the eaves and meeting underneath the soffits — there were roses curling back downward like fountains and made curtains around that sad building — there were ground roses spreading along the tracks — there were thorny roses at home in the weeds — roses that were color book pictures on forgotten trees and roses outside the lines climbing on a warehouse across the tracks and roses that demanded to lend what was it the fuck you knew and roses with colors and shapes and wild crayon roses that hit your sight lines until you were blind with color and those colors tore the retinas off your eyeballs with little regrets for the looking.

Tomatoes... So many tomatoes! From the minute of seedlings you helped start in a greenhouse shack with scabbed windows and stolen framing from the casino job site... to planting them in the Jersey-land earth with swampy ocean breezes singing against your back...and on through the harvest burst — where all those neat and planned out progressive rows of plants from those months ago took to the wild and expelled red fruit from overgrown leaf stock...

Can't you just see what's going on she said.

What's that?

Plant mythology.

Beans and onions and greens -

Oh yea she said.

Plus the cannabis plants — tall well thought buds — silent green photos from the pages of High Times magazine — like the weeds — moving toward the light to stay alive — feeding on nitrogens and water waste — old fashioned seats — nature in ditches — like monks chanting sutras to be forgotten until the time was right to be dope — like the weeds hidden in the heavens...

*

Tara George made an oasis from scratch. She bought a small land on the sewer's end of Jersey-land that was classified as dead on the county maps and she turned it righteous.

The casino fought her over shit permits. In court the casino lawyers argued for the right to dump on her land for economic activities deemed critical for activity.

Colonel Shots took to the talk shows day one day on the boardwalk — ocean winds blew his gorgeous orange hair to the sky and revealed the stitches that wealthy men incorporated to disguise their baldness with an ugly wig — and on the shows he despised Tara George Sands as a total bitch loser standing in the way of progress.

Jersey-land asked her to yield as a matter of fact and so maybe move away with a reasonable compensation package before eminent domain kicked her ass.

*

She fetched seaweed from low tides on a sherpa pack and gathered fish heads from the cannery before the crabs got them.

She bargained haircuts for truckloads of topsoil.

She even went out on a date with a guy for a truckload of chicken shit.

As long as the chromium in the soil stays down then we'll be okay she said.

It took years she said — but finally I got the loam I was looking for.

*

All around her strange little house was this industrial mess. Say if Tara George Sands held the pastoral in mind body and soul and made that so on her strange little acre — then Jersey-land politics was Dante's subway into hell and burning salt on her life.

*

…the sun is up the sky is beautiful and so are you….

*

What to say but to crib from a Beatles record?…

*

The road where she lived — Martha's Break — the last road off Arch Street had been forgotten for years. Then one day massive amounts of fill — bad concrete from China — dirt to question where and what it was made from — and shady building debris showed up.

And the bridge construction over the bay to Delaware soon began.

Trump cranes swung against the sky like gigantic insects looking for prey. Trump bulldozers turned over wetland muck worth centuries of wetland life into temporary roads. Trump signs strung out barbed wire. Trump sentries walked the borders and exchanged words with the oil workers and checked arms.

And parked in the yard near Arch Street were a suspicious group of trailers. Ripped up metal things that were dropped from dumpster trucks one midnight — with a sloppy door that didn't close and one window below the shit stack but the shit was connected nowhere — and no surprise the trailers were painted a weak hazy yellow — like a cab color — and underneath the lousy paint job were the markings in splotches from a corporate name.

350

One night we snuck up close to the trailers. They smelled.

Across the tracks from Tara George was the other lone human outpost.

Across the tracks was Smiling Bob Jersey-land Transmission Specialties.

Don't let your gears drag on the road.

Me and Smiling Bob she said — we're in the same business.

How so?

Getting things back on the road. We're in the future business.

So what's the promise?

A future she said meant you take time out of behavior and not be stuck with your head up your ass.

Oh.

*

Gravity worked both ways. It attracted. It repelled. Time was opening. You saw it. You were about to turn into the future. But why was the question? The future was scary and that unfortunately was a promise and an argument's way to provide a tome between lovers. First we talked ourselves into a lusty equilibrium that brightened in the sky. And then one day we backed away from the corners we talked ourselves into.

Sky was home you said.

Not in my house she said.

*

That maroon halter- top she wore was undeniably hard to disagree with. It stretched across her ribs and hung tightly from armpit to armpit — a garden outfit with a damn good fit. Dark rayon material — smooth to the touch — that drooped away underneath her arms like a ribbon tied around a gift. And Tara George Sands knew what your eyes saw and she let them roam until gravity dropped them from their sockets like apples from Newton's daydream.

And from your perspective it was like this — let's get the eyes and language working on the same row — one simple embodied voice —

351

progressive — networked. Let's just get to the outcome. Let's make time so rudimentary that in the end it doesn't account for much.

But It's a process she said. You just can't go there.

Why not let it stand there by itself?

But then she said you need a bunch of promises to keep it there. This is not an event. It is necessary for you to make mistakes! Please. Go. Go and fuck something up!

But what you asked?

I don't know she said. Go fuck something up...

But you said you didn't like mistakes. You didn't like making them. You didn't like establishing them. You didn't need to live up to them.

If it doesn't work out then you pull it out she said.

Mistakes meant losing track and having to go backwards you said.

Tell me — what do you have to lose track of?

Everything you said!

Even though you knew that was nothing.

Mistakes meant backing up. Losing track and having to go backwards...

So what's more simple she said.

Losing track and going backwards... losing track and going backwards... and when you make mistakes it's like — your day gets messed with — all sorts of baggage and fucking life suddenly gets dragged back into your day and gets thrown in your face like this was some fucking contemporary situation and you lose track and you're going backwards and you fall into some house or some shit where you once lived and it's a place full of stuff you didn't do so well with in the first place and that didn't turn out well in the first place so you try and grab your head and try and blow it off and try to forget about it and mistakes meant backing up and losing track and having to live backwards and living backwards gave you baggage and mistakes meant moving backwards and you felt more stupid than ever — backing up — re-inked — creepy — a cartoon balloon across your head — mistakes meant appearance — backing up and re-living...

Well aren't you determined she said.

Not really you said. You believed in an endless summer....

Do you drool when the bell rings?

352

Yes you said.

Actually you thought you might have a decent life as a cartoon.

*

But it was the opening — did you step through — or did you not?

Sex alone wasn't a warranty enough to handle the equation tough enough for you to be determined — and to reach across a promise land into some kind of border land without you on the losing end for your reach. Why was it you thought? What was it? When you sleep beside another person on a nightly basis you revealed yourself — but often as such you feely delivered... the self she was after...

And you could lie. You could turn the word fabricate into something comic personal and then inhabit that word with blinders. But no matter what- a lie shook out for nothing.

You could be your self....

You could be a calculated boredom that pretended to be your self...

You could be wondrous ordinary and aroused and who was that...

Conversational to the sound of her voice...

And it never required strangeness...

Like we were driving together one day — sitting in the front seat together — listening to the radio and eating breakfast egg sandwiches together — drinking coffee and getting high together and on the way to visit her great aunt.

Great Aunt Biscuit now lived in a new swamp town off Exit 27. The old farm house — the old mule acres — the graveyard that was filled with three hundred years of ancestors buried there — Great Aunt Biscuit was the last standing... She was targeted by

Colonel Shots... destroyed by Colonel Shots and his Big New Map. Jersey-land would no longer be the garden state but a guarded state.

Great Aunt Biscuit was on the cusp — healthy enough to manage a garden and grow something — along with herself she said! But Great Aunt Biscuit was old and by formula she was too limited to grow anything that made cash for Jersey-land. The past season zinnias tomatoes and onions and eggs and the big herb — brought her fifteen thousand dollars last year on a bad market. She was destroyed. There was a formula for success. Great Aunt Biscuit was on the edges because she failed to reach a percentage — the two percent that separated failure from loss.

Colonel Shots seized the property.

Eminent domain — what was that?

Great Aunt Biscuit lived in a strange room… a room… that's where she found herself…. an affordable room…. a concrete block house off exit 27… all her life she hated exit 27…

Square and weird — painted with silly flower murals on the block walls outside and duplicated with the same fucking murals painted inside on the same block walls -that was her room. Great Aunt Biscuit kept breathing…. breathing…. breathing was good — breathing Biscuit said was defiance — breathing was crops… breathing was a long living contact with the earth… breathing was Great Aunt Biscuit… breathing meant sky you realized… when you talked with her breathing cheered her up… sky … sky was there….you asked Great Aunt Biscuit: do you understand sky?

She nodded. Great Aunt Biscuit was crazy… that's what her papers read… so the act sustained itself… her voice didn't require perfection nor did her silence prove to be a burden…Great Aunt Biscuit wanted to know shall we have a tomato sandwich together?

*

And the tomatoes we had…

Fruits from the sky she said.

Homeland you said was Jersey-land….

Great Aunt Biscuit made us a feast…

The tomato sandwich… worth $7 on any exit west on the Jersey-land Parkway … the everyday tomato sandwich…. worth $7…

Great Aunt Biscuit made the sandwich… the tomatoes made Great Aunt Biscuit… and that's what made the sandwiches. Cops bought sandwiches. Blind Charlie bought sandwiches.

Great Aunt Biscuit was sky.

But when was she dropped?

And why didn't you know?

Where was the signal you expected?

*

We drove together in the front seat for hours. But really by that time — time did not matter.

Tara George was behind the wheel. How to make it questionable … driving in the front seat for hours… no talking — but not silence — born a Jersey-Land kind of way … mostly having nature thoughts and driving on the Parkway and not paying attention… static love crackled — but no proof… popcorn was a sensual feeling… as it was two people without qualifications to be anybody… but drawn each to themselves and subsequent drawn each to the other… you drive for distance… for the long run… you liked the fact… you were evidence… not only memory… you were there… but once that was done you were memory again--- so you kept at it… kept showing up… kept yourself being evidence before you were done… before you were unable to escape and cast as support in some theater of the erotic… a funny bones love thing… driving off a ramp with no exit number… nowhere tomato sandwiches… tomato sandwiches tagged as a center… she dated one guy in high school and that was enough for her to try and engage some myth-less enterprise that was called dating… literally she touched anything and sheltered it and made it grow… And in all fairness we did those things and often enough for you and her to live under an illusion that we had circumstance to fall back onto if danger hit… However there was an apt vex of sorts between us — an awning with a tear in the lining above a window against the weather — we liked greasy paper bags from take out windows…. fried fish clams potatoes and squid… a jug of wine on the cheap… a big old fatty… caving our images into the cooling sand… settling Jersey-land with our clumsy bodies… like we were immigration and were made from sky and tissue… the first invaders ever to set foot in mind … frozen … last glare of the sunlight … the nuclear fast ball… hot reds sweet cheek pinks and sex me yellows… our very own hometown star… just a few light years… behind our reach… was a light… somebody else on the other side of that light was watching us… light years beyond their reach… not only did Jersey-land possess soil so good it was envied like around the world she said — but we also lived where that soil ended she said but also she said we lived on a satellite coordinate where the Atlantic began and Jersey-land ended — and not only did that make sunsets great but also she said — while tossing back some clams — she said being here made us an edge…

What was this edge you said? Like standing on a flat earth or some shit…?

No you sweet dummy she said — tossing back some clams — handing you back the wine… crushing buds for the next fatty… the sweet desirable rope smell…. the vintage herb smell… refined but not processed… cared for but not exaggerated… this edge was where sky earth and water collect us she said.

What from there you said? Tell me the edge — name me the edge — and all that. Take me to the edge!

Living on an edge she — that's where messages come from — and that's where messages arrive.

Earth sky and water she said… passing you a newly rolled fatty…. That was an intersection were forces collided she said… New things formed she said because there were differences she said and those differences crashed head to head and sooner or later there were other ways to do things than there was the day before.

Funny but you never considered Tara George Sands to be sky. But she was talking sky like she knew it.

And that was a bit of a quiz. Where was Tara George Sands?

*

What do you remember she said: What's important when you remember?

We were on our third big old fatty.

Everything's important you guessed and said. But you know — you weed some things out.

You didn't know how many opposites it took — to conjunct a situation as she said… what did that mean… and you know why even hear it… if you have no meaning about what it means…

… In that truly hungry sense she said — the out of control reach inside our bellies and where that reach takes us… Do we remember and go forward and share a meal like a family? Or do we just forget and trance walk through the dismal and bright satisfaction of having so many different supermarket choices?

Give food to people she said!

No doubt you said.

You handed her the fries. No more squid. No more clams. Just the last greasy paper bag that held our nutrients …close to close… another healthy swig… what meant our bodies… sand hornets flew into the air… they were angry because we flopped too close to their nest … her eyes peaked and her lips smiled. Tara George took that swig — red wine spilled across the corners of her mouth and sprayed the air while she laughed.

You nabbed yourself at times — you let yourself in at times — when somebody else thought about her what you thought about was that you were already thinking…

You were nobody. But you knew that. But you welded onto eternity more than those other guys ever were.

What are you saying.

Food on the beach you said.

Don't be like that she said.

Why be cautious at this time you said.

You think too far she said.

Well you said there's only an answer for so long. Give me the question. You know there's a question you have and that has a shelf life for only so long.

*

What was suggestive — physically intelligence was a carnal letdown — some of the very qualities that brought us close together — were the same things that were not only comfort and wonder but at the same time had us look at each other and ask- what's up? We longed for something else...while we slept together and our eyes woke up together... and we were confused with sex and in love with sex and sex was our address ... she looked back at you... from a place you did not want to recognize... but similarly you knew this place and it existed at any time ... so she placed you there... or you walked into it... you were always walking into things.... Maybe romance ended too quickly... talked too much... maybe love was lost... going backwards.... Like maybe the onset of love pushed things away... she was gravity because you were in love ... gravity was sky just in time... Tara George spun your head...sky was upside down... so you fought gravity... you saw gravity was going to win.... You were in love and sky began to haunt you... but that was wrong... you were left being in this strange world and so you were cut out to be in love by the demands of that world... you were left off in a world where people were in love... and you were expected to test the ground for ideas... to contain yourself — to get senseless and then get senseless over someone's body ... express yourself with thematic associations like the movie screens and go wild over someone's body... before the call came to go back home...

She said let's get more clams later on.

You agreed. Food that came in greasy paper bags was the best food the world offered.

But it haunted you. Fucked with you. Maybe and maybe and maybe it said... Not the food so much but a sweet blueberry tone she curled off her lips when she wanted something.

But what you didn't expect to happen was this: how far from your head you ended up.

Don't **think** that way she said.

What's wrong with thinking that way?

Okay she said. The first night we met — you asked a perfect stranger to suck your cock.

The hope was — a voice said — someone to say hello to you said. Besides — you were the perfect stranger you said.

The perfect stranger she said...Do you think that — that's what makes our bodies feel like light…being the perfect stranger… Is that how you feel… Are you the perfect stranger… and would that make you manic… do you contain sadness… or do you believe you're not believable… or do you have another way to live…do you know about that…do you ever imagine you're like this ore that needs to be mined daily …lustrous above ground…but in the dirt you're small…the perfect stranger she said just what was that…a cross between anger and beauty…the inviting eyes… the vanilla milkshakes and dark rum at the Nut House and the crack across the face you got that said you have to work for it mister…the fun culture where we turned one another into mouth verbs that spoke stars by the galaxy each time we used them…I am not the perfect stranger she said…I would like to be…but I'm not…

That seemed enough you said. It was just a choice of words. Seems like a lifetime ago…

I know she said. But sometimes the dynamics turn weird.

Yea you said…I got an idea.

And that idea would be: what she said.

You had an idea you said that it was imaginary for her to say that your way of being alive was so straight ahead and it was kind of retiring.

What about the same pizza you order each week she said.

Well you said — beyond the emotions — if you wished to talk in equations — then the pizza maker was happy that somebody liked his pies enough to make return calls — the delivery guy was happy because he got a tip and some dope for his troubles racing around the neighborhoods — and at the end of this well supported food chain was a moment — and that moment was the best deal — the deal you made in Jersey-land… and you don't have to give an answer —

I've met monks with more variance to their days than you have she said.

*

That was her way of saying ergo this ergo that…meaning that she looked at you and after looking at you over time she developed questions that questioned her commonplace way as to how she looked at you. It was a state something like distrustful or something.

Your own everyday take on grandeur and the neighborhood wasn't enough you guessed for her to make it fit somehow.

Each day Tara George Sands wrote an epistle on an old blackboard that she kept in the garden near the asters. A bunch of words she said. And once she wrote them down and made them solid she took a step back and looked at them. A bunch of words made the future she said.

For you — summer evenings were episodes in a daisy chain.

*

After our jobs optioned out for the day we'd meet up at the railroad shack in the evenings. And then for hours we'd fuck around in the earth — as Tara George called it — weeding and packing seaweed around the plants and watering and hauling the basic load that made stuff grow... nude gardening was the best mistake for relativity you ever had the chance to wonder about.

*

Things of that nature... A functional destiny... something in the garden... afterwards we walked to the beach... swam in the waves in the evening. After the lifeguards left for the day we settled back on the beach and smoked a joint and watched the tide move within a moon yet to show in the sky. Chloride fouled dolphins swam off the coast like drunks.

*

We walked home along Perry Street and bought flat bread from the mad Syrian and his food cart... we went out to the docks and bought the catch of the day off the boats...we cut down vegetables from the garden to make dinner with... naturally the everlasting bottle of wine waited on the table.

*

We retired for a soak… a second hand claw foot bath tub that settled on the lawn and was flanked by tall goldenrod and surrounded by three trellised walls of hyper-flower bougainvillea and was all but invisible from outside sight… complete with solar water heater and homemade plumbing made from an old fish barrels and painted a midnight blue that seemed like it needed a starry night to keep going and there was a television like this was an outdoor room and we watched the ball game while we floated in the bath … and…you thought… but you didn't want to think…so you thought were the gods bowling for dollars in the heavens?

We floated — was there a better word for escape —ending the day made your bones go numb and your eye sight loosen and all the questions vanished like the daylight taken out of the sky after the sixth inning. Then we slept — and then we dreamed… Sometimes we had the same dream… other times we did not. But the dream was the bomb. You saw a blueprint… she saw a method for taking apart the lines… you wanted sanctuary… she heard a bell ringing on the horizon and answered it… calm flat waters that were made for a simple boat fit you fine… she launched armadas into the sea… a constant search for different trade routes…

*

The last time you saw Tara George Sands was an evening in October.

She just flew into Jersey-land from some international agricultural explosion conference in Bangalore where she met with holy types and talked spiritual dirt for several days. The basic idea was to cover the earth with gardens…

The last time you saw her was an evening in October and she flew in and you were making food.

Squid — bait food — squid that was battered in fresh eggs and cream and breaded from yesterday's loaf ground into crumbs and roasted in the fire pit — garden tomatoes and basil and garlic in the sauce — meaty slices of sweet onion — the squid deep fried and sizzled inches deep in hot oil to a bullion color and then you had a lemon zest and a spirited dusting of hard cheeses from the Italian Market on Neptune Avenue for garnish…

The evening was there. Same as before but that's how you thought about it. You lived inside an atmosphere that made sure the evening was always there.

That was the last time you saw her. And the last time you didn't see her. All in the same time — that was the last time that you saw her and didn't see her — because she never came home that night.

Too bad the evening was still there.

*

the coffee mediations

You were looking at a photograph taken from a parking lot atop the Grand Canyon.

With it were letters from Eden Jones twined around one another. It was funny listening to her — like her words on the page were the same voice in your own throat.

Satellite nuclear destruction makes me nervous she said. What if all those deals break down she said and I'm on the road with nowhere to go and the world blows up? You know what I mean. Here I am out here in the big west — surrounded by all the space in the world — and know what — I miss the subways. Not that I want to be in a subway right now — I'm lost in space! But what I do miss was that feeling that the train will be late. I'll be waiting next to the tracks. But just like that — without feeling like I obey anything — I feel like I'm doing all right again. And that's what this day has been like. Fucking highs and fucking lows like one thing tries to out prove the next and so on and then you try and adjust to the slips in your head like today I had lunch at a diner called Hag Eats and I ordered a grilled cheese and it was cooked on the line with a dozen other lunches and so on and so I try and improve on what's next but I'm tired of that so I took a few of those pills you like.

*

So here I am sitting on top of the Grand Canyon. And I thought when I was young I really liked St. Theresa but that was before I found out about Greta Garbo. But I also loved bushy plants without flowers and also sharpening colored pencils and arranging them afterwards. I'm worried over what happened after I left. I did what I had to do. I know that sounds bad. But I was never quite sure if things were fine. You know my grandfather. There was no way to do him wrong without doing everything wrong. And so on my option was to leave or get found out. I miss the boardwalk. It seems like paradise now. But I still can't figure it out. I'm not a moody person. We have something in common between us. But I can't define it. Part of everything starts with my family. Suddenly I had a job. Part of something else starts with you. And saying this makes you happy. And I'm also saying this makes you dangerous. You know my grandfather. What did you do with it? Come clean with me. I shot that guy. You got to stay hometown and I had to run. I know you took it. The cousins trusted you. I shot a guy. You took from my grandfather. Where on earth are we? Do you love me?

You are all sweetness and light — for me you're all sweetness and light — but you are also a thief. You stole from my family. And I shot the guy who wasn't the thief. Right out of high school a cousin put a gun in my hand and told me: here's the choice… and never said anything else to me. So I shot the guy and that guy should have been you. Do you love me? I hate to say it — that I killed for you — but I did. I remember climbing trees in Brandon Park. And swinging in the branches and eating sandwiches and settled into the trees where we looked over the ocean and we felt face to face. I know. But suddenly death has something to do with our life. And while I like to swing in trees — I'm marked. I want to swing in trees again.

*

Time runs into itself out here quicker than it usually does. There's nothing around but time! Unless you count the gift shop and the parking lot and the cast of sillies also tired of driving and out of their cars and stretching their legs. But this place is way lonely and also way beautiful. You say something to yourself… and I'm looking out over a big cut in the earth… and it's like you feel that I need to use less words to talk about it. I spent last night here in the parking lot…Parking lot lost! That's what the signs at the parking lot say anyway. No overnight sleeping signs.

Park closes at sunset signs and no open container signs. Government employee types rousting people mostly teenagers really though. Whatever I slept here last night. Nobody kicked me out before the stars came out. I woke up and stood on my head in the parking lot. Reversed polarity and all that you do to look some other way and say what was that about? And why do places get closed at sunsets? And why just when the stars were coming out?

And why was it — why did nobody — not kick me out from the parking lot on top of the Grand Canyon? How could I sleep through the night on the truck hood? Was I something powerful? I have my guns but that's not the point. The day I left and drove off — you called it my unknown and lacquered space– but to me it had to be tomorrow.

Remember that you stood at Third and Mulberry like some channel buoy? And I know you broke in half over my sweet ass. And I know if I need an ounce of blood one day you'd give me a pint of your own without thinking. Save that blood for yourself. Because I'll give you mine... but only when that day allows... it's like I got no percent...at the moment I'm unemployed and can't show myself... who knows... next day I may have a job. I didn't ask for this. I did a cousin and mostly my grandfather a favor. And so now I can't stop without wrecking what I need. Where is it? No one else knows you have it but me. Where does that put us? Do you love me?

I know you do. And some ways that worries me: how dare you understand? How do you know? I remember you standing in the rear view mirror...like someone disappearing without a being behind them. Was this trouble or not? It's strange but I believe I'm at the Grand Canyon and looking upon a wonder of the world. But what really strikes belief for me was having coffee and eggs in the Grand Canyon gift shop and checking my phone. Everything's wild right? But what's that got to do with me? I shot a guy over a business deal for my family. And you're aware the guy never woke up after. It wasn't a bad piece of work — but then I thought: what does this have to do with me being here? And even if I wasn't here it wasn't like I wasn't focused on the situation at hand. Somebody asked me to discriminate when everything else seemed plausible and had its own explanation.

*

There was a story here in the local paper. About a woman flying an airplane through the Grand Canyon. But her plane runs out of fuel and she crashes someplace totally remote. Eventually the search and rescue people find her — and she's still alive but critical. Apparently she's like this famous geologist with like this mad devotion to rocks. That's what she does. She lived to check out rocks. So the question people are asking is: how did she run out of fuel? Was it bad judgment? Maybe she just ran out of fuel and accidents happen? But it's the way the response was made... that's what I think lately.

And I'm on the hood of the truck spacing and critical when this RV pulls up beside. The brand was a Land Yacht. I've seen them before and they do justice to the saying: elegance through mass production equals your home on wheels. The thing was huge — big enough to house families — and two people step out into the glare. And it's like they surveyed the world outside from leaving the monster they've been driving in for the past day without a break. How high can you fly?

The woman looked around and said this place was a waste. Why are we here?

The man laughed — and the woman jumped on him and said like what's this about that a million people a year see this?

That's exactly why we're here the man said. Can you actually resist the Grand Canyon he said?

But this was a fucking parking lot she said!

At that point the man took her picture and kept laughing.

And she was right in a way. Nature was caught you know in some weird time museum with its metal plaques and raised letterings with explanations and descriptions of scenic wonders and warnings not to stray off the path if you headed down into the canyon.

Maybe it's meaningful. But do I need to know how many people died in the canyon over the years? And then you take that with all the years the Grand Canyon's been around and suddenly I felt like I didn't make any sense. This place doesn't fit the scale of my mind it's so fucking big.

Why are we here the Land Yacht woman said?

At that point he took her picture again and was laughing again.

I want a bistro for lunch and a club for supper with dancing in the night and I want a place with a bank where I get cash from an automatic teller she said.

Do you want to take a hike he said?

Give me a break she said.

That's because we're arguing he said when we're supposed to enjoy how beautiful things are.

Give me a break she said.

I didn't have anything to do with it he said!

Were these people like tragic because they wanted to be that way or what did they imagine it or what was said when they drove away in their boxy crate burning oil and it waddled side to side and I'm guessing they're pouring drinks for one another now and wearing strange hats and talking with their hands thrown up in the air as though beauty took a place with anger and you know that beauty and anger were swapped down the road and like exchanged for something else they probably made up with as much influence as the next gas station. I don't know.

*

But you know what? Kids were out and painting the Grand Canyon. You put some money into a telescope thing and looked across the rim you made out a tag: some crazy name taken with it's spelling and sprayed on rocks that were like twenty thousand years old.

Do you think what happened? When all this flirtation stops what then? Do you think when you think about me? I wonder whether or not if you do and if you do what do you think? I bought some earrings the other day from a guy at a bus station and had coffee from a vending machine and sat down in the brightest yellow chair I ever seen. It looked like a mustard color gone viral and remade hundreds of times over. There were like dozens of these chairs in the bus station. Sheeny daffodil or crossing guard markings on the street: but I couldn't decide about people in the bus station. I mean a bus station was like an oasis in the middle of nowhere. So I bought these earrings from a turquoise family. Do you feel worrisome? About what happens next do you feel worrisome? I like to think I do. So I listened into this foursome sitting at a table near the ticket window. They were drinking beer and looked hot and tired — work stained in the late afternoon shadows with hats pushed back on their heads. What was the question somebody said?

Does it matter? I mean the answer he said.

Well another said as long as our small aluminum friends keep showing up on time — at the table — I guess that's what counts.

Killing us –another said finishing his beer. What about the divorce rate? What about terrorism? All that shit keeps climbing he said and finished his beer.

What another said? You mean you're breaking up with your wife?

No he said and not like that.

What's the question another said?

Well I guess that amounts to failure another said! You need to know the question!

Four cowboys were sitting around and drinking beer and talking — but I thought Eden Jones said — were these guys real cowboys? What if they were hired in a season by the Department of Tourism? I've seen fake cowboys before she said: all rhinestone loneliness and good-looking boots and staring in profile across a mesa....

Yea man the first cowboy said we all got lives — no question about that.

As long as our small aluminum friends show up on time I'm good another said. I don't really care all that much outside what I got. But what's the question?

And so on. And so I moved on and found another table to listen to.

It's always so depressing a gal said.

Get over it another gal said.

Yea your right — but it's never easy and today was a never easy day.

Some days are never even like that another gal said. You look somebody in the eyes and give them the lab results....

Exactly the gal said... and twice today... no way around it. Here's your lab results and what they mean: congratulations you are now infected with the world's most popular disease... And you tell me to get over it? I can't do that.

Yea another gal said I know what you mean. I figured the best thing to do was to look out for myself. What was I supposed to do?

I'd ride it a gal said. How many years do you have left?

Well a gal said I did meet this guy at the lab and I thought screw the results!

A cowboy named Evan said wait a minute you met this guy in the lab and you're holding his life or whatever in blood result and you're saying you want to take this guy out.

Already have she said!

Don't you wonder a gal said with a grin and a beer can.... don't you have to maybe slow down and think about it...

And wonder about what the gal said. All we did was go to the movies and eat Italian afterwards and then we drove out to the rim and got stoned.

But this was a guy from the lab a cowboy said.

And what a guy she said. And anyway she said it's like you got to fuck them to meet them...

Unless you walk around in a dream all day long someone said ...

Well we got to the rim parking lot and got stoned...

That's a beautiful thing a cowboy said...

Not much better than that another gal said...

Yea another gal said but some people just work to get around...

No the gal said he wasn't embarrassed- zipped or unzipped...

Hell yes a cowboy said ...

Straight up and nowhere else a gal said... gotta have it like damn cold beer and pit roasted pork on a Sunday afternoon...

Gotta have it another gal said...

When you need to have it another gal said... roast pork and cold beer...

Yea the gal said I fucked him twice that night... who knows... he wasn't definitive only positive ...

I'd stay away from the definitive another gal said...

*

Do I belie this question Eden Jones said? I met this guy. He had a softball game that night and invited me. Would I hang around another day and watch the game and afterwards we'd go to a barbecue. From Jersey-land to beyond the Pacific Ocean there's always a softball game to be played somewhere right. It was so fucking ordinary you had to be captured right. How do you say no to beer? And no to mad barbeque platters was crazy.

And then you're a stranger and someone you don't know invites you to forget about things and hang out. And you can't say no because suddenly- no — no was like just a word — and no had no place in the travelogue — as long as I moved and kept quiet and kept my chances low that I might be found.

He said his name was Tony Rox. Wow I said so your name rocks. Like Tony Rocks.

It wasn't like that he said: it was spelled with an X. Tony Rox: Excavating and Landscape and Grave Service. Find the cost before you dig and then call Tony Rox for a quote.

So I said okay. I'll go to the softball game. He played right field and batted fifth for the New Desert Bandits. In the third inning he collapsed. He fell right over someone said. Both benches rushed out to help him. He was shaking violently on the outfield grass like some personal earthquake was inside him and was crushing fault line after fault line inside his body. And as I watched him from the stands I had this immediate feeling that Tony Rox was going to die in the bottom half of the third inning with the Bandits up by two runs. And that made it kind of tragic. And you know sensual in a way you don't normally understand.

Once the ambulance arrived and left — I went to the barbecue and ate and drank with his teammates till late and so decided to spend another night on then rim and fall asleep on the hood of the truck. Before I fell asleep I watched the fibers in star constellations spin away from us.

In the morning I talked to the doctor from the emergency room. Tony Rox was going to be fine. From what I make of it — the environments ganged up on him and brought him down. Too much work in the heat — little or no hydration — too much beer to drink — a mediocre 248 average — eyeballing me like I was some blood pressure gauge — plus he was a white pill addict and he ran short on pills and so he didn't have a daily cover to protect him from all the thoughts he didn't want to think about.

And I swear when I saw him in the hospital — with all these electrodes taped to his head — all I could see was this dreadful silence. Like when you run the last card in solitaire and you know you can't win the hand. Like staring at a television for no good reason. How long have I known you? Plan ahead and take notes you said. And then one day what? You bring flowers to a guy you hardly know with over-exhaustion?

So I was at the bus station. The oasis in the middle of nowhere — you remember? I bought some earrings from this guy. You made these I said. Yes he said. I made them. And that knocked me out because I was at the bus station and feeling lonely. I bought earrings. I always buy earrings. Like I've been knocked out of the sky that's why I buy earrings and that's how I get knocked from the sky because I fall in love with things like earrings.

I also got tan leather boots to kick up the dust and a wide buckled mineral studded belt to have and to hold what pleases the wandering eyes and naturally I got a cowboy hat that I crushed off the shelf.

*

My grandfather said be aware. Don't trust him and don't trust his clan. Why I thought. My grandfather said you now have enemies. All this is beyond your own life. Who the fuck was this Tony Rox he said? And he just happens to be in the bus station selling trinkets at the same time you were passing through? I don't like it my grandfather said. Don't trust him.

Oh come on. You're paranoid I said.

And that's why I'm still alive my grandfather said. And what we don't like we'll tell you what to do about. That was depressing. But as I wound it around in my head I found a sudden lightness there in thinking about it. Obviously I was trusted. I knew how to do the work. But what was the price? Was it a pair of earrings? And how could stones that were sky colored and had veins of blue rivers worked into a cheap bauble and that hung on silver stems and were for sale on a little stand in a bus station be worth a life? Is that what it took? There was nothing to forgive.

And I remember Sister Crumble going on about how impossible it was to love a thing. And that it was a sin to love a thing. But I love these earrings. And so do I have to kill for them if I love something? Be mindful around my grandfather. Everyone's a suspect. But you're close. Tell me where it is. I know you have it. And I believe you imagine it's some kind of ticket. But you can't get anywhere with it. Even if I ditched all my phones my grandfather would still find me out. That's just how it is. A long time ago you stepped into something large. Running errands from the fish store on Friday nights…passing something from one pew to another on the occasional Sunday morning mass… getting the K-bus when a certain bus driver had the route and then taking his money before you even rode to the next stop…listen friend what I'm saying is you are deep into this. We both are. So why not we drift alone together and call it even?

I hung around the hospital until Tony Rox was released. He said he was born around here. He had native linkage. This was his home he said and waved his arms across the surroundings. The way he put it there was no such word as frontier in his language. We've always been here he said. Everything we see and everything we feel was endless. That's how we belong. Our life has no translation. The bus station was frontier he said: a cash word for trading with the whites: cheap whistles and small mirrors: how you might take a landscape and twist it for five bucks.

So I asked him: what do you think about the Grand Canyon?

It's a land blessed by nature he said. Nothing he said outlasts a desert.

What about like Antarctica I said. That's pretty outlasting there I said.

He looked at me and laughed like his face was an act of kindness. Ice melts he said. His eyes brightened. We drank our beers. Let's take a ride he said.

At that point I was embarrassed that maybe I was using too much sunscreen.

Come on he said. We'll see open spaces and deadly creatures and my ancestors.

Come on he said and I'll show you the sights. We'll get more beer.

372

Some real food later at my cousin's hole in the wall cafeteria off the highway: real food real land good price.

And I thought — since I've been out here — driving on a lane that turns into another lane but it's still the same long road — that maybe I'd change my name. Undergo some experience that meant something to my travels and become that experience with a new name. Happens all the time out here.

I liked the Midwest but what I saw there wasn't a name change there for me. And it had to wait for you to come across it. In other words you need to find it and you need to figure out how that fits you. And I was thinking: what have I gotten myself into?

No offense Tony Rox said but for all the white people he met they turned into fools. You have a fine name he said. He laughed for a moment and looked off into the sky and then said maybe this was new business... Tony Rox name change agent... vision quest guaranteed... you want antlers...you want feathers or mystical teeth... no problem ... I've been around before time and every name you ever need was here in the desert.

I looked at him and said I'm not a fool.

Sorry he said. Didn't mean anything by it. But so many people come out here — like the bus tours — and lately the helicopters — and they mistake what they're looking at. And then the helicopter flies off across the skies and the bus pulls a U-turn and I'm inside the bus station selling earrings and the passengers mark off another destination accomplished.

Why do you sell earrings? I mean you got bulldozers and all that stuff...

You're a funny gal he said. My family always made jewelry he said. The earrings are buried in the land. I'm tied to that. Come on he said.

To save you the suspense no I did not sleep with him. Tony Rox was a handsome guy no doubt. Cool long dark hair and a faint smile and shifty hideaway eyes that sprung out when he looked at you and needed you to look back at him.

And then I remembered Sister Crumble again — in a personal hygiene class — girls she said in that voice that sounded like she'd just been hit in the throat with a baseball — don't choose a man.

So we drove off in a beat up jeep. We drove into places I never thought existed. Roads that weren't on maps got smaller and deep into canyon walls like shadows. Red canyon walls you swear were dead ends — but they opened onto a weird blond twilight place and behind the colors was another shanty dirt road that we drove. Hawks wheeled around the skies and spun out of sight and then took off into the air. I saw lizards watching from cracks in the rocks like they were parts in the features of the rocks. Ever seen a lizard? That's some old thing... Remember when we saw Valley of Time at the Bandbox? That's what lizards are like but without the special effects but they're cool but what did I know out here? We came to this old village — or the old remains of a village — how do you age things — so we parked the truck and started walking down another skinny dirt road. Wasn't the desert all dirt anyway? What good was a dirt road in the desert? Not roads anymore Tony Rox said: paths he said. Living paths.

*

We had beer and some chewy beef food and took our time as walked and ate oranges we bought at the bus station. I had a guidebook and it refered to the canyon as the hot mark of time. But I had a doubt to what I was looking at. We kept walking downward toward someplace that seemed bottomless from above. At every turn we made we had to squeeze between narrow openings in the earth itself. Then we came to this rounded boulder. He said we were at the bottom of the canyon. Old water made this he said. His ancestors sat on this same rock. And it was like round and smooth without seams or cracks and damned if it didn't look like it was set there on purpose.

So who was here before us I said.

You have to call it something don't you? That meant they'd have to call us something in return Tony Rox said.

Who are they I said.

The canyon walls he said.

I've seen something like this before I said in the Midwest. Isn't that why we look at things...we need comparisons... to set us straight... but you have to call it something. Otherwise how do you recognize a rock from a bleached out skull?

There was this small hilly place in the Midwest. Quiet rolling for-est-land. You'd see a trout fisherman with a coffee thermos in the streams if you saw anybody. And shy deer eating in forgotten apple or-chards nearby to dead farmhouses rotting in weather after weather. That was a spot like this I said. You had to work to get there. But once I got there I had these unexplained feelings. Mostly I think it's about being out in the open. Freaked out. But what I mean is there are places where you hear words. And where's the talking coming from? But what knocks me was why doesn't everyplace talk? That's the question I asked Tony Rox.

And he said well maybe you have an over-publicized view about nature.

I looked at him and said all right. But you were born here and your people were born here and have always been here since time began as though nothing much has ever changed.

Something like that he nodded.

Why do I hear the words then? Do you?

Yes and no he said. And not to be confusing he said. But when you say what are the words — and what I say they are the rocks living and breathing — what we should be asking is where do they come from?

I looked at Tony Rox and said words come from the sky. They just echo off the rocks.

The rocks are the words he said laughing. The sky echoes the rocks he said opening us a beer. That's the way we are he said.

Sure I get that I said. But out here nothing changes. With sky every-thing changes. He looked me in the eyes. We tipped beers and opened wrappers with cheese food sticks and stood listening for a moment. Si-lence was essential — in sky and in rocks — silence was the big clue to everything. Without silence — what were you? A toasted loud mother-fucker — with neither sky nor rock? And what are these cheese things I said.

My cousin makes them he said.

They're good I said.

Yea Tony Rox said.

And that's just what they are: cheese things.

But he said you describe it as something unusual. That's the differ-ence. Out here we've always heard it.

Maybe I said. But where I come from there's all this interference and that fucks with the signal.

Tony Rox laughed. He had a grand confident laugh and one that brought me to this landscape — like I was here to recognize the questions I had. But what did I know?

To me he said it's always there. Like when I'm trying to watch television at my uncle's house and conversations are going on everywhere and people are dropping in from outside to get something to eat or bringing something to eat and there's yelling and laughing and arguing and you're trying to concentrate on a re-run of Hawaii Five O because you need the space to be alone for a minute. What you're hearing in these places are whims and luxuries and accidents and the lives of everyone whose lives have ever been and gone in a place before you. For me it's a given. Why you hear it certain places and not others I can't answer. I don't know but it's marvelous that a white person hears them at all.

I pulled out the guidebook and read to him about revolutions in the earth's crust and the violent upheavals and how geology defines where we live from where we don't.

Look out there he said.

Where I said. Nothing seemed like out there from down here on a boulder. I didn't get it. I looked back at him.

Tony Rox said it's like everybody wants… everybody wants but that's no surprise… everybody wants a sudden image they've been searching for and when you come close to it it's like you ask what do I do now? And then you think for a minute and look around and say I got it. But you're not like that. You question what you found.

Yea I said to him. But your uncle's got satellite television and that's where everyone you know heads to spend a night and do you think you're witnessing the imbalances of the 20th Century in a place remote as it could be among thousands of years of intrigue and divine ecology? No matter where you go you're connected to it. That's what I'm thinking separates you from me.

So what do you have he asked? Besides your guidebook…

Hey the guidebook has gotten me this far!

No doubt he said.

Right I said. How drastic that seemed. That anything I knew was something to be contained years from now in a place that I did not know.

Tony Rox pulled this little stove from his backpack. We ate powdered soup and minute rice and fresh chilies and cornbread from his cousin. What would be perfect now would be a bath I said. Water's hard to come by he said. So after dinner I liked to think I floated on the desert floor and was up to my neck in the deep far waters of outer space.

Cassiopeia and Ursa Minor and stars after stars we don't have back in Jersey-land — they were there of course but we never saw them. There were probably more lights on the ground in Jersey-land than there were stars above us. We rolled joints and got stoned and switched on our camp lights. Tony Roz read native poems and cousin prayers and job statements where he needed to be this week. According to my guidebook — we have a poor location inside our galaxy. It had to do with telescopes and all that. But how could you not feel at home? What did location have to do with it? We stayed up most of the night. The guidebook said — even with the most powerful tools available to modern astronomy — despite our best efforts we were still unable to see all there was to see clearly. Don't you think they should qualify that? How could we be wrong and poorly located when you're sitting underneath the stars? Such objects the guidebook said — meaning the stars — were more than furious bodies of light and home to explosive hot gases. The stars have played roles in communal and human understanding — withstanding the pressures of science philosophy and religion to come up with and offer explanations and ready answers — and bring paradoxes and brilliant qualifications and aspects of nature that we constantly look outwards upon to make a space for ourselves within the framework of what exists above us. The stars — the guidebook went on — were housekeeping in the wild... an architecture to probe the depths of memory... the unfinished slice of the pie... a fertile resourceful intensity that once taken properly will revolutionize our beings... the repository for human insignificance... envy of the gods... the stars it said were a near stumble into death and the warm sweet opening that cradles you during sex... and as I was reading it I thought it was no wonder. Are you pagans I asked Tony Rox?

No man we're not pagans.

Why not?

Because we don't need to be he said.

That must be okay I said. Not needing to be anything I said. Really what he said was we don't need to be. Oh I said. But I didn't get the difference and he went back to reading his book so I left it at that until another time. If there was another time even. So I paged through the guidebook until I found my notes. A pagan was someone who lives out. A secondary definition was one who delights in sensual pleasure. That's what the root word for pagan means. And truly I could raise apples and make cheese and grow incredible pot and worship whatever season came over the horizon. Then the lightening began. Holy fucking shit! What's going on? Tony Rox said not to worry. But I worry as a course of life I said!

That lightening won't get down here he said.

How do you know I said?

Relax he said. Lightening hits the bus station and its flag pole first he said. The flagpole was grounded he said. What did that mean? Well he said electricity hits high and goes low. What did that mean? Down here he said we were at the bottom of the spike.

What happened I said before the bus station was there?

That was simple Tony Rox said.

What I said.

The canyon he said took lightening and made it rock. It was written on the walls.

Where I said.

Turn around he said.

I looked behind me and shined my flashlight.

This was better Tony Rox said. He pulled some twigs from his pack. Jumping down off the boulder he found some tinder. After that he got some pinyon branches. Sanctuary he said. I'll replace them in a day or so he said.

Soon we had a small fire at the bottom of the Grand Canyon and I thought go think.

Mad lightening flashed overhead. What to say — the sky broke in half and then there was a moment's dark and then the sky flashed and the dark halved again. We sat around the fire in silence and watched flames make shadows on the wall. That small warmth from a few branches passed right into me and I held it inside throughout the night. It was strange. We were sitting on the bottom of the Grand Canyon around a small fire — and up above the rim a lightening storm exploded like bottle rockets and left holes in the sky. Did things travel quicker in the desert? Did lightening find its exposed mark on a boulder before it found a smaller rock to strike? Was lightening even expected to strike? Tony Rox lay still and was singing. What were you doing I said.

Early people he said. Look over there.

Where I said.

Turn around and look over your shoulder to the left he said. Where was left? Don't worry he said. Just turn around.

But I worry I said.

Just look over your shoulder he said.

And I did because I figured Tony Rox was an okay guy. Plus all I had to do was pick up a phone and within an hour my grandfather would kill him. But that wasn't the point. I turned around and what I saw was amazing. When the lightening flashed and spread across the canyon walls I saw pictures. They were crude how they were drawn. But they were drawn like they explained whatever things they were about. Stick figures with circled halos for heads and triangles I guess to be torsos. Weird horse-like creatures ran past on the rocks. And there were handprints everywhere — climbing and scrambling and overlaid and it reminded me how people crush into a subway car. So where were they before this I said.

Electricity brings them out Tony Rox said.

Nothing in the guidebook said anything about aliens I said.

Not aliens he said. Early people. This is where the world began.

Down here I said was the beginning of the world?

No he said not down here but out here. This was just a station he said.

So what happened after here?

Nothing happened after here he said. All around us happened. That's what happened. Down here he said — was — just a hot mark of time.

All right I said. I gotta wrap my head around this and that's gonna

379

take a while. So why are we here? Why have you brought me here to the beginnings of the world?

You showed family Tony Rox said.

How so I wanted to know.

You came to the hospital and waited he said.

Yea I said but you guys were losing in the fifth like what 11-2? Anyway I worried about you.

Yes he said but you showed concern. And so it was my aunt who said that I should take you to the bottom and pray for lightening. My cousin — what food we ate tonight was old as the rocks — he knew — and he left us a feast.

Beef sticks I asked?

Early food Tony Rox said.

Before time I said.

No he said but something well before that.

*

Am I getting sentimental? But do you miss me? Maybe the lightening...and what a night... terrified and elastic and left somewhere between the present that we understand and some location that made itself up before time and at the same time was time before there was time to wonder and that left me to wonder what the fuck were we doing because let's accept it that other worlds exist and they have nothing to do with us but we know about them but we won't know fully about them until something else happens that we can't fully grasp at the moment and that difficulty and those questions set us in motion. Do you need to hear that I miss you? Was a confession all that it takes?

The next morning Tony Rox dropped me back at the bus station. Back in time I said.

You'll always be out of time he said. Try the muffins he said. My cousin runs the concession.

So I bought a bagful of muffins and filled both my thermos with coffee and drove off the rim of the Grand Canyon down into town. There was a cinnamon roll that was especially hot and gooey. And the coffee made my eyes roll the way I imagine tomorrow to always be. At a stoplight I pulled up next to a pick up with some kids in it and it was like I fell in love just looking at them. Dope smoke — open windows — loud music like nobody cared if there were any consequence to any things done.

Stone free... to do what I want...if I stay too long people try to pull me down... stone free to ride the breeze... listen to this baby... got to got to get away...I can't stay... and I had that download... and I'm not the only soul accused of hit and run and I'm lost in cross town traffic and I'm stone free and I'm confused on the edge of the desert with another muffin and a coffee and a big old fatty and I was totally in love with what I was doing and I suddenly felt that I was totally in love with you but I had to go because there's a bigger love that I ain't found out yet and I guess I'll leave it at that. Xo...gotta go...Xo...no place else for me...Xo...

*

Did you find what you were looking for? Was it there to begin with? Haphazard meanings and arguments from silence that from time to time you opened a suitcase and looked into and from time to time what you re-found was a little crawl space where you lost yourself- and from time to time that loss filled you with an intoxicated way to remember.

However — to have a memory was a dangerous business.

Getting shot through the chest for interest...

Being kidnapped for interest and taken out into the Atlantic around midnight and thrown overboard...

Small caliber bullet...the tide was going in... horror tricks... professional hands not an amateur hour... and it was great to imagine you were no good dead... people wanted you alive... but it was no fun getting shot for what you knew...

But we were back in the neighborhood — after years where we lived nowhere — in exile — being chased — moving like the weather at about 600 miles every 24 hours — like how those buzzards followed you around and showed up in the sky unexpectedly and circled overhead...

After Blind Charlie died the cousins took over and there like a snake's head was Bobby Alfredo… a hot head with enough brains to fill a small toe and a nasty face with a gap toothed grin.

It was Blind Charlie that sent the raven-haired woman on the job and gave her the inheritance.

But it was Bobby Alfredo who couldn't stand for that. There was trouble just by saying his name out loud… lord of the cousins he called himself… Bobby Alfredo.

But it was the raven-haired woman who had the list. She had her grandfather's book.

She had the word below her heart. And that opened the doors she needed. And at the same time that word was enough for her to kill others with no questions asked.

Bobby Alfredo didn't have that word. That's why he was a loud mouth. He spent years hunting us just to get that word. But since he was dumb as shark bait — wasn't that where you end up — what he never realized was — there was no word.

Blind Charlie would never do that. Tattoo his granddaughter? It was a joke — and a deadly one — so when the raven-haired woman said she had a word — that meant nothing.

*

And having nothing meant she was protected.

And Bobby Alfredo kept looking for that word…

And as long as Bobby Alfredo was alive and looking for that word that meant we were hunted.

The arithmetic was simple. In the beginning you fell in love. But there was no way to turn that falling in love into a definition. So the only thing you knew was to walk around and watch your back with a head full of sky- and on good days dig the clearance.

You tried — but one plus one never equaled two.

There's no end to love you told her.

Yea there was she said.

That's impossible you told her. It's never enough. But it does not end. So you put the suitcase away and tried to forget about everything and wait for her to call. Some little white pills helped slow you down like there just might be a pot of gold over the rainbow. You disappeared into the movie channel and watched the Bride of Frankenstein again.

Nobody dies really you thought because we're dead already.

The fuzzy logic of narcotics rolled up your spine and that made you linear and premeditated and you don't really run into things it's just a figure of speech to career a mind but that didn't make any sense so you took more pills and mixed them with wine and decided to go outside and rake some leaves as a strange exercise in normality and other memories from other times flattened your head and you laughed at the thoughts of them being serious at the time and after that you really didn't do much raking but just leaned on the rake for what it was worth and went timeless for a while and gathered in all the arrested colors of autumn in a pile you had nothing to do with.

What ever happened to your ideas? What a silly thought to have this late in the game.

But here's what: to stay in the neighborhood forever. Deliver pizzas and clean windows and work hard against the forces of hate — didn't you say that to her?

Can you remember now?

Sure. Why forget it?

Because you have that habit sky said.

You stared into a carpet of yellow leaves — some with burgundy edges — some with a pale green shoot showed in the veins. It was funny about all these leaves. You said something to her at the time. Maybe like fallen leaves — like middle age satisfaction — it's waiting and only made visible by someone else. Yellow leaves with burgundy edges and pale green veins — was that you but really you thought it was about her and it was ridiculous but you heard the ocean and the waves and that was like a distant swing back toward you because you never know and why where all these leaves and you realized you were on a street like blocks from your house with a rake and you were combing sidewalks for leaves and you told her long ago what you felt and sky agreed and then some kid asked hey old dude can I help you out and you said thanks but no thanks and he said why not you don't need help and you said I'm raking leaves because it's autumn and the colors are spiritual and who are you the kid said the designated street sweeper and you said no please don't go what's happening was music did you ever listen to sky you wondered and the kid said no old dude I don't have that on my playlist...

*

faster than gravity

Marshall Tate and his crowd were warming up — tossing footballs in the brilliant autumn air and discussing strategy — riding a two game win streak going into this Saturday.

Three games in a row would be a lift for Marshall and his squad. They hadn't won three in a row since a softball tournament in April.

Everybody took the leagues in the J.L. Chaplin schoolyard pretty serious — perhaps too serious — but hey — beating Marshall Tate and his crowd remained the measure of the day.

And it wasn't really a league in a way you might imagine a league. No uniforms no referees and all that crap. It was just a concrete schoolyard where we played our games.

In summer — after the classroom hell fires died away along with your attention span — and the last class bell rang its own funeral note — the days were longer in the sky and the nights were free and the streets buzzed with dance tunes from ice cream trucks — we took to the J.L. Chaplin schoolyard to pick up our lives where we left them.

Usually the schoolyard was basketball with the hoop magicians in the morning. Then slow pitch softball in the afternoon. And in the evenings it was touch football to work off any sweat you had left in you.

And after the evening football game it was always toying with the girls and drinking in the shadows and laughing at your home life and the cops constantly looking at you with spotlights tearing away at your privacy. Later on we'd run into the waves and swim out and back around the channel buoy.

But today it was Marshall Tate and his boys. Nothing was better. They had a good enough team to travel to other schoolyards across Jersey-land.

Loser buys tonight Light Skin Billy said.

You motherfuckers were doomed Rhino the Bob said.

Losers buy Light Skin Billy said.

And you thought about combinations otherwise... like imagine Marshall Tate and Off Broadway Jack in the same backfield... that would be amazing and get us any game in any schoolyard in Jersey-land.

But thinking like that was Cripple's job.

What you did was imagine and wait for sky.

*

But what was strange was the way we were divided and pigeon holed. Why was this so? Were the niches we were afforded all that small? But there were street lines not to cross. Who lived where was more important than who you were. Go figure — but look at all the civil wars... What was more cynical: What was more degrading: What fucking worked best: a dynamic backfield or third rate skin tones?

*

Off Broadway Jack tossed a long spiral. A Coin brother caught it on a dead end fast run.

Rhino the Bob was stretching a stocky muscular body and talking to himself in tongues and smacking his forehead with his palm. He looked like a packing crate about to fall off a high shelf and harm someone below.

The sunlight was beautiful. Sky told you that and you believed what sky said. You watched it rip J.L. Chaplin's brickwork in half — hot orange highlights up top near the roof and deep blue shadows below on the concrete. Sky didn't lie.

Light Skin Billy kicked the ball high and showed off his leg. Eddie the Chevy walked under it and judged the ball into his arms showing off his eyes.

Over at the gate on 65th Street Cripple limped into the schoolyard with his chunky leg brace like a poster boy for the March of Dimes.

Cripple's idea was to get on Groove Stand at Wagner's Ballroom. He'd shake this bad leg thing with the regular dancers and be discovered as the

386

Funky Cripple. And from Channel Six — local time — Cripple and his moves morphed into a nationwide dance craze. He was famous. He had millions of fans and made millions of dollars. He started a business to manufacture custom-made leg braces for healthy kids to wear for them to copy Cripple's dance moves.

Cripple was our manager... our sideline talisman...

About time Cripple — Marshall Tate said.

Cripple looked at Marshall and said well as the clock unravels that's how the boss travels.

Don't get caught in the trash Marshall said. He looked at Cripple and gripped the football with his big hands that seemed like they were strong enough to squeeze a diamond from a lump of coal.

Winner keeps the quarter right Cripple said.

Shit Cripple your family was so poor you can't remember what a quarter looks like. Your mom combines shopping and praying and hopes the money comes true before she gets out the door and gets caught for stealing.

Tails Cripple said.

Marshall Tate flipped the coin in the air without taking his eyes off Cripple.

The quarter twisted in the air like a drunk leaving the 20th Century Club and talking to himself because no one else listened.

Cripple was supposed to catch the quarter out of the air and then slap it on the backside of his wrist and expose which side came up. Instead he let it fall on the concrete and stared Marshall eyeball to eyeball.

Okay Cripple said we kick to you and we take this goal. Cripple left the quarter on the ground. There was no reason to pick it up and play god with it.

Cripple backed us into an end of the schoolyard where the afternoon sunlight was behind our backs and shone direct and bright at Marshall Tate.

Naturally they didn't trust us.

Naturally we didn't trust them.

How did nature get involved with a touch football game?

Were we solving the same problem twice?

Shit Cripple said.

Yea I know Marshall said.

When do we get out?

Soon as we kick the ball off the better everything is.

What happens if we walk away and don't kick off?

We can't walk away dude. That puts us in a bad place.)

Strange thing was that conversation never happened. That talk never took place.

You saw it. But it wasn't real. Each Saturday afternoon before the first kick off it happened. And you saw it happen but the way it happened was that Cripple and Marshall talked inside a fog. You heard them. Ghosts — talking behind Cripple and Marshalls backs and trying to make sense from tragic human forms.

*

Cripple was small and wordy to Marshall's big and scary body. And Marshall didn't like that. He knew with one swing he could crush Cripple in half. But Marshall was afraid when Cripple talked. And the more he talked the more Cripple respected Marshall. It was a totally fucked up situation and one that seemed endless in sight.

Cripple stood on the sidelines grinning into space. The afternoon sunlight hit the braces on his teeth and turned them into a machine-like gleam — like he was the brain behind some killer robot in a comic book.

*

A Coin brother teed up the football.

Rhino the Bob held his beer bottle shaped index finger on the ball and tilted it downward on the concrete. Rhino was a champ at not moving the ball. That was key. Holding it steady. And a Coin brother might put the entire force of his leg into the kick but Rhino the Bob never moved his finger. His finger was broken a few times but he never let go. He couldn't let go. That's how he was: a stupid death waiting to happen and so a certain threshold of pain was a necessity for him...

The Coin brother took a few steps back and then kicked off toward Earl.

The ball sailed high and away — odd and graceful — end over end through the sky. Earl caught it easily and moved up quickly behind his blockers — behind Richard White's massive body as the apex of a wedge running toward us.

The inevitable collision between teams running toward each other happened like it should happen but you couldn't figure out why it had to happen — between teams and who knows what that meant — between teams whose identifying jerseys were not so much a specialized shirt that you wore on your back but the more generalized condition of a world you wore from inside out... with odds to play as to what side of the street you lived on. And after some nice footwork Earl was tagged around the thirty- yard line.

Different ideas — maybe that was all that it was — different ideas like different streets to live on — and that becomes some fundamental thing — like who we were or who we are and who gets knocked down and stays there and who gets up...

Following each game opening kickoff President Bland tore a page from Soul On Ice and left it at the first down marker to start the game until the elements swept it away.

And what was funny was all this business about scoring. We never had defined goals in the J.L. Chaplin schoolyard. Touchdowns were scored across goal lines at the metal railing at one corner of the building near 65th Street and at then other end it was a telephone pole outside the fence on 20th Street. All this was simultaneously hard to establish and defend against — since the goal posts were drawn on an imaginary line — but the telephone pole lined up directly with first base on the softball field — which was a yellow square painted on the cement — and the metal railing — despite the arguing — was obvious where it was situated.

Two plays later they scored.

How does Jimmy Dark Wave do that so easily?

He slipped behind Marcus X on an in out move and caught a neat pass from Marshall Tate on the ten and walked in and scored like Marcus X wasn't even there. Easy pickings.

Damn. Hard to prepare a defense when an afternoon began like this. And with their score we had to give up our sunlight advantage.

Light Skin Billy kicked off for them.

It was a fucking beauty that backed Off Broadway Jack against the fence. He picked up a great block from Eddie the Chevy who flattened Byron stone cold on the ground. Off Broadway kept moving to his right — running hard and deliberate — quick stutter steps and head fakes and trying to set more blockers on the way to the goal line.

But Curtis Gunner was right on him and made the tag.

And after doing nothing with the ball for three plays we punted it away.

Soon we were down 4-0 and heading nowhere like we died and weren't coming back.

*

Playing lousy was possibly the easiest way ever invented to answer questions about your skills. The schoolyard repeated itself because it owned our attitudes?

*

Cripple paced the sideline — shaking his head and reminding us playing bad was one thing — but getting slaughtered was a backdrop for chumps!

What am I? Am I some forgotten message? Take a look around fools! Them motherfuckers are laughing. And you don't figure for shit. You're sloppy when you got the ball and look ridiculous when you don't. What do you want me to do? Flap my arms up and down and cheer?

Light Skin Billy laughed and boomed another kick that sent Off Broadway Jack back to the fence again.

See Cripple yelled! We got it now. Billy can't even kick the ball out of the schoolyard!

*

Rhino the Bob looked square down the field. Their kickoff defense came rushing toward us. The expression on his face was something so familiar that it still frightened you whenever you saw it. It was like you were taken away from your own position on the field and he extended you into his eyes. Rhino the Bob took no prisoners — especially when he was angry and down 4-0 and his best intention was not to stay out of trouble.

*

The look in his eyes — with all its destructive forms intact — was furious. There was no tomorrow for Rhino. Beer tonight for sure — but there was no tomorrow to live for this afternoon for Rhino the Bob when he was pissed.

*

The football came our way and Rhino growled as we dropped back to make sure Off Broadway caught the ball. And this resolve — where you were caught inside Rhino the Bob's eyes was a mind fuck. You felt it so necessary to obey it and hang with it through the return. We needed a score… and Rhino the Bob knew the way. And his resolve meant your mind and balls had to show up at the same time in the same place — aka a weird valley of spiritual courage to have your ass knocked down on the concrete if necessary. Rhino was primal. He was more or less a simple matter even if he was volcanic and pressurized. Where was Marshall Tate? Where was Bob? And in a sense just on the flat of it you admired them both. But once you logged on into Rhino the Bob's eyes there was only one standard: a senseless and overpowering need to knock down obstacles and make your intentions clear — from the fence at 20th Street to the goal line at 65th. And that point of view — the super hero juvenile handsome and nasty type — stood in the way — once the ball was caught…

*

Suddenly your thoughts were gone. You and Rhino flattened Marshall Tate and Marcus X took out Light Skin Billy. You looked up and saw Richard White and Jimmy Dark Wave closing in from the left. Off

391

Broadway Jack saw it also and dropped it down one sweet gear into hesitation and then sped off with his legs pumping and his lungs swallowing all the air in the neighborhood. And after we ran over Marshall Tate — Rhino stepped on Marshall's chin — we turned our attention toward Richard White and Jimmy Dark Wave…. And hit them hard enough for breath to disappear.

*

Rhino the Bob carried you senseless.

*

Suddenly all your thoughts were gone.

*

Does it take an instant for anything to be made physical? After we ran over… and hit them hard enough… a pile up followed and there was something you felt on Saturday afternoons… it was something you expected… but never quire defined… it was like force only met at the odds and ends and never gambled over anything in between… there was a pile up that you left you on the ground… a parcel to a collective — solid and harmonious and smacked again in the head… but that afternoon it disturbed you… maybe you looked at the future… smacked in the head again… sad and venture-less young boys… Rhino the Bob grabbed you by the armpit and we were airborne…were we angels… neither calculations nor a residence in a physical body…but how can you travel through the air when you don't want to… because somebody was stronger than you…and where was all this free will you've been taught…could you believe you were flying in a touch football game… we flew into them and wiped them out… and they flew ass backwards and smacked their own heads on the J.L. Chaplin schoolyard concrete… but we scored right?

*

Cripple lit up a cigar. That's how we do it he said! How you like that Marshall!

A little early for that smoke Cripple.

I smoke them when I got them Cripple said. And you look foolish down there Marshall.

Rhino the Bob was up on his feet and was swinging and kicking wildly at the air like an intelligence that went lost. There was something invisible in Rhino's head that he was slapping in the face and tearing apart again. You always wondered what that was. What made Rhino the Bob mad?

He went over to the sidelines and grabbed Cripple's cigar. He took a long deep draw. He stood over Richard White and then blew smoke in his face. Then he did it once more.

There was something with that boy Marshall Tate said.

And it was true — Rhino was a head case. Were you obliged to defend that — because he was your friend — because he lived on your side of the street? Maybe only he could see what he was hitting.

And as things were compounded by events surrounding them — Reds walked into the crowd and wanted details and details about the details. He smoked a Kool. What other brand would he smoke? He gestured with it and talked behind it as though he were writing smoky hieroglyphics on the air and expected everyone to understand what he wasn't saying.

*

Dig me up in this ambush of emotions?
Why did the world to make you nervous?

*

The next thing Light Skin Billy teed up the football. And it wasn't until a Coin brother called you a jerk off you realized what the sound was. But didn't sounds need a destination? Was it a fact that life drifts like a well-kicked football? Would you even notice the drift if not for some outside voice calling back you in?

Small beautiful things… frozen in the sunlight passing over the schoolyard in shadows and in even brighter shadows…everyday inconvenience… funny sky… time out of mind or the other way around… your head was singing…. your head was the audience…

The Coin brother kept yelling.

How did you get here? Not that it mattered. The dropping football hit you in the face about four inches below your reveries and bounced off your face and landed into your stupefied hands.

And then you ran with it.

Cripple was yelling… Eden was yelling… the hoop magicians were yelling… seemed like the whole schoolyard was yelling in a single din… and it struck you that all this noise was telepathic and was feeding you and if you were getting fed well enough was that a signal you could feed your thoughts back to someone else… and you thought run toward someone else and hand them the ball and reverse the field and confuse everybody… it was brilliant… you looked at how a score for us all rung in your eyes… there had to be somebody picking up your eyes because you were now telepathic and you were now the schoolyard… so you ran to the left carrying the ball on your hip… your head singing… thinking all the while you were devious and crafty and had the proper sign calling attention to what you looked at as the obvious.

Eddie the Chevy saw you and ran toward you

But wait you thought! You were throwing thoughts! Why couldn't he see that! Eddie you thought take this gamble… then it was like no way this was happening.

No Eddie don't use the block! You're getting the wrong signal! Here! You take the ball and reverse the field and catch them by surprise!

But then you saw that was not about to happen…. There would be no football exchange… no one big thought… like consciousness taking place in a textbook handoff.

Naturally we fumbled. The ball went off Eddie the Chevy's shoulder and did the stupid things footballs do when footballs hit the concrete. They bounce out of control. They go nuts. Footballs on concrete act like Gary Reset did last year when he found out that he was not going to summer school.

And as bad as it got — Sweet Onion Earl scooped the ball off a bounce — and walked into the end zone.

You know what — it was strange.

*

Cripple yelled. Reds yelled. The whole schoolyard yelled.

You fucked that up! But wasn't fucking up worth more than doing nothing?

*

In the air above the J.L. Chaplin schoolyard — your head singing — blue air fine afternoon — what you heard — getting lost in a familiar place — what you heard was your confusion messing with your sense of eternity — you wanted to believe — but that seemed to have some opposite interest at heart. Maybe this was the heaven they told you about? A place where people jeer because you made a mistake and at the same time they regard you as highly sensitized because a mistake was made and therefore because it was made you were worthy enough to be bothered with. Heaven was instant replay! The play happened in the past! But why couldn't you undo yourself from things? What was the big deal?

*

Richard White stood over you like a mountain. His deep heavy breaths shook the air. Shit you thought. Richard White was going to hit you. And if he did — the lights went out. But he didn't. Instead he swung his eyes at you. And that was good enough for you.

Marshall Tate walked over. Nice play he said. It takes skills to do that he laughed.

395

Tell you what he said. Let's bet a pint. You back your boys and I back mine. Just a friendly pint he said.

You told Marshall you didn't need ridicule at the time.

No dude he said. Just a friendly bet between you and me. Whatever happens no one's the wiser.

Inside Marshall Tate's eyes you saw his dream staring you in the face. One day he was going to run the neighborhood.

Deal you said.

Solid he said.

Was there hope — play the neighborhood differently — keep to yourself but probably not — get out low but get out but probably not — pick a winner pick a loser even — it didn't matter — we were solid objects — your head was singing — suddenly the world was flash cards — you couldn't read — there was hope — you might win a pint tonight — another path — not to follow but to explore — you head was singing — snacked your head on the concrete field a little blood over the left eye they told you — how was that singing — the only broker involved was the difference between us all — deal you said — and if you have such little trust the questions don't fade away — but if he owed you some-thing there was a bit of status involved — what was the score anyway?

*

the coffee meditations

Relax she said… it's an old bullet wound.

Sure.

One afternoon you were sitting on the boardwalk and doing nothing. Doing nothing but sensing the environment and feeling the pressure that went with past mistakes.

The raven-haired woman hadn't called in two days. Her sat phone took no incoming calls. Blind Charlie's enemies grew into serious numbers and they were still after the package. And she was still employed — wiping them off the earth — like picking fruit — and having them leave the planet prematurely. She had a tattoo written in a flowered script that wrapped her waist from the spine to her navel and read: what's a nice girl like you doing in a place like this?

Blue October sky — the old Atlantic — you came from somewhere — the weather will change — waves slapped on the beach — crushed diamonds in the spray reflected sky — what you really needed was to strip down to nothing and feel the air on your bare ass skin and then rush off and dive into the waves — but you're old — you can't run — but you can be nude — it's a delicate time — after they finally removed the bullet — after like twenty years ago getting shot — too delicate to remove at the time — you felt overdressed and needed to strip down — even for just a while because things were endless and you didn't need miss them — the way starlight gathers in a place you smoked a joint and some passed over little dog all hungry looking and practically disemboweled with a dirty coat recognized a friendly when she looked back t hou and hopped up on the bench beside you — was pizza good — yes she thought — you fed her bites so she wouldn't vomit and immediately it was like her world was rocked — just bites — take it easy — don't worry about the town — we split a couple slices — did emotion equal eternity — we stretched out on the bench- a paw across your hand — crazy — you were holding hands with a dog — poor creature — so what was better than a beautiful day at the ocean and holding hands with a homeless dog...

A sailboat passed beyond the breakers like a Japanese woodblock print captured in motion.

Eons of leverage and time in a landscape and an afternoon in the simple ride of the world and what you needed was to get out of the house because sky told you everything changes and so you needed to go out of the house... another skywreck afternoon.

You asked the dog — hey what scared you?

She was asleep and snoring.

Sky and seawater... reflected... you overheard the dog breathing...a sailboat drifted outside the breakers...a slender hello... you wanted to rent a movie... you fed a mob of seagulls what was left... it was strange... you knew what the dog thought... she wouldn't leave the bench with two slices resting in her belly and probably having the best dreams she's had in days...

Was there anything more to be offered?

What amazed you?

You needed to rent a movie.

All she did was to stare down at her toenails.

Finally you walked away toward the harbor.

You don't understand she thought.

Yea you did. Come on you said.

Now you had a dog. She had a wicked grin and she trotted beside you to the video store like old friends.

Outside the store she waited for you. You rented the movie you wanted. She was there to greet you.

Walking off the boardwalk — this homeless dog you just met — grabbed your fingers in her teeth and yanked.

*

faster than gravity

And you thought what more happened before the day was gone than you owing Marshall Tate a pint or Marshall Tate owing you a pint?

Saturday afternoon — planet schoolyard — what if all the scores were numbers without meaning —with no stretch of the imagination or a potential to define you — a place where we might quiet down and wonder about things — wonder about things other than the way we lived them out…

But one look at the air — between Richard White and Rhino the Bob — or a Coin brother and Curtis Gunner — or between Eddie the Chevy and Sweet Onion Earl — you saw something like face to face storms kicking up — nasty horizons jawbone to jawbone — and so what else — where else was the force of athletic tension left go but objects moving and objects resisting?

But it was our ball. We now had the kind of working position to do something with it before they did.

We faked a run at Richard White and then pitched outside to Marcus X and who ran well and made a substantial gain.

Marshall Tate and his boys dug in.

Richard White snorted at Rhino.

Light Skin Billy kept his sharp eyes on a Coin brother.

On the next play Off Broadway Jack stepped back to pass. Eddie the Chevy hung along the sideline and looked like he didn't know what to do like he did normally.

You drifted toward the middle where Curtis waited and greeted you with a forearm to the jaw and floored you.

Downfield nobody was open. The play was busted. Off Broadway scrambled — pumped faked once — reversed direction — waved for Eddie to run — dodged Earl with a quick smack to Earl's head — however for his efforts Off Broadway and his moves were about to be shut down for a loss…

Suddenly a shrill and acne laced voiced screamed louder than all the noise in the schoolyard: Ville Ville! The Ville's coming!

Marshall Tate and his boys froze.

Eddie the Chevy slipped off the sidelines and ran downfield.

Marshall and his boys swung with the Clang. And if the Ville were invading the schoolyard — Marshall Tate and his boys didn't have the numbers to stand them…

And the Clang and the Ville were like sworn gangland enemies — it all belonged to some fucked up blood feud from like a century ago that both gangs still supported…

But there was no Ville at the schoolyard.

Eddie the Chevy ran underneath Off Broadway's pass and caught it and scored.

Crippled laughed and lit up another cigar and puffed more smoke rings in the air.

Marshall Tate was none too happy. Marshall Tate was absolutely without a word.

Marshall Tate was wronged — the schoolyard saw it. Cripple suckered Marshall.

*

That score don't stand he said and never will…. lame shit Cripple he said… you run your mouth but someday your mouth gonna be run up your ass…

Cripple laughed back and smoked his cigar. Cripple was crazy.

The score don't stand Marshall said again.

What's the matter Marshall? Did you get fooled?

It was difficult to know — what Cripple thought. But when he thought it was the rest of us who got into trouble.

Cripple laughed again and said fuck that Marshall — the score stands.
Then you must like losing Marshall said.

*

You looked around for possible opponents. You didn't know how to fight anyway.

Mute Sammy was close but he had a wicked left jab.

Sweet Onion Earl always had a blade with him.

And there was no way you wanted a piece of Light Skin Billy.

And cruel was often the word used to describe Jimmy Dark Wave. He once broke into a house and beat an elderly social security type with a pair of hedge clippers and stole a cup of coffee and an English muffin.

Fuck it you thought. For all the good it was going to do you might as well tangle with Richard White and get it over with.

*

the coffee mediations

When we got home the dog was hungry again. Plus she stunk. She smelled like the scratch lands at low tide digging for petro-crabs and shrimp without legs. Which led you to believe you was hanging out with the oil workers. And if she was hanging out with the oil workers there was good enough reason to believe she'd been tortured for fun. And if she was tortured that led you to believe you would not torture. Seemed like a fair exchange. But even if it tortured her — the dog was getting a bath. All you had was dish soap or bleach or the raven-haired woman's shampoo — and it seemed dish soap was the better option. It was a struggle but finally you got her into the shower. But how do you dry a wet dog off? There were splatters everywhere on the walls and you had to chase her from room to room with a towel but that made you feel at home for unexplained reasons. At least the dog smiled and seemed to get it.

But what did you have to feed the dog? You settled on scrambled eggs and yesterday's muffin. She chowed it down without a thought. It didn't surprise you that much you because you made good scrambled eggs and the muffin was a sunflower and date from the mad Syrian's bakery. Afterwards she walked around the kitchen a couple times and then fell over and passed out.

Would it be that everything you did was that easy.

Glad you only had two bullets taken out. The third one might have killed you.

You hit the pipe and took some nod time.

*

A day from now they're headed for the airport...

A day from now whatever they know as familiar will be left at home...

A day from now these middle-aged inductees with spare tires and double chins and thinning hair will leave the world they know for another world they hope they can believe in...

Fathers and carpenters local fire fighters and little league coaches and trout fisherman casting flies in the streams of their dream...

They don't look like warriors or soldiers because they're not...

They may be patriotic and ready to serve but how many of these would-be grandfathers would be able to duck and cover under hostile fire in a foreign land and then turn up battle worthy for the long haul...

When was enough going to be enough for this latest war?

You opened you eyes — blinking them — again — and scratched your head. The television was on which did nothing for cohesion.

And there was the dog. She was sitting on the floor beside the couch.

What was the deal you thought?

No the dog thought. Let's go out.

*

The temperature had dropped out of the sky — much cooler than it had been twenty minutes ago — too bad a little piece of mind hadn't dropped along with it — but what also fell were fat snowflakes. They came down fast and thick and they were so beautiful to watch and coated you and the dog with such a wet snow that it clung to us like we developed second skins in a flash.

We walked along Mulberry Street and back toward the ocean. The dog seemed to know where she was going. So why not be pulled along — dependent — like the number of answers you'll never have the time to question — pulled along by a dog you just met.

When the sky changed colors and shut out the tavern gray afternoon light — the dog stopped. Her ears shot back and her head rolled in circles.

Inky dark clouds swept above us quickly from the south... luminescence behind the clouds glowed in silhouette like fingers about to drown — all fringes and outlines of clouds flying and evening sky dying… but what happened… what happened to the soft traipse of the snow and the way we went… like fools in love…unnecessary… the snow made it that way because the snow was unnecessary and that made us great… the snow coming down fast… you lost everything but to remain still… in a memory your head was singing… you had to leave before you got old… the snow treated you better than a memory did and that was scary and ecclesiastic across the stops… so what was the point raising sand with a same old feeling…

Let's move the dog thought.

No you thought. This was something. Besides where do we go from here?

The clouds swallowed the afternoon… nothing left…the streetlights came out of hiding…the dog shook… the snow fell and you shook your head… no you thought stay because … we had a little more time… there used to be hopes… just a little more time… we'll make a fool out of this… hey the snow was like crying… your head was hard to find… troubles were coming on strong… no use testifying… can't wait for the sunshine… a thief had no friend… but everybody had snow today… just stay here before the night unwind to time going by… the dog hung in… winds picked up like a steady bass line opening a show… no you thought this was something…nimble and brute…late sailboats got back in the harbor and rocked unsteady in the nappy waters and titled against their moorings like toys in a sick child's bathtub… when you find out what to do sometimes it's too late… you can't find the clue… no you thought stay…

The dreamy voiced snow ended like it began — born from nowhere and gone to nowhere.

Fisherman on Wharf 3 checked their radios.

Across then harbor the Coast Guard station raised several storm flags. Taken together and added up they meant alarm: high winds — long tides — wicked rains.

On the radios multiple storm warnings went out: the hurricane that was being watched over the week was now the hurricane that spun off the coast down south and had now gathered itself and picked up a warm surge and was now blowing north east and scraping the coast as it went.

Sky was happening. Did you have the questions anymore?

You explained that to the dog. She was free to go. But you had to stay.

Suddenly the rain fell in a hard wind. A blowing hard wind made the rain suddenly.

We were soaked and lost. The rain would kill us. The wind blew us sideways.

Sky was happening.

Sky reached back and would not forget you.

Get off the wharf you fool somebody yelled!

The dog grabbed your fingers and yanked.

*

faster than gravity

You imagined the Ballantine beer ads all over the city — on television — on billboards — on the sides of the K-bus — blue-green lettering with three gold ovals linked in a chain — yu thought it was like the new math we were supposedly learning in school — the intersection of sets — whatever they were — by eighth grade it was far too late for learning — one symbol placed through another to highlight areas in common — and further how utterly odd it was to be falling below a cloud of blood –all down in a hurry — we needed a score badly.

The taste inside your mouth was like a stream of sewer water. As usual you began searching your mouth for the appearance of any lost teeth.

You looked up. Richard White said don't you stare at me.

Did he expect you to accept this just because he was a giant?

And don't be smart either he said flashing his big knuckles in the sad air.

You looked up at him and told him the last thing you would ever be would was smart.

Why did blood taste so weirdly unforgiving?

Richard White a thug because his brother was a thug and his older brother was a thug and his old man was a thug.

Rhino the Bob was a thug. He simply enjoyed it.

Reds was a thug because he wanted to line his pockets with gold and land in some far off place like Oz.

Cripple was like a thug on acid bringing hallucinations home to him and carrying them out like pigeons eating crumbs from trashcans and then flying above the street to shit on everything below.

Look what you did to his mouth you yelled!

Boy got what he deserved Richard White said.

Rhino the Bob had a gash in his lower lip about two inches wide and was bleeding like an open hydrant.

When Rhino tried to breathe it looked ugly and painful. All his mouth did was whimper and gasp — at what seemed unexplainable — like there were two mouths now — one the genuine article he was born with and the new one he'd just been given free of charge from a sucker punch.

Fuck you Richard!

Hey little man he said. You need to watch your mouth. Like I said — that boy is not right.

You hit him and he wasn't looking!

Richard White appeared ready to cleave the heavens and bring the schoolyard down around him. And it was sad to say but he spat upon you.

And sad to say that you spat back at him from below on the schoolyard concrete — an mess of ungainly blood and indigenous nasal fluids landed on Richard White's knees — the size of which were like those hubcaps on the new Pontiacs everybody's older crew were driving. For a moment you imagined being kicked square into death and being launched into the scary land of no understanding by Richard White's size thirteen shoes.

You — he said — pointing an index finger the size of a police truncheon — you — little motherfucker — and then he turned and walked away…

Very strange… spooky even… you looked up and watched him walk away and you didn't understand it but were you supposed to think about it? Like what was death? Did you just miss it? Or would it still be around to collect you later?

You felt around your face for your nose. Was it still a straight line? Maybe a broken nose might seem rugged? Broken nose boy — the snot runner — the boy with the sad golden eyes — and while lies were advisable to get you by — you lost what you knew.

We did not own the score. We did no own the day. But hey — that's ridicule!

Word would happen that Marshall Tate and his boys were solid. They kicked our ass today.

*

Poor Rhino the Bob and what a mess his face was in. Sad-lipped and empty eyed and losing blood in a rush from his mouth when he didn't even talk that much — knocked out cold — a rude sudden darkness like a birth — what do you do with an unconscious madman on your hands — Rhino wake up!

Could his lip be stitched back together in time — before it was too late and it went off on its own?

You'll never play the clarinet dude!

Try kissing Denise tonight!

We didn't know what to do with him. Rhino the Bob had never been knocked out before. We never saw him like this before... Rhino the Bob was our young boy... he was the one who knocked other people out.

*

After you got on your feet — and after the one-way elbow from Mute Sammy — he handed you a business card that read: hit you good motherfucker — as though mentioning the obvious and explaining the details made any difference — although they say that your business card was a reflection — you got to your feet and wobbled about and hoped for days to come.

Wake up Cripple said.

Yea Reds said: what do you want: enjoy the sun forever?

Well you said. It's not like you've been saving this up for this.

Mute Sammy walked back over to you and flipped you another business card: say your prayers.

Save my prayers you asked?

Mute Sammy didn't flip you another card.

Why save your prayers?

Maybe saving nothing was the answer...

*

Cripple dripped a beer can onto Rhino's face — made fake holy signs and muttered fake holy words like priests do over the dead.

And blessed be — the refreshing waters from a beer cued Rhino the Bob and his entry back into the world. It was after all a reference point he understood. He swung at the air and that's when we knew things were okay. Rhino spat blood and nearly chocked on it.

What down was it he said. We all looked at him a little strange.

What the fuck he said.

Then he felt his lip — or maybe his lip felt him and said here's the catch radius and here's some pain and guess what more was on the way — first with his fingers — then moved his tongue around it — but the lip he once had and knew it wasn't there anymore. He looked around for an explanation… what the fuck…

And that's the problem with these moments. They change just like that. And you can't get a handle or what where or why — only wake up to see how things have changed while you weren't looking. How do you design a system like that and expect it to last?

*

Plain and simple you owed Marshal Tate a pint of cheap wine.

I know he said. You lost.

You looked back without saying anything. But you had to say something. You needed to speak words. The facets of the neighborhood were built on saying something in the face of things. But what might happen — what happened if you said nothing?

Anyway — you told Marshall it would be in the bushes this evening by the orphanage.

I was hoping for a more personal delivery he said. What's up hiding it with the bushes? That shit is kiddie-city amateur night. Have some respect dude. Show up in person and deliver.

Sure you thought. Like Marshall Tate had respect for anything he couldn't overwhelm.

But still — a debt was a debt and a debt needed to be paid. But fuck it — you didn't write the book. Why was it time and again we're held to someone else's words? It was your debt alone and did not belong to some ancient formula. But you thought about it — and Marshall was right on this one. Hiding the pint in the bushes was kiddie-city — and besides the last thing you did not want was for Marshall Tate to imagine that you had no heart. Better to come out of the shadows and have a taste for that… sky was there…sky cued the organist…

You told Marshall where you'd be — Avenue O and 65th — you'd be in the shadows more on the 65th side — away from the streetlights and the trolley corner.

See you then he said brushing a stout index fingers inches before your eyes.

*

Rhino was up and around — groggy and sore — everyone looked at him — who the fuck else should we look at Cripple said — yea Reds said get up and get with the atmosphere and shit — but Rhino wasn't listening — you could see that — he sat up and explored his brand new mouth — tenderly which surprised you — cautiously- his stubby fingers poked around his gashed lip and came away with blood on his fingers — what the fuck… what was this …

The blood poured over his lip and soaked his jersey. The palm of his hand wasn't able to hold it all so there was more blood soiling his pants.

Did you jerk off or what while you were out?

How you expect sneaking them bastards into the wash?

A hoop magician stopped by — ball in one hand and soundtrack in the other. Boy is fucked up he said. But the hoop magician had a kit — and from it he took out scissors and tape and shit from a tube and patched up Rhino the Bob's lip best he could. Before he left he searched in his kit — then he lit one up — took some deep breaths — and gave it to Rhino.

Y'all boys are strange he said.

We beat them next week Rhino the Bob said.

No man the hoop magician said without turning around. You boys beat nobody.

Not so Cripple yelled!

Yea Reds said what you think this is clown paint!

Rhino finished the joint — smoking from the side of his mouth. What? Nobody had an answer.

You know he said how you got a plate of eggs and then they're cold?

You know he said how when you got a fudge bar and how they last longer than an orange popsicle does?

Let me tell you about my baby he said.

Really he said it only hurts when I laugh.

The bells they be tolling he said.

It's low expectations — it's high hopes — but everyone here knows when you need the answer to question 3 you motherfuckers are stealing my homework — one problem after another you can't answer but you get away with it because you take me at my word.

Fuck that Reds said. You're high.

We stood Rhino the Bob up on his feet. He wobbled. He pushed his hair back with a bloody hand and left fingerprints across his forehead. He spewed disgusting fluids across us all.

You lost some teeth Reds said — like this information was some remarkable insight.

Reds grinned like a guy who sold used teeth for a living.

Rhino's lip was swollen enough that his speech began to slur. Possibilities here he said. With less teeth more room for food — don't need to brush those teeth — and I won't have to kiss Aunt Betty until the stiches come out...

And no getting communion till your mouth opens proper a Coin brother said.

Yea no holy wafers!

Rhino the Bob motioned for us to gather up. Overhead there was a beautiful afternoon sky — the sky of middle autumn — blue enough to enslave your eyes — sky made you wonder — about dominions and titles and how to be clear...

Rhino held his hands aloft. He looked funny — all fake and serious at the same time like some odd administrator nobody listened to — like the way Father Grabaoy blessed the nine o'clock mass after it was done and everybody was out the door — a sad raising of the hands that signaled and asked: have I failed?

Do we come back next week he asked?

Amen.

Double Amen.

Settled then. We regroup and find a strategy. And we need a play as fucking good as the last one they had!

Amen all the way home.

I got money on it amen.

How many little rituals were there to have and to believe they mattered?

We just can't ever quit Rhino said.

And there it was. A moment for quiet genuflection after having gotten the shit kicked out of us. Brief terrifying peace entered our hearts. It was way too quiet. Was there anything left to care about today? Now it was just us- alone in the schoolyard — the sky going away over the rooftops in sad colors that made you scared — the sky rising for the night and that's where you needed to be — how many neighborhoods and how many young boys did it take to set things right — because was it all the young boys from the past who fucked things up — but what did that mean — did we have shit on our shoulders — but where did the responsibility for that shit come from — we needed to come out of this on the other side alive — but was anybody home to take the call... but we had to leave the schoolyard for the strange netherworld of home and the evening meal...

Listen up Eddie the Chevy said. I need money now. Ace don't give anybody credit. Don't know why but that's what it its. So if you want to drink tonight you need to give it up.

Rhino the Bob threw some dollars at Eddie the Chevy and ran off saying he needed more than stiches.

We dug into our pockets and gave up what we had.

Money was already a mystery — from our parents — from gambling on the corner — what was it made from but promises you might not keep?

Shit Eddie said! We got like thirty bucks!

Party tonight Cripple said.

412

You owed Marshall a pint you said.

That's your problem Reds said.

No you said. It wasn't. What you owed belonged to us all.

Reds stonewalled you.

Fuck that you said. Word be true you'd just go over his head and meet Ace Macdonald and settle things. For a lousy fucking pint...

*

Hey man you going to confession?

Aw fuck that's right.

You looked at Cripple. What was it made him confess... why did he bother... what was sin to Cripple... why in the world did he bother... And so together we dragged Reds along and chewed up the pavement — searching for our rainbow — but what we knew waited us was the holy penalty box at church.

We left the schoolyard by the gate at 20th Street. Mercenaries — the others — checked us out while we passed. Can't blame them. They had to eat too. But they weren't about to eat at your expense. Besides — Reds flashed them his gun.

*

Afternoon brought on the last rays of sky and dropped them onto the west — slanting and golden — slowly drawn by the mysteries of orbits and now operated in the Chinese dawn. Above the row houses and flat tar roofs evening eased sky away from the neighborhood. And within the last remaining sky you felt like some least understood differential from those sets from the new math we were supposedly learning in school.

Out in sky you saw evening — slanting blue and sugar golden — deep shot reds and easy gray -it was alive — sky flushed you out. Sky made you remarkable. Sky kept you healthy. Sky was sad.

*

There was a big tree opposite the schoolyard on 65th Street. The remaining sunlight ran through its branches and left its shadowy memories of a tree in autumn on the peeling stucco walls of the house behind it. And maybe that was how you thought. Like this tree was made from memories. It was a big sad tree growing alone on a street corner. Dogs and bums used it as a post in the world to piss against. And the way it broke apart the pavement as it reached upward and grew — like the small space of dirt on a Jersey-land block it was given to live was not space enough — so the tree kept reaching and growing until it pushed apart the sidewalk and that was cool because the tree didn't quit. And when the city remade the sidewalks — like those fashionably urban renewal ideas that kept making the rounds — straighten things out was the idea — well fuck that- the tree kept breaking new sidewalks and moving into sky and scratched away at the dirty air and the funny tasting rain — because somewhere — beyond where the tree stood on a street corner it had been someplace else before and broke apart the neat concrete lines urban renewal constructed in a square around it. And because it was a big old sad tree — everybody carved initials and names into it — to affix what we imagined in time with the tree.

Names initials and hearts carved into the tree — in the beginning — with those stupid kitchen knives we stole — the hearts we had — the carving was eternal — and depending on your handiwork — it might you get laid at the Lots — but so many hearts were now blackened over with a scar on the bark like the tree was squeezing it's girth past everyone else's declarations of life and the tree couldn't be bothered with the past.

And there was always a plus sign between the names. You name and Eden's name was carved there. Some days — when sky was healthy — when you were sad — you went back to the tree when no one was around and re-dug our initials.

Whoever carved names into the tree — when they broke up — they hacked away at the bark. Did that mean if you killed the language you did away with times and names and that made them forgotten?

Why was there no minus sign? If plus signs connected names — what happened to minus signs to disconnect names? Was the tree a fortune-teller? If we stayed close to the tree would things work out?

Were trees like this one on the other side of the world? And if they were there what types of neighborhoods were attached to them?

And why had all the other trees on the block been cut down? And nothing left but rotting stumps? Ant colonies lived in them below ground now — rather than our names growing higher each year while the tree spread toward sky. Maybe the stumps were like grave stones — calling attention to the last tree standing — calling attention but who cared unless your name was carved onto the last tree standing.

*

And across 20th Street — from the last tree standing — was the horribly wrong house. There were plenty of families in the neighborhood who never did well. But the horribly wrong house was there from the beginning like some fucked up cousin of genesis.

Dank Tom Herbert stood against his house window looking out and gurgling a beer still dressed in yesterday's dirty work clothes. He hadn't changed his duds since Friday when he got off work. He hadn't showered or shaved or done anything since Friday after work but drink beer and get weird for his troubles. Torn-up flannel shirts that couldn't tuck in around his stomach any longer and old jeans smeared with grief that for years died to be washed and the cheapest t-shirt with body odor rings under the armpits like a bad polaroid of Saturn — Dank Tom Herbert worked until Friday — drank until 3am Monday and never bothered to change his clothes and never woke up from his drunk so he was dressed and good to go. Dank Tom Herbert was a construction worker who at the end of the day never built anything — he carried bags of cement down into hell for the new parking garage — the union paid good for his labor — he was another ghost who paid his dues.

So you watched him. If everything was a mirror where did that leave you?

He drank a beer. He inhaled a beer. He sucked the life from a beer. He primed himself for the weekend. Before he swatted his wife for not getting out of the way. Before he yelled and crushed the beer can on his head and screamed bloody welcome in his voice and kicked his son

Cruddy Joe in the ribs. Before he yelled at his daughters — small rascal faced and love affair Linda and crooked tooth cheat Betty Ann — for not making his food fast enough when he wanted it because their mom was punched and was crying in the corner of a dark room. Before anything happed in the horribly wrong house — Dank Tom Herbert went to the refrigerator and grabbed another beer and staggered to the bathroom and pissed into the toilet like a bastard.

You couldn't remember a time when trouble wasn't in spades at the horribly wrong house.

Cruddy Joe was either up on the roof huffing glue or walled in the basement and booting heroin before graduation.

Linda Joe and Betty Ann started to traffic themselves — wearing false bras and bar room high heels — looking for studs with one foot still in grade school.

Mrs. Dank Tom Herbert wandered the neighborhood in pajamas and tragic worn felt slippers — phantasm rings under her eyes and chain smoking Lucky Strikes and talking to tobacco clouds around her head that reminded her how thin she was when they first married.

You looked up at Dank Tom Herbert as we passed along 20th Street below his door.

He stared back at us like he always did: completely annoyed and mean — stationary in the window like a refection that wouldn't move.

*

I know you don't know shit Reds said to Cripple.

You thought: how truthful things can be when the exceptions made otherwise.

Cripple gave Reds a wise up slap in the chest.

It made you wonder. It made you look at Cripple. When he wasn't looking. That meek look on his face made you wonder. It made you look at Cripple when he wasn't looking back and made you wonder about the stock of brains he had behind the aquarium thick lens of his glasses.

His cheeks puffed up. He lowered his eyebrow ridge down under his glasses. Cripple titled his head almost sideways on his neck so the acne on his cheek just barely grazed his thin shoulder. Was he really a cartoon?

He lit a cigarette and blew smoke at Reds. If this were a spy flick you would be dead because I'm the counter-spy. If this were a prison flick and I am the governor then your request for a stay has been denied and you will be executed tomorrow in the electric chair.

If we need to steal something Reds said then I'm the one to do it.

*

The light settled weakly in pale white blue to bring a few stars out over Avenue S.

Sky was great and bore you in.

Up Avenue S. was such a line of cars — both parked and travelling — a steady line of cars — stretching — exploding — pregnant with dinosaur fuel — from the boardwalk parking lots at the beach and beyond to the last bus stop at Mount Airy where the big roads took over. There was a line of cars you've known since birth and they've never since stopped. And that line went out in the evening and came back to park every morning. Out and back — out and back — like patterns in the brain of a junkie.

But they were so fearful weren't they? Wasn't that it? Maybe that was why they kept moving. Cars don't want to be stolen. Cars don't won't a milk crate heaved through their windshield. Cars were futile cars and where people have cars then people will steal cars and no order and no security will matter if there was only one person left on earth holding a car.

Cars were like jealousy. Cars were like the sex you never had.

And Cheapy King Used Car Lot was across 20th Street. Like a bonanza of ill pickings underneath strands of bare white light bulbs — Cheapy King had cars for sale that bums wouldn't even take a shit in. Cars for sale that Cheapy King bought somewhere in exchange for an abortion. And real live Mercurys so heavy with so much raw steel it took a gallon of gas just to open the door and sit down. The worst abandoned cars — the bread and the butter... was standard for Cheapy King. Cars we played tag across — denting hoods and roofs — kicking them for fun —

stomping on them — we jumped from car to car to avoid being tagged and tried to break a mirror or rip off a radio antennae- that's the type of cars the were. Cars that inspired no ownership... ancient cars with push button controls... cars your grandfather drove on the farm... cars in the grave... cars that kept coning back.

Cars that no one bothered stealing so Cheapy King tried stealing your money by selling you a car.

There was a Plymouth that looked like the day after Pearl Harbor and some Dodge with enough rust holes it might have been shot in the Saint Valentine massacre.

Buying a car from Cheapy King was like cutting your throat to avoid shaving.

*

Across 20th St. from Cheapy King was the Liberty Belle Tavern. You walked through one door and got yourself bombed and then later walked across the street and drove away in a bomb. What was more perfect?

It was easy as a streetlight and funky as an attitude.

Cars? You want cars? Sweetness believe it we got cars. We got so many cars that one day in a year we herd them out to the suburbs just so we remember where the streets were.

People got cars on their brains. And that's why they steal cars and that's why they love cars. People see cars in their dreams. You need to steal what you love.

*

An old car dreamer staggered out from the Liberty Belle door onto the street and burped in the night and fumbling for a cigarette he didn't have in his Cadillac leather coat. He stunk like his last whiskey and the cave-like air from the bar he'd been sitting in all day.

Young boys he said pass me a smoke.

Reds winged this old dreamer a Kool. He swung at it with reptile-like hands but he was already out to lunch and drunk. The Kool hit him in the shoulder and fell to the pavement. He seemed satisfied. He was anybody's fool. We left him like that — on the corner like the last drunk standing wobbling around and trying to reach down to the sidewalk for his free cigarette.

*

We walked over to the church like the fake penitents that we were. Unless you did nasty crimes like rape or murder — the rest of penance amounted to sins of the imagination like cursing and disobedience — and who was ever wise enough to feel sorry for that?

And the doors of the church hardly made a sound when you muscled them open. However once inside and you let the doors go — they slammed shut with a dull thud-like echo. What that sound did was to leave you to imagine that this place was a trap.

We blessed ourselves from the holy water font. The dead eyes of the saints as wordless sentinels of the faith in marble statues stood life size in the vestibule eyeball to eyeball with us. How do you look at a saint in stone? How do you understand what you see?

Not that we took this holy water business seriously. It's just a reaction when entering the church. You walk inside and bless yourself without thinking about what you're doing. Canonized men in stone with palms outstretched in greeting welcomed you. This holy water business was nothing more than a tweak of fear that kept you looking over your shoulder.

So we blessed ourselves. And stepped into the side aisles of the church — rather than then main aisle where you'd be seen and where the wedding and funerals marched to the altar. Four priests were on duty inside their respective confessional boxes.

Someone coughed. The sound was amplified and held inside the stone walls by the tight church silence and seemed to encourage loudness and held a sound like a cough until the echo was deafening and fucked with your ears.

We stumbled into our pews like outcast. In our hearts we tried to believe...but that leap to be included — there was nothing there.

419

So we decided each to try a separate confessional booth — hoping to split some difference and whittle some time in this sad and programmed behavior. We didn't care about sin. Sin was bounty. Why be sorry?

Cripple went to Father Carey. He was an old guy and kind of deluded and took his time over the balance of penance.

Reds went to the Monsignor and that meant Reds was out in a flash. Monsignor had no stomach for sin.

And there was a hell of a line at Father Stan's box. He was a decent guy but you worried about him.

And that left Father Grababoy… the dark night of absolution was yours…

*

So you left the stiffness of the pew and navigated the church quiet with your shoe rubber squeaking on the hard tiled floor. Holy silence was the most dreadful place to try to be alive in. Your thoughts became overwhelmed. You felt nowhere. Dead air in the church whistled through your head. There was no handle on things because you can't hear your thoughts. Wasn't this supposed to be the straight up enterprise where everyone involved made a deal?

Other parishioners walked slowly past –they were like creepers with their mournful gaits that dragged and slowed them down against the feet they used.

First up was the priest booth to confess. And then it was up the altar to recite the penance. Supposedly we carried the burdensome knowledge about what we've done wrong and what it takes to make it right. Of course when we left the church and went back outside and it was time to sin again. Week to week this was our variation on some divinely inspired comedy.

Inside each priest booth sat a sales rep from god. Outside the booth he was just a guy with a plastic collar around his neck. But once inside that booth he was transformed. He made judgments about bad guys and protected the innocent with just a word.

For an entire afternoon he sat on a cloud and heard tales of lust and swindles and how neighbor failed neighbor. The story goes we don't understand enough about what we know and through our ignorance we knew how it was and we then got led around for no good on the hooks of demons because we didn't know what to do about the things we were told to confess. And this was where it got confusing.

What good was sin unless it was going to do something? After you admitted it in some faked-up presentation what worry was there when worry got dumbed down and that came dumbed down to some blissed guy giving advice on a cloud? Wasn't that what liars were for?

And week in and week out you wrestled to find a balance.

And week in and week out you couldn't find a grip.

Maybe this eternal life stuff– one-way or the other — maybe it wasn't going to work out.

Either way it seemed a stretch.

If there were forces for good — if there were forces for evil — what happens if neither one of them shows in the middle? What kind of game was that? Where was the backbone in that?

You took a place in line outside Father Grababoy's booth like you were waiting for chops at the market butcher shop. Four irksome-like souls were in line ahead of you — counting rosary beads or playing with earwax.

And each week you tried — you tried to imagine — how god divvied up like this. Was god even working today? Four booths — each one was a singular transmission agent for the word — each one simultaneously was transformed into the word — and not simply parts and pieces to add together like a Mister Machine erector set that once built was set clumsy along and walked over the kitchen linoleum floor with the lights in his head flashing and his arms pumping — but the genuine article inside each booth — occult and enjoined and impenetrable — a place beyond — where our heads were told to follow.

*

But imagine the backfield inside the mysterious and dangerous booths…

*

God ran the football!
God passed the football!
God blocked the football!
God caught the football!

*

Quarterback god took the snap and pitched wide to halfback god who was running strong and looking to cut up the sideline. Suddenly halfback god pulls up quick! Halfback god was going to throw it! And flanker god was streaking down the hash marks with nobody near! Halfback god tossed a wobbly spiral downfield and flanker god had it! Flanker god went into the end zone untouched for a score! And fullback god danced with quarterback god in celebration!

*

Enormous strangeness...

*

What were your sins for the week? You needed to come up with a list and memorize it before you went into the booth. For some it was a serious to do to admit the wrong doings they've come to bear — and kneel at the altar rail and say their prayers before they moved on. For others it was another motion to go through and this was called penance. It was impossible to know. If it was just for sin what was the point in that? Can't we all agree that we all die and leave the rest alone? May the high agony keep us and get us a free car wash etc.

Why didn't we realize it was necessary to punt sometime and then forget about it before it came back around and bit us in the ass for all it took to think about it.

*

High up on the vaulted arcade ceiling were the new murals. Below the arcade was a canopy — a roof structure above the altar space and the statues — supported by four arched columns that were newly gilded — and underneath the canopy were small versions of the new murals that were painted on the big arcade. And above the windows were Lunettes — a smaller canopy with a smaller mural above a saint — arms outspread — greetings — a fellow in stone — standing behind the poor box — with a place to kneel and candles to light as prayers for the beggars outside the doors. Jersey-land was being initiated as the new Calcutta.

*

Cripple's father — said why pay a fortune for signage? What ever happened to good old white ceiling paint! Explain to me why I have to pay for fancy colors?

*

High on the arcade ceiling — above god the hurt — beyond the math of prayers collected from each confession and the agony that a better idea might be real — the Monsignor raised his voice in sermons for a year and said pony up! And so now we had murals above our strange heads —for comfort like that's what Jersey-land needed. But we had naked cherubs floating through open windows with paper scroll announcements — saintly depictions of life — small devotional interludes walking in gardens or bewildered in thought — lots of naked cherubs — somebody was big on nude children sans genitals. How did a cherub pee?

And above the altar — above the canopy — high on the arcade ceiling — there was a stenciled message in broad rose-colored letters with gold leaf highlights scrawled around the edges. It was written in Latin and came off the ceiling like fighting words.

LABORARE ET ORARE.

Translated it comes off as: work and prayer.

But where were the saints coming from today?

 Where did they live? How did they earn their money?

What LABORARE were they employed at?

And what did ORARE sound like today?

*

Week in and week out this was how it happened

 You get these ideas that might play out and give you answers but then the holy silence inside the church slammed into your head and shut you up.

 And you've tried the opposite- — trying to think among the noise. You rode the subways and the buses looking for clues among the debris and the language from one end of the line to the next. You've snuck into professional sporting events and sat among a cast of thousands hoping a wild senseless party might abandon you and roll you over and maybe open some kind of door to the senses. You watched television while listening to the radio and calling someone on the telephone. The same deadness always seemed to happen.

 What did your thoughts mean? Cliché number 1 right?

 No. There is always something that didn't make it. So you complain about it like it's your last breath.

 Suddenly it was time again — had a week gone by already?

 Now it was your turn to slip inside the god booth and kneel before the perforated screen — in darkness — in boogeyman light — waiting for the god booth to hear you out. On the other side you can hear some-one else and their murmurs. It's supposed to be deviant to listen in on someone else's sins but everyone does it. You don't know why. What's left for surprises?

 The screen in the god booth you talked through was this sad plastic barrier stained with the breath of thousands from the past. It was like speaking through a thin and creepy layer of something old and yellow like the color of a sick dog's tooth. When you were young you toyed with the wildest fascination to peek closely through the screen — to see if you couldn't get a picture — what the god booth actually looked like. Was it exactly like Father Grababoy and how dim might that be? Was it dressed up like someone's dad in the rare suit worn on special occasions? Or was there nothing at all you might recognize but just a halo-like thing listening in the void between heaven and hell? The only thing on the other side between you and eternal life was a fuzzy silhouette like a badly developed Polaroid. It was another reminder what our purpose was here. We were here for talking. What we were not here for was any espionage nor a glimpse into the shady knowledge of the almighty.

But to this day you still try and sneak a look past the sadness and the screen onto the other side. It's just for the memories you suppose. You still listen intently for the sins other people have to say. Maybe you'll learn something. But you doubt this is a workable option.

At some point you just gave in and were satisfied the shadows behind the yellow screen were without question the god booth waiting to hear the treble in your voice.

And even if you gave in so what?

Obedience was just another word in the dictionary.

So when from behind the screen you heard the words — like they've been cued up — yes my child — you go into a well-rehearsed role the mechanics of which you learned a long time ago.

Bless me father for I have sinned. It's been two weeks since my last confession. I cursed fifty times. Disobeyed my mother ten times. Talked back in school ten times. Fought with my brother five times. I stole an eraser. I jaywalk every day. I give my friends a hard time when I'm in a bad mood. I fought in the schoolyard five times- you know- just little stuff. And I had impure thoughts fifteen times. For these sins and all the sins of my past life I am sorry. May the goodness of Christ come into my heart and may all my sins be forgiven. Amen.

You could recite that blindfolded. You could say that in your sleep. You could mouth the words even if you didn't have a tongue.

You just pick categories: like fighting stealing cursing etc. And then you add numbers to them. It gave your sins a little polish. It's like you wanted to give the god booth enough meat to chew on — but you don't want it to get out of control and gnaw away at you.

Who told the truth in the god booth anyway?

Why trust Father Grababoy and give him the benefit of the doubt with your secrets?

Maybe that's why the years and Father Grababoy remained in place.

If the truth were ever told all at once who knew what happened? Jersey-land might go nuclear and vanish.

For your penance my son say ten Our Fathers and ten Hail Marys. Also try and be more indulgent with your mistakes. It sounds as though the cursing and the fighting have the better part of your soul. Be calm and loving and accept — like our lord Jesus — which people are different and need to be understood for who they are — each as an individual residing in the house of god. Be kind to your mother and never question her for she has a difficult task in the home. In school obey your teachers for they are the holy representatives for the learning of god. And never jaywalk. And yes you must make restitution for the eraser.

Now my son — tell me — what are these impure thoughts?

Do they reoccur with frequency?

Are you bothered by what you feel or see?

Do you try and shut them from your mind?

Or do you take pleasure in them?

Tell me about them.

*

Why even mention it? Now you were caught.

The god booth does not give the ultimate whatever over cursing and fighting. But bring up questions of impurity and a rise happens and a candle starts to burn.

You told the god booth that you kind of you know thought about your girlfriend.

What do you mean my son?

That you thought about her and kind of you know imagined her — like in a bathing suit or something.

And what happened then — with these thoughts?

Nothing happened... how she might look — that's all.

426

There's no way you can explain it to the god booth. There's no way for words to come across in matters like this. How good it felt to jerk off last night. You can't explain that to someone holding court in the god booth. What pleasure was to someone who wanted sins?

And how often do you have these thoughts my son?

What sorts of troubles do they bring?

Are you able to control yourself?

Or do these thoughts get the better of you?

Why did you even bring it up?

What was so important about having this privilege into other people's lives? Must they know everything?

Yea-yea-yea you thought and made up some crap of a story. You had to get out. The god booth was starting to become way too small. No the thoughts do not bring you troubles. Just the opposite! But you didn't say that.

Yes you do control yourself.

But what did that imply? Who else should be in control? And you certainly weren't going to give anything valuable away.

It's like it's what you don't say becomes more valuable than what you do say.

And no you didn't have these thoughts often — just every so often! And they made you feel so fucking clean every time you jerked off! The last part you didn't tell the god booth since that would have detained you even longer in a small space closing in. What did it matter? It didn't.

Think of your girlfriend as a handmaiden of Christ my son. Remember that her body is pure and must belong to god. Even with your thoughts it is wrong to touch your girlfriend's body. You must try hard to conquer these thoughts as they are. These thoughts- they are temptations- and they are directed by the devil. Always keep your rosary at your bedside- and when the devil brings these thoughts to your mind- pray my son to the holy mother of god- and she in her purity will help keep your own thoughts pure and worthy of a son of god. Now go in peace with my blessing.

You opened the door to the god booth and looked up and saw night painted darkly on the church's stained glass windows. Why is it only light affects these windows? Wouldn't it be cool if stained glass windows glowed in the dark? How come nobody thought about that?

Imagine if stained glass windows showed different scenes from day to night? The way it was now — there were weak spotlights thrown against the high window — but you can barely make out what those windows were because nighttime had such a big push. And streetlights don't do much for stained glass. It has to be the big light of sky to make any difference.

So you made your way to the altar rail along with the other bone weary parishioners — to kneel before the high agony and recite penance — when suddenly your head went wait a minute… wait a holy fucking minute… you just listened to Father Grababoy read you the riot act and you took it? And now you were going to say buzz-buzz-buzz prayers like a fucking lab rat again?

*

Saying you're sorry but it did not matter as you stepped outside and took in a breath of evening air and that lifted your skull off its pins.

*

loose change

One evening — when it was that time — floating again — the dream time on earth and fueled by perpetual motion sky — narcotics — or any other way around — a man sat down next to you at the 20th Century Club. He introduced himself as Detective Shade.

Given any evening as it were you were nominally occupied and ruminating over the short end of things that were your thoughts and they were like a secret around you — a cool radiation built for no other purpose.

You weren't listening much — nor were you paying much attention to anything in general. It's just the way things were sometimes. You sat on a bar stool in a place called the 20th Century Club — in a pleasant enough experience called life on earth — passing below the radar and above the highest meridian — and you're bound to lose a moment or two — especially where other people were concerned. Not that you didn't like people. It's just sometimes they interfere with your thoughts. The way a parked car might get sideswiped or the way a phone might ring in a vacant apartment.

Not that any of this would do either of us any good. Shade? Shad you thought he said. Wasn't shad a fish and they made oil from it? Wasn't it used for something like arthritis? And didn't they call shad the poor man's salmon? Then you got it. He was a cop with a fishy name. That made sense but this guy didn't. What the fuck was up with this?

You were sitting around waiting for visits from extraterrestrials and a detective named Shad showed up? Where's the beauty in that? Because you were convinced there was beauty in space. If only these damn rocket programs didn't keep blowing up. There might be a transit to the stars one day — and in the event that happened — you wanted to keep your mind open to the possibilities. Maybe the drugs will turn out to be like surfboards to the heavens.

It's Shade he corrected.

He folded his newspaper way too carefully you thought. And the way he laid it across the bar and tapped it twice while ordering a drink- that had to give something away — didn't it? The way he was familiar — that bothered you because it gave something away. Something you couldn't name but it was something that had your nerve hairs standing on end.

He wanted some alley piss bourbon from the bottom shelf. Fast Eddie asked him once after looking him over if he was sure he wanted that — and because you knew Fast Eddie — you could be sure this guy was familiar to him as well.

But as it was Detective Shade looked like a man — who — when ordering cheap alcohol wanted cheap alcohol. A long dangling ash formed on his cigarette and dropped onto the lapels of his thoroughly below retail box store coat. He kept staring like something was supposed to happen. He didn't say anything but just sat there looking at you over the acetone in his bourbon. Maybe he was just another suited laborer done with work for the day and the day had been too much for him and now what he wanted was just a drink or two and a little conversation. But you didn't really believe in like minds when it came to a circumstance like this. Where a guy walked into a bar and sat down across from you etc. Maybe he was a hustler. Maybe he wanted to sell you something you weren't even thinking about. Maybe he wanted your money for something he was never going to show you. But you doubted it all — you doubted the whole entirety of it all — you doubted what you were seeing and if you doubted what you were seeing and if that was in front of you — then your brain can't be that far behind you can it now?

He finished his bourbon and ordered another. Curious thing about him sitting there was he didn't sip his drink and he didn't gulp his drink. He sucked on it like a kid finishing a nitrous oxide balloon. Care for one he asked?

Sure you nodded. But you never drank bourbon. That was a bad sign.

Letting this guy buy you a drink. Especially something that was bound to give you a headache in the morning despite any promises you made to the night before. Letting this guy buy you a drink was a bad sign and most likely some hare-brained scheme. No good would come from it now that it had you in its view. You imagined — through the clouds — this was a scheme not yours in the making and one that crackled with the static electricity from another human interest failure sitting across from you on a bar stool. But on the other side of the coin — the one we always talk about and base things like decisions upon without ever holding the coin we're talking about in our hands — what was the harm in a little misadventure?

Life on earth seemed predicated on the assumption or a vibration that normally you would be having one more drink. To this day have you ever met any life form without that way of being?

It was a way to cut into some understanding about other people's suffering. And hopefully it might diminish your own in the bargain. We were bottom weary anyway. And considering what a paranoid world it had become — and how we sit like vultures on barstools night after night waiting for the odd thing to happen — it was not surprising we scared ourselves into hiding.

And it isn't courage that's brought us here. It was the curiosity of the gods — played over in the low definition video of our heads.

We liked to figure and we liked to talk our way out a problem and we liked to gnaw on world the way dogs find crazy joy in bones. Everybody had their own little fear they liked to call their own — even if they were scared to death by naming it. You ask a thousand questions over what to avoid but you were still magnetized by what pushed you away. Maybe what we noticed was nothing more authentic than superstition was to a cave dweller. Maybe the gods invented the game: one more drink.... search your pockets for quarters to feed the juke box for music...come up with a philosophical discourse to reconcile with and ask yourself the big question: what did this guy want?

*

Detective Shade had tiny fleshy eyes and they were sunk backwards into a square head that was shaped more like container for odd things than what you might think of as a skull. Dog-like jowls flapped over the sides of his gray face. He smelled like sour aftershave and that smelled like a urinal flush. He ran his fingers over the crown of his balding head and lingered just slightly the third time around. Maybe his scalp was wistful. There had to be a comb somewhere in this to believe in. And a younger man's hairline that also needed to be there for this guy's head to make sense. What happened to the comb? You wanted to ask that. But it seemed an inappropriate question to ask after only one drink.

Let's put it this way Detective Shade: what brings you to earth?

I'll tell you a story he said. Three men were captured by cannibals one day and the head cannibal tells them the sad news — we're going to kill you and eat you and use your skins for our canoes. But the head cannibal -being a decent fellow — if you can imagine such a thing — offered them each a personal way to go out. Since they were going to die anyway they can kill themselves however they choose. With little alternatives they set about it. The European shoots himself in the head while singing. The Asian falls on a sharp knife and digs it into his gut and nods respectfully. The American asks for a fork. The head cannibal looks at him oddly but obliges and gives him one. The American then stabs himself repeatedly — in the chest — in the arms — in the legs — until his entire body was punctured with small holes. The American looks back at the head cannibal — hands him the fork and says: now go build your fucking canoes.

Maybe there's some difficulty here you said. Thanks for the drink. But what's up with that routine.

You don't recognize it he said.

No you said you didn't recognize it.

Have you ever noticed how people will say yes/no simultaneously while describing their thoughts? It's almost like they're born between opposites. They affirm and they deny — all in a single breath. It makes you wonder what the rules are.

Let me guess you said you're the head cannibal.

Hardly he replied seemingly though a little saddened by the thought.

So what's your problem?

That's part of my problem he said.

How big a problem?

Large enough he said to fit you in. Order us another. I need to go and bleed the weasel.

Being around Shade was like being taken by a tour guide on a disaster. What was it going take?

Why couldn't you have a peaceful night on the planet without Detective Shade appearing like a loud truck horn does moments before the crash and the exploding windshield?

Sky had little time for Detective Shade. And if veracity was moronic then Shade was a guy taken with his own transcendence. What he told you was that he had a gift for exceeding ordinary material limits.

There are levels he said — and when he spoke to you — he would say he was speaking from another level — and it was a level he said where you were not — and when he spoke from another level that meant you stood by what he said — and since you stood by what he said you were told there was a big difference between his existence and your own and that Shade's level and your level were never connected except by derivatives.

And by Shade's reasoning — what we held in common was whatever Shade wanted.

It was bullshit talk for the ages. Shade knew it. In the Detective-Ville of his own mind Shade was a supernatural bad ass — riding the neighborhood in that dull black cruiser and poking his greasy fingers wherever they didn't belong — and that was mostly in other people's business.

And that was what brought Shade to you. Detective Shade wanted something. And he believed you had what it was that he wanted. And the way Shade did business was sideways — he was never direct with you. It was like a matter of principle with him to be overweight with promise but never deliver.

Detective Shade was the odd man out in a game of checkers.

Detective Shade busted young couples for sitting on the boardwalk and then he stole their sad box meals for his own lunch.

Detective Shade loved to listen to himself talk — especially when he bought porn shots from the teenagers at Frank's Playland by the Sea.

You finished the bourbon and found two more placed on the bar.

Don't know why I stock this shit anymore Fast Eddie said. You doing all right he said?

Yea you said. You know how it is — when stink follows you around…

Got that Fast Eddie said. You need me to do anything?

No you said. But thanks.

Yea Fast Eddie said. The mindset and the scheme…

The clown and his dream…

*

Shade found his seat and did that weird sucking thing with his drink again.

Just the other day he said I heard that baboons think. Imagine that… Can you imagine that… a baboon… a thinking baboon… I can't imagine that Shade said.

And you never got used to this — no matter how often you heard it.

… you ever think humanity needs too many talents to succeed… there were only so many favors a person might do in this world for somebody else… so tell me where does anxiety go… it's a bittersweet jewel to reckon with …

What's on your mind Detective Shade?

Glad you finally asked he said.

It's never like that you said. No matter what anybody says.

Do you know what I hate he asked? It's the busy signal. Do you hate that? Do you hate that moment where — and when — you cannot get through?

You told Shade you did not have a phone.

I've never called you he said?

You told him again that was impossible since you did not have a phone.

That's too bad Shade said. Otherwise we could speak nightly. Get to the bottom of things. Make deals. Exchange money.

You told him again that was impossible.

You wouldn't answer your phone anyway if you did have a phone. Its people like you Shade said that makes staying in touch so difficult. What do you think — that messages were second rate?

No you said again you just didn't have a phone. Therefore it was impossible to answer. Besides you said there was no place to have a phone.

You lived in a condemned building. It was a breezy old building that housed the bus station and there was a reasonable chance the building might not stand tomorrow because it might be dynamited tomorrow. Amid the rubble the cheesy Phoenix would rise... with brand new names with something fucked up sounding like Surf Hedge Condos or the Atlantic Berry House...

Why invest in anything that kept you in touch?

The landlord figure — whoever or whatever that was — you never met anyone — not even a shadow — you paid cash monthly- a wonderful Somali family downstairs ran the sandwich shop — and somebody like a heavy Czech bouncer at the back door took your cash and spat at your heels as you walked away — so it was like you spent your dollars for history and felt foolish and wondered if you had a chance to get out before the dynamite took down the sky.

Why answer a message you told Shade...

Detective Shade listened. He shrugged his shoulders. Want this he asked?

Yea you said and took a big green pill from his hand and washed it with a sip of rat bourbon.

*

Listen Shade said. What does it take? What will it take? If you don't mind I'll ask my own question first he said.

*

Nearly four years exactly you thought — waiting for the pill to kick in — stretching time — night after night and if you took enough foreign agents into your bloodstream your memory might turn over on itself like some hallucinatory right of way and come up looking like the impossible dream and maybe that's what Shade wanted — as the pill kicked in.

435

Cocktail hour and the gods blessed the 20th Century Club.

Despite the mass hypnosis we shared — for getting rich one day and sleeping with beautifully advertised sex ideals- for being above the fray- and the delusions en masse we loved like living close in with the neighbors — there remained the day on earth — an exercise in running away — a certain leveling of faith — the day was going to be there tomorrow. We're all so terribly alike you told Shade. Visual annoyance... games with strings... what we ignore we will turn into.... how do you picture yourself you asked Detective Shade...did you wear a hangman's vest.... Were you able and willing to force open a sticky door... we're all so terribly alike you said how bout another pill and Shade ponied up and we drank more poisonous bourbon and Fast Eddie kept his eyes on you and you heard the sad worn out directions from the loudspeaker calling from the bus station: NOW BOARDING POINTS WEST: NOW BOARDING POINTS WEST...as though the announcements were for name calling and herding loss to open doors above the air brake settings...

Why did you picture yourself this way Shade asked?

At that moment a shotgun fired off in your head.

You were certain Detective Shade heard it.

The same old merry nonsense — you took Shade's dope and left him with nothing in return except for some old chatter he heard a hundred times before.

Why not picture how you were...there was a step and you can't afford to take it without questions.

Why do you picture yourself the way you do? That's been a puzzle for me Shade said. We've offered you many things and the things we offered would satisfy most people for a lifetime. But you — you don't take our offer seriously and why is that?

Hey you said I had the pancakes and bacon last week. They were great. Best pancakes I ever had. Bacon was fucking killer.

Let's talk about money and not talk about bacon and pancakes.

Hey you said. You guys picked up the tab. And left the tip...

Because you told Shade: The minute I give you what you want that's the second where I become a dead man and go below the surface with my eyes pecked out and caught in the lobster pots like another sad fuck sent down to the burial sites. So don't bother to answer your question.

I know the answer to my own question Shade said.

You're an investment oddity Shade said.

Try and cash me in you said.

Let's wait a minute Shade said. Give me a minute he said before we get wound around our difference where we needn't be — because we can work things out. When you look at it — if you look at it — we can skip the third degree — what I need is for you to tell me something.

I've told you for years — Detective Shade I have nothing for you.

What happened to the knapsack?

You told him — you took it down to the end of the boardwalk -where things have their day — and then you tossed it into a outgoing tide and that was the last you saw of it.

Why I meant he said was what happened to what was inside the knapsack?

Well you said that was a different story. Maybe I have it. Maybe it went out with the tide. You reminded him that the knapsack was your negotiating point.

That knapsack was your tolling bell he said.

Probably so you agreed.

Detective Shade picked up his glass and squeezed it hard. Purple roadwork veins creased across his forehead. Guarantees were not only out of the question but were in addition bad taste.

What could Shade guarantee? His pockets were ass deep into somebody else's money. What position was that?

Yes and no he said unclenching his glass and politely ordering another.

You have no idea what shit you are in Detective Shade said.

As long as the old guy was alive and the pizza shop was in business you were protected. But now he's dead — and the pizza shop makes

437

mediocre pies — and things aren't the same as they were so if I told you these situations changed –might be what I'm saying is that if certain information were passed on then a certain negotiating point might go away. And in the future there might not be any other negotiating points on the radar. Does that rattle your cage? And how was that pill?

The pill was excellent you thought. You had the satisfaction from that rare and foolish moment being high when despite being land bound in a day on earth you sensed in the warm hollow of your stomach you were tucked away safe… a dune somewhere — a crescent moon — a big iron skillet on an open fire cooking beans onions and potatoes and peppers — the Atlantic — looking over eternity…

Wait you said — you work for Bobby Alfredo?

You want another pill?

*

At some point — and one not too distant — things as such are going to be out of control. This was what I'm trying to tell you. This is why you need to tell me all there is. Otherwise try and picture this — what your face looks like in constant pain over a week's worth of time. Think what your body will feel like- — wrenched away from all delusions and all happiness — standing in a place where the end won't come quick enough because those who are bringing the end to your face are so completely fucked up about it they lose sight of the end game and just go on and on little by little and cut by cut satisfying the means. Listen to me and get this straight. This was no longer a circumstance existing simply between you and me. You will lose — and I might add for emphasis — very regretfully. Give this thing up or really — shit happens.

By now you were angry enough — and high enough — melancholy enough — maybe there's not a lot of difference — to understand what Shade's take on this was. The old ex-priest now feared for his own soul. Old markers had finally been called in on him. Why were you were wasting a good pill on this?

You looked at Shade and asked: so you're feeling this behind your back. They're going to kill you also?

It seemed that way.

Why now? And what makes you think I still have what you want?

Shade answered I know you have it. And why now you ask? The whole thing needs to go away. If it does not then you and I go away. Does it need to be broken down any further for you?

You never could tell — when it came to things like reductions. And now what — Shade was like sincere because he realized he was going to die also? And if they killed you both so what then? The knapsack wasn't worth dying for. But living was worth what it takes to get away with each day for nothing. How do you picture yourself? A question like that could fill anybody's head. It was already a ready-made fact by dint of birth that you would be swept up in it. You might be defined against all evidence by as much external crap whirling around you as you might be by walking down the street alone and minding your own business. Maybe the question needed to come across as more specific. Then maybe you might have some answers.

You looked at Shade from underneath the beautiful feelings that were your eyelids rolling through the room and you told him that it was songs: songs did it for you. Was that close to what he wanted? You always pictured yourself and that your life was better off viewed in someone else's songs.

Yes that was wonderful he said.

And that's human nature you said.

Hear me out he said. You are in this deep. It only takes a certain amount of faith here to turn your attention to what's being ignored. Try to imagine yourself not settling for less than a better life… okay — which you have to realize — you can afford to do.

But if you don't get this right this time- there will be no next time for you. This cannot be difficult for you to grab hold of.

Damn the pill was good. Because it was easy to blame your troubles well beyond the household of your own being so to speak you had the impression to say: so what?

You told Shade all along you were never interested in the symbols of a better life. In fact there was no better life. What were you supposed to do? Be like one of those storefronts that went bankrupt in the night without anyone caring and then next day everybody else wonders about it after it's gone?

Picture yourself as having a choice he said.

But that's just a convoluted set of free wills you replied — unable to get it right.

You listened to the pill and its rip tide…

This was a business deal Shade said. What we require here was a better handicap. Without it you and I are in the shadows. Do you realize how easy it is to die?

Well he had you there. You'd never been dead unless you didn't know about it.

A silence followed that under normal circumstances might prove difficult to overcome.

Here we were trying to come to grips with certain things. Like being killed.

What good was any of this going to do anybody? How lousy it would be — to end this way. Damn. You hated being in a corner. Not that this was the time for nostalgia — but you had to weigh everything against everything else. Shouldn't everything come into play? Especially when there wasn't a soul in this enterprise that you trusted.

Don't you hate it when you're alone Shade asked?

It was the worst thing you said — except sitting when I'm sitting next to you Shade you said.

*

Yea you told Shade you hated it.

*

You did hate it. Being squeezed — forced into trouble- squeezed and moneyed against your interests — totally fucked up — even if you had something held back in the rears for a rainy day or a trick up your sleeve — squeezed out from the middle and moneyed against your interests. But Bobby Alfredo? Even if you had something in the rears or a trick up your sleeve where you might hold them quiet without trouble — but what were you doing with them except playing at playing them out?

440

But…Bobby Alfredo…?

Wait… wait…

Don't tell me…

Bobby Alfredo and Shade were doing business together?

Back when it happened you saw Blind Charlie at the wake. Yea he was dead and lying pasty looking like yesterday's pizza dough. And by that time Blind Charlie was gone — that was the last time you saw him.

Days earlier it was the last time we spoke. You slipped in past the cousins at the hospital room door. Blind Charlie was praying with his last breaths and that was cool to sense how connected he still was. Even in a sterile hospital room — machines beeping — air forced in the lungs — constant fluids dripping through tubes into his arms — Blind Charlie held his dignity. But it was hard to tell the difference between his coughing and his laughter. On notice — the cousins said yes — Blind Charlie motioned you closer.

First off he said: do not fuck with her.

I treat her right you said. But else do you say to a dying man about his granddaughter?

Blind Charlie laughed or he wheezed and hit the bed with a fist.

You understand me?

Totally you said.

The cousins moved in and flanked your chair.

I understand you said and I tell you that I've done nothing wrong.

Except to fall in love Blind Charlie wheezed or coughed.

Okay I fell in love!

The cousins laughed and backed away into corners of the room.

Blind Charlie wheezed or coughed or laughed.

Second thing he whispered: do not ever trust Bobby Alfredo. Do you see these two men in the room?

Yes you said.

Well Blind Charlie wheezed or laughed: these are your cousins. They only like you right now because I tell them to. So let's recap: first: do not fuck with her. Second: do not trust Bobby Alfredo. And third — if you do these two things — you will not only have these two cousins behind your back — but every cousin at the pizza shop… are we clear?

It was clear. But so was the alternative.

*

Shade looked at his watch. Aging ambition — late time age skin flaps hung below the corners of his mouth — a bubble-faced loser in all regards with flaky skin tone and burnt tobacco hair — Shade seemed ahead for himself and adjusted the cuffs of his poor boy suit coat. He cocked his head and leaned it slightly towards you. Dead fish at low tide smelled better than his breath.

Let me ask this you said — after all the time — all the time you dogged me — why- suddenly — why now?

Let's get in the car he said.

It's a paranoid world you said and I don't like it getting in cars with Detectives.

Here Shade said light this up.

*

We drove around Jersey-land for an hour. We were killing time that much was evident. But why were we killing time? Driving around — you were prone to something — criminal intentions — or worse — Shade's frame of reference? This was a paranoid world you said and I don't want to be driving in cars with Detectives!

Stop worrying asshole Shade said. Besides — how many Detectives do you see? How many cars were we driving in? Light this up and calm down.

*

The Welfare Offices on Rose Street where Jersey-land never repaired the sidewalks was like a dead-on clue.

Shade said there were no answers here to anyone's problems. There were only mistake filled questions here — and they waited in line for hours — sometimes days — just to get in the door — just to fill out forms and get skanky advice.

Cash or nothing you said.

You're begging to see what I'd like you to see Shade said.

Cash or nothing and give me another pill.

I can do that but you owe me something.

You'll need to kill me first before I owe you anything.

And that sounded funny to you the way it sounded to your ears on the air. Straight up with no apologies but ridiculous if you thought about it.

Questions to mistake-filled answers: driving around and burning evening summer daylight: Millionaires' Alley and the beach front bars and the shit-faced intent prone to paranoid criminals or worse: chains of weary apartment buildings that clung for existence onto Millionaires' Alley because the casinos bred them like bastards and gave cheap housing to the ten thousand card dealers of the world and a prostituted work staff and the probation galley slaves making important food for critical news reports.

*

For a time you did not know what to say. Except to say nothing much happened on these roads. Unless you were prone to a criminal frame of reference because the sidewalks were a dead clue and they were never repaired from the Welfare Offices on Rose Street to the shit-faced beachfront bars on Millionaires' Alley because there were questions to mistaken answers like you found the summer daylight helped your head because the light extended out the windshield to the Atlantic and brought you back and you could die on the Atlantic swell enough but you could not die on Rose Street and so trying to find a thread of logic in between time there was an idea in play here and maybe it was the pills ganging up on you and maybe it was Shade kept saying stop worrying you asshole but maybe what happened was when we entered a ditched apartment building on Loomis Street because somebody inside owed Shade money and once we got inside there was this old dude watching a baseball game on television and he gave Shade a few dollars for his shakedown efforts but the poor old guy had little to nothing in his apartment but a fifty-four inch flat screen and a cold empty pipe on the kitchen countertop and you said to Shade don't fuck with this guy and Shade said why not and it was then that you began filling in the paint by numbers scene and the red exit you saw above the door and that said you should not underestimate Shade because he was a cop and that's where the fuel was and second this was another perfect place to demonstrate how the textures in the neighborhood were about to get plowed under down here at the bottom of exit 17 there was never anything built for years but an unfinished concrete ramp that was left and dropped off the night into the mud flats and the ditch lands.

*

You watched sky through Shade's filthy windshield. Clouds jumped from faraway rooftops down to the sea. Exit 17. Exit 17 ended nowhere. And let's take aside the visual annoyance — you were at the bottom of a broken concrete ramp that dumped into the ocean and that should be exit 17 and Shade's car was parked like two feet from the water.

Shade you asked so where do you live now? I know you moved and things are going to get way weird —

I have a bungalow. It might be on Congress Avenue. It might be in fucking Europe. It might be all in my head.

You never can be sure about information you thought.

A stringy Jersey-land vapor — crippled orange exhaust — drifted through the windows of Shade's automobile — a rusty silver blue dodge the size of a propeller airplane burning oil and sucking gas like there was no war going on in the old holy lands nor a death per gallon index here at home.

Streetlights flooded down from above. Shadows reached around the streets and alleys like craters across the sea of tranquility.

Across the seat as he backed us off an Exit17 the one that was there but the one that did not exist — Shade looked like an inflatable toy come to life in a horror movie — one minute the thing is dull and witless and then it grins like a cartoon duck from hell.

444

Don't you love summer Shade said.

He drained his beer can and tossed it out the window where it disappeared along with everything else. Check this out he said.

Shade's eyes took off from his head and settled onto two chicken leg girls.

Gawky aged teenagers smoking their older sister cigarettes — decked in high heeled plastic sandals and tight v-cut shorts.

And those shorts… some cheap overseas fabric … caught the jailbait lines of hidden ass and relieved them from the stint being nude in public — and that was where Shade and his eyes drooled.

Shade honked at them. He gave them some tongue.

Shade looked over at you and said what? You wouldn't poke that butterscotch? You wouldn't have that if you had the chance?

It was warped you said.

I've got photos I'll show you he said. There are some things when you look at them these things change your mind. What's not to like?

What if one of those kids was my sister?

Oh who cares about your fucking sister he said.

Shade would take eight bucks out of a dead man's pocket even though the guy only owed him five.

That's the trouble he said. Everybody pleads no contest.

You looked at him and threw a beer can into the back seat and asked him why attempt behavior anyway?

*

Shade was no dummy. He was however a very poor excuse for being one.

Shade had to be considering what his best move was? What if the next move he had was for Shade to kill you?

Why the fuck were you driving around with this guy?

What if you killed him first?

*

When you rode near the ocean- its bigness arrived in your head like a welcome mat and allowed you to curve and roll with your own small

445

thoughts. It was a precarious beauty for sure. Much like staying up with the night sky and feeling cool with the spectacle there. Feeling especially cool with the Milky Way above. Or having that slice of pizza after hours when the world spun around you and your footing was unsteady. But it was that last slice of pie with its hot cheese and spicy red sauce that reached inside you and touched what you needed on an otherwise second hand confidence night.

Did it matter someone was trying to kill you?

You had to get to your phone and call Eden Jones.

*

While we drove — and Shade salivated over prison time for fucking a minor — Shade said the problem with you was that you only saw god in the rear view mirror...

*

Nostalgia had a way that happened on its own on its own and showing up unnoticed.

Was there an order to any day?

Haven't the gods always made promises they can't keep?

The problem with Shade was: he was only a god in the rear view mirror.

*

During the summer months- when school was out and gone and forgotten — as you looked out Shade's car window at the evening — the scroll work of graffiti passed by — layering every last inch of public space available ... during the summer months you might be arrested for any number of offenses — however minor — despite the presumption of innocence described in the Constitution. Month after month Shade snuck about the layers of youthful Jersey-land. Month after month Shade broke the law with a single mindfulness — like some tragic worn out flunky.

446

Where would you be to this day without an influence from Detective Shade?

From his lousy shoes to his beat up cruiser Shade was a ready guy.

Even if the crime was no more than having the nickel meter run out on a parked car Shade spotted young blood and was there with a ticket before you knew.

He had a slow tail on you — because you might commit something wrong a week from now — and Shade hounded you now.

He parked his cruiser outside homes and waited all night.

He made anonymous calls in the dead skin night asking for dope when your parents answered.

*

Shade was lonesome and unhinged and you had to get out of the car.

*

When Shade looked in the rear view mirror he shook his head...
Why aren't you rich you said...
Because I need more than what I got he said...

*

One night you and Eden Jones were hanging out in some abandoned car. It was a Cadillac and was on 65th Street and had been for months and was big enough inside so we all used it as a place to chill and get high. It was like we didn't exist enough inside the car to fill this huge back seat. We looked at one another strangely. We knew. Being together in the back seat was being this pearl in the fucked up shell outside. We knew. We were stupidly alive and foolish.

When suddenly a flashlight banged against a cracked windshield.

Eden Jones said well looks like the exists were covered. She cocked her gun and put it back inside her pants.

Outside the car Shade frisked you.

What were you going to do with this?

Ace MacDonald gave it to you. It was a ceremonial thing passed on from an older guy on the corner onto a younger guy and today happened to be your day.

Only if it were true you told Shade.

It was there because it had so much verve riding in your pocket.

Shade held the sad love-rubber up to the streetlight and tore it open from its 50-cent foil package. I bet you would pay more than a dollar for this he said.

Yes you would you said and tried to grab the sad love-rubber back from his hand. But Shade was so filled with life that night that he snatched the sad love-rubber back from your would-be grasp and held it before your face — he toyed with it — he swung it like a bell —and then he dropped the sad love rubber onto the street and without a move or a thought otherwise Shade took the petty sole of his right shoe and ground the sad love rubber into the street.

Back inside the Cadillac — you knew Eden Jones had her southpaw down her pants — and if there was any noise from Shade outside — other than the usual bullshit — then she exited the car as told and looked Shade in the eye and unzipped her shorts — and let Shade focus in on a gun for a moment — and looking back into her eyes he saw a gun pointed at his head that was ready able and sure enough to be fired.

*

Later on after Shade got lost in the night — we cleared out of the Cadillac. But not before we tried and picked up what was going on inside the Cadillac before Shade and his villain routine broke our night apart.

We were back in the Cadillac — leaning towards one another. Eden Jones had no southpaw. Her shorts were zipped. We laughed… and we laughed… and what we knew was that Shade — the old ex-priest — was sitting on a bar stool off Beach Avenue and getting another chuckle before he died.

*

Bar stools leaned in emptiness and alone with his thoughts and when you add up all the years together and pulled them apart Shade was not remembering and his head was all fireworks and holiness and archives that lived in a fretful mind and that was not a synthesis to be but a ripped up way to be. And to ponder that nightly Shade poured himself silly nightly.

*

One night there was a party out on Dead Shore Road. Some vacant summerhouse set way out in the tide grass near the ditch lands where turtles swam in the muck like heroes and big herons walked about freely picking at the crawl from low tide. Somebody had the key to the house so we all piled provisions together for the weekend and went out to the long reaches of the bay — where the water stank — that sweet Jersey-land — to join together and be all right like the Who sang.

*

Stars rippled in the sky above the bonfire ... hot winds curved in time ...on a clear night across the marsh the faint sound of waves fell on bone-white sand... a taste like black enamel paint flaked off through the air... suddenly cars were braking in fast and hard on the gravel and stirring up the dogs... they probably came in from exit 19 and broke hard and fast and stirred up nocturnal August to bust a drinking party.

Shade stepped out from his cruiser. His fleshy jowls hung like fat strings off his face.

Some kids froze. Other kids ran away. Was there a difference how to approach the law?

And Shade's eyes were always too small for his head — odd little points in gravity that never went out. No way Shade was not in question. He helped himself while his minions scurried the area. But what was left? What arrest was left to use? There were plenty of monsters left and Shade was among them. But how many statutes in the law were there for arresting teenagers?

What was Shade at us for?

Underage sugar-huddles lying with the daughters of the unemployed... a bag of smoke that never carried a name and belonged to no one... listening to radio music under the moon... whatever we were plotting out here in the weeds — wasting time while growing up — that's what drove Shade wild.

What were we up to?

What we were up to on any given day in Jersey-land — which was to say the Jersey-land of our minds — that was difficult to for him to reason with.

It was a bad combination of times to knuckle under. Because one moment you were tripping with your mates... as neurons... as material... as far as we knew... and the next moment you were face-up to Detective Shade stuffing peanuts into his mouth and asking too many questions with his drool-lip smile.

Yea you were flying a kite in a thunderstorm you said — looking for reasons and pictures that might happen some other day since you were planning it now you said ...Well you got the dope from any older guy... you got the beer from an older guy... and we're sitting outside underneath the stars and listening to music... and being out in the open was an algebra of life — ratios that took you in — and you told Shade he could get off where he wanted... it was all the same JERSEY-LAND JERSEY-LAND UBER ALLES you dumpy gunslinger fraud.

A point of truth and then so what Shade said.

Listen here kids. Oh I know he said life turns so out miserable. But you know kids — it's not about today so much as it is about tomorrow — and the tomorrow after that — don't you see? It's bigger than what we know. We're just set up against a background. And it takes nerves — we need to recognize certain things — like who was strong and who was not...

*

And to think for a few bucks we could have this guy shot and turned into a paving stone.

While you were questioned and frisked out of existence by Shade it felt like the time you were lowered down a sewer at 20th Street to fetch a softball hit off the right base line.

And sometime after — when the beer and dope and food was gone and loaded into the cruiser — Shade pulled you aside and told you that we now had a carefully laid out set of instructions together. And you may go through mea culpa after mea culpa all you want but you're partially wrong because you got caught. You don't owe me anything Shade said. But from here on in — things get interesting.

Then there was a radio squawk and hiss from the cruisers and Detective Shade and his boys drove off.

*

Shade took a deep hit off the joint until the look on his face overflowed from the dope smoke in his lungs. He coughed it out and made a mess across his shirt — spewing phlegm and firing little bits off his lips like amulets. For good measure he did it again.

It was the worst of times — it was the best of times... Ever read that Shade asked?

You mean the book?

No you asshole not the fucking book!

The spray paint on the east wall at Frank's Playland by the Sea: it was the worst of times — it was the best of times. It's sprayed right there in black and white. You should check it out. You know — it's my place to watch ambition from the shadows. The spray paint kids are value added. They're always up to something.

I wonder maybe we grab things by mistake. One day you wake up and feel something odd enough to explain — something absurd — something with holding power. You ever get that?

Before you answered Shade said people see order. And in this order they want to believe. Like some unwritten fucking contract that said this works because number one there's sanity presumed belonging to it and second they want something. I can't do anything about number one but I sure can ply number two. That's the problem with faith Shade said. It leads to trouble.

When did you rediscover god you said?

I wonder if maybe rather than win or lose the purpose from the beginning was a never- ending tie. Technically right — that could be like a definition of infinity. Because if someone doesn't score the game continues in this round robin trap — believe me — what people want was to pay their money and be entertained and go then go when things were done and believe they been somewhere and done something tonight. You might also ague the possibility ending in a tie also proves a tie might also be impossible.

That's a lot on your plate dude. And more than I think you can handle.

*

We pulled up to the bus station where Shade had an interest to look after: dumb fools who jammed packages in lockers and then walked away and imagined it was easy to walk away and get paid.

Above the bus station was the apartment where you lived. It was like a Jersey-land of your own. The chemical wash of security lamps above the streets... a sad tree in the broken sidewalk... a trash can knocked over... framed in perpetuity from above... a long industrial hangover... buildings abandoned to insurance scams and lonesome winds that settled off the ocean... one big and inspired mistake you called home.

Detective Shade you asked do you feel confidence or regrets that your present environment allows the opportunity to develop your personality?

Fuck you he said. He smiled with a greasy look of simmering meat fat in his eyes.

Does this seem like a variation on other people's suffering?

No he said. It's a snake's world. You don't want to suffer. But I suffer little patience.

Shade you said do you find yourself up to shit?

Look he said. It wasn't me that killed anybody now was it?

Shade had you there. You often wished for a substitute take on what happened or what you knew but really there was none to be had because you already knew it.

You ever kill anybody Shade?

Less than I care to think about he said.

He was lying out his words. And his words were little enough to sound like an untied shoelace in the dirt — something flapping and loose with motion and posed a hazard.

Wouldn't it be perfect to have no past he said. Wouldn't it be wonderful — to have everything destroyed — all your personal records — even the dental ones... Boom — just gone ... no you.

People always get found out Shade you said. You leave a trail. You never killed anyone.

Fuck you he said. You are so mediocre he said wait here and slammed the car door.

Shade you called out! Some people you met and you share a great sense of early feelings! Was the money still there? Is that what you're asking? One thing doesn't necessarily lead to another!

Shade returned to the car and opened the door and said: I'll give you this question again: you live from payday to payday in this little notch you got going and you're covered in paint and fucking wallboard compound until you have that first drink and then what comes after that: belief?

It's a living you said. It's limited. But what's the damage I could do Shade?

I should cuff you Shade said.

Shade you said you are wish fulfillment run amuck.

Shade said we play the consequence for the benefit.

Perhaps my compulsion- toward deliverance- through patterns- has landed me in a state of human insignificance and all that- but as I see it- hindsight and money's prayers lend to themselves certain melancholy evidence to living. What you do not see here Detective Shade was the handle on things and who turns it.

And you just keep on hoping for the day when you win the lottery Shade said.

Then there are those days Shade when the schemes will turn nasty against you.

Shade clicked the car door shut and walked away again into the bus station.

*

So you sat in the dull no future cruiser — thoughtfully at odds with things in a general fucked up sort of way — sipping on a ready alcohol container the way you might e-mail a friend on a whim — and for a strange reason — and the best reasons to be found were strange — as you looked out the car window you felt a heartbeat around the sad body of Jersey-land. Just about everything that moments before had seemed artificially dedicated — faces hanging on heads going side to side — infested gulls on the corners eating sandwich wrappers — and suddenly you saw — it did not matter — how things fell apart.

Everything you saw lived its entire life right where you saw it. They just do and that was the good of it. There was no other place to go. Everything was here and near and dear to the particulars. Most of it overrated but this evening — well — it was like some places the clouds were brighter than in others. And a thing like the earth was calling you: bedrock and fossils and the engineering behind what it showed.

It was so easy to fall in love when there was everything to lose.

The night air — air if you dared call it that — saturated the open car windows and fouled the cruiser with chemicals and humidity. The particle stuff in the air was familiar and named to you because it had a taste you memorized from grade school. Chromium. Carbon Monoxide. Second generation copper arsenic fibers broke off from the rotting boardwalks and stuck to the humid evening while you waited for Shade. The table of polluted elements was a text every kid knew by heart. It had a place in the classroom above the blackboards and beside the cross and the flag and the oil derrick.

The tunnels were backed up again — that was the buzz on Shade's radio — commuters were knotted at the bridges — twenty- four hour traffic horns — chaos lane to lane — phantom drivers on twenty-four hour traffic horns — honking for respect and honking for fear — everyone's honking because they need an unreal true place... and honking from a car will do that for you.

Satellites high above the fray fed pictures back to a network of controllers seated at desks miles away from Jersey-land... trying to harness a congestion into a synchronized energy... trying with a highly tuned computerized intelligence to find the most effective means to get all these people in or out.

A trashcan rolled underneath a bus: before it was flattened and crushed sadly the message on its side said: Keep Jersey-land Clean!

*

Across 8th Street a bunch of young boys argued about tomorrow and whether or not it was going to happen. They all had guns hidden in their belts because all young boys had guns hidden in their belts — because all young boys want to be imagined like a face gone spectacular. It's a loud culture. Everyone's normal voice yelled at some maximum load across capacity to stay on top of someone else talking back. ... so why bother...

*

Across Waverly how many dog walkers this evening from the other exits were in town to buy dope and pocket a high from the locals? How many saw the family of beggars with their cardboard signs — anything helps — kindness is not a crime — in what must be another frightening night for them out on the town?

Taxis rushed through like wild bolts of light.

Runaway numbers were set to explode.

Below the statues of war heroes at Packer and 5th Street — spray paint names ran over the cast bronzed history of ignored events — three old souls sat passing a bottle of wine and listening to a radio not worth stealing.

Home was here and there was security and that was how generations thrived.

It's a snake's world Shade said leaning across the window. They say fighting is cruel and happens for dogs and beasts.

Who said you said?

The natives Shade said. They were here long before you and I were even sperm in the fucking universe. You're such an asshole. They were

455

farmers. Fisherman. Thinkers. They were friendly to neighbors but given a cause they'd mount a disaster against their enemies.

That leaves you and me out.

We're fucking immigrants he said.

And that like takes the top off your mind.

Fuck you he said. Now we rule.

Maybe you said the dead see the identical things we see. Maybe they watch us right now on the other side of the street. Maybe they don't even recognize us a place. Maybe they only acknowledge presence and leave it at that. Maybe it's like the way the living feel about who got left behind and now speak in tones about what's departed. Living to dead and back again but maybe not. But Shade something does happen. Physicality happens and loosens as we work through this. Let the dishes pile in the sink — isn't that what you're thinking? Someone comes along and cleans up later.

Shade slammed the car door and heaved himself onto the seat like a bag of laundry tossed from an apartment on Tuesday morning.

Shade you said go back outside and give those people some cash.

What?

I know you just got paid.

Fuck that.

Go on.

Don't fuck with me mister. I will shut you down.

Shade you just got paid big for peanuts. A little side action at the bus station — go on now and share the wealth. What ever happened to that old communal spirit? The one you once upheld with an oath or some shit? What would your former employer say? How's this play out in time when it's written down in the ledger of all things accountable?

Shade looked back at you. The past doesn't happen for me like it happened for you.

Give me the money then you said and I'll give it to them.

Fuck you why be concerned he asked? Why even fucking care?

You wouldn't understand the reasons in a dozen life times. Give me the money.

It's all the fucking same he said.

456

*

Shade drove out Broadway and veered left at the neon ice cream cone where all the used junkies on methadone gathered and sat around waiting to quit. Shouldn't someone tell them it's not going to be that easy?

From there he turned off on a dirt road. A billboard-like sign announced this was soon to be: Ocean Heights Community. Financed by Buffalo Ready and Da Nang Kindle Limited.

And Jersey-land was all flat land. There were no ocean heights. If anything at all it seemed we were several feet below sea level before we even started.

We drove down an old road filled with holes and slung with trees and stars looked through branches from above. It was a road where you easily walked faster than a car was able to drive and that made it murky why we were here and where we were going.

And all this cause and effect made you sad this evening. And yet you shouldn't be. Because you know what: there was no fault… there was only falling through the air again and again… memory pushing against tides…

I hate fucking traffic Shade said coming to a stop. It was a point well and blindly taken since the road ran out of space and ended in a rush of weeds that had been growing here for centuries. Traffic he said…and he let the phrase hang…you could kill somebody he said.

Yea Shade you told him there's no way out.

That's so untrue he said.

Like how so?

Like the other day he said I was in the supermarket and there was this middle aged couple. They fucking argued over everything in sight. Did this contain ten ounces or eight? How much pepper is enough? Can you believe the price of that watermelon? People like that have no fucking idea how close they come.

To what you said?

To mercy and forgiveness you asshole that's what I'm saying. Have some fucking clue about hell and the fucking concentration it's going to take.

We got out of the car and looked about. No shadows yet but the moon was on the rise.

We stood in the darkness listening to crickets and the bayside water trying to make waves but leaving only small breathy sounds on what was like infinity shushed on pebbles.

I like it here Shade said. It's not a dump yet. Ducks live here. You ever watched fucking ducks? I don't care in the end. Because something else always happens and fucks up what you think. But for right now I picture this. Something like it used to be…when it didn't matter…or fucking not but anyway the ducks at some point have to go because they're in the way. I like the ducks you know…I like it while they're here…

Shade you said it sounds like you're trying to be convincing.

That's just one of the problems he said walking away.

Shade you called after him this technical aspect carries us only so far. We'll never see the money. In fact — all this business — it's just an endorsement for imperfection! Certain moments never happen and this was one of them. Sadness was temporary. Sadness was eternal.

Yea well fuck you Shade said. Fuck you. You do not know what the fuck you think you are up against.

When you caught up with Shade he was leaned back against a small gnarly dune and smoking a cigar. On a drift of plywood washed in from the Atlantic he spread out four small glassine envelopes.

Shade you need more of a deck than that to play solitaire you said.

Less than you might think he said.

And let me guess you said: this brings us to this evening.

What we have here Shade said was not only a time out — but we'll say it's also bliss and a litmus test of sorts.

Like door number 1 or door number 2 you said.

Shut the fuck up and sit down he said.

*

You had a feeling: someplace inside there existed a future outside. And they happened at the same time. Pale white stars overhead…solitary habits…water sounds in the night… the absent mind… the clue…

Did you know Shade said that bank tellers no longer accept the paper tubes you used to put pennies and dimes in? It's way too much trouble. Or there's a specific day when they take them but you never know when that day is because they never say. And doesn't that fly in the fucking face in the first place that they no longer accept them? How do you cash out? Where did that idea ever go? The teller looks at me like I'm a fucking lunatic. The other people in line look at me like I make them nervous. These are people upon whom my face was neglect back at them and doubled down.

Nobody hopping in bed with you there Shade you said as a kind of solace to someone who was a fucking lunatic.

Whatever happened to actual money?

How much did you bring — in your paper tubes? Actual money you said.

About seven thousand dollars Shade said.

In change you said?

All there and accounted for an there was not a slug in the package It was like too much trouble for somebody to break open each tube and count it out. Where did service go? I was pointed to a machine where I dumped my money. Same result and I got no problem with the result — but why do you have to do things yourself when you go into a place of business? It totally fucked up my day.

Shade exhaled on his cigar and offered you an envelope.

Any one he said you pick.

And while the choices inside any envelope were probably the usual — horse tranquiller ecstasy — professional sport amphetamine — the latest Afghan breathing dust — you figured it best not to bargain with the goods from the hands of a damaged cop. This was a bunny you didn't want to pay later for.

Maybe another day you said.

Take one then for another day. Take it as a hedge for another day.

Dope was so hard to refuse — even if you thought now was a good time to refuse — but maybe this was the package that delivered you somewhere. You'd ask around to see if this cocoa mix was meant to kill you or not.

What do you see Shade said? When you look around — what do you see?

That was easy you said. Water was eternity. The Atlantic was a god but sky was your home. And by no fucking coincidence did they reflect one another. Water goes around the globe. Sky goes aground the globe. And the further they go and the longer they traveled a peculiar thing happens.

And what the fuck was that Shade said already into one bag.

Well it runs away. And two other cautious nervous types are now on the other end looking back at us. They're sitting an ocean away from us and sitting in front of their own ocean and looking back at us. It was like water carried with it a primitive television.

Wait a fucking minute Shade said. But fuck me — across the water — looking at people I never met on some other side of some other fucking ocean and they were looking back at me across a third ocean and what the fuck what was this some kind of fucking communion or some fucking nature mystic eyeball state of being? There was no time for this he said. Fuck me good and then some — does that make any sense to you…

What made sense to me was what I don't care about you said.

But what makes sense to me was a different story Shade said. What did you do with it? And what needs to make sense was where it is now… what did you do with it?

Why do you assume that you said?

You keep fucking with me Shade said.

And you keep pretending you care about keeping us both alive.

And if we don't play this thing correctly then we will be killed alive.

Tell me where it is Shade said. People want it back.

Why do you assume it belonged to these people in the first place?

Because I'm getting fucking paid to assume that!

Whoever's paying you Shade it's not theirs to claim.

All problems have a solution until they're not a problem to me any longer Shade said.

Who cares where it belongs or whoever it belongs to!

Tell me — what the fuck do you think you're doing? If we do not deliver this in a timely and fucking expedient manner — then without having much else to say about it then friend we are gone… assassinated by some kindergarten dropouts who wouldn't understand which way morning came from even if their own lives depended on their fucking ability to think!

That is not how it ends for me Shade said. Understand...

Shade does it seem like you been had? How many people in the neighborhood eat your lunch? Maybe you prefer it that way. What do you owe Shade? What's in your bones?

That was a long time ago he said relighting his cigar.

Evidence?

It's more than a passing embarrassment Shade said.

You told him there was no way you could have him on your hands.

There's no way either that you can't Shade said.

Why not just get lost?

You get lost he said.

No you said — because the people who cash your checks want you out.

They want you out too.

But Shade you said I have something to negotiate.

Shade pulled off his flask and coughed like he was trying to create a spirit from his defaults. He drew on his cigar and blew smoke filled air into a humid and little breeze.

*

Shade you asked: were you the most confused man alive tonight? Didn't you see it? Deeply sorry for the rough time you've had — like you can't be helped — like you're the original romantic — a bad credit guy —

Shut the fuck up he said.

We called a no mans land and both did an envelope.

*

Shade do you think it's possible — given the current evolutionary state of biology as we know it — do you think it's possible to fall in love with the same woman twice?

I don't know he said. I never was in love.

Well we're deep in the cosmetics tonight.

Shit you asshole we are going to die.

Shade do you ever feel pissed off that god let you down?

All I want is to be breathing tomorrow he said and eat a bad breakfast. You tell me what that costs. And god has little to do with anything friend.

*

Here's one for you. Walking across Washington Street two days ago you told Shade near the dug-up intersection at Lafayette — the only building left standing was the liquor store — and it was raining and windy and somebody walked by with an umbrella and the rain and the wind caught that umbrella. Suddenly the umbrella turns inside out and it's like this slacked and torn cloth flapping around a bent aluminum stick. It's a mess and the woman who had the umbrella dropped it and walked away. A minute later somebody else came along without an umbrella in the storm and without much thought picked it up and walked away with a new though badly shaped umbrella. Go figure. People were nuts. Your life was crazy.

What's left to offer you Shade asked?

You believed in sky. That's what you said.

We are so dead Shade said.

Of course we are. But this was no time for tears now was it?

*

Shade was silent and off to himself.

*

Small humid breezes worked inland off Delaware Bay. The Atlantic cut in wide and the Bay cut out a few hundred yards from the east and where they met was like the mystery where the bay ends and where the ocean begins.

It was the best ocean in the world.

Tides rose at your feet and you had no responsibility for anything. So what if there was nothing to compare it to — because you'd never seen any other oceans. But forget the other oceans. Maybe you'll see them one day but what if you never leave Jersey-land? What if this was the last and only turnpike where you rolled? And would you ever miss those oceans even if you never saw them? And fuck it — these were home page waves you lived beside. Jersey-land was born on shores before you were born and once you're gone the same shores will be right here. They changed with the waves. And that's what you knew.

With me so far Shade yelled!

Whoa Detective — how you feeling?

...gold... gold fucking light...out there...bars...atmospheres...wavy lines...quietly...in the scrap...when the smoke clears...I still feel it... the asphalt sky...

Shade you said that would be Delaware and its lights you're looking at.

Can't be anything else but Delaware he said. And what I'm thinking was he said was we were trying to move a mountain with a spoon. And we're on the wrong end of it. The wrong end of things fuck it you know that's where we are — but wait — maybe we're second guessing it — you know — I mean how the outcome is — and second guessing you know was like falling off a bicycle.

Shade you said we are not second-guessing anything together. But were you thinking about moving a mountain or falling off a bicycle?

I know he said but I could have a city block of bicycles stolen in less than an hour. The money's not great but you unload them fast. And I'm seeing it. We're about to die and I'm seeing it.

You looked at Shade and looking at Shade made you feel pointless and heavy-lidded. You wanted an answer. However reasonable — or not — or however brief or not — but whatever he said to you it had to stand on its own.

Hey Shade you free tonight — thus far. Now that you're living the dream and getting paid and living in the condo upstairs —

None of that is so Shade said. The dreams I live in are wastelands. The only time I get paid was when somebody threatens me. And the condo upstairs — you know you're bullshitting. You keep fucking with me. But who the fuck are you?

You told Shade you really didn't know.

Fucking great. You're my job. And you don't even fucking know who the fuck you are! So are you insane or some shit?

Shade handed you what was left from a burning joint.

There's a lot we can do he said — fingering the air before his face. Are you worried? I mean worried? What I'm seeing here was business. We have what they want. We need to get by for sure... but we sell what you got and invest that...

Maybe clarity was one thing... and talk was a personal bag of wind and emotions were revenge by design... and Shade was high and getting a sloppy heart... where the weeds run wild in parking lots ...and bedside alarms go off when you don't know what they're for... Maybe it was his eyes... greasy thin eyes that weren't right like runny undercooked egg yokes and how they shook on a stack of pancakes like embryos ... Shade's eyes were underdeveloped and off plumb to the rest of his head... runny fucking egg yokes but they were his infinities and his eye-balls and how he viewed time... tattoos without a place to rest...

This is business he said throwing the last of his cigar into the sand.

I know you think much of the market has slipped over to the designer drugs you and your hombres have found so — what's the word I'm after here — performance driven — that's fucking close enough. Well think again gland head — marijuana will continue to be a steady performer because you know- — bottom line — despite whatever anyone does to rip their brains apart — smoking a joint along the line- that will always be there to expand the whatever factor in those ripped-up brains. And this is where it's thinking forward. I'll rattle off a few things — disposable incomes- age quotas — lifestyle interest — trends in newcar sales — this is a database I have. These are numbers I have. And the numbers pay out. Shit man in eighteen months we break even and then the shit takes care of itself and starts paying off fucking dividends in two years max. It's the hopes it's the dreams it's the opinions they have — that we are about to exploit. And what I have was the raw stuff and that's what our fucking understanding is about to be about.

Listen up mister ex-priest you said — there was no way this side of hell that you were putting money in Bobby Alfredo's pockets

Listen you said. One evening the phone rang. So let's back up. Let's tell something across a flashback in time.

We don't have time for time Shade answered.

Then start swimming you said.

Not before we set this straight.

Then we back up. Which backing up in order to examine the problem — that namely appears to be consistent enough to apply to the second law of thermodynamics — whether processes do or do not occur in nature.

Fuck you he said. We are running out of time.

It might also be categorized as a generalization of experience.

*

I see expansion Shade said.

Be ready to have them call you a liar.

Want a drink Shade asked?

You took a pull from the flask he offered. It was never the good stuff with Shade. Always bottom shelf — that was Shade's act — that was how he got to be left alone and not bothered with. Who drinks with a crooked Detective with absolutely lousy taste in alcohol?

In the newspaper this morning you said there was a classified thanking Saint Jude for all his help. Isn't that funny? Don't you think so? Who would have thought a spirit fished through the want ads? One evening Shade the phone rang you said and a voice at the other end — altered and digital — said come walking by the West Branch Hotel. The voice said come walking by after last call at the 20ᵗʰ Century. There wasn't anything to do the voice said — there wasn't anything to pick up…Just walk past at a certain hour…

I am trying to stay alive here Shade said. Was that too much to ask for?

But hear this: There are census figures — analysis — Jersey-land census figures — they're reading messages and dodging shadows from the economy and driving about in expensive cars they believe they can afford — fucking franchise wannabees — fucking fragments — and what's epiphany about this set was their belief in speed and efficiency.

They want the sky pulled right up to the dooryard so they can walk on clouds. But they will settle for quality reefer and a big screen television as a side.

You sell appliances now you asked Shade?

Do not go fucking idiot on me. Not right now. We are going to be outlived. What we have now was an opportunity.

What about the phone Shade?

Inconvenient- even sad- and really he said — did it break your soul?

Souls don't break you said. Hearts break. Glass breaks. Souls were like sheets of rubber. They get twisted and warped by the time the shit that happens bends them around points of view. But they don't break. And yea the phone call laid me out.

That wasn't my fault Shade said. That was a consequence. One of many that happens when you make choices. You were convenient — just around the block as they say. And stop looking at me like that. You were perfect. Have you ever been perfect before?

Warm August rains fell on the bay water. You thought this sight was especially kind to watch — like a certainty of kinds — drifting into the light of a moon itself falling among the drifting clouds. Rainwater falling lightly in the late hours — another day added volume to sea levels come and gone.

Wild indigestible berry vines threaded themselves among low woody thickets — crawling through branches and advancing and reaching for something to entwine with. Some of the vines spilled out of the trees into the air and were now drooping and growing back downward towards the sand where they came from.

*

Shade sat against the dune — texting into his phone like some rocket kid absorbed into the marvels of a two-inch screen.

What actually happened you thought — now that you were looking at it — now that you could not get away from it — now that you having a drink at the sight of the new Ocean Heights Community: what happened was: hallucinatory development hit the neighborhoods and ripped out poverty — but that was done only with money interests in mind and as consequence bone-knifed perfectly good neighborhoods into death.

Enter Bobby Alfredo and Shade.

All along the shorelines Jersey-land neighborhoods were gang-planked out of existence. Mad cash rushed in and anted up against that first dollar that started the whole fucking mess going. Good luck on that one.

Think about the total genius of the species — the set of gravy train brains — the dull episodic ones — they who built a hotel a hundred yards into the ocean. And then figure what's the big deal: they're just waves. You think nobody saw that one coming? You think it was just coincidence? When one night the cold deep swells of the Atlantic kicked up like bastards and rode the wind into the Top Crest Mall and tore so many holes in the thing it had no structure left and two days later it fell over on its own and was gone down to the sea in legend.

What happens? When all the places to live disappear and were replaced and there are no homes left? And there was nothing left except butt-ugly rooms to rent in a casino.

Fucking rain Shade said.

It's not going to kill you.

There's an umbrella in the car he said. Go get that.

What you said?

Look he said I am not going to say please.

Let's get out of here then —

No he said. I like it here. And if I'm staying here then you are staying here. I need to finish this.

Let me guess you said. Whoever you talking to I'll bet they are not concerned with the heat death of the universe. And frankly that's an agreeable point. When time will be still was still a long way off. And shouldn't that make us happy? Picture when the curves of negative space-time begin to tighten. Don't you want to go out and do the things you enjoy because the biography of the universe will be repeated in reverse? Is it too much to say don't make a mistake because you will then have to watch re-runs of your own damn folly? The solar system was dying anyway. Expansion ultimately threatens something in its path. Isn't that who you're talking to Shade? Snap crackle and pop here. The shooter's not important. The shooter's never important. It's the wreckage what matters.

The meaning behind the shooter has long since been removed as a point of interest.

She shot you didn't she Shade?

She took your gun and shot you and then took the car.

Who were you working for then?

She shot the guy in the front too. Killed him. And that was no funny business either.

But you're a fucking liar Shade said. Go get the fucking umbrella!

You can't have what you won't get Shade.

It doesn't matter who I worked for then. Everyone's interest was mutual — and poisonous. So what.

But why Eden Jones you said.

That's easy Shade said: Blind Charlie. You know how people want to move up the ladder and all that shit. And so he was old. And the various mutual interests — and remember — they wanted him out of the way. And so he was old. But well protected in his pizza shop…and so was the girl but… these things end and what am I supposed to do about them… get involved? Hell no. I get paid and that's the story on that.

Shade you asked — why are we here? What's up with tonight?

My guess is there were scores to settle. That's how it normally happens. Look she had to be there. And you had to see her. Blind Charlie would believe you: that you saw his granddaughter. Even the same granddaughter you were fucking. Speaking realistically my thoughts on the matter were the parts involved outdid any possible sum. That's why that car stopped at your feet you asshole.

Right you said. It just does not matter you said.

What does it matter Shade asked? I will tell you what mattered you shit for brains. You looked into a car window. You saw someone. Someone who meant something to you that was who you saw. Were you looking at love? Because it's connected to more than business and you knew that once you saw someone through a car window. But you already know that. It's late at night and the phone rings — what fucking crap was that. But then the gun goes off. And you don't have the time to decide what love means.

Okay you said. But where does the car go… follow me… you're shot and dumped out the side onto the pavement — like a sack — you're nobody now Shade and you're leaking and worried... and you got a few bullets in your left shoulder and the number one guy riding shotgun was dead... so where does the car go Shade... how does the car drive... how does the car get away...

You are fucking crazy Shade said.

Should we have her shoot you again?

I don't give a ripe fuck about that girl. Just because she moves around a lot — well maybe even if she was afraid — but you add it all up... she always comes back. Was that love — or what?

How does the car get away Shade?

*

You have what I need and I want it.

One night the phone rang and that was what it took.

Listen you asshole this was not a bargain between you and me. And you think this was funny.

Everything's funny. Look at you. What is it? What do you have now?

*

Shade's phone rang — its ring tone like some low bit of organ music inside a digital sanctuary. He walked down to the shoreline with the phone stuck shoulder to ear while drinking from his flask.

A mess like this will never be over you said.

And then you thought: what if Shade was right. Did you really care about dying? Why be so hasty with principles anyway? Limitations — you had them — that was obvious.

Without them being there in the first place would you even have a place to begin?

What did happen to those cyanide pills we were given back in high school? One day these phantom oblong pills — like gossip — material-ized one day — along with the other lunch memos and the soda rations and the twice-failed beef that passed from school to school and came resting in a creamed glue-like sauce. The pills were the latest incarnation after the duck and cover drills from back in grade school. Just in case the other worlds attacked with rockets and troops — once you took the pill you had the disconnected opinion to do nothing but watch the wasteland unfold and be spared any further trouble.

The official position — and never quite spelled out — why survive — didn't seem like advice anybody rushed toward. When other worlds attacked — the official position was all about liability and fraud and who paid for the damage later on.

Why survive? Get out of the way… It seemed like that should be a damn good question to be knocked around — except it wasn't. Some tribal guys took the pill just to make sure it worked.

Eden Jones said afterward — by the old hollow maple tree in the cemetery night where she lived as a pretend kid: this was no time to go sober.

But where was she?

Driving somewhere.

There was all stuff you had to sort through. And you hadn't done it yet. And with it not being done all by your lonesome you tried to hold down the fort and keep Shade and Bobby Alfredo away.

But what do you do with it?

All this stuff will kill you — that's what Blind Charlie said.

Shade was down by the water still talking into his phone and for what you knew he was plotting our deaths while he dipped into the last envelope.

You imagined your life was a personal cosmology of sorts — the perfect step whenever you needed one — outside the herd — outside ambiguity and force — a simple life to be carried along and dissolve being. A lot of what you noticed went unseen anyway.

Time clogs. Time stabbed the dark. There was this stuff and what to do with it — and what it does — what builds on itself and goes haywire and does exactly the opposite from what you first imagined.

Of course you had it.

Everyone knows you have it.

Leaning back against the dune — looking for Shade — taking in the envelope and digging the August air — like sitting beside a grainy television set and watching the moonwalk while some announcer explained the math behind it all — you waited for a feeling to overtake you — an agent to sort out the monkey business.

Maybe love mattered.

Maybe worrying about the earth's rotation mattered too.

The great need presently was to gather the problems together and pull in the transmissions in your head. Shade was unable to zip his fly at this time of night. But Bobby Alfredo was prepared to blow you off the planet. What was more troublesome to distance yourself from? There was always something to lose and always a losing end to grab onto.

But the great need presently was not to lose sight and wait for that feeling to come like an old soul record.

*

Why die unnecessarily? At the end of the day all you really wanted was to go home and sleep in your own bed. Why was it you were the fool here? Shade didn't know anything. And Bobby Alfredo knew even less because he was nothing more than a genuine prick — obligated by blood to have a seat at the table — but the trouble was he wasn't satisfied with his share of the take. And that made him crazy with money he didn't own. Bobby Alfredo was out of control.

And for Blind Charlie — control — that intellectual chill — that spiritual bravado in dangerous times — Blind Charlie loved watching The Man from U.N.C.L.E. on television on Tuesday nights — control was the most obvious reason for staying alive.

And you were the fool because you knew what they wanted. Truth gets told in a questionable way: it's not a great reference point to be the fool.

But there was something that Shade said. And you might as well be dammed if you remembered what it was…

You walked past the West Branch Hotel like you were told to do — and there was the car like you were told it would be there and there was Eden Jones in the back seat looking at you like you hoped she would — and for the next few minutes while you stood between the Kimono Party Shop and a cafeteria style bakery at the corner of Old Court and

471

the brick alley — you didn't know who was firing or whether you should duck or not or play it out and see if you were oddly harmonious and quiet with the sudden gunshots in the car.

Maybe you were a murder witness? If so then that was the wrong line of work to be in. But maybe you jumped the gun here. Who said anybody was dead? And if nobody was dead then it was just some gunfire. And it seemed hard to pick out details following gunfire. There was a plan rolling and its momentum caught you. But shit like this always gets personal and that's why people die. And why we suffer in limited areas... we were the goods... the cache... headache personalities — freaks of nature... we knew there was a future. And seeing that car drive off that was exactly why you were dragged behind.

*

You called after Shade and said hey but that wasn't any use. He was talking on the phone in the rain with the tide slapping on his shoes.

*

All this stuff — what was the reason — why the need to sort through it was beyond you. Who the fuck knows? That's what they said at the 20th Century Club. Who the fuck knows...

*

Un-faced drug dealers in masks used your apartment like a convenience store. They showed up in posse and you left. An hour later a month's rent was on the table in a circumstance that never really happened. Plus they left a little behind and tightened you up.

Plus you liked some woman at the clinic.

At work the other day you were almost killed. The scaffold toppled over and went crashing down into the pews and you were spilled out against the Saint Jerome kiosk and knocked over candles and rattled the money- box. And then whoa — you got to the clinic with bruises and

472

cuts that need mending and there's a gal who sewed you up and you said tomorrow you would paint her onto the ceiling of St. Anthony's Church where you worked plus you said to her let's get out of here. You knew the best spot in the dunes to spend eternity. And you knew the pizza guy and he would deliver a pie for us while we sat and watched the tides.

Then there's the guy who lives below you on the second floor with his get-laid shirts and troll hair-do and who worked twenty miles inland at the sport's complex on Route 9 at exit 4A and who wrote these pornographic stories with the word steroid in each title and each day if you saw him he rushed after you and handed you a fistful of stories and wanted you to edit them.

All this stuff- but what use was power if you weren't any good with power.

*

Walking home you ran into the spray paint kids. They owed you a favor and they owed Eden Jones a favor and they owed Mantis a favor. You explained the problem. You needed some negative publicity on somebody else. For sure they said: truth don't take sides. You wanted a couple names tagged high enough for the public to view. What names they said. When you told them who it was they said no: they needed more money they said for those heads.

*

And do you know what I was just told Shade said pointing to his phone.

That we all talk to ghosts you said.

Look Shade said. Earlier tonight I picked up the phone. Was it too much to ask but are you still with me so far? Here's the point — I got no answer. What I got was a mechanical voice that said: hold the phone. It was like voice mail shit but only it was directed back at me. Then there was a click and then I got another voice. And that voice has followed me ever since — all night long or some fucking shit it calls me.

What does it say you said.

The voice said: what was happening: how was it going: did you have

473

it: did you know where it was: could you get it: why not: what's happening: are you responsible or not: will you deliver...

Shade you said it was obvious — in a world with constant entropy there was no change and thus life was impossible. And that's where we're living.

There were better ways to live he said.

And better ways to die Shade you said. Call off the dogs and buy us some time.

Sure he said. And how much time would you like? Maybe tonight? Maybe tomorrow?

No. Now you look Detective Shade. Eden Jones shot you in the car while she was in your custody. So tell me: why do you have a second chance?

Listen asshole: Bobby Alfredo wants the pizza shop. But there seems to be a technical glitch — he can't find out who really owns it — the legal papers are like lost and nobody knows where they went. And nobody can locate Blind Charlie's will. Nobody's found Blind Charlie's attorney. Ever since Blind Charlie died it's been like Blind Charlie vanished. But if you're dead Shade said — I guess the pain was there.

Shit he said I need to take this.

Shade walked away onto the shadows of the moon — a light rain fell on the sand — talking rapidly into his phone — pacing his sad ass through old seaweed lines and dead horseshoe crabs by the thousands.

Delaware night-lights across the bay shrunk and rose on the tide like artificial stars broken in time as they crested up and then waved back down.

What Shade wanted was understandable. But it was also impossible. And given the conditions that we faced that was also a problem.

*

Shit — you needed to think about it in some way that got you. But — what way? Do you just pick one out of the air and go with that? Funny — but the template that came to mind was from back in the day — back when you ran those scripts. You got them from some ship -wreck in the mud flats out in the scratch lands called Dr. Vest Hunter.

The first time you met him all you needed to say was I got pain and you got a script.

And then after that — boom- some brute force in the earth's neurons fired and you had pages and pages of legal drugs in your hands for twenty bucks. Bonanza. What's My Line. The Late Show. That's how it all felt. You made enough money to get high and buy a television.

Remember: going to the Nice Drug Company and handing the guy behind the counter prescriptions by the fistful all neatly folded in half like test papers. He was a baldy boney-nose apothecary man who looked like your father and like your dad there clearly wasn't any need to say much to him. It was the simplest transaction to imagine. Money went into his hands. Small 3x5 papers filled your hands. And for each script you paid five dollars for — on the boardwalk they went for thirty-five. You were alive in the culture working the free market through the eyes of the losers and tied with ancient commerce all at once. There were no barriers to deal with if you had cash the right amount of paper and then humanity rocked. And for as long as you had goods then there was a shine between you and other people. And that was the best. A kind of wavelength carried everyone along.

The question of the day was: get stoned or worry?

There were bankers hours and restaurant hours and bus schedule hours and heroin hours and nine to five hours for millions of people and hours that brought inspiration to a few and there were cop hours and hospital hours and subway hours that never ended and there were playground hours with the kids and hero hours and trashcan hours piled along the curb and serious hours when there were no other hours and down by the water hours and be-bop hip-hop hours after hours and dreary stoplight hours and cafeteria hours after the fabulous hours after a party and restricted hours the following day when you had to wake up and hours you could not face dragging on for sixty-one minutes.

It was a laugh to suggest everybody wanted something.

There was a large picture out there. We could fit into the sky. And it doesn't have much to do with our identities. Sky was wonderful. Sky made nobody unique.

But what happens when a day's troubles go into a hole and everyone falls all over each other and what do you do about the fucking thing because it's crashing down? Just yesterday a stranger shot a stranger on the

K-bus and so now what — there's one less stranger on the bus?

It's an old song.

And the further we got out in time — and this was necessary — to go out in time was necessary... What happens if eternity was a failure... the further we got out in time then our dull criminal transcendence might continually scare you shitless on the way out but further out in time we might drift along with the night and not compete with it.

For every script you sold you also kept one in the rear for personal use.

Remember: hanging around in the parking lot outside the pharmacy and leaning back on anybody's car and expecting the pills to flower and when they did your nerve endings grew less dense and you stood in place on the asphalt and felt like an architecture.

Up high on a cracked wall above the parking lot was faded sign lettering in lead white on hard red brick: Nice Drug Pharmacy — Orthopedic Shoes — Old Age Walkers — Artificial limbs — Real Vanilla Sodas-Your Needs Served Since 1909...

You weren't giving Shade anything.

And Bobby Alfredo got even less.

*

One evening the phone rang you said to Shade as he sat down against the dune.. So tell me about it.

That was the best deal I could make he said. What the fuck do you want from me?

You didn't know and you told him that. But you had suspicions and so you asked him how was it that you didn't die that night in the car Shade?

Because your bitch was a lousy shot he said.

No you said. She shot you in the shoulder when she could have shot you in the head. And what you need to figure out was whether she chose to do that or whether she was told to do that. Shade — you got two different points of view playing you.

And all you're doing is talking on your phone.

Listen shithead that was a murder that night and you saw it.

You told Shade you saw bright flashes in a car window that night.

You told Shade it was always too late to never see anything.

You told Shade go to hell.

Perfect he said.

Shade — was it your idea?

Yea he said it was.

But your idea didn't work you said. Any why was that? Why did you live and the guy in the front died? Why did the car get away — if this was your idea — so why were you dumped?

Because somebody bought past me Shade said.

No you said. That wasn't it. You were sandbagged Shade. There was no money spent on you by anybody. You were only supposed to get shot once — like a warning that this was business you couldn't handle. But you slapped Eden Jones in the face and that was a very wrong move on your part. Hence you got shot twice more. Same shoulder. Three bullet holes one after another with some burn time in between — how does that shit feel tonight? Are you embarrassed: number one — that a woman shot you: and number two- a woman spared your life. Shade — how do you act?

There was money Shade said. That's how I act you asshole. And you should know I keep revenge close to heart.

Just like a page from the old testament you said.

Some things are true and some things are certain and some things never see daylight.

Nice line Shade you said but at this point you can't cover anything. You believe you're going to die tonight. What do you plan on doing? Shoot me?

No Shade said I can't shoot you. Because you have what I fucking need!

I told you before Shade. It's not yours to have. And it's not Bobby Alfredo's business either. What I got — what I have — I took from a dead man and he was the original source.

All you had to do was babysit the thing Shade said. You let time play out and then you collect some fucking winnings when you deal it back in. First you're an idiot and now you're a fucking hero? No way man — you are dead — like me. Give up what you have. It's that simple. And we both buy time.

Shade: here's a simple question — do you trust Bobby Alfredo?

No I don't he said. But I'm paid to think otherwise.

For sure you said. What good did the truth ever do?

*

Listen he said this is not something I dreamed up. It's a fucking natural fact. Everything fails in the long run. And what you have taken was like a side step around the long run. Fuck you.

All you had to do for a couple years was to keep your mouth shut. Was that so fucking difficult?

And yes it was you told Shade.

As ever Shade looked like he was only capable to think low reptilian thoughts from the old center in his head- and try and flash wise off a pre-analogue pattern that always thought it was going to die.

Time was running out you said. How do you blow up time Shade? What do you do? You told him you didn't see him as a guy who ran away. But what was he hanging around for? What were you trying to do Shade? At some level you thought you had it figured. Wasn't that it? And then you try and run around Bobby Alfredo but that was going to take some quick doing. How did you feel Shade — what went through you head except what you couldn't believe what you saw — what happened Shade when you looked into that locker at the bus station and saw nothing inside? Who has you Shade?

Yea how so he said taking a drink.

Shade you need to think clear.

Well maybe for now I go into hiding. Maybe I spend the rest of my life on the run. Maybe I do nothing because there's nothing left. Maybe you think you're just some act that's been had and that was the story on that. And so one day once the breakfast carts went past on 8th Street — on the fucking morning show of the universe so to speak — with the cheap coffee from the Philly mobs and the sandwich wraps from the Turkish guy and the mango and avocado sellers from no country of origin but faced extermination if they were discovered — there was a loneliness planted around my feet like wet cement. Ever felt that? Fuck it. Feelings were like silver bullets in the movies anyway. They kill things otherwise on a roll.

Shade stared back at you. He reached in his coat pocket and pulled out his phone. He took another drink and handed you the flask.

And that's what fucks me up — I can't figure it.

Who knew? It wasn't my first option. I had no idea it was there.

But you took it he said. And that fucks me up. Because I don't have it and I'm supposed to kill you tonight. But I can't kill you! Oh I would kill you a dozen times over he said. But I need what you have.

But I don't need you Shade. You're not protecting me. All night long you're on your phone — what happens? You get told the same old shit: Shade you fucked up.

We're the human ones Shade — full of grace and so bonded to what we do.

Yea like how valuable Shade said. Give me a number you want and I can make that number work miracles.

And was that what you been doing all night on the phone?

No he said I was with some guy in tech-ville and was trying to have him bounce my GPS.

Turn off the phone you said.

Can't do that you asshole. Any number in that speed dial might be salvation.

Shade and his slow and benumbed eyes watched over the bay hunched up with his arms wrapped around his knees. Raindrops fell but they were unreliable. Raindrops fell but Shade never saw them. Raindrops fell on Jersey-land through centuries of sky through the evening but they were phenomenology and not the truth behind them.

Shade you asked you gone to the fishes yet?

He looked back at you — mostly he looked passed you — and took out a slim metal case from inside his coat. Shade's clothes were like a second hand skin — rumple and dirty looking — like car fumes or pigeon shit — and always slept in wherever he fell over for the night and crashed.

But his needle and spoon were another story. Clean and no guess work. Almost sacramental might be another way to put it. He picked out a bag of junk and got himself ready.

*

What I see was expansion he said. Back in the day people came here because they needed to avoid something else in the past that was catching up to them — like military conscription — political stuff — debts and criminal offenses — maybe they were even looking for a decent god... and we're the descendants from those fucking colonial assholes and when they got here — right here where we're now sitting — and what they found was like super abundant — fresh water...proper harbor land...woods and fields... good fishing... the whole fucking richness — check this out an unspoiled world — holy fucking glory — and in the unspoiled unbidden landscape they saw the word reflected back at them and that word was: cash. We're only in it for the money.

And that's why we're here.

Fuck Shade said they hunt you down and what then?

They won't do that. Besides they want me alive.

That's not how I hear it Shade said. Doesn't matter if you're alive or not and it doesn't matter if the girl is alive or not.

Then why are we here Shade? Can't bring yourself to killing me? Was that it?

Everybody talks to themselves Shade said.

I had a cousin once Shade said. The court papers filed on his behalf said he was a retarded farm boy with no personal history and unable to manage his own person or his own affairs. The state as it was seized him and he was packed off to the back wings of a hospital where the staff kept the book keeping records and the moon howlers.

What happened? If he were your cousin how come he had no personal history?

He wasn't that much of a cousin Shade said.

One night he walked away from the hospital. He made a camp for himself where exit 23 would be years later. At the time he could fish and grow vegetables and whistle because that's what he liked to do. One night a trooper shows up. You can't sleep here the trooper says. Why not my cousin asks? Just be gone in the morning the trooper says. You're a vagrant. What's that my cousin wanted to know? The trooper hit him across the head with a flashlight and told my cousin he should be grateful — because that's all he got and also he gets to leave.

How do you know this Shade? If he wasn't much of a cousin...

The fucking trooper works for me now Shade said. And he works for other people.

And I work for other people. And there are rules of behavior... and when that goes contrary you fracture the rules –

Yea you said. Shade wound himself out onto an endless philosophical current and got high. You want me out first thing in the morning. But that can't happen Shade. There's too much here — to just to pack up and then forget about it like there wasn't anything there to begin with.

There was no finding mercy with you was there he said.

Yea right you said. You kidnap Eden Jones and expect me to say thanks for the memories.

Well Shade said maybe the worst thing was we have was a memory.

Well Shade you said then I'm a refugee. One of your own- escaping from something holding a person back and looking at the bright land to get paid — you said it yourself — we're descendants.

And what do you get paid for Shade said — because you're in love with the girl and she's worth something? You want to get paid for fucking love? You want to get paid for that? Who do you think you fucking are?

Maybe you said. Maybe Bobby Alfredo gets his pizza shop. Maybe the money comes back. Maybe I own this development.

Fuck me Shade said.

Shade you said why be cautious when you're dead already?

I need to do this he said.

Of course you do you said. But right now Shade you're just a bit of information on a chip. There are natty sunglass types in fortified cars controlling your life and dealing every moment of your existence out into a market. How do you expect a return on that?

Simple he said rocking his spoon back and forth.

How so you asked?

I need to do this he said.

Oh right you said. What you need is some privacy now — some getting away time so you can relax and put the long day that was today behind you. You probably want to forget. You want to forget that Jersey-land — once a small city of hopes on the expanding seaboard of dreams — that Jersey-land Shade — where we're both from — where so many others came and had to make a difference because they were dead back in the old homeland — that Jersey-land Shade — has run its course and was out of time and was never real in the first place.

You never did like history he said.

Fuck you he said. Money built everything here. Money reclaims everything. And money was the ticket out of this shit. Stop and think for a moment. There are benefits here ...

*

And with that Shade was gone for a while and was lost in what he got out of a spoon.

Small waves from the bay flopped against the pebbles at shoreline.

He looked sad — like the sand around him was his casket and that was going to hold him together through death and burial. And who knows what else he had in that fuck-up head of his beyond his money trouble and beyond his sorrow. His rumpled ass suit looked presentable in the shadows of the cloudy moonlight as if this were a dress rehearsal for the real thing.

*

Maybe there was nothing worse than to have a memory.

A place where everything got caught up caught in its own backwash and rather than letting the past churn you into its own endless stream — you decide to take on the world.

But the question was: did it matter?

Would you fall over if you didn't remember things?

And where would the days go? Do they return like future theoretical experiences?

*

Maybe like she said: I want to be anonymous and see things for the first time.

Maybe there was nothing left to plumb?

Maybe it didn't matter but you doubt it. August birds were singing against the noisy gulls when she drove up to the party in a small brown automobile and wearing a white blouse that would never be mistaken for a funeral garment in a dozen lifetimes.

I'll be the beautiful stranger you said.

And I just got into town she said.

Hard to say really — but this did seem to demonstrate the absurdity that there were people willing to kill you on consignment.

*

Shade you said kicking him in the left knee. Did you ever wonder why the same products keep reappearing night after night on television? Have you ever questioned why suddenly everything has the same value? That's expansion Shade. All those overnight millionaires centuries ago — they made Jersey-land Shade — evolution's moneymakers let loose in the new world — engaged in a fantastic struggle against nature — where's my god and where's my money Shade — fuck it man all the miracles you talk about and all the success you want adds up to a hypnosis — we're bit players sent over from central casting.

What if this were the last night on earth for us Shade?

Shade was skyward and blanked on the Milky Way — nodded out in a sorry dent on some near extinct beach grass. It made you laugh. They were both settled in places that somebody else always stepped on.

You looked around and felt immediately stupid — a fog passed over you — the rain turned up and made the only sound you heard — why were you waiting at the end of an old beach road was a puzzle you couldn't figure. Nobody around for miles — nothing around but ocean and a gnarly tick-infested Jersey-land wood — it was like you were shipwrecked — drifting in open water — washed up on the beach — questioning the surroundings with a slim though rational clue that you were better off here than being out there — essentially stranded until you came up with a better plan.

483

And what about you Shade What do we do with you this time?

You kicked him in the knee again. What did it matter to him?

Shade lived on pain-killing medications. Conditions like his psychotic selfie that indeed he was the golden mean — the tattoo on his back from Ecclesiastes 7:18: who ever fears god will avoid all extremes — summed it up — and his blaze for young girls summed it up also and together they banged his skull into daily headaches and complaints with each other and so he replaced them with transcendence from momentary existence and a sleeping agent unaffected clear and homely and injected.

Shade's optic circus was still doing cartwheels in the Milky Way. His golden mean only turned up the volume on the comatose. You reached into his shoulder harness and took his gun. He had two other guns — one in the back of his pants and the other one in a left ankle holster. No big deal when he wakes up alone and broken again.

Then Shade's phone rang. You took it out of his coat pocket while he was still in the Milky Way. You needed a pass code. You took a guess and typed in — fuck you — and the phone opened.

How do we know Moses didn't lie you asked the phone? Maybe it was his job to lie. So maybe Moses punched his own ticket. Who else was around to say otherwise? And that's what you get when you go alone on the mountain — basic facts balance out. And down below there's a mob waiting to believe something because they're lost and hung out to dry by Moses by god by the whole operational schematic. So maybe Moses walks down off the mountain like this chilled cobalt sunglasses type. He's a visionary ensemble of cosmic speeds wrapped in a tinker's rags and he's got these two stones with language carved in each stone. Yo he says: just got these from god. The crowd goes wild and promises Moses gravy for the rest of his life if they can just see those stones. But what if Moses wrote those stones. And from now on Moses was god's sole rep on the planet. That would change everything.

Shade's phone said it did not care about Moses or who told the truth. Shade's phone said if it had to then it would shoot Moses. Steal the tablets. Shoot god. And not think about it.

Not the sentimental type then you said.

Not really Shade's phone said.

But what if we're in the good you asked?

Not my problem Shade's phone said.

What needs to happen? To avoid all this now — and to avoid it in the future —

Kill Shade tonight Shade's phone said.

What does that do?

It make ssome people laugh Shade's phone said.

After Shade was gone — then what happens?

There are people who do not like you Shade's phone said.

But what does killing Shade solve?

Not much Shade's phone said.

You explained to Shade's phone there were ten reasons each day to kill Shade but today you were lost to find even one reason. Didn't seem to be in the stars you said. Not a viable option you explained.

And you're running out of those the phone said.

Tell me you asked Shade's phone what's your take?

Shade's phone laughed. You almost didn't hear it but it was there on the other end of our electronic life. It was a laugh some alien would use. We want what Shade wants the phone said. Shade's phone said what do you have to offer me? And remember — you have to parlay this far enough to be effective. Do you understand that? No juvenile shit... no fast ones... no lies...so let's deal.

What's in it for me you asked the phone?

You get to live Shade's phone said. And that's all.

Then I lose everything.

What's your life worth?

You told Shade's phone no way. If you kill me then you never find it.

You're right Shade's phone said. Killing you brings us no good. However when we pull all your fucking teeth out of your fucking mouth — that's a start.

What do you want?

First off Shade needs to go. And second — as I've said — you are a thorn. You irritate people.

No you said what is it you want?

You have no answer for that the phone said.

Maybe you said — just to pass the time of night — you'd like to hear what I have to say. When you get done with all the Shades in the world — what do you want? Where's that big exit sign you always see in the movie theaters — where does that sign happen for you? Where does the assassin go at the end of the day when he's done working? What goes on when business was over and you were out?

Shade's phone laughed again.

Do you have any idea how expensive it is to live outside the neighborhoods? I want a place — just some place away from the fucking boardwalk and the Ferris wheel — without as much confusion too– without anxious smiles on the guys you can't trust and big hair on the girls you can't bed — fuck man I just want a place to go to where nothing much happens... but wait — hold that and let's say there's a stream nearby and maybe I take up fly fishing and leave behind the shooting people in the head business.

What if you said to the phone that you just might have property that suited what the phone wanted.

Careful the phone said. I might be your killer.

You couldn't kill Shade. That's what you told the phone.

It's not that hard the phone said. I could offer you a few suggestions...

Problem was you said Shade might have done you the favor. He's out cold as space on his end.

Shoot him anyway Shade's phone said. It's more professional that way.

What if I help you get out of the neighborhoods? Information was always handy. And cash was forever useful. And you told the phone you had plenty of both. If he wanted to keep working you could help with that. You had a place on Ben's River — a small comfortable sack near the water. There were options to choose from you said to the phone.

And what's your take the phone said.

Amnesty. Both for you and Eden Jones — we want the hunt called off. And Shade gets to see the light of day also — assuming he hasn't overdosed.

That's a tall order to serve Shade's phone said. Shade's a fool or some fucking clown and his only use tonight was to make up some damn story and get you onto the beach tonight. The girl was tricky and more than likely her time came later.

486

Hear this you told Shade's phone: if you were killed — or if Shade was killed — then the phone was dead. She'll kill you in less than a week. If she had to drive three days in a row without sleeping — just to look you in the face — well brother that's the face of death looking back at you and she's ready to take your eyeballs right out of your head.

All this is fine the phone said. I'm going to hang up now.

Do we have a deal you asked?

We have a deal only with me. And that assumes you live up to your end and provide that information and that cash and that small though comfortable shack at Ben's River. There are other people who consider you a thorn and Shade a fool and the girl is a dangerous risk. I'm only speaking for me. And that means tonight I call off the hunt or some shit you said. Tomorrow some other spike-head was going to be after you.

What I'm saying you said to Shade's phone was that I need an ally in all this. You already put yourself up for hire and hired twice tonight already to competing bidders. You told the phone what you needed was a steady hand. And why didn't you kill us tonight? Why did you make that phone call?

Because the phone said: number one — it's easy to scare the balls off Shade — he hates to die. All you needed was to explain to him that you're going to shoot him later in the day and fuck man that sets off a bandwidth in his head that he fills with worry. It's fun to toy with him. And second the phone said: you and I were destined to have a conversation tonight. Shade was chum. You were the tuna.

Let me ask the phone said. How does it feel? People want what you have. They don't want what you know. And that makes you a thief. If I look after you there needs to be more on my plate.

What guarantees did you get you asked the phone?

Here's a deal maker: you keep Shade's phone and tomorrow morning I call you. And tomorrow afternoon I move into Ben's River. If you have what you say you have then I'm you're man. But if you're lying to save your ass tonight then brother the hunt's back on with a warp.

All this is fine the phone said. I'm going to hang up now.

What about tonight?

Just start walking on the beach back to town the phone said. Don't get in the car and drive. That's a mistake everybody makes. Do not get in the car and drive away because you do not know who's at the other end of the road. Do you understand?

Yes you said to the phone. You understood.

Fine the phone said. I call you tomorrow.

*

Shade you said: wake your sorry ass up. But he didn't move.

You kept the phone and his guns and went through his wallet and took the cash and the good plastic and cleaned out his dope.

A small illustrated rain left the sky in filigree and blew inland on the wind.

It didn't take a dime store Buddha mind to realize that what you thought you knew was now different from what it once was.

*

You had to walk away from this and hug the shore. It was the long way back home but it was a satisfactory night for a walk. Generally all nights were times to go walking. Especially on those nights when you missed out on being killed.

Maybe the things that happened in the world and to the world were like the aftershocks from earthquakes. Shade was wrong. Memory was worth it. Jumbled troubled effects — imaginary funny ratios — redundant attachments — sex friends family landscapes whatever it took to manufacture an individual you thought about it while walking home in a mist-like rain and the low bay waves slushed on the pebbles. The fishing boats were up soon and then sunrise wasn't far behind. When you got back to the neighborhoods you'd pop into the 20th Century Club by the rear door exit and once inside you could have all the mediations you wanted to have on a bar stool in the morning. And then order Jersey-land eggs and bacon from the practice farms out Rt. 29 and great thick toast with real bee honey the mad Syrian made special for breakfast — and you'd drink mindless drinks until you felt it good enough to bop till you drop and safe enough to go back to your apart-

488

ment. Or until Fast Eddie said go home because the bar didn't upon until afternoon.

*

But due to natural complexities — and despite doing up an envelope you took from Shade — and clinging to the first noble truth that all life was suffering and not limited to plain old ineptitude — the rain picked up and so you sat underneath a tree to let it pass — and suddenly the dope hit your brain like an artificial intelligence and you were as free as gaseous light and maybe that as a deliverance landed you in a state of human insignificance and all that — a wish fulfillment run amok.

Yea. You rolled back and looked out window fronts in your eyes on the cold green Atlantic. Cynicism used to be enough to see you through. Morning happened again — that was a good enough sign to get on with. Stars in multitudes began to vanish. A thin sleek line of light separated the horizon and took apart the nighttime. Satellites high in orbit above the atmosphere feed messages and shadows to your phone. The coolest blue color you ever imagined slowly gained heaven's speed from behind the ocean and a brand new sky formed over the Atlantic and spread across Jersey-land in minutes.

What to do about Da Vinci's pizza shop was a question you had to analyze for its faults. It was also a pain in the ass to deal with. Bobby Alfredo was out. That much was simple. But Bobby Alfredo making trouble was not so simple.

And what angle was Shade's phone working?

Empty purple clouds drifted out to sea on the twelve lanes of the sky. The morning's commute would soon knot things tight at the bridges and the tunnels. Consequently everyone in their cars started honking madly. Shade was wrong. There was eternity. No matter how late it was we still loved sad songs. Your distant thoughts brought wishful thinking but fucking A they went off like theme parks waiting for you to develop. And didn't it feel that your small thoughts were details that kept recurrent and tried to hold onto a place that was constantly getting lost.

489

Eden Jones was missing. You felt very sorry for the sad-assed wanna-be whoever Bobby Alfredo sent after her.

Rice colored sand and reddish brown seaweed held the shoreline wave after wave. Sky owned everything. Without sky what use was there for the sunlight? Otherwise we were a burnt land. Leaning back against a washed up tree that pressed back against your epidermal layers of feeling. The dune behind the tree staring to cover over the tree with a sand clumsy measure about how peace and quiet worked.

The tide was grabbing Shade's ankles by now.

Bobby Alfredo was thinking in Da Vinci pizza's back room.

Eden Jones worked her phones listening to Bobby Alfredo think in the back room.

You swam out into the ocean.

*

A cormorant flapping on the skim of the water trying to take off... A dark swim... Incoming tide... The horizon and the moon and all that... Breathing hard and all that ... Seemed like you were moving into yesterday... Swimming into yesterday... The same as swimming today...

*

Who wanted the worry?

And that's what Shade wanted. He wanted you to have the worry.

Last night he said essentially we employ people to survive the short run.

And as he nodded off after his sweet-ass injection — he asked for a plate of spaghetti with hot garlic bread and the holy wine of god. We were the gifted animals he said beginning to slur his words. Or so we were told. We were the ones who burned time in our campfires. Campfires of the dammed we were told. But what — when — made — Shade nervous we burned those campfires but if three were the number when by the time you reached and who perfected the tomato to acceptable today and who invented the electric guitar —

Of the heroin addicts you knew Shade was the most literate.

Meditations on a boardwalk bench: surf's up.

It was as if you were a voice a voicemail machine and were stuck on a broken recording loop. And then you'd have only a single message to hear: your own voice asking — one minute please. Can you hold?

Behind you — across Beach Avenue — between the summer cottages — vacant for the season — the spray paint kids fired eggs at you from their wrist rockets. This was another good sign. Must be that Bobby Alfredo didn't like seeing his name tagged to walls and buses and being called out. So what? He hired the spray-paint kids to kill you with eggs?

If you had a place to stand and enough cash to use then you could move Jersey-land around to your liking.

No eggs hit you.

Maybe it was how Frank's Playland by the Sea was such a flat utility rectangle. The kind of industrial hangover architecture passed down the line from a century ago that lived a minute behind itself and tried to capture a certain esprit de corps of the time: namely: the warehouse. Inside were pinball machines and bowl-a-mania lanes and jerk off photo booths and shoot-a-clown in the mouth stands and how it was all good and blind fun to have. But what killed you was the paint job on the outside and how crappy it looked.

Once upon a time Frank's was painted a glorious yellow orange color that no one had ever seen before. Try and picture saffron on acid. We mixed it ourselves. We used discards from people's garages. Anything anybody had that they didn't want that had lead or arsenic or chromium in it we took it and mixed it.

We made the stuff by the five gallon buckets. Eden Jones called the color we made medium little Asyu.

Frank's Playland by the Sea never looked as good as it did that summer we painted it.

Blind Charlie owned the building back then.... which meant that you owned it now.

You also owned Da Vinci pizza.

You owned the Beach Avenue Movie House and its collection of movie posters and small retro-seated aisles and an old popcorn machine and its bright neon marquee.

You owned the nearby miniature golf course with its huge Neptune head and a hideous high pitched recorded laugh on the ninth hole that played on cold war era speakers whenever somebody missed a shot.

You owned a takeout clam shack near the docks and vintage deep-fry baskets and long shoestring French fries served gondola style in long paper boats.

And when you sat near the ocean — didn't matter whether it was day night or any hallucination otherwise — inside a skeleton and born to scheme — inside the sky and made to dream — all the reasons and all the cash money to buy a moment's loneliness didn't match up with what you saw. It all really belonged to her.

*

@ chest heaves@boulevard of hips
@ wide marshy grasses
@ strange nocturnal water life
@rotting boardwalk piers
@smoking alone in the dark

*

Sitting at a booth inside the Dirty Clark Diner you drank three coffees — each one was more driven and tasteless than the next — ate a dozen pieces of cheap white toast with a tab of butter on each — read a comic — smoked a joint — tossed back a pill — and across 21st Street in a tree there were six crows hanging together on a limb and across the inside of the window pane there was a smear of white paint that the crows passed through irregularly when their branch moved in the wind.

But it was your money.

The titles to the properties belonged to you.

The dope was yours. Those select bricks collected over Blind Charlie's years… they were now worth a fortune here in the future.

And the recipe for the sauce at Da Vinci pizza — yea you owned that. And what about a slice? Wouldn't that taste good? Maybe get a whole pie and start fresh? A slice you might get off the top of the oven. And maybe it sat there for too many minutes and tasted that way. No. What you wanted was just a slice — a hot cheesy slice.

But it was too bad... the conditions we all found ourselves in today. There had to be a winner. You simply could not walk into Da Vinci pizza and feel the real stuff and the better smells and order a slice. No. A cousin working the ovens laughed at you and took your name. Soon you didn't have a slice.

There was a place at Pine & Wooster that did okay. Augustine Pie.

And it wouldn't be too much to walk around for a few more hours until you went home. Walking around Jersey-land with a slice... time to get out and live... no brakes on the turn and let's have an enthusiasm for impact... it was your money...it was a figure eight course you walked into and suddenly you were in the stands at a demolition derby and setting back beers and foul water dogs with total strangers. Like they were kinship and this was the final get together. Afterwards we were bound for the heavens beyond the tremendous car crashes and old v-8 metal exploded and separated from fenders and car hoods hung rusted and crude and was applauded righteously in the stadium lights and you yelled along with your new cousins and we traded dope and it was like we were all out on the night in the ancestor tree.

Afterwards the beer let you down. When the subway hit Broad & Olney it was five after midnight.

*

You read a Green Lantern comic yesterday... she didn't want the money... it was just a conversation to have... aka a mnemonic street corner.... where her grandfather went down.... where you took a bullet and then wept over Blind Charlie the ground and dead... five good cousins were also down.

Damn a slice would taste good. Augustine closed at midnight. That left boardwalk pizza. That was enough to make you worry. And those

493

were nothing more than reheated plugs... those slices... artificial cheese and a red paste that tasted like car enamel.

It was still there and it was still here. When we were younger we traded beautiful suspicions about the world with each other.

Wasn't the perfect object a slice: born from hunger and desire and neon greetings.

You walked past Augustine just in case.

You thought you might have a chance with the pizza waitress at Augustine. No luck though. They were closed.

Why was it so much to want a place where the air opened up around you?

And if you had a slice and if it folded a lousy paper plate in half with grease heat and smells then you held a decent slice in your hand. . That slice carried weight.

But not tonight — Augustine was indeed closed. Nope — not tonight ...

But when you thought about it — maybe you did stay in the neighborhood forever.

Not to fix windows or to deliver pizza boxes — but to make pizza... send out pizza for delivery with new kids running the errand. Pizza was so on everyone's radar that a slice overtook apple pie as an American food.

Whoever owned Da Vinci pizza — you also owned the back room... whoever owned the pizza shop you also inherited Blind Charlie' tombstone — and with that you got to answer the question whether or not you would follow that up and bring hell with you.

You knew seven cousins that were still true.

Did you have the eyes of a stranger?

When Eden Jones came to town she'd kill Bobby Alfredo.

Shade had no ties that money wouldn't fix or if it came to his blockhead stubbornness there was a convenient overdose waiting for him — a shot in the dark and where we left him on the beach when the petro-crabs came out to eat and he was never to be seen again.

There was a lot to do- to make things right — somebody had to die — somebody else had to leave again — and when the killing was done you still held the paper.

Shit.

You walked along the back end of town up to the Coast Guard docks and got another dirty water dog and some fries from the take out shack. You went down to the beach and faced the night ocean and enjoyed your meal. Someone was watching you.

One evening the phone rang. Shade was on the other end.

Your first intoxication was on Crazy Elliot Horse Ale. Years later you were still driving your consciousness wild. Maybe personal satisfaction was the original eye opener.

There was nothing wrong with anyone coming into this world.

You sat for a while. And what you remembered was your bicycle one summer. And how it felt divine to have a wrench in your hands and your blinking teenage eyes reflected upon eternity and how to change a flat tire

*

One evening the phone rang and you answered it.
Just like one evening you walked back home.
They were connected.
Shade's phone kept ringing but you ignored it.

*

Arrivals from New York —
Departures to the Poconos —
All Exit 29 riders your bus has been delayed again–
Bus station loudspeakers barked like dogs outside your windows —
A strange bacteria that ate stone was busy eating your home —
A strange bacteria was busy eating stone buildings across Jersey-land –
Our heritage was disappearing said scientist Ralph Winston —
At Angkor Wat the dancer's feet were crumbling —
The big heads on Easter Island were bug eyed —
Fancy Greek monuments were shit holes for hydrocarbon endolithic fungi —
How cool how sad — your home — your shelter would never make it -

*

Of course you'd have to live at the bus station for the next thirty years. And it wasn't without possibility that might happen. But it all belonged to her. And she was silent again for the nth time in two days.

Anyway you slid in behind the big oversized wooden doors with two thick glass panels and an old world transom on top and tucked your sorry ass into a shadow on the cracked landing below the stairs. Shade was across 3rd Street. He was sitting in the front window at the Mani Ho Luncheonette. Detective Shade was busy piling a dozen pancakes and fried eggs into his face and scanning a newspaper like any other famished and dumb ass.

Inside the doorway you hesitated. You didn't want to go up the stairs to your apartment. You didn't want to go back outside the door. By now you figured Shade had regrouped.

And you had Shade's phone from last night.

If you didn't call then the phone killed you.

If you did call the phone killed Shade.

Inside the doorway the light was dim and got lost the further it traveled down toward you.

On the second floor landing a bare light bulb lit the semi-darkness above the landing. The light folded down the steps and followed the sad 60-watt glow to the bottom where it flattened out and stilled on the cracked tiles.

Inside the doorway you watched Shade continue eating. The air smelled like cheap get-laid aftershave and the cigarette butts from ten thousand lost souls. You didn't know what to expect upstairs. But it was a long day — or days whatever — and you needed to go home.

On the wall were a dozen mailboxes. Each mailbox had a name taped above the mail slot. When somebody moved out — and somebody else moved in — a different name was taped over the previous name above the mail slot. Names upon names — strangers gave way to more strangers — existence after existence — your home was a way station for wanted criminals and cosmic migrants and plain old ghosts –and each old name peeled off under the new tape but stayed on the mailbox — like there was too much magnetism for anything to fall away — like we were all still there living in the building and out of time.

496

*

Upstairs the dog was glad to see you.

You dialed Shade's phone.

What the phone said.

You told the phone there was a shack in Margate ready to move in.

The phone said I told you I wanted to get out.

This was a start you said. Plus you don't pay rent for a year.

And in return you want something for this the phone said.

We talked about that you said.

Can't give too serious a promise with only a shack in Margate as collateral the phone said.

Take it you said.

I don't trust you the phone said.

Nobody does you said. But this was a good deal.

This was a funny thing the phone said.

You'll love Margate you told the phone.

If I don't the phone said I'll let you know.

*

Beautiful October day...the phone rang... geese flew across the sky throughout the day... a sign the weather would change... you were locked into place... warm days never refuse attention... salt colors in the trees... sky reflected off the ocean with a hazy luminescence that moved your eyes... the dog grabbed your hand and we walked along and you were glad the dog wouldn't let you escape... walking along... a juiced up still life painting... motionless enjoyment as though the scenery were moving and not you and the dog... a sensual world was all... zinnias bloomed on cracked brown stems... tourist groups finding Jersey-land strange stopped in the mystery where they were and smoked long thin filters and read maps aloud... young girls flew past on bicycles... hair grace epidermal and shadows ... the dog ran toward the beach and looked brilliant running into the surf ... you saw this before... numbers inside an equation… music sounds… you were here before… burning sunlight… delighted blue … gleaming and material… signifiers tracked overhead… union of opposites… geese overhead and you walking… so much you don't know… a voice behind you called I'll be right there… it was tomorrow… you were still alive…

to be continued

Fomite

About Fomite

A fomite is a medium capable of transmitting infectious organisms from one individual to another.

"The activity of art is based on the capacity of people to be infected by the feelings of others." Tolstoy, *What Is Art?*

Writing a review on Amazon, Good Reads, Shelfari, Library Thing or other social media sites for readers will help the progress of independent publishing. To submit a review, go to the book page on any of the sites and follow the links for reviews. Books from independent presses rely on reader to reader communications.

For more information or to order any of our books, visit
http://www.fomitepress.com/FOMITE/Our_Books.html

More Titles from Fomite...

Novels

Joshua Amses — *During This, Our Nadir*
Joshua Amses — *Raven or Crow*
Joshua Amses — *The Moment Before an Injury*
Jaysinh Birjepatel — *The Good Muslim of Jackson Heights*
Jaysinh Birjepatel — *Nothing Beside Remains*
David Brizer — *Victor Rand*
Dan Chodorkoff — *Loisaida*
David Cleveland — *Time's Betrayal*
Paula Closson Buck — *Summer on the Cold War Planet*
Roger Coleman — *Skywreck Afternoons*
Marc Estrin — *Hyde*
Marc Estrin — *Kafka's Roach*
Marc Estrin — *Speckled Vanities*
Zdravka Evtimova — *In the Town of Joy and Peace*
Zdravka Evtimova — *Sinfonia Bulgarica*

Fomite

Daniel Forbes — *Derail This Train Wreck*
Greg Guma — *Dons of Time*
Richard Hawley — *The Three Lives of Jonathan Force*
Lamar Herrin — *Father Figure*
Michael Horner — *Damage Control*
Ron Jacobs — *All the Sinners Saints*
Ron Jacobs — *Short Order Frame Up*
Ron Jacobs — *The Co-conspirator's Tale*
Scott Archer Jones — *A Rising Tide of People Swept Away*
Maggie Kast — *A Free Unsullied Land*
Darrell Kastin — *Shadowboxing with Bukowski*
Coleen Kearon — *Feminist on Fire*
Coleen Kearon — *#triggerwarning*
Jan Englis Leary — *Thicker Than Blood*
Diane Lefer — *Confessions of a Carnivore*
Rob Lenihan — *Born Speaking Lies*
Colin Mitchell — *Roadman*
Ilan Mochari — *Zinsky the Obscure*
Gregory Papadoyiannis — *The Baby Jazz*
Andy Potok — *My Father's Keeper*
Kathryn Roberts — *Companion Plants*
Robert Rosenberg — *Isles of the Blind*
Fred Russell — *Rafi's World*
Ron Savage — *Voyeur in Tangier*
David Schein — *The Adoption*
Lynn Sloan — *Principles of Navigation*
L.E. Smith — *The Consequence of Gesture*
L.E. Smith — *Travers' Inferno*
L.E. Smith — *Untimely RIPped*
Bob Sommer — *A Great Fullness*
Tom Walker — *A Day in the Life*
Susan V. Weiss —*My God, What Have We Done?*
Peter M. Wheelwright — *As It Is On Earth*
Suzie Wizowaty — *The Return of Jason Green*

Fomite

Poetry

Fomite

Odd Birds

Micheal Breiner — *the way none of this happened*

J. C. Ellefson — *Under the Influence*

David Ross Gunn — *Cautionary Chronicles*

Andrei Guriuanu — *The Darkest City*

Gail Holst-Warhaft — *The Fall of Athens*

Roger Leboitz — *A Guide to the Western Slopes and the Outlying Area*

dug Nap— *Artsy Fartsy*

Delia Bell Robinson — *A Shirtwaist Story*

Peter Schumann — *Bread & Sentences*

Peter Schumann — *Charlotte Salomon*

Peter Schumann — *Faust 3*

Peter Schumann — *Planet Kasper, Volumes One and Two*

Peter Schumann — *We*

Plays

Stephen Goldberg — *Screwed and Other Plays*

Michele Markarian — *Unborn Children of America*

Made in the USA
Columbia, SC
06 May 2018